The Last Zulu Warrior

Published by Keldaviain Publishing

ISBN 978-0-9928599-1-6

Chapter 1

Emerging into the cold damp atmosphere of the western approaches, Ellen took her first breath of English air in more than two years. Shivering, she pulled her shawl tight about her shoulders, took several tentative steps across the gently undulating deck. From high above her, the lookout called out from his vantage point in the crow's nest

'Land ho,' he hollered through a battered pewter megaphone. From the Bridge Ellen heard an acknowledgement, the ship's horn hooted several short blasts across the cold and empty grey sea. Ellen reached the ship's rail and gripped it with both hands, took several deep breaths and took a few minutes to reflect. She was almost home, except she had no home, the interminable voyage had taken five weeks and now that it was almost over she could at least look forward to familiar streets and perhaps a familiar face. However, that seemed unlikely; she had lost touch with what family she once had and any happiness she did feel was tempered by the knowledge that once she reached London she would have to face her formidable father in law.

She closed her eyes for a moment, felt the vibration of the deck beneath her feet and peered out across the grey, barren seascape. Mist was rising and she could see very little, the swirling patches of grey confounding her eyes and so she decided to take a walk up the narrow flight of stairs to the deck above in the hope of a better view of England.

Released by her proximity to her destiny opposing forces fought a silent battle within her, one a feeling of liberation, the other apprehension. Although she was a widow, free of her overbearing husband, she still had to face Clarence's father. Edward Jameson was a rich banker who believed that just about everyone else in the world was beneath him and he did not hide his feelings. Married to his son, she had found life difficult as an officer's wife in the garrison towns and military camps. Left alone for weeks on end whilst Clarence did his duty, campaigning she had struggled to break the boredom, unsuited as she was to the life of a military wife. She was a product of London's back streets and a woman of her background, married to an officer in a cavalry regiment seemed improbable, and yet on reflection, she had been fortunate to meet and marry Clarence. Unlike many officers' wives, she did not have the benefit of a formal education, found it hard to mix socially, to cross the class divide though to some extent she had succeeded in that. She had worked hard, learned to refine her speech learn what she could of the etiquette expected of an officer's wife and she had begun to fit in. That was until the final battle, when fate had prodded Clarence into leading one charge too many in his quest for glory.

Reaching the top of the staircase, she steadied herself against the slow roll of the ship and was about to grasp the door handle, when suddenly it swung open and a deck officer almost collided with her.

'Sorry ma'am, mornin' ma'am, there's land on the port side, it's still a way off but it is England alright. Thought you might like to know. If you'll excuse me I have to attend to my duties below decks.'

Ellen smiled and the young man grinned back as he held the door open for her as she stepped out onto the windswept deck. Several other passengers were already there, leaning against the ship's rail, looking towards the land.

January 1880 in the English Channel was proving to be very cold, a stark reminder of the time, barely two years ago, when she had stepped ashore in Cape Town and feeling a twinge of regret at leaving South Africa's warm climate, she pulled her shawl tight around her shoulders. Memories of her first days in South Africa returned; she remembered landing a few days before Christmas and then the Ball. The officers of the Twenty-Fourth of Foot had arranged a New Year's Eve Ball and had invited Clarence as a visiting officer and of course herself.

Dressed in his smart blue uniform, her husband was dashing, confident and their introduction to South African colonial society had been a success. For her it was the beginning of new life, very different from that of a common parlour maid from the East End. Clarence was aware of her shortcomings and had taught her some of society's finer points, turned her into the beginnings of a Lady. He had insisted she attend elocution lessons, learn to dance, attributes he knew would augur well for his promotions.

She remembered the Ball, a glittering occasion with the officers in their best uniforms, the women in ball gowns brought from England. The event was one of the pinnacles of colonial society, Magistrates, Government officials and their wives attending in their best attire, each trying to outshine the other.

The regimental band provided the music and as Clarence danced her past the musicians, her eyes caught sight of a face she recognised. At first she was not sure, he seemed so familiar and yet, momentarily, she could not place him. As Clarence guided her across the dance floor she could not help looking back and then, shocked, it dawned that it was her cousin Georgie. She had not seen for several years, not since he was fourteen, not since the day the policeman had dragged him away. Was it really him? He was no longer, the boy she once knew but a sturdy good-looking young man.

She remembered vividly their days together picking pockets, and then that fateful day in Trafalgar Square. The shock of seeing him again had taken her mind off the dance and she faltered, missed her step and Clarence had scolded her. His sharp words had brought her back to reality and as Clarence whirled her away from the bandstand, she had not dared to turn her head, clinging to her husband as he whirled her round the room.

She wanted to catch Georgie's eye, see if he recognised her and finally, their eyes did meet. Smiling inwardly, she recalled the moment and then other memories sprang back to life. She remembered the hard times when she and Georgie had picked the pockets of the unwary, how they had escaped the Peelers after a passer-by had alerted them. They had been successful for more than a year until the day a policeman had caught Georgie stealing a pocket watch. That was the last she had seen of him until the night of the Ball and that was just about four years before.

She shivered, not at the memory but because of the cold, although she was wearing gloves she had to rub her hands together vigorously to generate some warmth and as the feeling returned, she recalled the time she had finally made contact with her cousin. He had told her of how a recruiting Sergeant had persuaded the Peeler to release him into his custody with a promise that he would join the army. He told her how he had learned to read and write, use a gun, play the drum in the Regimental band and it had made her smile with pleasure.

Then it was her turn to tell him how she had met Clarence and how she had come to be in South Africa. She had gone out shopping for the old man for whom she worked as a housekeeper, a rich old man who lived alone in a large property on Brompton Road. He had taken a fancy to her, lifted her from the gutter and given her a roof over her head. It sounded good but there had been a price to pay, a small enough price to escape the poverty and deprivation, to live in a warm, comfortable house with plenty to eat and have a few coppers to buy some half-decent clothes.

Then Clarence had appeared and become besotted, his clumsily attempts to sweep her off her feet at first embarrassing and then laughable. Smiling sweetly she had at first put up with his clichéd line of chat, finally managing to get away from him and had thought no more about it. However, Clarence was smitten and he had returned on each of the following days until he had found her again and the second time they met she allowed him to walk with her for a time.

Old habits seemed never to die and as they walked and he talked, she pondered on lifting his purse, or perhaps his pockets watch as he chatted incessantly, describing life as a cavalry officer and of his father, a successful banker. He had explained how it was an advantage for a young cavalry officer in need of support to have a wealthy father.

'I have the upkeep of my horses, I need expensive uniforms, and I have a hectic social life to finance. You know I need several hundred pounds a year,' he had said.

It was then Ellen began to show an interest and he became bolder.

'My dear, I should be honoured if you would accompany me to dinner this evening. I assume you are unattached judging by the lack of a ring in your finger.'

Ellen was sharp, intelligent and always on the lookout for the main chance, it was in her nature.

'Wot d'you suggest?'

'I could pick you up this evening, take you to dinner at Claridges or some other establishment you might prefer and afterwards drop you off at home. What d'you say?'

'I say that sounds a very nice suggestion but I 'ardly know you. P'raps it's not such a good idea,' she said, teasing him.

'Erm, not such a good idea, why, are you busy, perhaps we could meet some other evening?'

'I'll fink about it. Now I must be off as I 'ave work to do.'

'Work to do? My dear if you came with me there would be no talk of work to do, why you would have servants of your own.'

'Tell you what then, it's my day off on Sunday, why don't we meet over there by the park at mid-day and you can buy me an ice cream.'

'An ice cream, well if you insist, maybe... we could go for a walk in the park.'

'That sounds nice Clarence. Until Sunday then.'

'Until Sunday my dear.'

Clumsily he had reached out and kissed her hand, and she had chuckled to herself at his naïveté. He was pleasant enough, seemed harmless, but the idea that he would take her to one of the poshest hotels in London had scared her. She was from the slums, the Rookeries of the East End and she would be totally out of her depth. Her only experience of such places was hanging around in the shadows in search of a mark and then a familiar voice interrupted her thoughts.

'Good morning Mrs Jameson,'.

'Ah...Major Tompkins, good morning. How's the leg?'

'Oh fine, fine thank you, just a bit stiff this morning, the old hands tell me that the English weather will be the real problem.'

'I can imagine. Will you stay in the army?'

'Good heavens no. once I get my medal I will probably be discharged and then it's off to the City for me. I've had a good war, always an advantage when looking for a job in the City.'

The Major was full of himself, grinning broadly at the prospect of an easy life until he suddenly pulled up short, realising what he had said.

'Ah...sorry my dear, how insensitive of me, I...erm I am sorry if I was rather too ebullient, you must be feeling rather strained returning home a widow. I must appol...'

'No Major, no need for an apology, I am quite in control thank you. It has been a while since I lost my husband and I am coming to terms with the prospect.'

Falling silent, they both turned towards the rail to watch the coast of England slip slowly by until eventually the Major took his leave and Ellen heaved a quiet sigh of relief. For a while, she remained against the ship's rail in silence, mulling over recent events, contemplating meeting Clarence's father, and then of course, there was Patrick.

The stevedores of London's East India dock grasped at the heavy lines snaking out from the side of the ship and from her cabin, Ellen watched the manoeuvres. Then, quite suddenly, the familiar vibrations of the ship faded away and voyage of 6,000 or more miles ended and she realised that it was time to find a porter.

The ship was a hive of activity the like of which she had not experienced since coming on board in Cape Town. Officers marshalled subordinates, barking out their orders and high above cranes began unloading the ship's cargo. Ellen shivered, she had forgotten how cold an English winter could be but at least she had her shawl and her gloves and pulling the collar of her coat up to protect her neck, she turned towards the melee and to look for a porter.

'Mrs Jameson,' said a voice behind her.

'Yes,' she said turning to see a young man in a white steward's jacket.

'Morning ma'am I have come for your luggage.'
'Where do you want it?'

'Er..I do not really know. What do you suggest?'

The steward grinned, colonials always seemed lost when they reached England, full of confidence during the trip but once they landed life seemed to become more daunting.

'There will be carriages waiting by the dock gates. I can take your luggage on my barrow as far as that and then you can take a carriage into town. Where are you staying?'

'Claridges,' she said almost without hesitation.

Claridges it was and after paying the driver, she called a porter to take her luggage into the hotel and with some trepidation, she approached the reception desk.

'Do you have a reservation madam?'

'Er, no, my late husband always stayed here though and I'm sure you can find me a room.'

Ellen's heart rate kicked up a few beats and she smiled at the man.

'Your late husband, could I enquire as to his name?'

'Jameson, Captain Clarence Jameson of the Seventeenth Lancers. He was killed at Ulundi.'

Ellen feigned sorrow as well as she could.

'Ah Captain Jameson, Mr Edward Jameson's son, I am sorry; yes certainly we will have a room for you. Is there be anything else madam?'

'No thank you except what time is dinner this evening?'

'Normally guests visit the dining room between seven and ten in the evening but you can have dinner served at any time you like, what about room service? I can ask the floor manager to visit you and arrange chef to cook you something to eat in your room.'

'Yes, I think that would be a good idea, thank you.'

The man reached over, pressed the palm of his hand on the bell in front of him and within seconds, a boy appeared.

'Take Mrs Jameson to room two twenty four,' he said handing him a key.

To her pleasant surprise, the room was nothing like the primitive colonial rooms she had lived in for two years. The bed was large and comfortable; the furniture of high quality and it had a somewhat interrupted view of Berkeley Square gardens.

'Leave the luggage just there,' she said, offering several coppers to the boy and after he left, she walked to the window to pull the curtain to one side and gaze over the street below. A few carriages, a horse drawn tram, and several pedestrians passed by and for a few minutes, she watched in fascination. She remembered when she and Georgie had dodged round carriages and trams just like them making their escape. They had run for their lives to shouts of 'stop thief' over the bridge, down side streets until they could run no more and collapsed in a fit of hysterical laughter.

She could see it all, her mind's eye bringing the past back to life, the silk handkerchiefs, the police looking for the likes of her and Georgie. It all seemed so real until a gentle knock at the door disturbed her. 'Ah, the floor manager', she thought, going to the door and to her surprise she opened it to find not the floor manager but a bellboy of no more than twelve years, shy and awkward looking in his loose fitting uniform.

'Yes.'

'M...message for you ma'am,' he said holding out his hand.

'Thank you,' said Ellen taking the piece of paper from him. She looked at the note and prepared to close the door but the boy stood firm. 'Is there anything else, do you expect some sort of reply?' she said.

'Don't know ma'am,' said the boy rather sheepishly.

Why was he still standing at the doorway she wondered and then she understood, he wanted a tip. She had paid the porter on the ship for his services, given a tip to the hotel porter and now this lad wanted one too.

'How much do you normally get?' she asked him.

'Sixpence,' was the sharp reply.

'I don't think so, here's a penny. If you want any more tips from me, then do not be so greedy. Let me give you some advice, if the management of this hotel think you are upsetting guests you won't last long and you can wave goodbye to any tips never mind a sixpence.'

'Sorry ma'am, I only started today. I need the work to 'elp out me mum,' he said, tears beginning to form in his eyes.

Ellen smiled, oh how the memories were returning.

'Wait a mo.'

She went back to her purse and returned with a sixpenny piece, took back the penny and placed the small silver coin the boy's hand.

'Oh fank you ma'am fank you,' he said, a huge smile spreading across his face.

'Go on, be off with you.'

Ellen closed the door a wry grin on her face, remembering the time when she was his age and had nothing. They had lived from hand to mouth and she imagined how she would have felt if someone had given her a sixpenny piece. She looked at the note in her hand puzzled that anyone would send her such a thing and unfolded the piece of paper.

"My dear Ellen, I have just received news that you have returned from Africa. May I take this opportunity to invite you to dinner tonight at eight 'o' clock sharp in the hotel dining room when you may inform me of the details of my son's death."

It was signed Edward Jameson, Clarence's father, a summons more than an invitation. So, it had begun and the prospect of meeting Clarence's father for the first time left her feeling a little faint. Clarence had told her his father would not approve of her, but his passion for her had overcome any reservations he might have had. He said he hoped that in time she would acquire at least some of the airs and graces of an army officer's wife and then, and only then, he would introduce her to his father.

Reading the note a second time, she sat down on the bed to decide upon a course of action. She had not married Clarence for his money because initially she was unaware of the family; she had married him simply to get away from the old man who at first had been kind to her but in time, he expected her to do more than run errands, and so she had sought an escape.

She had realised in those few short years with Clarence what an opportunity she had to better herself and she had grasped it with both hands. Through a mixture of guile and hard work, she had transformed herself from a street urchin into the beginnings of a Lady. She had come to understand the motives and desires of the middle classes and realising Clarence's father would believe that she was simply after his inheritance she needed a story. She had never met Clarence's father, knew of him simply by reputation and, reading the note once again, she wondered how he could have known so quickly she was here in London. She began to feel unsure of herself, but one thing was certain; she must appear to be a woman of some social standing and a doting wife in mourning otherwise she could expect to be dismissed out of hand.

Looking up from the note she caught her reflection in the mirror and decided that she must wear dark clothes, appear to be still in mourning and then it occurred to her and that she should go down to the lobby of the hotel and set her watch to the correct time. It would not do to be late for her first meeting with her father in law.

She folded the piece of paper and after laying it on the dressing table, locked her room door, and descended the stairs to the lobby and as she approached the large clock she saw the bellboy again.

'Ma'am,' he said with a cheerful grin.

'Hello young man, I wonder, can you help me? I would like to know where I can find the dining room.'

'Certainly ma'am, follow me.'

The lad had a bounce in his step, buoyed by their little episode and was very pleased to assist the "Lady from Africa" as the staff now knew her.

'There is the dining room,' he said, as they came to a set of dark mahogany and glass doors.

Ellen peered through the glass to see several rows of round tables; each with a bright white tablecloth laid out with polished silver cutlery and sparkling glasses and found such splendour impressive.

'Thank you young man, here is another sixpence for your troubles.'

'But I thought you said...'

'Never mind what I said, I was poor once and struggled to make ends meet. I do not mind helping you but don't expect everyone else to be the same. Go on, off with you.'

With a grin the Bellboy disappeared and Ellen decided to have a walk around, familiarise herself with her surroundings. The hotel was sumptuous, far superior to anything she had seen in South Africa, awe inspiring to someone like her and she enjoyed every minute of her exploration until it dawned upon her that it must come at a price and then she panicked. How far her money would stretch became a concern because to pay for such luxury might be beyond her means.

Before leaving for England, she had met with Clarence's commanding officer obtaining the paperwork she needed. He had produced Clarence's death certificate, the discharge papers necessary to claim the small pension awarded fallen officers widows and the back pay he was due from his campaigning. As well as this, she was given access to the funds he had deposited with the quartermaster to cover the costs of the upkeep of his remaining horses. The horses had value too and after selling them, their saddles and tackle, she had a total of almost five hundred pounds. At the time, it had seemed a fortune but how long would it last if she stayed at Claridges? She paused for a moment to look through the great revolving door, watch the passing carriages and she decided that perhaps she should stay only a day or two, find a cheaper place until she secured her inheritance.

At ten to eight, Ellen looked in the mirror for the final time, adjusted the black ribbon about her throat and fluffed up the collar of her black dress, picked up her evening bag and made her way down the staircase to the lobby when the Bellboy appeared.

'Ma'am, I have been sent to tell you that a gentleman is waiting for you at table and I am to show you to him.'

'Oh, thank you,' she said swallowing hard, 'lead on.'

The boy walked three or four paces ahead of Ellen, held the dining room door open for her and pointed towards a table by a window where a middle-aged man with thinning grey hair and dressed in an expensive looking evening suit sat.

The man caught sight of her from the corner of his eye and swivelled his head towards her before rising to his feet and Ellen realised then just how much he looked like Clarence. He had the same weak chin, the darting dark eyes but there the resemblance stopped for this man was very much older, portly and with a complexion that resembled a strawberry.

'My dear, you must be Ellen,' he said,

His gaze was steady, intimidating, but he was unable to hide his surprise at Ellen's good looks and for a few seconds his defences failed him. How had his youngest son attracted such a fine looking woman he wondered? Money, it could only be money for Clarence had never been a hit with the women, tongue tied and awkward, no, money had attracted her to his son, his money, and his attitude began to harden.

'Please take a seat,' he said pulling out a chair for her. 'Waiter, bring a wine list will you. Let me introduce myself, I am Edward Jameson, Clearance's father,' he said bowing his head slightly.

Ellen smiled a little weakly and stepped towards the chair. She had noticed the look he gave her to begin with, she had seen it many times on a man's face and took comfort in the fact that she had at least one weapon could use should she need it.

'Pleased to meet you, yes I am Ellen, your daughter in law.'

'Quite, I trust you had a pleasant journey from South Africa.'

Before Ellen could reply the wine list arrived and Edward Jameson did as he always did in the company of women, he ignored them and ordered wine to suit himself. He considered himself far more knowledgeable about wines that any woman could ever be and believed it a waste of time consulting them.

'A bottle of the '68 Beaujolais, if you please waiter. Now, tell me the manner of Clarence's death, was he fighting the Zulu at the time, did he account well for himself?'

'Yes sir he did, he was a brave soldier. He was awarded a posthumous medal for his bravery and both you and I should be proud of him.'

She pulled a handkerchief from her sleeve and dabbed her eyes as if wiping away tears but she was simply avoiding the old man's eyes.

'It was at Ulundi where we lost Clarence. His fellow officers told me of how he led charge after charge against the Zulus killing many of them and unfortunately it was towards the end of the battle that a few desperate natives fell on him, brought down his horse and...' Her voice tailed off as shammed sorrow at those missing words.

Edward Jameson nodded, showed little emotion, and picked up the menu.

'The venison is very good here at this time of year,' he said, pausing as the waiter poured wine for his approval. He sniffed at the glass, took a sip, and rolled the wine around his mouth before motioning to the waiter to fill both glasses.

Ellen was hungry, she had not eaten since an early breakfast on the steamer and recognized that Clarence's father had little respect for his dead son and that her best course would be to go along with his suggestion and so, she simply nodded agreement.

'Good, then that is settled.'

Edward Jameson gave the order for dinner; smoked salmon followed by the venison and lifted his glass to his lips.

'Ah, a good year '68, try some, what d'you think?'

Once again, Ellen smiled sweetly and took the tiniest of sips from her own glass, it had a satisfactory taste, but she had no idea about fine wines.

'Mmm...that's a very nice wine, I congratulate you on your palate Mister Jameson.'

He grunted his thanks, not inviting her to call him Edward.

'Tell me a little of your life with my son in Africa, the weather, the landscape. What are the Zulus really like – savages?'

'I don't know much about the Zulus first hand Mister Jameson. I never got anywhere near the front line and the nearest I came to Zululand was working in the military hospital at Dundee.'

She managed a description of the landscape and of the military camp and began to tell Jameson what she knew of the campaigning when the food arrived and the conversation tailed off and they consumed dinner in a mood of silence. Both diners were acutely aware of the real reason for their meeting, Clarence's inheritance, and the negotiating that would go with it.

The venison was good, just as Edward Jameson had said it would be and Ellen ate her fill, leaving a little on her plate watching as the old man finished his off in style and then attacked the French cheese dessert and finishing off the wine and ordering a second bottle. Edward Jameson liked his food and it showed, his concentration fully on the cheese selection when Ellen managed several glances to study him more closely, not particularly liking what she saw.

'Have some cheese, it's delicious.'

'I couldn't possibly eat anymore.'

'Hmm...some wine, help me finish this bottle.'

'Just a drop, thank you.'

Edward Jameson poured a little wine into her glass and the rest into his own and Ellen watched as he demolished the great mound of cheese before making his way through the second bottle and leaving her astonished at how much he had consumed.

'Now to business,' he said suddenly. 'You are my son's widow and are expecting to claim on his estate.

Well, first you will need to prove in law your claim before you may realise any assets, which I can tell you now are minimal. The family's wealth is solely in my name and it is only upon my death that my sons inherit anything. George and Edward junior are in the banking business; both have done well enough for themselves, are unmarried and they have no need of my money but I am sure they will not refuse it when the time comes. It saddens me to tell you my dear; you have picked the poorest member of the family to marry. Clarence would normally receive a third of my estate that, under present circumstances, would pass to you, but I intend to alter my will to make them the only beneficiaries upon my death and you my dear will receive nothing. Do I make myself clear?

'Perfectly,' said Ellen in a quiet voice, and then she heard herself say, 'what about an allowance?' 'I loved your son and all I have now is his memory. Do you want your son's wife to end up destitute and on the streets when you are a very rich man Mister Jameson?'

She pulled her handkerchief from her sleeve and appeared emotional, noisily blowing her nose. Not used to dealing with a woman in such a state of anxiety, he paused for a moment, winced as if in pain and then scowled at her.

'No I will not allow that. I will instruct my secretary to award you an allowance of one hundred pounds per year, which should be enough for a woman like you.' he said, his face reddening noticeably as he fumbled in his waistcoat pocket and pulled out a small white card to pass across the table.

'Here, my card, call at this office in two days' time and speak with my secretary. He will make the arrangements. I think we have said all we need to so if you will excuse me I will settle the account and have a drink in the men only bar before calling a cab. Good evening.'

That was it, he could not even bring himself to call her Mrs Jameson, he just wanted rid of her and, slightly the worse for wear, got unsteadily to his feet. She bowed her head slightly with some dignity as he took his leave but inside she was seething. What a bastard Clarence's father had turned out to be, no wonder her late husband had been such an arrogant moron, it was obvious from where he got it.

Chapter 2

Unable to sleep, Ellen's mind repeatedly visited the scene from earlier in the evening. She had not expected such a severe rebuttal from Clarence's father, the bitter disappointment of rejection consuming her thoughts. She had expected at least something of value from Clarence's estate to support her but alone and friendless, she worried for her future. What should she could do she wondered and then Patrick came into her mind. He was strong, a man, and he would know what to do she was sure, but he was still in South Africa. She thought of Edward's offer, one hundred pounds a year, it might keep her in basic comfort but she feared it would condemn her to a life of poverty not much better than the one from which she had escaped. Groaning to herself, she turned her head from side to side in frustration and as the first glint of daylight poked through the thick curtains, she realised that she must leave the expensive luxury of Claridges and find somewhere more within her means.

She had hardly slept but somehow she did not feel at all fatigued and struggling from the unruly heap of bedclothes, she dressed and decided to go for a walk.

She looked at her watch, a quarter to six, the hotel would not serve breakfast until half past seven at the earliest and perhaps a walk in the morning air and then a good breakfast would give her the strength to face the day. She would start to look for a cheaper hotel or rooming house straight after breakfast.

Making her way along the silent corridor, she descended the stairs and walked through the entrance hall towards the big glass doors, the night porter acknowledging her as she passed and left the hotel. For a moment she stood, taking in her surroundings, drawing a breath of soot-laden air, almost tasting the burnt coal on her tongue. She had forgotten how foul the London air could be and for a moment missed the clean and unpolluted air of South Africa.

The street was deserted save for a few early starters, huddled and silent as they hurried past and as she made her way towards the Embankment and Waterloo Bridge and she remembered how it was when she had worked the patch all those years ago. In those last months and weeks, Georgie had been with her and young James as they looked for a likely trick and they had been successful, lifting silk handkerchiefs, and the occasional pocket watch until that fateful day. She had not seen first-hand the Peeler arresting Georgie, but James had and they had run through the square only to see the policeman and a recruiting sergeant frog marching the hapless Georgie away.

So much had happened to her since then, her life had changed so much and if Edward Jameson thought that he could send her back to that earlier life, then he was mistaken, she was determined that it would not happen.

Squeezing her eyes tight, she cast off those memories and concentrated on her immediate problem before turning onto the embankment. Traffic was light; a few horse drawn delivery vehicles and early morning trams trundling along loaded with sombre faced workers. A few pedestrians hurried past and to her surprise, she saw, coming towards her with his hands stuffed firmly in his pockets was the Bellboy from Claridges. He appeared still half-asleep as he shuffled along unaware of her, stopping suddenly as he almost bumped into her and as recognition dawned he said, 'morning ma'am. Have you heard the news?'

'What news?'

'Don't you know the gentleman you was wiv at dinner last night keeled over in the bar and they took 'im 'ome.'

Ellen's jaw dropped, Edward Jameson collapsed. She could not quite take it in to begin with and then her mind went into overdrive as she wondered what the implications for her might be for her, had Edward Jameson really collapsed? She looked into the boy's eyes and knew that it was true.

'No I didn't, where did they take him?'

'Dunno but I can find out if you like.'

'Yes please, I would like to know.'

'I can't stay, I have to get to work, I will ask in the 'otel,' and touching his forehead in a gesture of respect, the Bellboy hurried on his way.

So, Edward Jameson had taken ill and collapsed. How bad was he and would it affect their arrangement she wondered because if he was very poorly, died before changing his will, then she might still inherit Clarence's share of the estate after all.

Breakfast was a lonely affair; most of the other guests distant and keeping to themselves, no more than a nod or a reluctant "good morning" coming her way. So, she sat alone at the same table she had shared with Edward Jameson the previous evening, the news troubling her. She considered several scenarios that might transpire, first that the old man might recover enough to change his will but then he might forget to give instructions for her allowance. That had to be the worst case. However, if he died before he had chance to change anything then she stood a chance of inheriting Clarence's share of the estate. She must find Edward; see what condition he was in for herself.

Not knowing the reality of the situation increased her anxiety and as she consumed the last of her breakfast, she picked up her coffee cup and stared out of the window. What was it the commanding officer of the Lancers had said to her in that final meeting, what had he said? She had not paid too much attention, her mind was in such a whirl with everything else at the time, and she had difficulty remembering that last meeting. What was it he had said, something about a lawyer that was it; he had said she might need to consult a lawyer. What did she know about lawyers, nothing but perhaps she should find out and leaving the dining room, she went in search of the bellboy.

'Good morning young man I see you are fully awake now,' she said finding him near the hotel entrance.

His eyes dropped in embarrassment, the hours were long, it was no wonder he had looked so tired.

'Yes ma'am.'

'You haven't forgotten what I asked of you have you.'

'No ma'am, I know one of the boys who works in the office and I've already asked him to find out what he can for you.'

'Thank you; I'll give you another sixpence if you find out something useful.'

They smiled at each other, a proper little team she thought and for the first time she began to feel at home again in London. She had been one of the best pickpockets in London during her early life, a mixture of excitement and panic but she had always survived and she was beginning to feel that this new adventure might not be so different.

'Keep your eyes and ears open young man, find out what you can. I am going for a walk and when I return I hope that you will have some news for me.'

'Yes Ma'am,' said the boy anticipating a second sixpenny piece.

As Ellen left the hotel for the second time, she felt the faint warmth of the sun, forcing its way through the smoke laden city air and walking purposefully, she thought through her options, hardly noticing people or the carriages filling the street. She reached the river and paused for a time, watching as several barges passed by, letting her mind drift again to those days when she ran like the children that she could see playing. Her childhood had been all too brief, she knew that now, she had earned much of her family's living since she was nine years old and shuddered at the thought of the hardship she had endured, an incentive to make as much as she could of her situation. Mulling her thoughts over she made her way along the embankment for several hundred yards and by the time, she returned to the hotel, she had formulated a plan.

'Can I see the manager please?' she asked the concierge.

From behind the counter, the man looked up. 'The manager ma'am?'

'Yes.'

'Who shall I say?'

'Mrs Clarence Jameson.'

Nodding acceptance of her request, he left his seat and disappeared through a door to re-appear within a few seconds.

'He will be with you shortly madam,' he said closing the door behind him.

The door opened again and a tall, bespectacled man walked from his office.

'Mrs Jameson?'

'Yes.'

'What might I do for you?'

'I need to see a lawyer but I am new to London and have no introductions, perhaps you can advise me.'

'Hmm...that should not be too difficult. Please bear with me whilst I retrieve some information. Take a seat and I will be back directly,' he said pointing to a large leather armchair.

Ellen sat, waited, her lack of patience exposed by the drumming of her fingers on the arm of the chair and only when the hotel manager reappeared behind the desk did she stop and return to the counter.

'Here is a list of three lawyers I feel that I can recommend,' said the manager. 'Each has worked in some capacity or another for this hotel and as far as I know, we have no complaints. I have written the name of the person I dealt with from each firm of solicitors and their addresses. Here you are,' he said passing the paper across the counter.'

Ellen took the list, recognising at least one address, the Old Kent Road and decided that she would go there first to see a Mister Frederick Jones of Bartlett and Bartlett.

The horse drawn cab made its way along the Old Kent Road, pulling up outside an austere, dirty looking building tucked between a pub and a church, its once elegant stonework turned black by smoke from thousands of chimneys.

'Here you are Miss,' called the driver tapping the roof of the cab with his whip.

Ellen climbed from the cab, paid the driver, and studied the polished brass name plaques fastened to wall beside the door to the building. Bartlett and Bartlett, Solicitors, were on the third floor. She pushed the door open and walked into the dark interior, pausing a moment to allow her eyes to become accustomed to the gloom. The staircase stretched out in front of her and anxiously she climbed up to the third floor, coming upon the office of Bartlett and Bartlett solicitors. Cautiously she tapped on the glass, almost immediately a shadow appeared behind the panel, and then the door swung open making her start. A thin man of about thirty years old, dressed in an ill-fitting woollen suit confronted her with darting, inquisitive eyes and she swallowed hard.

'Yes?'

'I...I would like to speak with a mister Frederick Jones'.

'That will be me. Do come in.'

The man swung the door wide and allowed Ellen to pass unhindered into a surprisingly pleasant room. It had a good-sized window facing south and the sunlight it let in gave the room gave an altogether more pleasant feel than the rest of the building. At the room's centre were a large table and two spindly high backed chairs. Beside the window, stacks of papers stood on the floor and against one wall stood a chest of drawers but apart from that, the room was devoid of any cheer.

'Please take a seat. I am afraid you will have to excuse the mess; it is not as disorganized as it looks I can assure you. Now, let me introduce myself, I am Frederick Jones, everyone calls me Freddie. And you are?'

'Mrs Clarence Jameson.'

'Pleased to meet you Mrs Jameson, what is it that I can do for you?'

Ellen sat in one of the high backed chairs opposite Freddie Jones and began to explain her situation. She told him that she knew very little about lawyers but advice given her was that she might need to hire the services of one. She told of her husband's death fighting the Zulus and of her possible inheritance, omitting for the moment disclosure of her recent meeting with her father in law

'So, to begin we will need to find out what are the assets of your deceased husband's estate, property, bank accounts, and the like. Do you know where we might find that information? Do you have access to any paperwork that might help us? His will, do you have a copy of his will?'

'I just have these,' she said producing papers acquired from Clarence's commanding officer.

'I see, he was an officer in the seventeenth Lancers. You have here his death certificate and a simple will used in the field, there could well be a more comprehensive will deposited somewhere, perhaps with the regiment. Soldiers are pragmatic souls you know, most leave some sort of will before going overseas. That will be my first port of call, er that is if you wish to hire my services.'

Ellen did want to hire him, she liked him, his confidence was infectious, and she felt that she really did not have much choice unless she was prepared to trudge round the offices of the other names on her list.

'Yes, I would like to hire your services mister Jones.'

'Good, good, my fees are five shillings a day. I will send you interim bills as we progress. I have other work so do not worry if I seem to be weeks without any communication it may be that I only need to spend a day a week on you case. We will see. First though I will write a letter to the home depot of the seventeenth Lances and see what that turns up. Are there any other relatives we can contact?'

Ellen began to realise that perhaps she should tell Freddie everything and cleared her throat.

'Er...my husband's father, a man called Edward Jameson, a banker and two brothers who I believe are also in banking on the continent.'

Freddie's eyebrows rose a little at the name.

'Edward Jameson, I've heard of him, if it's the same Edward Jameson he is a wealthy and successful man as I understand it. Might we talk to your father in law?'

'I doubt it, he is cold towards me, and I do not think he will be of much help.'

Freddie rubbed his chin as he considered the information; perhaps it was too difficult a subject to pursue for now. He would save for later any searching questions about the close family, see what transpired as the case unfolded because he did not want to upset such a powerful man as Edward Jameson, not yet anyway.

The Bellboy jumped up as soon as he noticed Ellen walk through the hotel entrance and for her part, she could see that he had news for her. Instinctively she wondered that inquisitive eyes might be watching, Edward Jameson was a powerful man and how had he had found her so quickly?

'I have a letter to post, can you send the bellboy to my room in ten minutes please,' she asked the concierge as she passed his desk.

'Certainly madam.'

'Thank you,' she said with a smile and not long after entering her room, there was a tap tap tap on the door.

'You require a letter posting ma'am,' queried the bellboy as she opened it.

'Come in. You have news?'

'Yes.'

'The man who collapsed is back at his own home, they say he might only have days to live.'

The news made Ellen hesitate for a moment before she finally asked where it was that Edward lived.

'Moreton Place Belgravia, don't know the number but I can find out.'

'Well done, here's sixpence and not a word to anyone.'

'Your letter ma'am, do you want the letter posting.'

'If anyone asks I blotted the ink and will write another one. You can go now and if you hear any more you will let me know.'

'I will, fank you ma'am.'

The front door to the large imposing house was equally striking. Large, black and adorned in polished brass it looked a fitting entrance to house set in the well-maintained street at the heart of the fashionable district. Ellen had seen large houses before, worked in one but they were nothing like the buildings in this street and a world away from the Rookeries of her childhood. She wondered how people could live in such opulence whilst others barely survived in the gutter, dressed in rags and half starved. If there was a reason to should go through with her plan, then this was it.

Composing herself, she climbed the few wide stone steps to the door and gripped the bell pull fixed in the wall. She heard only the faintest sound of a bell as she tugged at the metal knob and wondered if anyone would hear her. Taking a pace back, she listened, waited and after what seemed an eternity; the door began to swing open to reveal a tall, stooped man in a loose fitting morning suit.

'Yes,' he enquired.

'I am Ellen Jameson, Mrs Clarence Jameson, your master's daughter in law.'

'And the purpose of your visit madam?'

'I had dinner with Mister Jameson only last night and heard this morning that he was taken ill shortly after we parted. I have come to see how he is and if there is anything I can do.'

'Master Clarence's wife,' he said more as a statement than a question.

'Yes.'

The man's eyes flickered, betraying some inner thought Ellen was unable to decipher and he opened the door a little wider, allowing her to step inside the house.

'This way, you may wait in the study while I see if Mister Edward will take a visitor. The doctor is with him and presumably will be the one to decide. Tell me, how old Clarence was when he died.'

'Twenty six years and three months.'

The butler nodded as if she had uttered a secret password and turned to walk slowly through the wide hallway and as she followed, she could not help but look around, amazed at the wonderful wood panelling, marble statues and the paintings spaced along the hallway. She had never seen anything quite like it and wondered fleetingly why Clarence had never spoken about his home and his parents. She was vaguely aware that his father was a rich banker, that his mother had died several years before and that his two brothers worked in banking on the continent but Clarence had never seemed particularly interested in the family business interested more in his horses and the regiment.

The butler opened a door, ushered her inside saying that she should wait here whilst he went to consult with the doctor and was gone less than two minutes before returning with a second man.

'Madam I am Doctor Spencer and I have been attending to Mister Jameson's needs. He is very weak and must not have further strain upon his heart. I suggest you simply sit with him for a while and if he speaks then by all means engage in conversation but, please, no more than say a quarter of an hour.'

'Thank you doctor, I will do as you say. I feel I must show support at a time like this.'

'Quite, quite, Thornton, be so good as to show the Lady to your master. I must take my leave now, I will return at,' he took out his pocket watch, 'seven O clock this evening after surgery. Good bye for now Mrs Jameson.'

'Goodbye doctor.'

'If you will follow me please Mrs Jameson.'

The doctor saw himself to the front door whilst Ellen followed Thornton into the hallway leading towards a wide and richly carpeted staircase. The two of them walked slowly, silently up the stairs, along a corridor to a room where Thornton rapped delicately on the door with his knuckles. Not waiting for an answer, the butler entered the room, a large room for a bedroom thought Ellen. Richly carpeted like the rest of the house the room possessed an expensive looking chest of drawers and wardrobe, a washbasin and a four-poster bed on which a pasty-faced Edward Jameson lay. With his eyes closed, his arms straight by his side he seemed lifeless, until he wheezed quietly as he drew a breath and the sight of him looking so helpless after his bombastic behaviour of the previous evening shocked Ellen. A man at deaths door replaced the brash, confident bully she had dined with not so long ago.

'I will leave you for a while madam,' whispered Thornton.

Ellen nodded and reached for the chair the doctor must have used, pulled it closer to the bed, and sat down.

'Edward,' she said softly.

There was no answer other than a short grunt as if he had heard her and this was his only means of communication.

'Edward it's me Ellen, I came as soon as I could.'

Edward Jameson grunted again and this time managed to say 'Mary, is that you?'

'Yes said Ellen, I have come to see you.'

'Clarence's wife came to see me y'know. Dreadful woman, she only married him for my money. She'll get none of it, what d'you say?'

Ellen did not say anything; calmly reaching across the bed for a loose pillow and picking it up in both hands, barely breathing herself, she calmly reached over the prostrate form to hold it firmly over the dying man's face. At that moment, she saw not a human being but an obstacle, and she knew that she had to remove that obstacle. Holding the pillow tightly to Edward Jameson's face until she was sure that he could draw no further breath she finally removed it. Satisfied with her devil's work she calmly replaced the pillow and peered down at the dead face. He looked little different from when she had first entered the room and feeling no guilt, sat calmly back in the chair to await Thornton's return.

For a moment Ellen shuddered, the memory of her crime briefly passing through her mind but after a deep breath, she shrugged it off and tapped on Freddie Jones office door.

'Mrs Jameson do take a seat, it must have come as a shock to learn of the death of your father in law. I'm terribly sorry.'

Ellen pulled a handkerchief from her sleeve and dabbed her eyes, drying invisible tears.

'Thank you Mister Jones, Freddie, I presume that you have news from the army?'

'That's not exactly why I asked you to come and see me. As I am acting for you, I thought it prudent to hold a meeting now that your Father in law has died. I have no idea as to the contents of his will but I do know that, Nicholas and Rodney his two remaining sons are the next of kin and I expect they are at this moment making their way home to attend their father's funeral.'

Ellen sat motionless, very much on edge, waiting to hear what else Freddie had to say.

'You, Mrs Jameson, as the widow of one of the deceased's sons are in line for his inheritance and I propose we approach the firm of solicitors handling Jameson's affairs and lay claim. It may well be that you could inherit a third of the estate but we will not know that until after the funeral and Edward Jameson's will is read out.'

Storms in the English Channel were not unheard of at this time of year but a force nine was a rare event in springtime. Captain Cape had ridden such storms on many occasions and secure in the knowledge that he was the best captain in the fleet, he would he do his duty as he always did. His job was to see the passengers from the French railways transferred to the English side, he had a schedule to keep, and from the bridge of the Star Line ferry, he gauged the state of the sea. Although the waves were high and breaking, he felt his ship and his experience would see them across and decided that they would sail tonight.

At the same time, in the waiting room of the ferry terminal a young Englishman sat with his feet astride a leather valise watching a man approach.

'Hello old chap, thought I might see you here, glad you could make this ferry. I did not fancy travelling alone tonight. Bit of a storm brewing I believe and you know I'm not a good sailor.'

'Nor me. Did you know that Clarence's widow has turned up? Got a telegram from father's solicitor saying she will be attending the funeral and has some lawyer or other who is demanding to be at the reading of father's Will. What d'you say to that?'

'Damn cheek if you ask me. What are her chances?'

'I don't exactly know but I telegrammed old Tom Campion with the same question and he seems to think, if I've read it correctly, that the estate is to go to surviving sons or at least that will be his line of argument.'

'Hmm...I like the sound of that. Clarence was unfortunate to die out there in Africa fighting the natives but we are just as unfortunate to have a hussy for a sister in law. Squeeze her out I say.'

'Hear hear old chap. Look they seem to be starting to board, let's get a move on.'

The channel storm swept northwards during the night and by daybreak had brought showers and strong winds over London. Pedestrians held on tightly to their hats and even the newspaper seller struggled to keep hold of his wares.

'Read all abht it read all abht it, cross channel ferry sinks with great loss of life. Read all abht it read all abht it, cross channel ferry...'

Ellen was walking along the street towards a line of hansom cabs when she heard the newspaper sellers call. She was in plenty of time for the funeral and had made an effort to look the part in her long black coat and black veil. Freddie had said that it would be best if she were the showpiece and he the mouthpiece, he said that he would accompany her to the funeral and afterwards to the office of the executors of Edward Jameson's will.

As she made her way towards the cabs, the newspaper seller's cries became ever louder and she decided to buy a newspaper to while away the time. Settling into the leather seat she gave instructions to the driver and a few seconds later the cab lurched forwards, the clip clop of the horse's hooves echoing across the cobbles. Unfolded her newspaper she scanned the front page and was immediately drawn to the headline "Cross channel ferry sinks in storm" and underneath in smaller type – great loss of life. She read on:

Yesterday, sometime shortly after leaving Calais, a fierce storm overcame the cross channel ferry King George. Reports of strong winds and high seas state seem to suggest that the ferry should never have left port. Her captain, one Captain Cape, though a well-respected and highly experienced seaman should not have risked the crossing until conditions had eased. Eyewitnesses have stated that waves were coming over the sea walls of the port and even less experienced seaman could see that the conditions were dangerous. Luckily, the ferry was only half-full or the death toll would have been much higher.

Our correspondent in France has had sight of the manifest and passenger list and he reports that several prominent people have perished including sir Frances Havers, the well-known member of Parliament and his

*wife and also two brothers, the sons of the prominent
banker Edward Jameson who himself....*

Ellen's mouth fell open, Nicholas and Rodney both
lost at sea. How dreadful she thought and then her mind
turned to Freddie Jones and the reading of the will.

Chapter 3

The moonlight was just bright enough to discern the terrain as the troop of mounted men led by Major Marter cautiously followed the native trackers across the uneven ground. They had been on the trail of Cetshwayo for more than a month following one false lead after another and to make matters worse Captain Lord Gifford and his patrol were somewhere in the vicinity following the same quarry, determined to steal their glory.

Georgie was alert for any sound outside their invisible perimeter. He had been fighting wars and campaigning in South Africa with the British army for more than five years, a veteran of the bloody Zulu war and now seconded, for a time, to the Dragoons of Major Marter. He peered into the darkness, young eyes detecting the movement of the trackers and with gentle nudge of his knees, coaxed his horse forward.

This was no time for private thoughts but he could not help wondering how Patrick and Ellen were faring since they had last seen each other. Patrick was his closest friend in the army, a year older, a big strong Irishman and he missed his company. They had served together ever since their days as boy soldiers at Chatham and had been almost inseparable ever since. Patrick had left his native Ireland to escape the famine, enlisting in the army at the age of fourteen and Georgie, forced by circumstances, became a boy soldier six months later.

The war with the Zulus was as good as finished; the regiment were returning home, Patrick amongst them and Georgie did not know when, or even if, they would meet again and as Patrick and the rest of the regiment headed home Georgie remained in Africa. He was to help train a newly formed squadron of mounted infantry together with several men of the Twenty-Fourth's mobile force who had volunteered to remain behind for a six-month spell of duty. He pursed his lips at the irony of it, volunteers; the regimental sergeant major had said, making it clear that they were to be volunteers, threatening them and offering to drop charges against accused men to fill his quota. Then there was Ellen who had turned up so unexpectedly as the wife of an officer in the Lancers.

Her husband was a stuck up cavalry officer not at all the sort he imagined Ellen would ever fall in love with. However, it had soon become evident that she did not love him; even his own brief dealings on the training ground had left him disliking the man. He had tried to speak with Ellen but an officer's wife was out of bounds, a private soldier could not converse alone with an officer's wife. Even so, they had made contact, he had discovered a little what had happened during the years since he had last seen her and then he had introduced her to Patrick.

There was a rustle in the bushes ahead of them and Georgie brushed aside his private thought, turning his head towards the disturbance. Two native trackers appeared, dissatisfied Zulus who were no friends of their King. It had been surprise to learn that not all the Zulu warriors were prepared to die for King Cetshwayo, a cruel and vindictive despot. Ahead of him, the Major had reigned in his horse and was waiting for the trackers and after a short conversation, they melted back into the bush and the Major addressed his subordinates.

'Sergeant it appears that there is a village up ahead. The trackers are convinced that we will find Cetshwayo there. I will ride up to that hill over there to reconnoitre the valley for signs of life. Sergeant Adams, you and two troopers accompany me whilst you, Sergeant McNamara, muster the rest of the troop and await my orders.'

The Major urged his horse forward followed by the Sergeant and the two troopers, Georgie dismounted, turned, and walked his horse back along the line to whisper the Major's instructions and one by one, the soldiers dismounted. Georgie returned to the head of the column, pulling the horse along behind him and led the troop towards a small clearing.

'Have we got him this time sarge?'

'I don't really know but the Major seems to think so and those two trackers were very excited so I would say we are getting close.'

There was a murmur of approval from the men close enough to hear, Georgie's eyes flashed in annoyance and he pressed his forefinger against his lips signalling silence. He knew the trackers were good but equally, Cetshwayo's own loyal tribesmen were just as competent and, concealed in the undergrowth of the kloofs and ravines, might see them, and warn the King. Then the sound of someone or something forcing its way through the thicket alerted Georgie to potential danger and he unslung his carbine from his shoulder. Some of the men heard the noise too and similarly positioned themselves ready for action but the disturbance simply heralded the Major's return and in the grey light of the dawn, his horse emerged from the dense undergrowth at the far end of the clearing.

'Men, there is a group of huts no more than a mile away in that direction,' he said pointing. 'Our trackers are keeping an eye on any movements while we take advantage of this early hour to catch them by surprise. Ndwaka tells me that he believes the King is in one of the huts and thinks that there are only a few older men with him and they are all still sleeping. We will proceed on foot. Sergeant, take half the force and circle round to the far side of the huts to cut off any escape. We will give you a signal on the bugle when we attack but if I can, I will try to end this peacefully. Mister Ofterbro, are you ready.'

'Yes sir.'

Martin Ofterbro, a colonial who had known the King from childhood had volunteered as interpreter on the mission. Young and inexperienced he suddenly realized that he might be in the thick of the action and the thought seemed to unnerve him. He began fidgeting with his horse's reigns and looked at the ground with unblinking eyes.

'Mister Ofterbro, are you alright?'

'Ye...s sir.' He managed to stammer.

'Good, then let's get started. Sergeant, I will give you fifteen minutes to take up your positions before we move out. Go on foot and keep the noise down, we don't want the old fox escaping again do we?'

Georgie saluted, said nothing, and waved his arm in an arc, indicating to the troopers to follow him and within seconds he and his men disappeared into the bush.

'Mister Ofterbro, stick close by me and do not worry I think that there will be little trouble, particularly if you can convince the King to come quietly. We will send in the native troops first, they should calm things I think.'

Martin Ofterbro looked at the Major with a stiffening resolve and he nodded. The Major acknowledged the gesture and led his men towards the side of a ravine where the soldiers picked their way carefully through the undergrowth and over the uneven ground. Eventually a small cluster of native Beehive shaped huts grew out of the mist and from the bush, one of the scouts emerged and approached the Major.

'They all eating, no one on guard. I think the King has lost his bodyguard, only old men and women here. We look inside kraal and find no problem. King is in this hut,' he said pointing with his assegai at a hut in the middle of the compound.

'Sergeant Adams, take the native soldiers into the kraal, quickly. We will follow on behind. Mister Ofterbro, I think maybe we should try a gentle approach once we surround them. Are you prepared to go into the village and speak with our quarry?'

'I can try sir.'

'Good, let's see if we can end this thing peacefully.'

The Sergeant signalled to his native troopers and the advance into the Kraal began, passing first through the flimsy gate used to keep the few animals in the compound at night and on to guard the exits from the huts.

'Impi, Impi,' shouted a voice from somewhere in the kraal but it was too late, the native troopers were already in position, and the bugle sounded alerting Georgie and his troopers.

In the compound, the Zulus were giving up without a fight, concerned only that the native troops were stealing their possessions and in his hut, a patient King Cetshwayo awaited his fate.

'Now Martin, call out to him, get him to come out peacefully.'

'Oh great King of the Zulu nation we have come to find you, come to rescue you from your plight.'

'Who speaks,' boomed a deep voice. 'Who dares to say he has come to rescue a great King?'

'Magwegwana, it is I Martin Ofterbro, son of the missionary a friend of many years. I have come with many red soldiers to take you back to Ulundi and safety.'

'You call me by my childhood name yet I am not a child. What rank the soldier's leader?'

'He is a major, Major Mater.'

A major, I am of Royal blood and I will surrender to only a general. I will die here; I have no wish to be taken by the red soldiers, the destroyers of my Kingdom.'

'Magwegwana there is no hope, you will surely die if you resist. I am here as an emissary, as an interpreter to tell you that you will not be harmed. The soldiers of the great white queen have instructions not to harm you unless you resist. Please oh great King come peacefully and we can put an end to these troubled times.'

For a few moments, there was silence, then, from the hut's entrance emerged a giant figure of a man, the King of the Zulus. Cetshwayo was tired of running and clad in only a loincloth, a wry, dejected look on his face he accepted the inevitable. Raising himself to his full height, he stood proudly before his captors and surrendered.

News of the King's capture had spread rapidly throughout the land, leaving his loyal supporters disheartened and weakened. The Usuthu, his Royal clan, had come to expect privileges and favours not normally granted to the rest of the population but now they were no more. To others it was a time for quiet rejoicing, the cruel yoke of Cetshwayo cast aside, no longer oppressed them, no longer must they live in fear of the witchdoctors, and suffer their cruelties.

'Father, you have heard the news of the King?'

'I have my son, it is a sad day, we have been destroyed by the redcoat army, and now the King is taken. I do not know what will become of us. We are free of the Usuthu clan but what will the British do, what taxes they will impose upon us I do not know.'

Mondli picked up a stick lying beside him and poked at the glowing embers, scattering a cloud of sparks into the air between himself and his favourite son. Glumly he stared into glowing embers, seeing nothing but hardship for his people and he felt that he could carry the burden of leadership no longer, his strength was waning, and the time was drawing near when his sons must carry the burden.

The two companies of the Ninetieth Foot assembled before the array of tents acted as the show of force Wolseley felt necessary to intimidate the gathered Zulu chiefs. As the representative of Queen Victoria's he was master of the Zulu lands and he would impress upon the gathered chiefs the need for change and mindful that some might take the opportunity to seek revenge he had instructed several squadrons of mounted infantry to patrol the perimeter.

'What do you think they will do sergeant, now Cetshwayo is caught?'

'I don't know. Rumour has it that the Kingdom is being divided up so no one chief will have much power,' said Georgie.

'What about that John Dunn feller, they say he has twenty wives and more than fifty children.'

'Fifty children, they'll take some looking after I bet. I hear he has a lot of land and many people working for him. He is a rich man all right and I would not wonder he would be a lot richer when this *Indaba* is over. Come on let's have a look over there I can see some movement out on the road.'

The troop closed up and Georgie took them at a slow trot towards a group of natives walking towards the encampment. As they neared the newcomers, he brought the patrol to a halt and looked them over.

'Alright men, let them pass, our orders are not to antagonize the natives, just make sure they are not too warlike,' he said pulling up alongside the group and looking them over.

The leader of the Zulus acknowledged Georgie with a raised palm and behind him a group of perhaps twenty men dressed in simple loincloths and carrying assegais came to a halt. They looked a beaten people, undernourished, typical of the groups seen arriving during the past two days and Georgie indicated to the troopers, motionless on their mounts, to let them pass. He had fought against these people, and had been in awe of them at times on the battlefield. Brave, well disciplined, earning the respect of the British soldiers but now they were a sad sight. After their victory at Isandhlwana many had worried that the Zulus would overrun Natal, yet ultimately they were no match for the firepower ranged against them.

'Don't look so fierce now do they,' said a trooper.

'Naw, gave 'em a good thrashing in the end didn't we,' said another.

Georgie listened and shrugged his shoulders. Most of these men had not seen the real, raw side of the war, they were not long out from England and those that had seen action were only involved in the latter stages at

Ulundi and had not seen what he had seen. He cast his mind back to that sobering morning when they had marched away from Isandhlwana, past disembowelled half-naked corpses of the 24th Foot. Many were friends, their faces still fresh in his mind's eye, faces he could never forget, comrades resting in the hard African ground forever. He would not forget them, not as long as he lived.

'Sarge, some more coming.'

Georgie snapped out of his morose thoughts, his eyes following the pointing finger to focus on another, larger party of natives approaching from a mile or so away. They were only partly visible above the long grass, and he could see that they had a wagon with them.

'Ready men, follow me.'

The troop closed up and at a steady pace headed in the direction of the strangers, intrigued at the sight of an Ox drawn wagon in the midst of native Africans.

'There is a white man with them sarge.'

'Yes I see him.'

This was a much larger party than the previous one and there was indeed a white-man at their head riding a grey and sporting a fine bushy beard.

'Good morning,' hailed Georgie.

'Morning,' came the reply.

'I take it you are heading for the *Indaba*.'

'Indeed soldier.'

'And who might you be,' asked Georgie, alarmed at the strength of the man's followers, many of them sporting modern weapons.

'I am John Dunn, come at the request of Sir Theopolus Shepstone.'

The mention of that name was enough for Georgie. 'Mister Dunn,' he said saluting, 'we will accompany your party into camp.'

John Dunn bowed his head in acknowledgement and nudged his horse forward. Behind him, his own mounted men closed up and behind them came the Ox drawn wagon. To the surprise of the soldiers from under the cover popped as many as twenty faces, women, boys, and girls of differing hues. It looked as if John Dunn had brought his whole family for a day out.

The main proceedings of the *Indaba* took place under the shade of some Jacaranda trees, the British soldiers forming an impressive backdrop as they stood to attention. The dignitaries and government agents sat in the shade on their folding canvas chairs and sitting cross-legged, facing them, were the Indunas. The headmen of the kraals had gathered from across the vast plains of Zululand to hear the fate of the great Zulu Kingdom, welded together by the father of the nation, the great King Chaka. His dynasty had lasted a mere seventy years, dominating this part of Africa, fighting the Xhosa and the Boers but they could not defeat the might of the British Empire and now the victors were carving up their country as if it were a sacrificial bull.

In the midst of the dignitaries, the imposing figure of the High Commissioner rose to his feet to address the gathering. His task was to inform the chieftains of their fate, to tell them how the authorities intended to divide their land, who would rule over them.

'People of the Zulu race it is my duty to inform you of the outcome of the deliberations of the Great White Queen's government and how your country will be governed from now on. There will be a strong military presence over the Tugela in Natal should you not adhere to the Great White Queen's wishes.'

The natives sat in silence and Wolseley continued, pausing occasionally to inspect his papers and to allow the interpreter's time to get his message across to those who did not understand English. He told them that the authorities were holding the King in the castle at Cape Town and that he would not be returning. He told them of the partitioning of the country, of which Induna would control which area and as he read out the names of those selected a murmur swept through the gathering. Some approved, some did not, and finally he produced the legal document enforcing the plan, inviting those Indunas who were to take control of the partitions to come forward to sign it.

Of the thirteen areas allotted, John Dunn was to receive the largest and as the chiefs came forward, Wolseley once more read out the terms of the settlement. They were to abolish their military system, they were not to import arms, all trade was to pass through Natal, and capital punishment was to end.

Already some were scheming, ready to promote their own agendas. Subservience to the King was the core of the old Zulu system and no one Induna had a right keep taxes but now all that had changed.

Georgie watched from a distance, his section grouped with the rest of the mounted men and set apart from proceedings ready to contain any trouble that might arise.

'Things seem to be going well enough sergeant,' said the Major in overall charge.

'Sir.'

'I want you to stay here for a while after sir Garnet has finished, give them plenty of time to disperse before you stand the troop down.'

'Sir.'

'I have some urgent business to attend to so I will leave you in charge for the moment.'

The Major nudged his horse forward and moved away at a slow walk in the direction of some tents and a wagon shaded by a singular Thunder tree.

'That's John Dunn's camp,' thought Georgie, 'What's the Major doing fraternising with John Dunn?'

He had little time to consider the Major's movements because the *Indaba* began to break up and some angry looking Zulus surrounded one of the government agents.

'Bring your men corporal,' he said, 'could be trouble brewing.'

The soldiers kicked their mounts into life and followed Georgie who deliberately rode close to some Zulus busy berating a white with anxious eyes that demanded he intervene.

'Break it up you men,' he called out as the troop forced their horses between the White man and the natives.

'Thank you soldier, it's alright, these men have grievances, and I am trying to explain where they should take them,' said the official. 'It was a little worrying so thank you for your timely intervention. I do not know what would have happened had they pressed me harder. They are not happy with the settlement but I am afraid that it is just hard luck. If they decide to stir up trouble I am sure you will quieten them down with a few volley's what, just as you did at Ulundi.'

The man grinned weakly before walking away and Georgie watched him go, incredulous at his attitude. For the first time in his life he began to wonder about the people in charge, as a soldier and politics did not concern him, he was here to take orders and not to question the reasons why nor think about the consequences but he could not help feeling that the Zulu's had received a raw deal.

Chapter 4

The Zulus returned to their kraals in sombre mood, in the knowledge that the British and Colonial powers had sealed their nation's fate. The once great and powerful nation of the Zulu lay in ruins, carved into thirteen Kinglets, administered by the twelve paramount chiefs most likely to adhere to British rule and the Whiteman John Dunn, a confidant of Cetshwayo until the war and then he had backed the British and was now reaping his reward.

It was not what Mondli wanted to hear, they were not of the Usuthu clan and had never been particular beneficiaries of the King's favours, but even so, he preferred the return of Cetshwayo to the white man John Dunn.

'Dumisani, Nkosinathi, Somopho, we are no longer expected to submit to the Royal house of Usuthu, the White man Dunn is our new King. Our crops are poor, the herd is dwindling, and I know that soon men will come to take even this from us, to exact taxes we will struggle to pay. My sons you must be strong, you must be cunning and clever and try to outwit these new rulers, or we will starve.'

Mondli was a proud old warrior, a man who had served his King all his life but the changes imposed upon him were almost too much to bear and he fell silent, and the thought of their future weighing heavily upon him.

'Father I have heard these words already, I have spoken with my brothers. We will take half the herd and hide them in the forest as soon as we see strangers approaching. We will do all we can to protect them,' said Nkosinathi enthusiastically.

'Brave words my son but these are difficult times. We do not have the white man's guns to protect ourselves and if they so wish they could destroy us. We will hide what we can but I fear obedience is our only chance of survival.'

Nkosinathi clenched his fists in anger; he had been through a lot during the past year. In a very short time, he had grown from an innocent, hopeful youth into a hardened warrior, felt the pain of total and utter defeat, and suffered hardships that meant he could never be the same again. The final battle at Ulundi had drained his strength; the guns had decimated the regiment and numbed his soul and he had been lucky to escape alive.

The regiment's spirit had been broken; they had turned and run, pursued by horse soldiers who slaughtered them at will and then one had caught up with him. Breathless and exhausted he had faced death as a warrior should, turned to look his executioner in the eye and in those few brief moments, as he prepared to join his ancestors, something inexplicable happened. The soldier, instead of shooting him, raised his gun and allowed him to escape and he knew that he would never forget the look in that White man's eyes and as his anger finally subsided, he spoke to his father.

'We will do as you bid, you are the head of the family, and we bow to your commands. We will find a way to keep the herd should the Hyenas of John Dunn try to take them from us.'

Mondli nodded, his eyes lighting up at Nkosinathi's brave words. 'You make me proud my son; it is a time for cunning and stealth. I have seen famine in the land before and I fear its grip. We must avoid conflict, save ourselves.'

For six months after the partitioning of the country the people of Mondli's village worked hard planting mealie and beans, the herd recovered some of its losses and it was the quiet time of year. It was a time of relaxation before the hard work of bringing in the harvest began, the cattle were in the lower pastures where the grass was still sweet, and Dumisani was taking time out to rest.

Sitting astride the branch of an Umbrella Thorn tree, he pulled a small horn from the slit in the lobe of his ear ready to take a pinch of snuff. Lifting the back of his hand to his nose, he was ready to take his first pinch of the snuff when a dust cloud rising above the crest of a hill drew his attention. Inhaling the snuff, he watched the cloud grow and from his vantage point made out a group of horsemen heading through the valley. Swinging his legs over the branch, he dropped to the ground to set off at the run and alert the rest of the herdsmen scattered about the valley.

'Quick, men are approaching, men with guns.' He
called out. 'We must alert everyone. Keep an eye on the
animals, I will go to the kraal and tell of their approach,'
and after reaching the Kraal, Dumisani breathlessly
blurted out his news and the more Mondli heard the
more his brow furrowed.

'It is as I feared; they have come to take our cattle.
Find Nkosinathi and bring him here.'

Bowing his head in acknowledgement, Dumisani ran
from the kraal and towards the high pasture in search of
Nkosinathi, eventually finding him standing sentinel
over a part of the herd.

'Nkosinathi, Nkosinathi, trouble, riders are
approaching. Riders, many of them with guns, father
says they are from John Dunn.'

'Go back to the kraal; tell all you see to arm
themselves, these men will not take any cattle without a
fight. Go now.'

Dumisani left and Nkosinathi called to one of the
boys helping him before setting off in the direction of
the approaching riders. He was angry and determined to
fight but as he neared the crest of a hill, saw the size of
the group and their guns; he recalled his father's words
and decided to turn back. Times had changed, they were
no match for the White man's guns, he had seen that at
Kambula and at Ulundi, and although it would be a
glorious fight, he knew in his heart of hearts that they
would lose.

Wasting no time he turned on his heels to run to the
kraal where he found Dumisani together with the men
of the village was waiting for him. Each carried his

assegai and shield and beside them stood Mondli, his face contorted in anguish and from the look on their faces, he knew that they did not have the stomach for a fight. He felt powerless, impotent and the realization that the warrior creed of the Zulu race was finished crossed his mind.

'We will not fight them Dumisani my brother, men of the village, we will follow the advice of our chieftain and use our heads to outwit these bandits. I will confront them and try to pay them as little tribute as we can,' he said seeing that John Dunn's men were no more than four hundred yards from the kraal. They were approaching at walking speed, appearing benign, but Nkosinathi knew they wore a false face. He walked towards them arms folded, blocking their path but the narrow trail was no obstacle, and grinning in triumph, they simply turned their horses to pass either side of him, leaving a forlorn Nkosinathi helpless in their wake.

He had achieved nothing; he had not stopped them, not even had a chance to bargain with them, they had simply outflanked him. Tears of frustration welled up in his eyes and he raised his arms skywards calling to his ancestors for help. It was no use, there was no answer, no sign and the riders reached the kraal unhindered, and with sadness in his heart, Nkosinathi followed them to see all that Mondli had feared was coming true.

A white man was leading the group and he addressed Mondli in the Zulu language. 'John Dunn sends greetings and to tell you that many things in this land that can never be the same again. He is the Induna over these lands, from the Mhlatuze delta to Babababgo in

the west he is the rightful representative of the White
Queen, her officials have decreed it and it falls upon the
him to collect taxes and to retrieve the Royal herd from
those who have taken it.'

It was true, when the British and their allies defeated
Cetshwayo the clan of the Usuthu had secreted the
King's herd, dispersed it throughout the land, but now
the cattle belonged to the Great White Queen.

'If you have any of the Royal animals and mixed them
in with your herd you should give them up to me to take
them to the government officials. The law says that you
cannot keep them. So, Mondli, tell me where you are
keeping the King's cattle.'

'I have no knowledge of the King's herd; since the
defeat of our King no member of the Royal clan has ever
set foot in this kraal. We have no part of the Royal herd
here.'

'You lie Mondli,' said the man, his eyes dark, and
threatening, 'I will do nothing now, but when the moon
is full again I will return. By then you will have
inspected your herd and any Royal cattle amongst them
you will turn over to me.'

Mondli looked sad, beaten, his sons and the few able
bodied men of the kraal were no match for these men
with their horses and their guns and he knew he would
have to begin paying tributes or his kraal and his people
would be destroyed.

BANG! The retort of the elephant gun reverberated
across the valley and its lethal package of lead sped
across the open veldt towards the great bull elephant. At

first, the animal appeared unharmed, not faltering in its headlong charge, but even as it crashed through the bush its life was ebbing away. The bullet had smashed easily through the thick skull and entered the animal's brain to ricochet around the skull, smashing pulsating blood vessels and grey matter to pulp.

John Dunn stood his ground, a second elephant gun at the ready and was on the verge of shooting when the grey behemoth stopped dead in its tracks. Slowly it sank to its knees, remaining motionless for what seemed like an eternity to the hunters, before finally falling onto its side, a solitary leg kicking weakly into thin air and then it was still.

'Phew, bagged that blighter what,' said the Colonel. 'Thought the beggar was going to do for us.'

John Dunn gave his guest a tactful look. He had experienced the event many times, killed his first elephant when still in his mid-teens and now the Colonel had made his first kill he understood how he was feeling.

'Well done Colonel, I will have him butchered and brought to camp. The head will make a fine trophy for your castle back home.'

'Ha, hardly a castle, but yes, he will go well in the house, just above the doorway of the grand hall. It will impress my military friends I'm sure.'

'You've managed quite a mixed bag during the hunt Colonel; you must feel pretty satisfied with yourself.'

'By Jove I do. I must thank you for your hospitality mister Dunn. If there is anything I can do for you, just ask.'

John Dunn smiled in the knowledge that he had gained another ally in the establishment. 'Might I suggest we return to camp, perhaps a whiskey or two before dinner Colonel?'

'A splendid idea Mister Dunn.'

'Johnjo put two chairs under the canopy of my tent and set up the drinks for our guest. Colonel I am sure you would like to try some of the game you shot today; my cook is going to roast a joint of the buffalo for tonight's dinner.'

'That would be wonderful; I will look forward to that.'

After giving instructions to his men, Dunn led the Colonel towards his tent at the centre of the small camp. He had invited him to join the hunt several weeks beforehand, a well-tried tactic he employed to glean information from his guests, invariably people of influence with valuable information to help further his ambitions.

'I had the whiskey shipped in especially from the Cape, it's one of Scotland's finest I believe,' he said as the two men made their way into the camp, passing natives already skinning and preparing carcasses shot during the day.

'Your good health sir,' said Dunn handing a well filled glass to his guest.

'I must congratulate you Mister Dunn, this is a fine whiskey, and as good as I have ever had, even in the officer's mess back in Blighty.'

'Thank you, I have been thinking, the Zulus are subdued for the moment but what will the British do should there be some sort of reaction to the settlement? Will troops be stationed here?'

'Don't think so, under the terms of the agreement the army will retire over the border into Natal. It will be up to the magistrates in each district to try to keep the peace with the aid of each Induna and his own men. The plan, as I am sure you are aware, is for us to withdraw and concentrate on confederation with the Orange Free State and the Transvaal. The Boers are the problem now.'

'Yes I understand that. So you are saying that any internal strife should be taken care of by ourselves?'

'As I understand it, yes.'

'Another drink Colonel?' said Dunn draining his glass as his mind worked overtime. The state of affairs as it now existed suited him perfectly.

Georgie untied his horse's reigns from the picket line and pulled his animal towards a group of troopers standing beside their own horses ready for the day's manoeuvres. Each of them had the young and innocent face of a newly arrived recruit from England, the sight causing him to sigh because it was his task to turn them into hardened fighting men. The army had changed in the short time he had been a soldier, the lifers, men who spent almost the whole of their life in the army, battle hardened and experienced fighting men had all but gone and replacing them at an ever-increasing pace, were the young and inexperienced raw recruits he saw before him.

Not far away, sergeants Alwen Jones and Bill Smith were in a similar situation, the three of them in sole control. Sergeant Jones, ever the one to pick up snippets of gossip had discovered why the Captain was absent; he was accompanying the Colonel on some big game hunt and had left the sergeants to train the men. At first, they had grumbled over a beer in the Sergeant's mess until Bill Smith suggested that they could do just as they liked until the Captain returned.

'What are you suggesting Bill?'

'Well Sergeant Jones, without an officer in our midst we can set the training regime to suit ourselves.'

'In what way?'

'Think about it. We can send the recruits off on all sorts of manoeuvres while we put our feet up.'

'And I suppose take as long as we like over our dinner,' added Georgie.

'That's right. Maybe we could rotate, have some time off. Two of us can manage this lot.'

Georgie shook his head in disbelief, what was the army coming to.

'It's no good you shaking your head. If they can swan off to shoot elephants then surely we can have a few perks.'

Georgie kept quiet, he was unhappy at the state of affairs but reluctant to engage in an argument. His fellow Sergeants had campaigned against the Zulus and both of them knew how important discipline and training were. He was disappointed that they were becoming so lax, feeling strongly that they should prepare these boys as well as possible in case of any further fighting and with that thought in his mind, looked over his charges.

'Right you lot, let's see what your made of. Corporal, ride to that bluff over there and wait. Each man will ride towards you and then back here so we can see how they handle their horses. I suppose you're all expert riders,' he added sarcastically.

A murmur spread amongst the recruits as one or two realised they were about to be exposed and Georgie sighed. He remembered the time when he had volunteered for the mounted Infantry; he had said that he could ride yet he had never even been on a horse. Still, he had managed and had become expert with a horse and now he watched as Corporal Williams rode the two hundred yards or so to his position.

'Mount up. You soldier lead on and the rest follow on my command.'

One by one, the recruits set off towards the corporal as Georgie watched. It was not a particularly scientific approach to training but he would at least know if any of these youngsters really were unlikely to make the grade. It did not matter that they were not particularly good riders more how they handled themselves, how they could be moulded with discipline and training.

The horses and riders streamed away and Georgie nudged his horse forwards to trot after the last of them, watching how each man sat, held his reigns, and controlled his horse. Drill sergeants were not softly spoken men and were unlikely to give recruits a easy time. However, Georgie was different, believing in proper training, the kind that got you out of trouble and as he looked each of his charges up and down, he made mental notes.

'Not bad, you surprise me. Right we will try trotting a little faster and cantering before we knock off for dinner. Watch how I sit and hold the reigns, easy enough if you're not being shot at.'

The men laughed and Georgie and the Corporal exchanged knowing glances. It was going to be a long hard slog but they would do their best.

Chapter 5

In the darkness of the night the only clue to the location of the tightly grouped huts were silver shafts of moonlight dancing off their thatched roofs. Surrounding them, the protective wall of thorn bushes was almost invisible and not a sound permeated the scene save faint snoring and the occasional movement of the cattle.

The inhabitants of the kraal, exhausted by their toil, slept the sleep of the dead. Everyone helped with the work of reconstructing a way of life decimated by war. Even young men who would not have even considered working in the fields only a short time before helped with the planting and weeding the new crop. The whole village was contributing and slowly they were succeeding in restoring some semblance of normal life. The harvest had been moderately successful, the herd was finally beginning to recover but even so, there remained a shortage of food and weakened by the rigour of their toil the villagers found solace only during the hours of darkness.

In the corral, silent cattle stood waiting for the new day to dawn an occasional throaty snort or a stamped hoof the only clue to their presence, a peaceful, idyllic scene. Nevertheless, outside the compound lurked danger and at least one of the animals sensed it. The animal, uneasy at the strange new scent drifting through its nostrils stamped its hoof and let out a deep mooing sound, disturbing Nkosinathi's slumber.

Opening his eyes, straining his ears and unsure of what had disturbed him, he lay perfectly still. The cattle were milling about he could hear them; something had disturbing them, something or someone. At first, he feared it might be a large predator and rubbing the sleep from his eyes reached for his assegai in the blackness. His hand felt the shaft and gripping it firmly he crawled towards the entrance tunnel, emerging into the moonlight and a world of silence save for the one cow. His eyes, already accustomed to the dark picked up a movement near the corral fence and the hairs on the back of his neck stood up. It was a large predator, he was sure, and with his heart in his mouth and holding his spear at the ready, he crept slowly forward.

The shape was larger than he would have imagined and then to his relief, he saw it was a native. The man was about to open the corral gate and Nkosinathi tried to recognise him but could not. Holding his spear at the ready, he moved towards the intruder, his bare feet carrying him silently towards the gate and then a second man appeared.

Sure only that they were not of the kraal he leaped into action, taking them by surprise, first swinging his spear to catch one across the head and send him senseless to the ground and then he turned his attention to the second. He was so quick that the man did not have time to react and within a split second, Nkosinathi had him pinned against the corral fence and the blade of the short stabbing spear against his throat.

'What are you doing, who are you?'

The man stared at him, silent, the fear of death in his eyes and Nkosinathi jerked his blade a fraction into the man's skin.

'Tell me, who are you,' he said again but before he could extract an answer a voice spoke from behind him.

'We have come to take the King's cattle that do not belong here,' and then Nkosinathi felt the coldness of a rifle barrel against his naked back.

Shocked, he stood stock-still; he had little choice, and released his captive. He had rushed headlong to protect the herd but fatigue induced by a lack of food had clouded his judgement, he had acted too quickly. Then he saw that there were several more shadows moving between the huts, men he had not noticed earlier and now he had the price.

'That's right my friend, drop your spear and turn around.'

Nkosinathi obeyed, letting his weapon clatter to the ground before slowly turning to face his captor and by the first grey light of dawn looked into the sneering eyes of a Whiteman, the same White man who had come to the kraal only a month before demanding the King's cattle.

'Why do you invade our kraal, who was it sent you to rob us.'

'We are not robbing you; we have come to take that which does not belong to you.'

'All these animals belong to us, to my father.'

'If you are not happy then you should take your grievances to your chief, John Dunn. I am taking those cattle that I believe are from the Royal herd to him for safekeeping. When he has gathered in all the animals, belonging to the King's herds, he will take them to the representative of the Great White Queen, the rightful owner. You are well advised not to resist for we have many guns and we will use them.'

The sound of voices awakened the sleeping villagers and Mondli who appeared at the entrance to his hut. There was little he could do except watch in disbelief as the raiders began singling out animals, herding them from the corral and expression despondency spread across his face.

'They have taken nearly half of the herd,' he said wringing his hands. 'What are we to do; we have little enough food as it is, we cannot fight them, and we do not have guns.'

Nkosinathi came and stood beside him. 'Mondli, my father we cannot let John Dunn starve us to death. We cannot slaughter any more the animals and weaken the herd for that is the road to ruin. I will take the ablest amongst us and search out wild game to feed us. We will hunt as our people did in the time before Chaka. I have an idea; we will trade for a gun and bullets to kill springbok until we can harvest the next crop and it will give the herd time to multiply. They have not taken the best bull and that may be our one stroke of luck.'

'My son you speak with hope, you are young and you have not yet seen real starvation but I hear your words and they give me strength.

The number of cattle John Dunn's men were bringing in from the kraals was growing. The lands granted him by Boundary Commission were vast, encompassing many Zulu kraals and homesteads and now that he had the power, his men were raiding the settlements. The King had ordered the Royal herd dispersed to loyal kraals during the upheaval and on the pretext of recovering those animals Dunn's men were taking any they fancied. They said that would hand them over to the White Queen's representatives but in reality John Dunn would keep them for himself.

Leaning against the rail of the great corral, the lord of southern Zululand watched the new arrivals enter the compound.

'You have done well Willem, there must be upwards of five hundred animals in there, and we're not finished yet. You have still to take cattle from the kraals to the west and then we will start taxing the mealie crop.'

The renegade Boer grinned, showed his blackened teeth as he nodded his approval. He had recovered the largest part of the herd penned in the corral and his rewards would spur him on to take more from the Zulus. He was a tough and dangerous man originally from the Transvaal who had left under a cloud and with little in the way of prospects had done a little gun running during the war until he met John Dunn and had not looked back since.

'Boss, I see many things out there in the bush. The war is over and the Zulus are trouble no more. The old ways are reasserting themselves, I see traders from the south crossing your lands. Maybe we should try a little trading ourselves.'

'Ha, all in good time. I know about men heading north with guns and whiskey. I don't want to be involved in that trade, the authorities might take a dim view if we are found out. I have a better idea.' Pausing, he smiled at Willem frowning, not understanding. 'I have a plan to award licences to those traders that cross my land to reach the northern territories. We can take the goods we need instead of money, say ten per cent of everything they carry, guns, whiskey, cloth, utensils; they will be trading everything they can. The Europeans are bringing more and more goods into Durban and shipping overland to the Boers in the Transvaal. It is a profitable business and we will have our share. We will form two patrols, you will take one and my son Rabanina will take the other and together you will patrol my borders.'

Willem nodded and his face cracked a crooked smile as some understanding dawned upon him. The once fierce tribe of warriors he pushed around with impunity were one thing but to intimidate whites as well was another, especially if they were British.

Dumisani and Sibusiso looked down at their brother sitting cross-legged and whittling the end of a branch to repair the corral. He had called to them and now he broke his news.

'Dumisani, I am leaving the village, our father is not well, the loss of his cattle is affecting him greatly and with the people going hungry he feels there is no way out, but I will find one.'

'How,' asked Dumisani.

'Have no fear brother, remember we are warriors. I will go in search of a gun, find something I can trade or maybe I will simply steal one from the white men.'

A look of horror spread across the face of Dumisani. 'That is a dangerous thing to do my brother; if you are caught you will be killed.'

'I will not be caught, I will be careful. I have faced death many times and I have survived and I intend that I will live a little longer.'

Jumping to his feet, he looked his brothers over, thin and with sallow eyes from lack of nourishment and knew he must do something. He had not escaped deprivation himself but he was different, always positive, always cheerful no matter how heavy the burden he carried and he was blessed with a fine physique, a true Zulu warrior.

'The herd is smaller now and does not need so many of us to look after it and we have already planted the crop. You will not need me for a time. I will talk to our father of my plans and I will leave before the sun returns.'

There was little more to say, the village was struggling, Mondli was slipping into depression and more than anything, it pained him to see his father in such a way. Mondli had always been strong, always knew the right path to take but he was not the same man anymore and so when he came to sit with his father he decided to tell only part of his plan.

'My father a great evil has come to the land, we have lost much of the herd. You have lost sons fighting the white man and now the village goes hungry. It is my intention to go out and seek food from the plains with my spear just as our ancestors did.'

Mondli looked at his son with tired eyes; the loss of the King, the uncertain future they faced had taken its toll, he had seen the herd diminish and felt impotent when it came to stopping the raiders. With his wealth decimated, did not know how to counter it and as he looked at his son he saw a strength he no longer possessed.

'You are our only hope Nkosinathi; you have proved your courage more than once. I am weak, I feel my ancestors calling me and now it is to you the clan looks for salvation, it is you who must lead them from the darkness in which we are trapped.'

'Your time is not upon you yet my father, have faith. I will do my best, I will leave tomorrow before the sun rises and seek that which we desire. I will go first to hunt game and then I will go to the white man's kraal and take back that which is ours.'

'Brave words my son but you cannot fight their guns alone.'

'I will not fight them, you said that we must not fight as we have done before but find a different path, one of cunning like the crocodile, wait and when the time is right, pounce.'

Mondli managed a smile, his son's words giving him strength to carry on and he reached out to touch Nkosinathi's arm.

'You are a special one my son. Be careful, do not let the white man intimidate you with his threats, bend with the wind as the sapling that grows to be the tallest tree.'

The first yellow rays of dawn raced across the landscape, silhouetting the distant mountains, a backdrop to the vast fertile plain Nkosinathi called home. Today though, he did not see that beauty, only the task in front of him as he ran with the loping gait of the Impi, his mind focusing on one thing and one thing only; he must take for himself one of the white man's guns.

He knew Chief John Dunn had become very rich when a friend and ally of the Zulu King and then as the enemy. He lived in a sprawling farming community, not the close-knit beehive huts of the Zulu but a series of European style wooden houses with corrals for cattle and horses. That was the difference; they had guns and horses and with such animals could travel further and faster than a man could on foot, faster even than an Impi and Zulu's spear was no match for their guns. Nkosinathi knew in his heart of hearts that unless the Zulu adapted to the white man's ways they would not survive.

As he ran, he began to wonder how he might be like them and then he noticed some old tracks and slowed his pace. He was sure the tracks were of his father's cattle, the ones taken from them not more than a few days before. He looked up at the sky, across to the distant mountains and called out to his ancestors. 'Oh father of my father give me the strength to take back that which is ours, help me understand the ways of the white man so that I can steal from him that which he has stolen from us.'

As if in answer, the sound of thunder from a distant storm in the mountains rolled across the plain and he shook his assegai, truly believing the spirits were with him and for many hours more his pace did not slacken.

As the lone runner neared John Dunn's settlement he saw men and women working in the fields and others with horses moving about and thought that perhaps he should hide his assegai and approach unarmed. Finding a prominent tree, hid his spear, and calmly walked towards some men loading a wagon. He feared their guns, he was unsure of their reaction on seeing a stranger and felt his best chance was to appear a lone, unarmed native and not a potential threat.

The ploy worked, the men were not alarmed, simply curious, and as he neared them, a native called in his own tongue.

'Who are you, what do you want?'

'I am Nkosinathi of the Magwaza, I come seeking work.'

'Well you had better go over there to the big corral; you will find a man named Rabanina talk to him. Can you speak the white-man's words?'

Nkosinathi looked at the man, his eyes giving his answer.

'I see that you cannot. Rabanina speaks our language but be sparing with your words, he prefers the white man's tongue. I have learned their tongue, it is useful.'

The native man appeared sympathetic and Nkosinathi wondered if he had been on the side of the whites during the war as many disgruntled Zulus had. To know their language and to be working closely with them meant he must have lived amongst them for some time. He pushed aside his thoughts and approached the corral, taking note of everything he could see. Most of the men and women of the kraal were black or coloured; many were of the Zulu and, like himself, unarmed, a surprise as those who had taken part of the herd had carried guns and he had expected that all John Dunn's men carried guns. A woman looked up from her work and cast an appreciative eye over him but he took no notice and walked nearer to the corral. He felt his chest tighten with expectancy, his plan was working so far, but he had not reckoned with being in the midst of so many potential enemies completely unarmed.

'Hold stranger, said a voice in English.

Nkosinathi did not understand, did not realise someone was challenging him and carried on walking.

'Hold I say,' and then again, "*bhabha*" and this time he understood.

Obeying the command, he stood still and waited for the man to speak again. White men expected obedience from their black servants and workers and although it was against his nature to bow to the whites, he knew that he must.

'Who are you and what do you want,' said the voice
again.

Nkosinathi turned and looked at the man, shocked to
realise he was neither white nor black and yet was
talking down to him.

I am Nkosinathi of the Magwaza and I have come
seeking work.'

'Indeed, what kind of work?'

'Anything you can give me. I am strong and can
labour, I know the ways of the herd, I can....'

'Hold, that's enough. We have plenty of labourers
and cattle herders and do not need anymore. Can you
track, can you track men?'

Nkosinathi's nostrils flared a feeling of pressure
building inside him. Of course he could track men, he
could track anything, had he not grown up a warrior,
roamed the wilderness and lived off the land.

'I can track a mouse, a man is easy.'

The half cast threw back his head and roared with
laughter, calling to some of his fellows.

'This boy can track a mouse, what say you to that?'

The men laughed weakly in agreement, it was folly
not to. This was Rabanina a son of John Dunn and a
man to fear. As luck would have it, he was already in the
process of forming a border patrol, instructed by his
father to form a border patrol of men they could rely
upon and he was in need of a good tracker.

'We will test your belief in yourself, not a mouse, but
a man. Find me the one who made these tracks,' he said
pointing to several footprints nearby.

Grateful for the chance to prove himself Nkosinathi rose to the challenge, walking slowly back and forth before finally squatting down for a closer inspection. He was looking for signs of age to determine how long ago their owner had left them, to judge the weight of the man who had made them and create a picture in his mind. The blades of grass flattened by his quarry had not yet sprung back so the tracks were fresh and he did not wear shoes and his feet were small. Looking in the general direction of the path of the tracks it appeared that whomever he was following was not far from the corral. Following the faint marks he noticed others crossing, obscuring them and they disappeared completely and he stood still to imagine his prey. The tracks were straight, with purpose, only meandering when entangled with other footprints. His prey was mixing with others and looking up he saw a group of men standing by a wagon and amongst them a boy carrying a water gourd. He looked at the ground again and slowly, walking forward he saw the tracks reappear, pointing like an arrow towards the native boy. It had to be him and as he came close to the boy he could see that the footprints he had tracked were his and satisfied, patted him on the head. The boy spun round, a look of surprise on his face and from the direction of corral, Rabanina shouted his approval.

'You truly are a tracker boy, you will join my force. Take him to the bunkhouse, give him some food for he looks half-starved, and then find him a place to lay his mat. He will come with us tonight,' he called out to one of his men.

Nkosinathi understood enough, they seemed to have accepted him and he felt relieved but he was puzzled as to why Rabanina wanted him to become a tracker, wondered how he had convinced this man so easily of his tracking abilities. He lowered his eyes as Rabanina spoke again to one of his men, and then he noticed that he wore some European clothes and guessed he was more white man than native and was it possible he knew very little of the art of the tracker.

'Where have you come from?' asked the native showing him to his quarters.

Nkosinathi was unsure how to answer, to say he was from the kraal of Mondli might arouse suspicion, men might be here who were part of the raiding party and he did not want to be recognised.

'I am from the north, I was with the uVe regiment during the war and did not want to return to farming, my father has died and my brothers did not want me around anymore so I decided to come here in search of work. I hear the Induna, John Dunn hires black men.'

'Did I not see you recently, when we took cattle from a kraal to the east.'

'Maybe, I don't remember you but I have stayed in many kraals on my journey. I am of the Magwaza; a lot of us look alike.'

The other man chuckled, it was true a lot of the Magwaza clan did look alike but then so many others did too, perhaps he was mistaken. Shrugging his shoulders, the man introduced Nkosinathi to the cook and left him tucking into a bowl of maize porridge and after eating Nkosinathi felt so much better. He decided that he would like to wander round the settlement and see what he could find and was amazed at the size of the corral. It contained more cattle than he had seen since the gathering of the King's herds at Ulundi. John Dunn must truly be a rich man because as well as cattle, he could see a corral of horses and his curiosity got the better of him.

'What are you doing boy,' said a man standing by the corral.

Nkosinathi did not quite understand the man but was already beginning to pick up some of the Whiteman's nuances and knew that the man was challenging him.

'I have just arrived here. I do not yet know my way.'

'Oh you don't speak English.'

'No, I do not know the ways of the white man and do not speak his tongue. I have come from afar to find work and I am to be a tracker.'

'I have heard the son of Dunn has found a tracker for his patrol. That must be you.'

Nkosinathi said nothing.

'Well I am Johnjo, John Dunn's servant and I look out for his interests. You should keep to the bunkhouse and not wander. We have had thieves here and you do not want to be thought of as a thief,' said the man, his dark eyes sparkling with pleasure and running his finger across his throat to indicate the fate of a thief.

Nkosinathi managed a suitably admonished look and walked towards the bunkhouse. He had seen a lot in a short time, noted that there were so many cattle that it would be impossible for anyone to see that a few were missing. How to steal them was his next problem and he was still wondering when Rabanina caught up with him.

'Tracker, gather your things together in the morning and report here as soon as it is light, understand.'

'Yes.'

The sun was already well above the horizon when the band of a dozen native men left with Rabanina in the lead. All were well armed, rifles slung across their backs and long bladed knives hanging from their belts as they headed out across the veldt and on foot, accompanying the lead animal trotted Nkosinathi.

Once they were out of sight of the homestead Rabanina sent him on ahead to look for trails, hard work to begin with undernourished as he was, but food was plentiful and in only a matter of days, his strength returned. As he grew stronger, he was able to keep up his loping run for hours on end and covered many miles in his search but in the end, the trails grew cold.

It was Rabanina's first patrol and not much happened, they did not find any smugglers but in future, his father would expect more. Rabanina was happy enough, he had learned the best way to patrol, staying high in the hills and staying inside the tree lines but he could see that to follow the trails more quickly Nkosinathi should ride a horse and when they returned to their base he instructed one of his men to teach Nkosinathi to ride..

Nkosinathi had never been on a horse before and it was with some apprehension he mounted a horse for the first time.

'Don't let it know you are nervous tracker or she will throw you off.'

At the man's words Nkosinathi gritted his teeth and let his body relax, feeling the power under him and within a few hours of instruction he became competent enough and on their second patrol, he accompanied them on horseback staying with Rabanina until he needed to take a closer look at the tracks. When that became necessary, he would hand the reigns to one of the men and disappear into the bush on foot to follow a spore and when he did, he would lead the patrol to the smugglers. When they finally found them, there was sometimes an argument, occasionally a fight but always Rabanina's patrol would come away with a large tribute and only then allow the traders to pass on their way.

It soon became evident how good Nkosinathi was at finding the traders and the men began to trust his judgement. They began to mix with him a little more and around the campfire each night, he managed to pick up some English, able to converse to some degree in that language he one day he asked if they would show him how to use a rifle. At first Rabanina was reluctant until Nkosinathi explained that he felt vulnerable tracking ahead alone, armed only with his short stabbing spear. He explained that not only did their quarry concern him, but also predators roaming freely. Rabanina shook his head, there was no need for a tracker to carry a gun, and if there was any trouble, his men could take care of it.

More often than not, the patrol would head south towards the border with Natal, towards a crossing place Nkosinathi had found that was becoming the main trade route into Zululand. Men from Natal had seen profit in the new order, seen possibilities of enrichment through trade, smuggling guns and tradable goods and it was Rabanina's job to make sure his father received his fair share of the spoils.

One day they made camp as usual in the shade of tall, leafy trees and as the sun sank over the distant mountains the men settled down to a meal of dried meat and cold maize porridge and Nkosinathi lay on his mat looking at the stars. He would be the first to leave in the morning and he wondered what the new day would bring. Rabanina had decided that they would search unfamiliar country in the hope of coming across a trading party and explaining that he had received word that men from Natal were often in that part of the territory.

Just before the dawn, Nkosinathi rose from his sleeping mat. Rubbing his eyes, he looked east towards the first grey hint of dawn, faintly silhouetting distant hills. After rolling up his sleeping mat, he slung it over his shoulder and set off on foot towards those same hills leaving his horse behind. It would be of little use in his search for man spore because the grass was tall and he needed to look closely at the ground. If there were men out there then he would find them.

Quietly he walked out of the camp and a few yards away, saw the horses and their overnight guard. Grinning mischievously, he decided to test his skills his bare feet moving silently across the ground until he stood behind the man and gently laid his hand on his shoulder.

'Uhh...you surprised me,' said the guard in mild panic. 'Lucky I didn't shoot you.'

Nkosinathi smiled to himself and thought that although these men were tough they would not survive for long if an Impi came across them.

'Sorry my friend. I am going out to look for tracks and could not resist surprising you.'

'Never mind surprising me, isn't it smugglers you should be surprising.'

'Tell Rabanina I will look out for him coming, he knows where I will be.'

The man nodded, still shaken by the ease with which Nkosinathi had surprised him and as quickly as he had appeared the Zulu melted into the bush.

Clearing the trees, he reached the grassy plain and at a steady loping run, headed towards the gap in the hills. Constantly his eyes searched the ground for tracks, for signs of disturbance to the long grass and then in distance, he heard the cry of a Hyena and the squawk of birds taking to the air. The country was new to him and he was following a trail he did not know and, gripping his assegai a little tighter, was well aware that he needed to be ready for anything.

The morning was uneventful, the trail unused for many weeks and overgrown in places but he kept on pushing forward towards the pass and as the sun neared its zenith, he paused to rest. The grasslands were giving way to the bush and he saw a kopje from where he could command a better view. The hillside, covered mostly with scrub, sloped steeply, and after scrambling over lose rocks he reached the summit and a better view of the landscape. He took hold of a low-lying branch of an Umdoni tree growing nearby and pulled himself up to settle comfortably in the branches, invisible to anyone looking his way.

In the bright sunshine, he could see for a mile or more before the shimmering heat haze confused his vision and he had to shield them. He looked first towards the pass, then he looked back along the trail for Dunn's men and some way off caught sight of them, black dots on a sea of dry grass and he estimated that it would be some time yet before they reached him. Deciding that it would be a good time to eat, put his hand in the bag tied about his waist, took out some maize, and dried meat and it was then that he noticed the movement.

The men and horses were near the gap in the hills, a pass that was the only way through and he watched them for several minutes as he chewed on the dried meat. They were at the extreme of his vision and he was unsure of their numbers but judging by their movements, they were men on horseback, not just large animals. For several more minutes, he watched and then he turned to see the progress of Rabanina and the patrol, seeing that they were not far away.

'Tracker, have you seen anything yet?' asked Rabanina as Nkosinathi dropped to the ground in front of him.

'I see men over there, maybe four, or five, heading down from the pass. They have mules with them and I think, carrying heavy loads.'

Rabanina's eyes lit up, mules, carrying heavy loads; they would earn a rich reward today.

'Good, we will find them and see what they have for us. Nkosinathi, which do you think is our best path?'

Nkosinathi held his arm out to indicate the way and put his finger to his lips to warn them to be silent.

'Take two men and lead the way, I will follow a hundred yards behind with the rest of the patrol. Find a suitable place to confront them, somewhere with advantage for us, where they will know that resistance is futile.'

Nkosinathi nodded understanding and set off in the direction of the Pass, trotting ahead of the two mounted men and after several hours, he saw something of interest. Holding up his hand, he signalled the men following to halt and he then left them to creep forward alone. His eyes had noticed a faint wisp of smoke rising from a campfire where the smugglers had stopped for the night. After a brief look around, he quickly backtracked to where the two riders waited.

'What is it?' whispered one.

'Smoke from a camp fire. Can you see it?'

'No.'

'Over there.'

The man strained his eyes, eventually picking out a faint wisp of smoke and nodding his head. 'Wait here, I will go back and tell Rabanina what we have seen, and find out what he wants us to do.'

Nkosinathi heard him go but did not look round; instead, he concentrated on the smoke and the terrain ahead of them. It would not be easy catching these men, the wooded hillsides afforded some cover, and it would be difficult to take them by surprise.

'What have you seen?' asked Rabanina riding up to Nkosinathi.

'A campfire, over there, behind the hill, I saw something earlier and I think that not all of them are in their camp. I think I should take a closer look.'

'Are they are making their way towards us?'

'Yes, but they will not be coming this way until early tomorrow.'

'Good, we will ride on and position ourselves ahead of them, camp for the night where the trail drops into the valley and wait. Nkosinathi go and make sure we are heading to the right place. It will be no good if they take another trail and we lose them.'

Nkosinathi replied with a nod of his head and set off at pace across the uneven ground, diving down the sloping side of the Kloof and trotting through gullies. Keeping below the ridge as much as he could in case their quarry might catch sight of him he eventually came across their camp in the valley below. Men and horses gathered round a campfire, four men, their mounts, and a line of perhaps a dozen mules. Obviously, they were smugglers, they had their goods piled upon the ground leaving the mules to feed on the scrubby grass, and he toyed with the idea of having a closer look. It would be too risky he thought, he was sure that they were not the only ones here, he was sure he had caught a brief sighting earlier in the day of at least one more man scouting ahead of the party and after watching them for a while, stole away again to find the patrol.

At first light Rabanina's men broke camp and moved slowly and silently through the valley with Nkosinathi ahead of them scouting the ground. He had explained the situation to Rabanina; they had discussed where the best place might be for an ambush and now Nkosinathi led them to a small clearing where Rabanina briefly explained his strategy for the ambush.

'Go and keep an eye on them Nkosinathi, if they deviate from their expected path let me know as soon as you can. They will not be able to move very fast with a mule train. Go.'

Nkosinathi darted off in the direction of the smuggler's, up the side of the ravine and emerged not far from their camp. Clambering across the loose rocks and through the thickets, he came across a tall tree and climbed into the branches for a better look. Sitting motionless, his eyes searched for movement and then there they were.

The mules were the first to come into view, not a quarter of a mile away, dark grey against the sandy coloured rocks of the escarpment and making slow progress. From the bush, a white man appeared on a horse, threw a noose over a recalcitrant mule's neck, and encouraged the animal to take the trail he had predicted. Confident he knew their intentions; he slid from the tree and darted noiselessly into the bush to report to Rabanina.

'Show me them.'

Nkosinathi led Rabanina's horse up the sloping side of the Kloof to point towards the approaching mule train. Rabanina reached into his saddlebag and pulled out an ancient telescope, lifted it to his eye and brought the scene into focus.

'I see them, a white-man is leading mules, and they are loaded with something. I think it is time we took a closer look. If we let them enter the clearing, they could spread out and put up a fight, out there they have to move in single file. We will confront them now.'

He wheeled his horse round and totted back towards his men, beckoning them to him.

'You four ride on and position yourselves behind the mules and keep out of sight for as long as you can. Cover us in case of trouble while the rest of you follow me.'

The four riders detailed to ride shotgun cut through the undergrowth and headed down the sloping side of the Kloof remaining out of sight of those below. It was their usual tactic, a small party would break away to cut off any retreat and to add support to the main group should they need it.

Nkosinathi took the reins of his horse from one of the men and leapt into the saddle to follow on behind and they were still a hundred yards from the mule train when lead rider spotted them. He yelled a cry of alarm and lifted his rifle to his shoulder and the others did likewise. It seemed that there would be a fight and Nkosinathi braced himself for the inevitable crackle of gunfire. It was many months since he had found himself a target of the white man's guns, the memory of those days still haunting him.

'You are trespassing on our lands,' Rabanina shouted as the smugglers came within earshot.

'Who are you?'

'Men of John Dunn. This is his land and you are here without permission.'

'We do not mean to trespass; we are traders heading for the Transvaal. Will you give us safe passage?'

'For a price.'

'What price.'

'You can buy a licence to cross our lands in safety.'

'We are happy to do that,' said the man lowering his gun and turning to say something to his men and one by one, the others turned the barrels of their rifles skywards, an indication that they did not wish to fight. Rabanina nudged his horse forward, picking his way down the final part of the slope and onto the trail just ahead of the mule train.

'Tracker, go back along their trail and see if we have missed anything.'

Nkosinathi understood, swung his legs and dropped to the ground, handed his reins to the next man and disappeared into the undergrowth. Regaining the trail, he searched steadily for anything unusual, examining a mixture of tracks and hoof marks left in the soft earth. The tracks left by the mules and the smuggler's horses were plain to see but after ten two hours of searching, he spotted an inconsistency. There was another horse, five in total and yet he had seen only four with the mule train.

Puzzled he stopped, held his breath, and listened, his eyes flitting from side to side in search of movement but there was nothing, and then it occurred that there was there no bird song, they had stopped their refrain, and he sensed danger. Straining his ears, holding his breath, he listened intently and then, from somewhere amongst the trees he heard a movement. Someone was making their way through the vegetation ahead of him and again he looked for a sign of movement. A shadow seemed to move through the trees and then another and his heart leapt. There was a man leading a horse, the fifth man, and he guessed that he must be part of the mule train. He was probably riding apart from his fellows as their eyes and ears in case of trouble and it seemed that he had detected them and was coming for a closer look.

Nkosinathi held his breath, watching as the shadows moved slowly between the trees a man, and his horse moving silently, almost invisibly. Nkosinathi could not help but admire his field craft and moved to within fifty yards of the man. He was a native, not a Zulu and he had stopped, was standing quite still, and was listening. In the distance Nkosinathi could just make out the voice of Rabanina voice, it looked as if the patrol had cornered the smugglers and he was negotiating the price of the trader's licence. There were eight men on patrol with Rabanina and he wondered what this one man could do against them.

The answer came soon enough; the man was not prepared to fight them, slung his gun back across his shoulder, and turned his horse round to retrace his steps. Pulling the animal behind him it was obvious he was not going to fight but flee and Nkosinathi hidden amongst the vegetation moved as fast as he could after him. Silently his bare feet carried him closer and eventually the rustle of leaves told him that the man was close by. Nkosinathi could see the path he was taking would take him close to a sunbird tree with its long branches stretching out like a giant hand.

The man was not aware of him he could tell and with his mind racing; he outflanked his quarry and sprang up into the branches. Within seconds, the horse appeared its rider still unaware of his presence and more intent on making his escape. Bent low over his horse's neck, the man began kicking at its flanks urging it on and as they came on, under his hiding place, Nkosinathi leaped from the tree. The horse was picking up speed as it passed Nkosinathi missed landing astride, instead sliding over its back and towards the ground but a strong arm struck out and caught the rider around his neck and the two men fell from the horse. Crashing to the ground, Nkosinathi was the first to react, locking his arm tighter round the man's neck and rendering him helpless. The man's arms and legs flailed in panic and then, with a swift movement of his arms, Nkosinathi's grip changed and he twisted the neck with enough force to snap the spinal column and kill the man.

Not waiting to inspect his handiwork Nkosinathi immediately leapt to his feet and raced after the horse. It had slowed its pace and within a hundred yards managed to catch hold of the trailing reins and pull the animal up short. His blood was up, coursing through his veins at an alarming rate and forcing him to take a few minutes to calm down. With his breathing under control and his heart rate near normal, he pulled the horse towards the body lying near the tree and for the first time since the war, he felt like warrior.

Looking down at the corpse he saw that the man was a native all right, probably Xhosa by the look of his clothes, a mixture of native and European attire. A bandolier hung about his chest, his gun lay a few yards away on the ground where it had fallen and Nkosinathi quickly retrieved them, slipping the bandolier across his owns chest and then he picked up the gun. The strap was broken, but he could soon repair that and without a backwards glance, mounted the horse. If they decided to come looking for him he would be long gone

Chapter 6

The Graslaagte farm was big, almost six thousand acres but the land was not as productive as Petrus De Wit would have liked. His father had settled these lands years before, after the great trek, the time when the Burghers had decided that enough was enough and left the Cape. Too many Uitlanders and too many British colonists had begun to overwhelm their simple way of life and so they had trekked northwards to look for new lands to settle. It had not been easy; many had perished, overcome by unforgiving elements, starvation and war with the Zulus.

Petrus kicked his horse none too gently in its ribs and set off at a fast trot towards a group of springboks he had been watching, grazing, unaware of his presence and upwind. He calculated that there was sufficient cover for him to get within rifle shot and bringing his pony to a halt behind a small hillock, he slid expertly from the saddle. His mount was obedient, would stay where it stopped and pulling his wide brimmed bush hat tight onto his head, he lifted his rifle from his back.

He guessed he was at least two hundred yards from the grazing animals and sinking to his knees, he adjusted his rifle sight. The day was warm, still and the gentle breeze that had accompanied him all morning was dropping away. He knew he did not have a lot of time, if the wind changed the animals would discover him and as if answering his fears, one of the bucks lifted its head and sniffed the air. Something had spooked it and Petrus knew he had little time left to make the kill.

The animal paused for only a second to assess the danger but it was enough. Petrus aimed at the animal's chest and squeezed the trigger, the shot catching the animal squarely in the chest and throwing it backwards to the ground. Without thinking, he swung his rifle a few degrees and fired a second shot to bring down another animal, then the rest turned as one to zig zag at speed across the open veldt and another shot was out of the question.

Jumping to his feet in triumph, he ran to his pony, leapt into the saddle and galloped towards the fallen springboks. They lay no more than a dozen feet apart, both with a bullet hole in the head and he was pleased only that he had shot them cleanly.

Jos De Witt sat on the veranda of the stone farmhouse he called home smoking his pipe, watching his son making his way along the narrow track. Petrus pulled up his mount in front of the house, looked at his father, his bushy beard obscuring most of his features, and he knew that he could expect little praise on his return from a successful hunt.

'What you got Petrus.'

'Two fine springbok Papa. Mutti can make us a fine stew and Annika can make me a new jacket from the hides.'

'You better talk nicely to your sister if you want her to make a new jacket for you. Christiaan already asked her to make him one.'

Petrus shrugged his shoulders; trust Christiaan to beat him to their sister's favours, an expert at skinning and curing hides. When it came to making jackets or breeches she was the best for miles around, no one could compete with her skill and now to his disgust, his brother was at the head of the queue.

'I will Papa; I will buy her a new dress when I get some money.'

The old man frowned, his forehead practically the only part of his face not covered in the tangled grey hair.

'Money, don't you be thinking about money, dat is against the way of the Lord, a thing for Uitlanders.'

'Sorry Papa,' I will ask her to make two jackets and trade one for a new dress.'

The old man's frown subsided and he said nothing. The youngsters were getting silly ideas and they needed to stop before it caused trouble, there were more pressing things than new clothes. He had heard only that day that a meeting was to take place in a few days' time to discuss the British proposal for Federation. He had heard that Piet Joubert was coming from Pretoria to address them so it must be serious. He would bring it up then, his fears for the degeneration of youth, money indeed; they should not be thinking of money, money was the way of the Uitlanders and against the creed of the Dopper.

Petrus knew not to antagonise his father and with no more than an obedient grunt, he led his horse towards the small outbuilding to discharge his cargo and from the house, his mother came to watch.

'Mutti I have shot two fine Springbok for the pot. I will hang them in the shed to let them bleed,' he said walking into the house.

'Good boy Petrus I will ask Annika to skin them when they are ready and we will make a stew with some corn and potatoes. The rest of the meat we can dry for the bad times.'

The bad times, Petrus shrugged his shoulders, they had struggled through the dry winter months when the great game herds had gone north, too far away to follow and hunt, and it had been hard. The land was plentiful but not very productive; the crop of maize and potatoes had not been good and had reduced them to scavenging. They had eaten the last of their dried meat long ago but this year would be different though, he knew it.

'Little brother, I hear you had a good kill today, two springbok. Soon you will be a better shot than me,' said Christiaan walking in through the door. 'Papa told me you were back when I finished chopping logs.'

'I am already a better shot Christiaan; I killed them both within a second and with my sights set for a shorter distance.'

'Very good, I tease you; I know you are the best shot in the district. We will need your marksmanship when we fight the British.'

Fight the British, do you think it will come to that?'

'Me, yes I think so. Look at their history, always getting into a fight, always wanting to be boss. They are pushing for this federation business but I know our leaders do not want it and the Orange Free State will stay neutral should it be war.'

'What's this about a fight?' said their father entering the house.

'Christiaan says we will fight the British, what do you say Papa?'

'Maybe, I know they do not want federation in Pretoria. We do not want it here. We live well enough by our own rules and we do not pay taxes. You can bet federation with the British will lead to less freedom and more taxes.'

'Will we fight the British Papa?' asked a softer voice, a woman's voice.

It was Annika, Jos's daughter, twenty years old and the second of his three children. She was a fine looking girl with blonde hair and a body made strong by the physical labour of the farm. Mostly she helped her mother with the cooking and cleaning, with the planting and the harvest and she took care of the animals when the boys were too busy and made the clothes they wore.

'It's not for women to discuss,' said her father.

'Hmm...'

Annika was as obedient as her brothers were but had an independent mind and a fiery temper. Even though she was supposedly a weak female, Christiaan and Petrus had a healthy respect for her, after experiencing their sister's wrath on more than one occasion.

'No sister, it won't come to a fight, Joubert and uncle Paul will see to that will they not papa?' asked Petrus.

'Maybe, though it will come down to a vote of the people. The leaders are visiting outlying settlements and farms to gauge the strength of feeling and ultimately it will be up to a vote of the people to decide. There is nothing to decide though, the British and the administrators from Natal have put no proposal to us – yet.'

For twenty minutes or more, the menfolk discussed the coming meeting, the disaster they believed the British would try to inflict upon them and the women retreated into the kitchen. Mutti listened, her hands white with flour as she kneaded a batch of bread dough. More than once, she had heard of threats to their existence and always they had prevailed. It would be no different this time.

'Annika have you seen the animals Petrus brought home today? He says he wants you to make him a fine jerkin from the hides.'

Annika's eyes flashed. Her brothers were good at giving her jobs to do, could they not see how hard she worked, it was coming to the point where she had just about had enough of them.

'A jerkin, he will be lucky if I knit him a pair of socks,' she said just as her brothers appeared at the doorway. 'And what about you Christiaan, you want one as well. I'm busy in the fields I have no time for making jerkins for my two idle brothers.'

Both Christiaan and Petrus grinned at her; it was part of their little sister's charm – her temper. She was feisty, strong and a good worker, the kind of attributes a Boer man valued in a woman and no doubt, one day, some good Boer farmer would take her off their hands.

'You don't talk like that,' said Jos, following his sons into the house.

Annika gave him a respectful and, at the same time, an indignant look before returning to her chores in the kitchen.

'You have upset her papa,' said his wife, 'she is of an age, and you should let her be.'

The old man shook his head in begrudging agreement, he was just as afraid of his own wife as his sons were of their sister and grunted to himself, a rare smile creasing his face – that was family, and he would not be without any of them.

Several weeks later found Annika sitting with her mother in the shade of the veranda; she had just about finished the jerkin for her brother and was holding it in front of her for a last inspection when from the corner of her eye she noticed riders approaching.

'Mutti, a man, look over there men on horseback and coming here.'

The two women stopped their needlework and strained their eyes, the strong morning sunlight causing them to squint until Annika's younger eyes made out more plainly the figures. There were four of them, the one in the lead wearing a black frock coat and a wide brimmed hat that obscured his features whilst the others were dressed as any burgher would in rough woollen jackets and the ubiquitous bush hats. Who were they and why were they coming to the De Wit homestead?

'Go and find your father and brother, bring the gun.' It was a natural reaction, after so many years of struggle the Boers were left with an inbuilt suspicion of anything outside their daily experiences. Ever since Blood river the fathers had drilled their children in the art of self-preservation, mistrust of Uitlanders and an ability to handle a rifle and drilled as she was, Annika dropped the jerkin to the floor to hurry and fetch her father and Christiaan from the back of the house where they were chopping wood.

'Papa, Christiaan, come strangers approaching.'

The two men looked up from their toil and a worried look spread across Jos's face. He was old and tired and did not want any more trouble in his life but his son had the energy and fire of youth. Christiaan reached for his rifle propped against the wood store and looked at his father.

'We must be ready Papa.'

Jos looked back at his son and snapping out of his complacency, reached for his own gun and followed his two children. Whoever these strangers were they were in for a shock. Christiaan led the way and at the front of the house, he found his mother waiting with a relaxed look upon her face.

'These are Boers like us. I think that maybe we have visitors and we should think more about entertaining them than shooting them.'

'Who are they; I do not recognise any of them. Do you Christiaan?' said Jos.

'No Papa but they are waving, I think they are friends.'

The four De Wits stood together on the verandah as the strangers came on and soon their features were plain to see and each had the serious look of an Afrikaner Burgher.

'Jos De Wit,' called out one of the men. 'It is I Johannes Swanepoel; we come to talk to you.'

'Johannes, I know you, welcome. Who are your friends?'

By now, the riders had reached the farmhouse and were dismounting, tying their animals to the fence and turning towards watching faces. The one called Johannes stepped forwards and held out his hand in greeting.

'Jos, this is Piet Joubert, he has come to talk to us about the partition.'

Hearing that name caused Jos's eyebrows rise. He knew all about Piet Joubert and looking more closely at the older of the men saw that there could be no mistaking him. Piet Joubert, one of the leading politicians of the Independent South African Republic of the Transvaal, a man who had led them when president Burghers had travelled to Europe to raise funds for the railway to link landlocked Transvaal to the sea. Everyone knew of Piet Joubert but it was the first time Jos had seen him in person.

Annika and her mother reached between the men seated at the table and retrieved dishes wiped clean with the last of their bread.

'Vrou De Wit I do not think I have eaten so well for at least a year, I congratulate you on your fare.'

Annika grinned broadly at the compliment given her mother by one so famous whilst her mother blushed with embarrassment. She was not used to compliments, her husband expected her to provide good wholesome meals and was a man who did not give compliments to anyone about anything – but then he was not a politician.

'My we sit a while on your verandah Jos and smoke, I have some fine American tobacco with me.'

Jos looked across the table at his guest and smiled and from the corner of the room, Annika chuckled inwardly as she saw her father, a man toughened by the harsh Boer life turn into a puppy in the presence of Mister Joubert. She risked an extended glance at the man the Boers revered and could see something in him that told her he was one of greatness. Piet Joubert looked up at her staring eyes and smiled, he was used to people looking at him, he knew that he was something of a celebrity but that was not what drove him on.

'Gentlemen you have all been introduced, we are all Burghers of the Transvaal we are all Doppers worshiping the same church. Here fill your pipes,' he said pulling a soft leather pouch from his waistcoat pocket and putting it on the table.

The men filled their pipes and went to sit on the verandah, the older men in chairs, the younger ones at the edge, their legs dangling through the spindly rails. Piet Joubert sucked gently at his pipe, savouring the taste for a few moments before exhaling the sweet smelling smoke. Petrus had been out hunting when the men had arrived at the farm and had returned home surprised to see so many people in his house. His father had introduced him and to Joubert and those who were accompanying him and now he sat on the verandah floor with his brother as the great man began to speak.

'I can tell you that we intend to throw off the yoke of the British. Ever since annexation a few years ago they have pushed us further and further into a corner. At every turn, they restrict our freedom to do as we please, live as we please as an independent nation; it is time to take our country back. We have ridden many miles during the past few weeks; we have talked with many of our citizens to search out opinions and gauge the mood of the population. Resentment towards the British in Pretoria is well known, but what is not so well known is the mood out here and I have come to hear for myself from people like you Jos.'

Jos nodded his head slowly as he listened to Piet Joubert; he knew from his conversations in the markets that change was afoot. Rumours abounded that the Volksraad was discussing the restoration of the Transvaal's independence and with the Zulus crushed the British army had removed a major threat to their existence. Perhaps now was the time.

'The Burghers have planned a meeting of the whole nation at Paardekraal in one months' time. We will decide then, as one nation, the path we will take'

'Will it be war?' asked Jos solemnly.

'Ah…do not be too pessimistic, let us see what happens. The British have not made any proposals yet, it is just talk at the moment,' he said, his face giving little away.

Inside the house, sitting as close as she could to the slightly open doorway Annika listened to the men's conversation. She appeared to be busy with some stitching and unconcerned but that was not the case and although it proved difficult to hear some of their words, Piet Joubert had the most to say and his voice was loudest. As a gifted orator, his voice was strong and clear and Annika sat nodding unconsciously in agreement with his arguments.

Paardekraal, a small farming community fifty miles to the south west of Pretoria was the place designated for the gathering. The Boers had a long tradition of freedom from authority; they rarely paid taxes and resented bitterly having to pay them to the British. They lived free and unhindered lives on their extensive farms where petty regulation was unheard of, and to Paardekraal they came in their thousands. They came as individuals, families, some on horseback and others in their lumbering Ox drawn wagons, in total more than six thousand people, practically the whole of the Burgher population, determined to have their say.

For almost a week, they hammered out their demands for the restoration of the republic, elected new leaders, formulated the proclamation; the women played an important part. Sharp tongued and quick witted they cajoled their menfolk into standing up to the British and amongst them Annika was particularly vocal.

'We have suffered enough Petrus, the British have taken everything, and we will fight them to take back our country. You and Christiaan, you will fight them will you not?'

Petrus looked at his sister and saw something in her eyes he had not seen before; her clear grey eyes sparkling with passion, a fire burning within them. He was not immune from the oratory that had so inflamed her, but he was just nineteen with little awareness of politics. More interested in riding and hunting he could not help but hear the arguments and eventually he began to ask questions as they sat round the campfires until well after dark. He listened as the informed and those not so well informed spoke of the annexation, of the history of the Afrikaner and their struggles. He learned about Jan Van Riebeck and the first settlers from Holland and the old men and women amongst them, children during the great trek, told of the hardship they had endured in search of a better life. How they had moved away from the interfering British, driving their lumbering Conestaga wagons across hundreds of miles of unforgiving veldt until they reached the Orange River where they believed they had reached the Promised Land.

'My father and my uncles walked in front of the wagon most of the time, only using their horses to scout ahead or hunt for game to feed us. My brothers and I, we looked after the sheep and cattle we took with us. I can remember the times we had to stop because the Oxen could not pull the wagon any further; all of us had to help unload it to make it light enough to move on, and then we would spend all day carrying furniture and cooking utensils back to the wagon. It went on for months,' said a gnarled old man.

'Months is right Willem, we thought it would never end,' said the old man's wife sitting on a stool beside him.

Willem's eyes stared into space as he recounted the time of the Great Trek, finally falling silent as the ghosts of the past came alive in his mind.

'You are remembering Blood River husband?'

After a short pause, 'Ja.'

Willem's face contorted in pain as, in silence, he remembered those who had not lived to see their promised land. His wife looked at her husband with understanding eyes and then she looked at each of the others sat around the fire, one by one, and looked them in the eye. She expressed the strength and resilience inherent in the Boer psyche, instilling in those that did not already possess it a feeling of togetherness with the White tribe of Africa.

'Were you there when Dingaan lured our men to their deaths and what happened at Blood River?' asked Annika.

'I was at Blood River,' chirped in another old man, 'with my father and brothers. God was with us that day. He had forsaken Piet Retief and the others when they went to the kraal of Dingaan to talk peace, but we exacted a divine retribution from those savages.'

There was no pleasure on the man's face; he was simply stating a fact. They were a deeply religious people, Doppers, and they believed fervently in the divine will and that God had led them to these new lands. Whatever hardships and setbacks they endured the will of the Almighty helped them win through and they truly believed that they were a chosen people. They were modern day Israelites and they were escaping bondage at the hands of the British not the Egyptians.

Petrus shifted his weight to find a more comfortable position on the ground next to his sister and looked up at the old man with his long grey beard. He knew about the massacre of Piet Retief's party at the hands of Dingaan's warriors and was intrigued to know more and as if reading his mind the old woman spoke again to her husband.

'Stephanus, you have an attentive audience of young people. Tell them what you know of Piet Retief of the massacre and of Blood River. They should know of our history from one who was there.'

Stephanus paused, looked at his wife, and slowly nodded his head.

'I was not with Piet Retief's party who went to meet Dingaan; if I were I would not be here now. The Zulus are a treacherous people, not to be trusted under any circumstances. They lured Piet to their Kraal with promises of friendship and then massacred the whole party, clubbing them to death and leaving their bodies for the wild animals. The next day he turned his warriors on the rest of us, scattered groups of wagons all waiting for Piet's return. Of course, it never came, just the Impi came to kill over five hundred of us, but those that had laagered the wagons as a precaution survived. My father made us fill the gaps between the wagons with thorn bushes and to this day, I believe it was that which saved us. If just one of those screaming savages had managed to get amongst us, I think we were done for. I lay between the wheels of our wagon alongside my brothers, shooting at the Zulus whilst our mother and sisters reloaded our guns. The attack must have lasted more than an hour but in the end we had killed many of them without loss to ourselves save a few cuts from their assegais.'

'What happened next, when was Blood River?' asked Annika.

'One thing at a time girl,' said the old woman, 'it was months later we fought them at Blood River.'

Stephanus was into his stride; he had had the good fortune of not losing any relatives and had seen only a few of the Voortrekkers bodies, he had helped to bury them but even so, the experience had deeply affected him. He pulled his pipe from his pocket and slowly began to fill it, his eyes staring into the darkness and his audience, impatient for him to resume his story, looked at him until finally, he reached over and pulled a burning twig from the fire to light his pipe.

'We had a hard time for many months, Piet was killed in February, and the fight at Blood River did not take place until just before Christmas. We spent those months together in one big laager and this time everyone put thorn bushes between the wagons. The older men would ride out into the bush most days to search for game to keep us alive but we were prisoners of a sort until word reached Andries Pretorius and he mustered volunteers to come to our rescue. We were in desperate straits when they arrived but Andries had organized everything. They brought food and guns and we were soon ready to take on Dingaan. Five hundred of us set off into his territory and at the Ncome River we laager the wagons. Andries made us position them near a Hippo pool in such a way that the Zulus would have to attack over flat ground on a narrow front and it was there that we killed a great many of Dingaan's warriors.'

'How many did we lose?' asked Petrus.

'Six, we lost only six men and as victors we claimed new lands for ourselves and raised our flag.'

Chapter 7

The lone rider approached at a steady trot, his horse lathered in sweat and dust after an arduous journey. The man dressed in a plain loose fitting jacket and wearing a wide brimmed hat, appeared as a man who knew this country. After his hard ride, he had reached the outskirts of Pietermaritzburg and Fort Napier and narrowing determined eyes, urged his steed towards one last effort.

A hundred yards away, a squadron of mounted soldiers riding two abreast approached, impressive in their red tunics and white helmets and at their head, Georgie eyed the approaching stranger. Noting the man's appearance, he could see that something was not quite right; dressed as a farmer he had fastened about his waist, an officer's leather holster. Farmers did not carry pistols, not in military holsters anyway. This was a military man attempting to appear inconspicuous, a messenger, a spy perhaps and he had come from the Transvaal where Georgie was aware already that there was a problem. For some days, rumours had abounded that the Boers were unhappy under British rule and that there had been some sort of upheaval.

The man rode past and Georgie, chewing gently on his bottom lip, watched him pass and for a moment, wondered what this military stranger was doing in Pietermaritzburg. Something was brewing he was sure, he had seen men like the stranger come and go before and it was usually a precursor to trouble. Shrugging his shoulders he cast those thoughts aside, his days in Africa were ending and it was of no concern to him. With little more than month left training recruits he would soon be on a ship and heading home after seven years soldiering in Africa.

It had been quite an experience for him, a poor lad from the East End of London with only the prospect of destitution or prison. He had come a long way since his life as a pickpocket working crowded streets with his cousins at times with barely enough food to live on. He sat up in his saddle, looked across open, flat veldt. There were no grey, decaying buildings blocking his view, no smog from a million fires filling the streets, the ghostly warrens that they inhabited. Here was different, very different, the veldt stretched towards the peaks of the formidable Drakensberg Mountains, pale against the horizon and standing sentinel over Natal Colony.

'Sergeant, what do you want the men to do?' asked the Corporal interrupting his daydream.

The men of the platoon had been in his charge for more than a month, his third batch of raw recruits since his arrival at fort Napier and these were no better than the last lot. Twenty young men he and Corporal Phillips were to school in the ways of the Mounted Infantry. They were supposed to turn them into a fighting force in only a few short weeks, a hopeless task, but he thought; at least their uniforms were in good repair. Most had not long come out from England and not had time to show signs of wear but the horses were a different story. Neglected and in need of a good feed, the nags were in a sorry state, but that was the quartermaster's fault and not his. After the regiments rotated of at the end of the Zulu conflict, and a lack of funds, they had left only the dregs of the regiment's compliment of horses and the promised feed had never arrived.

'I think we will take it easy today corporal, let them do all the work.'

The corporal grinned; a Shropshire lad a year younger than the twenty three year old Georgie and like him he had been in the army since he was fourteen years old. A useful soldier and good with horses he did his best to help Georgie mould their charges into some sort of coherent fighting force.

Georgie raised his right arm as a signal for the column to halt and then he wheeled his horse round to face the troopers.

'Gather round you men and I will tell you what you will be doing today.'

The young soldiers, a mixed bag ranging in age from seventeen to twenty-three, came on at a slow walk to surround the two NCO's. Most were from the poorest parts of British society and the recent army reforms, shorter service periods together with a lack of work at home had combined to provide a way out of their hopelessness.

'Today we will practice riding and shooting at the gallop, though judging by the look of some of these animals we maybe should only try it at walking pace. You have been drilled in all aspects of the role of the Mounted Infantry and the most important of these is killing the enemy, so today we will try some target practice.'

He paused to look the men over once more, most of them were attentive and interested, but as usual, troopers Cooper and McKenzie had their minds elsewhere. He had not long before leaving for home and he wondered if he should let them carry on and not worry about them or should he do his duty and try to turn them into Mounted Infantry. He made his mind up fast.

'Cooper, McKenzie!'

'Yes sergeant,' said two surprised voices in unison.

At least they were responding. Now what could he give them to do that might make them wake up?

'You see that tree over there?'

The two soldiers looked across the open ground to where the sergeant pointed.

'Yes sergeant.'

'I want you to go over there, go round the tree, and come back here.'

Cooper and McKenzie looked at each other and grinned, it looked as if they were to have an easy time of it, the tree was about half a mile away, and a leisurely ride out of earshot of the sergeant would make for a pleasant start to the day. Pre-empting the sergeant they began pulling on their horses reigns to turn them towards the tree in the distance.

'Hold it, dismount.'

They stopped their turn and looked uncomprehendingly at Georgie, wondering why he wanted them to dismount? However, dismount they did to stand relaxed and waiting for Georgie to speak.

'Stand to attention; you are supposed to be professional soldiers. Do not lounge about like that or you will be peeling spuds. Do I make myself clear?'

'Yes sergeant.'

Standing hurriedly to attention, their faces in a moment changing from relaxed and content to ones filled with apprehension they waited for the sergeant to speak again.

'Right then, off you go, double time to that tree, round it and come back here. You two take hold of their horses until they get back,' he said to one of the recruits.

The jaws of the two soldiers dropped open as the task they were to perform became apparent and solemn faced they turned to begin the double tempo march to the 'Left Right, Left Right' of the corporal.

'That should keep them out of trouble for a while corporal.'

Corporal Phillips said nothing, simply looked at the sergeant whose reputation for toughness and discipline was well known. Georgie made an impression on all who knew him, his hard work, determination and record fighting the Zulus had earned him the respect of all who knew him. He had campaigned right across Southern Africa, seen men die, comrades, men with whom he had served since his days as a fourteen-year-old raw recruit, the experience had made a man of him, and these two yobs were not going to get the better of him.

'Corporal have the men spread out into skirmishing order and we will ride at a steady pace for a mile or two in that direction.'

'What about Cooper and McKenzie?'

'They will be alright, a bit of exercise will do them good and if they think we are leaving them then perhaps it will teach them to act more like the soldiers they are supposed to be. I want to practice skirmishing tactics today. You take half the men and I will take the rest but first let me tell them what is expected of them.'

He lectured the soldiers for half an hour, explaining in detail the manoeuvres he expected them to perform. They were the eyes and ears of the army, he said, and it was their job to scout the terrain ahead of the main body. They were to look for the enemy, search out the best paths for the lumbering Ox wagons and by the time they were ready to remount, two red faced and breathless soldiers had returned to the fold.

In subdued mood, tired from the day's training the troopers fed and rubbed down their horses. The sun was fading fast and their minds were on their own stomachs, they were anxious to visit the mess tent for their dinners. First though they had to suffer an inspection under the watchful eye of Sergeant McNamara and only when he was satisfied could they leave their horses.

Most of the young troopers congregated in the mess tent, sitting at the bare wooden table to hear more details of the expanding rumour spreading through the camp. The simple farmer with the officer's holster was indeed a military man. He was the one to bring news of the Ninety-Fourth's disastrous engagement with a Boer force at Bronkhorst Spruit, a little known river up country towards Pretoria.

'I heard from someone I know on the staff that half of them were killed or wounded. Nearly all the officers,' said one of the men.

Georgie looked up from his plate of boiled mutton. He had heard the rumour, heard that a disaster had befallen a column making its way to reinforce the garrison at Pretoria and now it seemed that it was true. Were they finally at war with the Boers, he wondered? For weeks, he had been aware of trouble brewing, seen elements of the army despatched to re-enforce isolated garrisons and he had heard of the gathering of the Boers. Where was Paardekraal he wondered, chewing on his last forkful of mutton?

'Sergeant.'

'What is it Cooper?'

'You are to report to the Major.'

'What now?'

'S'right sergeant,' said Private Cooper, his face expressionless in case he might find himself walking several more miles in riding boots, a chastising experience and not one to be recommend.

Georgie dismissed the trooper, drank the last of his beer and sat thoughtfully for a few moments before rolling a cigarette. He placed it between his lips and felt for his matches in his tunic pocket.

'Jonesy, have you got a match?' he asked the sergeant sitting opposite.

'Here you are Georgie. Funny, you have to see the Major,' he said passing his box of matches across the table.

Sergeant Jones had been in the army long enough to know the signs and he looked across at Georgie for a reaction. Georgie lit his cigarette and leaned back, not looking at Jonesy and yet well aware of his gaze and after a brief silence dropping the half smoked cigarette on the floor and extinguished it with his boot. Standing up, he straightened his tunic just as two soldiers not long from England passed by and he realised then just how worn and bedraggled was his own uniform. The bright red of his tunic had faded in the African sun and a patchwork of repairs performed by his own unschooled hands covered the elbows and he was ready to go home when he stepped into the Major's tent.

'Sergeant McNamara come in, take a seat.'

'Thank you sir.'

'Now you will be aware of some minor disturbances, the business with Colonel Anstuther's ninety-fourth a few days ago.'

'Sir.'

'Well it looks as if we will be in support of General Colley to counter these Boer rascals.'

'Up country sir? I am supposed to be leaving to join my regiment back home when H.M.S. Humber arrives.'

'Fraid not sergeant, not for now. Your attachment to the Fifty-Eighth is not ending just yet, we need your expertise and experience for a while longer. Major General Colley is assembling a force at Newcastle. The few Dragoons still here and our Mounted Infantry together with a few other available units will comprise the mounted squadron. However, we have a problem; there is an acute shortage of good horses, as I am sure you are well aware. I want you to see the quartermaster and between the two of you, see if you can get hold of some decent mounts. Dismissed sergeant.'

Ellen looked out of the arch shaped window that reached up almost ten feet to the high ceiling and looked out at the traffic passing by. The hustle and bustle of central London fascinated her, carriages and horse drawn trams vying for space, pedestrians dodging in and out between horses, their hooves clattered noisily across the granite paving. It was windy and raining and great puddles were forming on the uneven surface leaving pedestrians and their umbrellas struggling to negotiate their way.

'Your tea madam.'

Ellen's attention turned to the waiter, his long white apron a contrast to the greyness outside.

'You did say a pot of tea and two cups did you not madam?'

'Yes, thank you.'

The waiter placed the tray on the table, transferred the teapot and scones onto the placemats, and left Ellen alone with her thoughts. The tea would remain warm enough for a while; she could wait a little longer, but where was he? Glancing out through the rain-streaked windowpane, her heart skipped a beat as she caught sight of a familiar figure. He was hopping across the road in a vain attempt to avoid the puddles and she watched for a few seconds until he disappeared from view. He was behind a heavily laden wagon and she found herself straining forwards to try to see him and realised then how much she had missed him.

The afternoon was dark and foreboding, the December rain miserable and depressing and the teashop's solitary gaslight offered little enough illumination to lift dampened spirits. She picked up the teapot and began to pour the tea and right on cue, Patrick walked into the room a huge grin on his face and to her, it was as if the sun had at last begun to shine.

Surprisingly, it was the first time she had seen him dressed in civilian clothing, the red serge tunic banished, replaced by a well cut tweed jacket and the white Foreign Service helmet exchanged for a smart black bowler hat.

'You want me lookin' loike one of those posh bankers do ye?' he had said when she had offered to buy him a coat. 'I don't need any of those posh coats. Haven't I managed all these years in a jacket and an oiled cape?'

She had smiled to herself at the time, unperturbed at his dismissal of her offer. He had been in the army since he was fourteen, tough and weather-beaten and it was no real surprise that he showed contempt for soft civilian ways. A week earlier, she had gone to see him in Chatham, spending the day with him before he had to return to barracks and she had to catch the train back to London. They could only spend a brief time together but in those few hours, they had made their plans. After ten years' service Patrick was finally leaving the army, seeing out the last few days of his service at the barracks in Chatham where it had all started for him, saying his goodbyes to comrades with whom he had been through so much and today, at last, he was free.

He had caught a glimpse of her looking at him through the window as he made that last dash between the traffic and it was that which had put the grin upon his face. They had not seen a great deal of each other during the past year even though they were both in the United Kingdom. The regiment had returned to its barracks at Brecon, miles away in the Welsh hills and, apart from regular letters, she had seen him only twice in all that time. The first time he travelled to London for a day, the second, he had taken the last of the leave due to him and for two days, they had lain in each other's arms. Ellen had booked them into a hotel well away from Claridges and prying eyes where they had let their passion run its course, rediscovering each other and cementing their love.

'Patrick, have you thought what you might do when you are no longer a soldier,' she had asked him and he had looked up from his plate of kippers, puzzled, not sure of her meaning. He had been a soldier ever since he was a youth, ordered to do this and ordered to do that, never really thinking for himself – unless of course his life was in danger but even his training took care of that.

'What d'you mean darlin' girl?'

'Have you thought about a job, how are you going to keep me?' she teased.

Patrick stopped chewing, his face expressionless, and his eyes moving slowly from side to side, the only indication that his mind was active.

'Keep you? To be sure I will find a way, don't worry your pretty little head about dat.'

Ellen smiled to herself, he was still the impetuous, optimistic Patrick she had fallen in love with and she knew in her heart of hearts that he would find a way, but she had other ideas.

'Patrick.'

'What.'

He was chewing again, his thoughts more about breakfast than supporting her.

'What *are* we going to do when we are together and you are free of the army?'

This time Patrick kept on chewing, wolfing down the last of his breakfast and after a gulp of tea, he dropped the fork onto his plate.

'What are *we* going to do? What do you mean? I will have a little money from my discharge an' I am going to do nottin' for a while.'

'And then what?'

'What?'

'And then what?'

'What do you mean?'

'Patrick we can't live together like this for much longer. Either we live separately, I find a job or...'

'Or what?'

'Or we get married and live together, but if we do how will you keep me?'

'Married?'

It was then her questions began to percolate Patrick's mind. A soldier did as the officers told him, ate when they told him, slept when they told him, in fact it was alien to the ordinary soldier to think at all for himself and Patrick was no exception.

'Married,' he exclaimed again. 'Now why would we want to get married?'

Ellen felt a sudden pang, perhaps he did not want to be with her after all.

'Because we're in love, that's why.'

After a short, thoughtful pause, he said with his cheeky Irish smile.

'As good an idea as any I suppose.'

Slowly he placed his plate on the bedside table and put his arm around her, pulled her towards him, and kissed her on her forehead. Ellen looked up at him and smiled, she would not tell him just yet that he need not support her, but he had cleared the first hurdle.

The troop rode in silence towards the setting sun and Fort Napier, a single line strung out over several hundred yards and a second horse accompanied each man. At the head of the column rode Georgie, deep in thought, concerned that the horses they had so recently purchased were not up to scratch. They looked tired, were smaller in stature than he would have liked but they were all they could find. The previous year the majority of the Dragoons and all the Seventeenth

Lancers had left South Africa; the army had sold off most of their horses leaving only a few decent mounts for the force that remained but now there was a new urgency to bring the mounted sections up to strength. The sound of approaching hooves disturbed his thoughts and he turned in his saddle to see the Quartermaster ride up alongside him.

'Sir.'

'Carry on sergeant, looks like we will be back at the fort soon,

'Sir,' answered Georgie aware that the officer was somewhat agitated.

'You know, ever since I have been out I have never failed to wonder at these corrupt colonials,' he said. 'The will drain the army of anything they can, given the chance. Ask high prices when they know we are in need and then they cheat on weights and quality and they do not seem to do much fighting do they; no it's our men who die out there not them.'

Georgie kept his peace, privately agreeing.

'You are very quiet sergeant, is there a reason?'

'Sir, I was wondering about the horses. Will they stand up to the rigours of the march?'

'Yes...I see your point. Still it is the best we can do for now. What if I see if we can get hold of some oats to feed them on, will that help?

'I think so sir, the thin grass out here hasn't done them much good has it. Perhaps a better feed for a day or two might put some stamina back into them.'

For several weeks, more the sergeant and the Quartermaster combed surrounding farms and homesteads looking for horses to bring the mounted sections up to full strength. As Georgie had feared, the quality of the animals the purchased was not good although things did improve eventually. a little while later some better quality horses arrived from the Cape and Georgie was happy that he was finally able to allot his recruits horses that could stand up to the rigours of patrol and soon after they were on the march north.

The journey was uneventful, flat grasslands stretching towards distant hills and on that first morning, as his horse snorted and swung its head from side to side Georgie looked towards those hills. Soon the land would begin sloping upwards slowing the wagon's progress as they negotiated the kloofs and ravines and he knew that if the persisted rains came then progress would come to a grinding halt. He had campaigned for too long in this hard and unforgiving country to expect anything less. He looked up at the sky; searched for ominous black clouds that foretold of heavy rain ones, to which he had become accustomed. The violent storms that raged across this country soon could cause rivers to flow with an intensity that made them impassable, tracks would turn to mud and the wagons would sink to their axles. He seen it so many times before, days of misery and backbreaking work and he realised that he was becoming tired of campaigning.

Lifting his field glasses he scanned the horizon and in the far distance, the foot hills of the Drakensberg, hazy grey and amongst them their objective, the pass at

Laing's Nek. Behind him his section of mounted infantrymen sat in silence until one called out to him.

'Sergeant, riders approaching.'

Georgie lowered his glasses, looked round, and saw The Major, accompanied by a mixed party of mounted Infantry and a few of the unruly looking Natal Mounted Police appearing over the crest of the hill and heading towards them.

'Cooper,' he said to one of the men.

'Sergeant.'

'Take Private Jackson with you and keep a sharp lookout from that hillock whilst I see what the major wants.'

The trooper kicked at his horse's flanks, waved at the private to follow him and the two of them moved off to the forward position leaving Georgie and the two remaining members of his section awaiting the arrival of the Major.

'Sergeant, we are going to set up a forward observation post on...,' he looked round, 'that hill over there where your men are already heading. I want you to take the rest of your section and form a vedette keep an eye on those hills. We think some Boers are there and if they try to interfere then you have my permission to shoot them.'

Georgie saluted and signalled to the remaining members of the troop to follow him to where troopers Cooper and Jackson were already keeping a watchful eye.

'We've been ordered to stay here for a while, better to dismount and one of you go and look after the horses,' he said to the watching soldiers.

'Are the Boers here then sergeant?' said Cooper.

'We haven't seen any.'

'I don't expect you have, not likely to stand up and wave are they. Spread out a little and find a good position with a view towards those hills – and keep out of sight, we don't want to signal our presence.'

The soldiers dismounted, handed their reigns to Private Jackson, took up their positions and Georgie lifted his field glasses to his eyes. Scanning the immediate vicinity he could see nothing, if the Boers were anywhere near then they were invisible. Shifting his line of sight he caught his breath as he noticed a movement and carefully focused the field glasses for a better view. Several riders had appeared over the crest of a small hill and as they came into sharp focus, he recognised their red and white uniforms as Mounted Infantry.

For many minutes, he monitored their progress as they made their way across country disappearing once more before emerging from a ravine to head in their direction. Eventually he was able to make out the lead horseman and as they came within hailing distance he called out.

'Jonesy, any sign of the enemy?'

'No, not really,' replied the Welshman. 'We saw some of them well off, but that would be about ten miles away. Their patrols are still a long way off.'

'Good, I had wondered about the chances of an ambush.'

Corporal Jones grinned at Georgie and looked back over his shoulder at the country he had just vacated.

'Every chance I would say Sergeant McNamara. In this is the kind of country a man could hide here for years, though these Boers are not really fighters. They are not really up to taking us on and I reckon that after firing off a few shots at us, they will run off, eh?

Georgie said nothing; the consensus seemed to be that they would have little trouble dealing with the Boers when it came to a confrontation and he hoped that was right.

'Well we are going back to camp Sergeant so I will leave you for now,' said Corporal Jones lifting his arm to sweep it nonchalantly forward and the patrol moved off.

Many miles from the vanguard of the British force the Commandant General of the Boer army walked with purpose towards a group of men talking in low voices. He took out his pipe, stuck it in his mouth, and stood waiting for them to acknowledge him. He was the commander only by common consent, the commander of an army of farmers not partial to taking orders and he would not dream of interfering in their conversation. Most of them were older, experienced men toughened by a lifetime in Africa, men who had lived their entire lives surrounded by hostile peoples and he knew there was little he could tell them. However, they were polite, kindly men and their conversation fell silent as Piet

Joubert struck a match and lit the tobacco and they all looked at him.

As he exhaled the sweet, sickly smelling smoke, his bright clear eyes looked at each of them in turn from under bushy eyebrows and then he spoke in deep, methodical tones.

'Our scouts positioned in the hills to the south, about ten miles away, have reported the arrival of the British column. They have observed them making camp near Laing's Nek and we expect that their patrols will soon come looking for us.'

Several of the Burghers nodded, they had discussed the probability that the British would have to send a column to secure the isolated forts they had laid siege to and to relieve the garrison at Pretoria. Commandant General Joubert had always believed any army entering the Transvaal must take the road through the Nek and it seemed that his was a well-placed belief.

'What do you want us to do Piet?'

The Commandant drew a mouthful of smoke from his pipe and exhaled, the cloud obscuring his sun beaten leathery face for a few seconds and then he spoke. 'I want the patrols doubled; I want our men to keep out of the sight of the enemy as much as possible. We can judge with some certainty their strength. They are on the march; we can see their column, count them almost to a man. However, they do not know of our strength, we have our fighters dispersed amongst the hills and a commando of around eight hundred men has assembled at Heidelberg ready to ride at a moment's notice to reinforce the few scouts already positioned around the

Nek. We can, we must, keep them guessing. It is my belief that they will overestimate our strength for a while, not try to attack straight away, and that will give us time to call up those reinforcements. Go to your commandos and organize them, send for more men and report to me here at regular intervals. We will see what kind of an army the British have.'

Amongst the listeners, Jos De Wit nodded slowly his agreement with the commander's interpretation and then the group began to disperse and he walked towards his pony and climbing into the saddle, pulled on the reigns to turn the animal towards a group of younger men.

'Christiaan, Petrus, come we must return to our post. We have work to do.'

Christiaan and Petrus had been catching upon the local gossip but responded to their father's command by running to retrieve their tethered ponies.

'Papa, what was decided?' asked Christiaan as his son's horses came alongside his.

'Nothing we did not expect.'

There was a brief silence, Jos was a man of few words and his sons knew not to press him but Petrus was young and impatient.

'What do we expect papa?'

'Hm...can you not see?'

'We are to attack the British in their camp?' questioned the youth impetuously.

Jos looked across at his son and frowned.

'We do not attack an army like theirs, they have field guns. No we wait and we watch.'

'Field guns, I have heard of those. What are they Papa?'

'They call them artillery,' said Christiaan. 'I was talking with some of the men and they told me they had seen field guns in action during the war with the Zulu. They say they are dangerous, they can shoot much further than a rifle and kill fifty men with one shot. We don't want to be attacking an enemy with weapons like that little brother.'

'It is beginning to get dark, come boys, we will return to Inkwelo,' said Jos gazing out towards the mountains and nudging his pony forward. Christiaan and Petrus did likewise, falling in beside their father and the three of them trotted at a steady pace.

The camp of the Ermelo de Witt commando nestled in a hollow half way up the side of a hill and as they approached, several men came to meet them. Jos's younger brother Jacob together with his three sons and several more men from their district.

'What news brother, what was said?'

'The enemy is making camp at the Nek and is ready to try to pass through. Tomorrow we move our position to overlook the Nek, find good firing positions and wait.'

Jacob De Witt nodded slowly spending a few moments reflecting before reaching into his pocket for his pipe, lighting it and through the billowing smoke cloud addresses Jos in a serious tone.

'Jos, we are leaving in the morning, I need to see to my animals and tend to the crops. The womenfolk can manage only so much. We will be back in two days.'

Jos nodded a stony acceptance, a peasant army sometimes had priorities other than fighting, and there was very little he could do about it.

'We come back in a few days Jos,' said Jacob.

'Ja, you go now and we let you know where we are when we move from here.'

Early the following morning Jos watched as his brother and nephews leave, their ponies picking their way steadily over the broken ground before disappearing from view. Lighting his pipe he looked eastwards towards the flat-topped hill of Majuba and beyond to the Nek and as his tobacco burned its last he rallied pipe the remaining volunteers.

'Break camp comrades, we have orders to move towards the Nek, to watch for the British. When we find ground with a good field of fire, we will make camp again and wait for the enemy.'

The men said little, they were a tribe of few words, most used to a solitary life on their farms and one by one, they led their ponies onto the track leading towards the expected battleground to mount up and follow on behind Jos.

The track led up a gentle slope to the hilltop and from there they could see right across the valley to where other commandos were already heading.

'It looks like the whole of our people are mobilizing Christiaan. I have never seen so many Burghers at any one time said Petrus.

His brother riding just in front of him turned round and gave him a stern look. 'It will need all of us to throw these Uitlanders out of our country. It's an army we are to fight and the sooner we rid ourselves of these intruders the better. We will soon have our chance.'

Christiaan was angry, passionate, and had a steely determined look on his face Petrus had never seen before and it fazed him, confused him and he avoided his brother's gaze, riding quietly for the remainder of the journey until Jos raised his arm and called out.

'We go there, the high ground over there and make camp.'

The men of the depleted commando followed Jos to the place he had picked and below the crest of a hill, tethered their animals, and found comfortable resting places overlooking the next valley. Jos told them their job was to lookout for any enemy movement, any patrols the British sent out, and most of all to keep out of sight.

'The Commandant General says we must not show ourselves or the enemy will see that we are not so numerous and feel confident enough to attack. There are commandos on their way to help but until they arrive, we don't want to get into a fight. Leave the ponies here and spread out, find a good position and keep a lookout. If anybody sees anything, then tell me.

It was a boring occupation, with no sight of the enemy for several days not even animal or bird movement to entertain them. It was as if the wildlife knew what was coming. Alone with their thoughts, the men lay in the long grass, invisible and silent until Petrus called out excitedly to the men nearest him.

'I can see a dust cloud. Over their look, Christiaan, Hans, Claus, look there,' he repeated pointing his finger.

'Where?'

'There.' Unlike some of the older men, his young eyes had near perfect vision, able to detect the slightest of movement when he hunted game and now he had spotted something. The dust cloud was faint, more than a mile away and rising almost invisibly above the bush. As each man's eyes followed the outstretched hand, they too became aware of something.

'Papa use the telescope', said Christiaan.

Jos rolled a little way down the crest of the hill before getting to his feet and reaching into the leather pouch slung across his chest, felt for his battered old telescope. Pulling it out he fully extended it and returned to his position ready to have a closer look at the apparition. Lying flat, he poked the telescope through his grassy surroundings and squinted through the glass but his eyes were not as they used to be.

'Ag, mine eyes are watering, I cannot see properly. Here Petrus, you look, tell me what you see.'

Petrus came to lay outstretched beside his father and, aiming the telescope towards the point of interest in the valley below, he slowly moved the lens in and out, twisting the instrument until it brought the subject into focus.

'Red, I can see some red colouring in amongst the long grass and the scrub. Redcoats, yes Redcoats on foot.'

'How many,' asked Jos?

'I can't tell but I guess upwards of fifty.'

The advance guard made its way along the trail ahead of the wagons, and as they came on more infantrymen joined them marching four abreast, then mounted men, officers, and behind them lumbering wagons began to appear. The British army had arrived.

Petrus described everything he saw, Jos's face changed little, his dark, implacable eyes revealing nothing of his thoughts. He believed that they were one of the most forward outposts and this was likely the first sighting of the approaching enemy and he asked Petrus to give him an idea of how many men he could see.

Petrus's mathematical skills were not of the greatest but he managed a rough count and hurriedly Jos scribbled it down on a piece of paper.

'Petrus take this note to the Commandant General. You know where to find Commandant General's camp?' '

'Ja,' said Petrus nodding his head and taking the piece of paper from his father. 'It will take me at least two hours to reach Piet Joubert's headquarters Papa. I should be back here before nightfall, will you still be here?'

'I don't know Petrus; it depends on what the enemy do. We will wait as long as we can but if we have to move then I will tie a piece of cloth to this tree here. If you see the cloth then don't come any nearer, go back to the Laager and meet us there.'

Petrus nodded again and picked up his hunting rifle before setting off on a crouching run towards the Ponies. The ride to Commandant General Joubert's headquarters would take him down the valley and up over the hills to the north, an easy enough and he hoped that Commandant Joubert would not detain him so that he could return by nightfall. If there was to be any fighting then he wanted to be part of it.

Far below the watching Boers, red-coated soldiers in good spirit were marching easier than previous days, the terrain undulated less, and the rain had held off. The ground remained dry and firm the waggons were making steady progress and each infantryman was relieved he did not have to struggle with them through the mud.

'At last a day when we don't have to haul the wagons,' muttered a trooper.

'And rumour has it that we will be making camp, a proper camp where we can rest for a few days,' said another.

'Will ye look at those hills,' added a Scottish voice. 'I haven't seen anything like that since I was a boy in the Highlands.

Eyes followed the soldier's gaze towards the Drakensberg, towards a single, square-topped hill standing sentinel over the pass of Laing's Nek and for the twentieth time that day struck up their rendition of My Grandfather's Clock. Most of the soldiers had never seen action, baby-faced recruits not long out from England and their first time on active service. It seemed an adventure to many of them, coming from deprived backgrounds with little prospect of work the army had offered an escape and their singing carried across the valley until the platoon Captain raised his hand, ordering them to cease. Several hundred yards away

Mounted Infantry returning from had suddenly appeared out of a depression.

'Lieutenant Mills take charge whilst I meet these fellows to see what they have to say,' said the Captain nudging his horse forward to meet them and across the valley, hidden behind the crest of the steeply sloping hill, Christiaan saw the riders too. He had taken over from his brother, scrutinizing the countryside through the aged telescope.

'Papa, some riders, look they are heading towards the soldier boys.'

'What...where? Let me look.'

Christiaan handed the telescope to his father and pointed towards riders making their way towards the mass of red and white. Jos peered through the telescope, picking out as much detail as he could but they were too far away for his old eye to recognize much other than that they were British soldiers.

'Here Petrus, tell me what you see,' said Jos handing the telescope to his son.

'Some mounted men are riding towards them and it looks like an officer is riding to meet them.'

The officer reached the Sergeant in charge of the patrol and each saluted the other. 'Where have you come from Sergeant?'

'Up towards the Nek, our orders are to keep a lookout for enemy movement.'

The captain nodded. 'Anything to report, have you seen the enemy?'

'Yes sir, we have come across one or two Boer patrols out in the hills but they were a long way off and if they saw us they certainly didn't come for a closer look,' said Georgie lifting his helmet and using the sleeve of his tunic to wipe the sweat from his forehead.

'If I catch you doing that again sergeant I'll have you demoted back down to corporal. I expect you to be smart and soldierly at all times. Discipline Sergeant, discipline, which is what makes this army what it is and it will be discipline that sees off this rag tag Boer mob. Do I make myself clear?'

'Yes sir,' said Georgie rather taken aback.

It was the hottest part of the day and they had covered a lot of ground since sunup, climbing the steep sloping sides of Kloofs and picking their way through unfamiliar territory. Georgie had worried about the possibility of an ambush and now this toy soldier's reprimand was doing little to endear confidence in the officer corps. Replacing his helmet, he saluted and out of the corner of his eye, he caught a glimpse of a smirking Private Cooper.

'Sir, if you will excuse us I have to report to the staff officer.'

'Certainly Sergeant, carry on.'

Georgie saluted again and signalled his men to follow him towards the staff officers to make his report. Not only had they been on the lookout for enemy movement but also had searched for a safe and easily defended area to make camp for the night and several miles away they had found one.

The order came to move on and the strung out column made its slow progress towards the campsite where Infantry units were set to work clearing tangles of undergrowth to make space to laager the wagons, a defensive tactic learned the hard way again the Zulus. The soldiers worked to the company Sergeant Majors barked orders, unloading tents and equipment, mules were unhitched, the mobile kitchen fires lit and at the edge of the camp Georgie halted his section.

It had been a long day, leaving the main column after an early breakfast they had travelled miles across country, up into the hills and with only hard biscuits and water for sustenance, they were hungry, the sight of the kitchen almost too much to bear, but the horses needed attending to first.

'Sergeant McNamara.'

Georgie looked up from inspecting his horse's saddle sores to see Major Brownlow, the Mounted Infantry's commanding officer approaching.

'What have you seen out there Sergeant, anything of interest? I have had reports from several sections already but you were the most advanced patrol. What have you seen?'

'Sir, I've reported to the Staff that we came across a few riders scattered across the skyline well to the north and there was some movement on that hill over there,' he said pointing to the flat-topped hill. 'I saw horses and men up there but the Boers manage keep themselves out of sight most of the time.'

'Yes they are good at field craft I will give them that. Tomorrow we have orders to scout the area towards that mountain, amongst the trees, a good place for our Dutch friends to hide. We do not want any surprises do we Sergeant?'

'No sir.'

'Rest the horses and get something to eat but I want you back out on patrol before daybreak. We are staying here tomorrow to rest the Oxen and for the General to consult with his Staff officers but sergeant, report directly to me on your return and I will inform the general.'

'Yes sir.'

Georgie saluted and led his horse towards a grassy patch to allow the animal to graze for a time but it would have to wait a while before the feed wagons arrived. The rain was returning, drizzling at first but it looked as if it would turn into a downpour and he pulled up the collar on his tunic. He had lived in wet clothes for half his time in Africa and shrugged his shoulders at the prospect of one more miserable night and then he wondered why Major Brownlow had insisted he report to him first, he had always reported to the Staff officers so what had changed?

The rain became heavy, Georgie put on his oiled cotton cape to gain at least some respite from what was to become a miserable night, and just before dawn, he was back in the saddle and leading the section out towards Laing's Nek.

At around eight o clock that evening, Georgie's weary patrol returned. The rain had not stopped and for the past half an hour lightening had flashed across the sky.

'There doesn't seem to be any smoke rising,' muttered trooper McKenzie a few yards away from Georgie.

'Don't expect any hot dinner tonight lads; they can never get the fires to light in these conditions. I've seen it before.'

Some of the troopers began to grumble but their mutterings were short lived when Georgie turned in his saddle and glowered at them. The Troopers knew better than to show dissent and after tying their horses to the Picket line they took off the saddles and fed them what they could before heading for the mess tent to try the biscuits and bully beef. If experience was anything to go by though, they would need a mug of tea to soak the biscuits otherwise their teeth might break.

'Bloody weather, will it ever stop raining,' queried Corporal Jones sitting at a table with his men and munching on a biscuit.

'Has it ever been any different Jonesy?'

'Yes, I can remember when we were chasing Cetshwayo it was hot and it hardly ever rained.'

'Hmm...hot alright, bloody hot. As I remember, you were moaning about the heat back then. Are you never happy Jonesy?'

'Happy, what in this army, not often Georgie,' said the Welshman with a grin.

Georgie grinned back. He had known Corporal Jones for most of his time in South Africa, campaigning together the length and breadth of the country. At the same time as Georgie, the army had seconded Corporal Jones to the Fifty-Eighth the two of them remaining behind when Twenty Fourth Foot had left for home to help train recruits for the Mounted Infantry. Corporal Jones had not always been a Corporal; he had Sergeant on more than one occasion only for some misdemeanour to return him to his present rank. This time the punishment had not only involved demotion but he was to remain behind when the regiment left and he was finding it hard to bear.

'Tell you what Georgie boy; I'm none too happy with this lot. Something is not right.'

Georgie sat opposite Jonesy, his eyes narrowing. 'It's not like the old days is it, these youngsters are willing enough, but something is missing.'

'No tradition, none of the old campaigners left. Since they brought in short service and got rid of the lifers the army has gone downhill in my opinion.'

'Button it Jonesy, the Lieutenant is coming our way. We don't want to be accused of mutiny do we.'

Corporal Jones looked behind him to see the Lieutenant and turned back to Georgie, eyebrows raised in mute statement. In return, Georgie gave him a wry grin; the ways of the army were no mystery to them, they knew when to keep their mouths shut. Good soldiers both, who would obey orders no matter how stupid they seemed, but they were not happy.

'Ah, you two.'

'Sir,' they said in unison, saluting smartly.

'Muster your men; your orders are to scout a mile or two from camp at first light. We are receiving reports of enemy movements and the General would like to know what we are up against.

Chapter 8

Messengers still crossed the lands of the Zulu, although not now from the King. Now they came from the new chieftains appointed by the great White Queen. Not many days after the great *Indaba* a messenger of John Dunn arrived at Mondli's Kraal with his message. The new Chief, John Dunn was demanding taxes amounting to almost half the mealie crop. An exorbitant amount that would leave them to go hungry during the lean months and they would have little choice but to slaughter more animals from the ever-diminishing herd, a serious blow to Mondli. Without his cattle, he would be a poor man; unable to afford to marry off his sons and greatly diminishing his standing in Zulu society.

'I hear what the great white Chief Dunn says but the crop is poor, the war against the Whiteman left us with little in the way of seed and with so many of our warriors killed we have struggled. Does he want us to perish and be unable to pay any taxes in future years? Tell him we have no more to give.'

The messenger, impassive, sitting cross-legged by the fire said nothing, his job was merely to relate his chief's message.

'I merely bring the message; it is not up to me to bargain with you Mondli. If that is your reply then that is what I will tell the white chief but be warned he does not take kindly to those who attempt to usurp his authority. Do not be surprised if he sends his son Rabanina to collect the taxes due. Rabanina is strong and has many followers with guns.'

On hearing the messengers warning Mondli blinked, the only outward sign that he was worried.

'Tell the white chief that his demands are too great. I cannot pay so much without my people going hungry and I will not let that happen.'

'As you wish, if that is your answer then I shall tell the White chief.'

The messenger, rested from his journey and having delivered the message rose to his feet. He had experienced this same situation before, and he knew what the eventual outcome could be.

'May the spirits of your ancestors be with you, and now I go to deliver the message to other Kraals.' He said standing up ready to leave.

Beside their father, Nkosinathi and Sibusiso looked on with admiration for he still had the fire of youth in his belly and he still held his head high. Nevertheless, they were in desperate straits and defiance against Dunn was foolish.

'Father I think I know of a way. Tell the messenger it shall be as the White Chief asks. We will pay the taxes; we will give up more of our crop.'

Mondli's eyes flashed, Nkosinathi seemed to be usurping his authority, but it was Nkosinathi who had kept them going when all seemed hopeless. With his horse and gun, he had hunted the forests and hills for game, bringing home meat for their bellies. He looked at his son, his eyes not quite so bright, his confidence dented and weighed down by his responsibility to his people he acquiesced.

'My son has spoken, it shall be as you ask,' he said.

The messenger stood and walked impassively towards his horse.

'You look down on us,' said Nkosinathi angrily. 'Are you not of the Zulu, do you have no compassion for your fellow Zulu?'

'Yes I am Zulu of the Sikhakhane, the King's Usuthu clan took everything from us and made us suffer, and so we sided with the British during the war. Now things are different, the old order is no more and we each have to find a new way. There is talk of war between the white tribes, the Redcoats, and the farmers to the north. I wish you good fortune but you should beware,' said the messenger beginning to mount his horse.

You talk of war,' said Nkosinathi catching him up. The messenger had brought bad news, had told of the changes in Zululand, the power of John Dunn and now war and he wanted to know more. 'Tell me of this trouble.'

'At the house of Dunn they say the redcoats are marching from Newcastle at this very moment to crush the *iBhunu*.'

'The *iBhunu*, the white tribe, the scourge of our nation?'

'Yes, those who take our land from us,' said the messenger and with little softening of his attitude he turned his horse towards the kraal entrance. 'You do well not to resist my friend, there is talk of more trouble in the lands to the north, and if the *iBhunu* are triumphant they will try to take more land from the Zulu.'

'Will the white Queen's army not defeat them as they did our own nation?'

'It is expected that they will.'

The messenger kicked his horse's flanks with his bare heels and without a backwards glance rode out onto the plain and Nkosinathi watched him go. His mind was in a whirl but before he could explore his thoughts any further, his brothers caught up with him.

'Nkosinathi what have you done, our father is distraught, you have promised that we will pay more taxes to the Chief John Dunn. We will starve when the bad times come, we cannot produce more crops, the herd becomes smaller each year,' said Sibusiso angrily.

'Have I not brought game to feed us when times were hard little brother?'

'Yes, but this means you must kill more and if John Dunn discovers you are taking what is rightfully his he will kill you and then we *will* starve.'

Nkosinathi looked through the open gateway, past the horse and rider, towards the horizon and his eyes narrowed. How indeed, he wondered, was going to fulfil his promise to pay more taxes. The anger that had welled up inside his chest was the same anger his father felt and like his father, he had wanted to resist. He knew that to show defiance would bring trouble to the Kraal and they had enough problems as it was.

With nostrils flared, he drew in a sharp breath and felt the adrenaline flow through his veins and intensifying his senses. He felt angry, a controlled anger, the kind of anger that had helped him survive the war with the British. Then it came to him.

'Little brother I have a plan, I will leave the village in the morning and I will find money to buy cattle and mealie. They say the lands to the east are less troubled and more productive than here in the Kingdom of John Dunn and I will buy cattle and mealie with the Whiteman's goods.'

Sibusiso was speechless, he knew his brother was a special kind of man and looked up to him, but this was a baffling statement. He knew that they could not pay such a high price without going hungry and yet here was Nkosinathi telling him that all would be well and that he would buy cattle with the Whiteman's goods. What Whiteman's goods, how could he, it was impossible?

'My brothers, do not despair, I have seen many things these past few months, I have seen the ways of the Whiteman, and I have seen the value of his coin. I have a horse and a gun and I can speak a little of his language so I will go amongst them and earn the coin they covet so much. I will be careful have no fear but whilst I am gone you must hold together for I know that to lose everything will destroy my father and he is not yet ready to go and see his ancestors. I will leave tomorrow, be strong my brothers.

The first of the men passed between the trees, his horse carefully picking a path through the brush and over the loose stones littering the ground. After fifty yards, he stopped to allow those following to catch up with him and from the trees came another man leading the first of six mules and then a third White man brought up the rear. The mules were heavily laden, a large wooden box strapped to either side of their backs, and as they came out of the trees they became aware of lush grass surrounding them. At the best of times they were bad tempered and disobedient and at the smell of the grass began a dry throated he-hawing demanding to be allowed to graze.

'It will be dark in a couple of hours Jake, how about making camp here for the night. It's pretty difficult ahead, look, up there, the slope is steeper, and it looks like we might not find as good a place as this.'

The one called Jake nudged his horse forwards and pulled up alongside his companion, his eyes searching the clearing and hillside ahead of them.

'Yes, I see what you mean, plenty of grazing and there is a stream over there look. William, hold up,' he called out to the rider bringing up the rear. We are stopping here for the night.'

The man William waved acknowledgement, slipped from his saddle to pull his horse along by its reigns, and secured it to a low hanging branch. The others followed suit and together the men began lifting the heavy loads from the complaining mules, leaving them to graze happily away and then they set about lighting a fire and erecting a small tent.

Within minutes, a blackened cooking pot was hanging over the fire and they settled down to smoke as their dinner of mealie porridge cooked and a battered coffee pot heated up some water. After a hard days trek across hostile country it was a welcome relief, leaving the men as content as their mules and two of them lay back on the grass relaxing. The one called Jake sat cross-legged by the fire and re-filled his pipe.

'What the...' he exclaimed, eyes wide in surprise.

He began to get to his feet, his two friends alerted by his exclamation tried to do likewise but they were too late. Nkosinathi had his gun pointing straight at them and ordered them to stay where they were. There was no escape.

'Who are you?' asked Jake.

'You smugglers; you trespass on the lands of John Dunn. I ask the questions.'

Nkosinathi's eyes never left those of Jakes', his gun held steady and threateningly and then he put the index and little finger of his left hand between his lips and let out a slow warbling whistle, the sound of an Orange Ground Thrush and all the time he watched Jake's face. He knew that the men would have heard that same sound since crossing the border into Zululand and would wonder. Slowly they made the connection and he took grim pleasure watching their confused minds make the connection, believing that someone had watched them for days. Jake's eyes narrowed and an apprehensive look spread across his face. The other two men simultaneously made the same connection and as Nkosinathi took a step closer, William's hand instinctively went to the holster fastened about his midriff. The Zulu had anticipated that he might meet resistance and that one of them might try something. With his eyes still on Jake, he swivelled his gun towards William who suddenly thought better of any heroics and moved his hand away from his gun.

'What do you want?' asked Phillip the third man of the group. 'Who are you and what do you want?'

Nkosinathi relaxed, secure in the knowledge that he had the better of them but he did not drop his guard. Instead, he walked towards them, indicating with the barrel of his gun that they should move closer together where he could watch them more easily and with Jake motionless under the threat of the gun the other two shuffled towards him on their backsides. Nkosinathi spoke again in faltering English.

'You trespass on the land of the John Dunn and you have not permission. You must pay.'

'H...ow much? We will pay, just don't shoot,' stammered Jake.

'I not shoot and you will not pay...yet.'

'What do you mean?'

'I am of the Zulu and I know this country, I know where the men of John Dunn patrol these lands and I can take you and your mules along secret, ancient paths to safety in the north.'

The three men looked at each other incredulously and then up at Nkosinathi whose face had broken into a broad grin.

'How, why...er...what do you mean,' asked Jake.

'I know this country and I am a tracker, I can take you safely through Chief Dunn's lands without you having to pay him. But you will pay me.'

'How much will we pay you?'

Nkosinathi let his rifle butt slip to the ground, the barrel resting against the crook of his elbow and he showed both hands and spread all ten fingers and thumbs.

'You pay me this many cattle.'

'Eh, cattle, you do not want money?'

'I have no use for money but I need cattle for my father.'

'How will you guide us, what if we kill you while you are sleeping, what if we don't pay you?'

'I don't sleep, you will not see me unless I come to warn you of danger and you will pay me because one of those boxes will stay with me until you do.'

'What do you mean?'

'Tomorrow or the next day I will come for one box. It will stay with me until you pay me.'

'How can we trust you?'

'I see men like you pass this way before, you will come again and then you take the box. If you cheat me I bring John Dunn's son to make you pay and you will pay him much more than you pay me.'

The men looked at each other, furtive glances passing between them and then Jake looked up at Nkosinathi.

'We agree to your terms, ten cows will be worth a lot less than John Dunn's demands for sure. What now?'

'Eat your food, sleep and I will return to show you the way and I will take one box.' What you called?

'Me I'm Jake, this here's William and he's called Phillip. What's your name?'

'I have no name.'

The path was nowhere near as steep as Phillip had imagined; the Zulu led them several hundred yards up the slope to begin with and then set them on a level path along the side of a narrow valley, invisible from below, where the ground was soft and relatively boulder free making the going easier for both animals and men. They were making good progress after the difficulties of the previous days and were slowly warming to the idea of using a guide and when they stopped at a small stream to allow the animals some respite, Nkosinathi disappeared into the bush and Jake spoke to William

'What do you make of the black feller?'

'Amazing, it seems such a simple idea and it will save us a lot of money. I bet we can pick up cattle for a few beads from some natives. If we had to pay John Dunn, I reckon his price would be extortionate. We knew that when we started this enterprise. Don't forget we have been worried his men might stop us and cost us our profits.'

'It's true, maybe they would try to kill us and take everything, and these guns will be useful to anyone, not just Zibhebhu. What about the Boers up in the Transvaal, they will need more guns if the rebellion intensifies. Maybe next time we should bring more ammunition than guns.'

'That's a good idea. Hey Phillip, listen to this...'

Nkosinathi pulled up his horse and jumped down from his saddle, commanding Dumisani and Sibusiso following on behind, to stop.

'They are nearby, follow me to the stream and we will surprise them.'

Leading his horse Nkosinathi and his brothers made their way down the sloping ground to the bank of the stream and for a mile followed its course. Finally, a faint wisp of smoke rising through the trees led them to the gunrunners' camp and it was time to put the next part of his plan into action.

Appearing as if from nowhere, Nkosinathi startled William as stood beside him.

'Oh...!' Where did you come from?'

'I come from there,' said Nkosinathi pointing to the bush twenty feet away.

'You are invisible sometimes, I didn't see you. You almost gave me heart failure.'

'So, you're back boy. What do you want this time?'

'I come for one of those boxes,' said Nkosinathi pointing to the munitions boxes piled up against a stout tree near the grazing mules.

'And what if we decide that we don't need your services anymore?'

Nkosinathi held two fingers to his mouth, blew steadily for a second or two, recreating the bird song, and from the bush came an answering call, and then another from a different part and Nkosinathi watched their eyes. He was satisfied at their reaction and could see that they firmly believed he had many accomplices hidden in the surrounding bush with seemingly little chance of escape.

'My friend we made a bargain yesterday and we will not renege,' said Phillip

'Ren...?

'We will leave you one of our boxes until we pass this way again in a month's time. Now what exactly do you want us to do with the box?'

'When you break camp in the morning, leave one box by this tree. I will be scouting nearby and will return to guide you.'

He was gone as quickly as he had appeared, ducking into the vegetation for cover and, other than a feint rustling of leaves; it was as if he had never been there.

'We didn't agree that we would go along with him,' said an angry Jake walking towards Phillip.

'Be sensible man, he has probably got more natives out there than we can handle and anyway didn't we find a simpler route today because of him. I think he is worth employing.'

'I agree Jake, the man has proved his worth and if a handful of beads is all it takes to get hold of a few mangy cows what have we to lose?'

Jake could see the sense in what his partners were saying but even so, he did not like it. There was something strange about a native who appeared from nowhere and dictated what they should do. How many more of them were in the bush? He took stock, for a few seconds his mind worked overtime and beginning to believe that there really was a whole Zulu Impi out there, the hairs on the back of his neck rose up.

The first orangey glow of the rising sun spread across the landscape as Nkosinathi led his horse into the small camp and from fire, William looked up and said 'you want a coffee?'

Nkosinathi nodded, tied his horse to a nearby tree, and with his gun lying across his bent forearm took the battered mug offered him. The men at John Dunn's ranch had joked about not being able to manage the day without their coffee and he had taken to it.

'Where do you want us to leave the guns,' asked William ready to lift a box.

Nkosinathi's heart skipped a beat. So the boxes contained guns, a valuable commodity and he realised how such a valuable commodity could help him fulfil his promise to his father and with a deadpan expression swung his rifle barrel a few degrees to point to a tree.

William grunted understanding and nodded to Phillip to help carry the heavily built box and land it with a dull thud beside the tree and it occurred to Nkosinathi that one of the mules was going to have an easier time of it.

'Say my friend it's all very well leaving the box here but what if someone comes along and finds it?'

'We cover it with a few branches and grass. It is not on the path and in a few days maybe the tracks will disappear.'

'What about your friends out there, will they not take it?'

'What friends, I am alone?' Jake exhaled through his teeth with a low, barely audible whistle. Was this native really by himself? If he was it was a relief, he had not relished the idea of natives shadowing and outnumbering them. As if reading Jake's mind Nkosinathi added, 'I am alone here but I have friends there.' He swivelled his eyes as if to indicate that the forest was full of his accomplices and smiled inwardly at Jake's reaction.

An hour later, the mules were again complaining, struggling to cross the uneven ground with their heavy loads. The lead animal stopped in its tracks, refusing to move until the sharp crack of Jake's bullwhip changed its mind and ahead of them Nkosinathi led the way. On foot and pulling his horse behind him, he picked his way through the undergrowth finding the easiest path for the mules and all the while listened to the sounds of the forest. He worried that one of Dunn's patrols would find them and he did not trust the white men following, they were still deep in John Dunn's territory and danger could be lurking behind any tree.

For half the night, he had scouted a wide area around the White man's camp looking for fresh tracks and had found none. It was reassuring but if he were to earn his fee then he needed to make sure nobody saw them. He turned and looked back, relieved to see that the mules were making good progress and waited for them to catch him up.

'Take this trail towards the crest of that hill and then down into the valley,' he said to Jake.

'Where are you going?'

I am going up there,' he said pointing to a steep sided kopje. 'I go to see what moves then I will find you and show you a good place to stop for the night,'

Nkosinathi mounted his horse and kicked at its flanks, urging it towards the hill and climbed up above the tree line to look out across the landscape. For an hour he sat motionless, the only movement that of his eyes constantly scanning the vista searching for movement but apart from birds circling there was none. By mid-afternoon, satisfied that there was no immediate danger he descended towards a cleft in the hills at the edge of the forest to meet Jake and the mules. It was the edge of the forest, grasslands stretched for miles and he knew they could be visible from a long way off. He had to lead them along an old watercourse cut into the landscape if they were to remain unseen and at the same time, almost ten miles back along the trail, Nkosinathi's brothers finished secreting the heavy wooden box in a cave Nkosinathi had found.

After piling up boulders at the entrance, they had uprooted several small saplings to replant them and screen the cave further. Nkosinathi had told them they must do this because freshly cut branches would rot and turn brown, giving away its position. Lastly, they cut small branches, stripped them of leaves, and used them to sweep away all sign of their activities.

Chapter 9

The jangle of loose tack and the horse's hooves thudding on the soft earth signalled a patrol leaving camp. Increased reports of enemy movements had prompted the General to order ramp up in patrols to gain a clearer picture of his elusive enemy. The mounted force was not as large as he would have liked and had forced an increased workload on his men. Georgie had led his section out of camp several hours earlier taking them as far as the flat-topped hill overlooking the approaches to Laing's Nek, almost five miles from the camp and deep into enemy territory.

'Their patrols are getting nearer,' he said, lowering his glasses, 'that's the fourth one we've seen today.'

'Don't look much to me sergeant,' said trooper McKenzie

'Have you ever been in a fight McKenzie?'

'No, but they do not look much do they. Whenever we get close to them, they ride away. Scared I reckon and how will they go on when the artillery lads give 'em something to think about?"

'We will see trooper, but beware, do not expect them to run away, when it comes down to it they know how to fight.'

He lifted the field glasses again and focused on a group of Boers leading their horses up the side of a steep ravine. Scruffily dressed, with large bush hats on their heads and bandoliers across their chests they were too far away for him to see their faces. He swung the glasses away from them in a slow arc, traversing the slopes of the hill and soon spotted tiny figures looking down at him. From what he could see they had positioned themselves well, covering the approach to the Nek and it would be wise not to underestimate them.

Behind him, he heard his men muttering between themselves, egged on by McKenzie and feeling angered by their lack of professionalism decided that it was time to discipline the trooper. He was becoming troublesome and causing the others to take their mind off the task in hand and that could be dangerous for them all. He would wait until they returned to camp before disciplining him but for the present, he felt his best option was to spread his men out, keep them away from each other.

'Spread out in skirmishing order,' he said, 'keep alert. You McKenzie over there and you two cover the flank.

The arrival of the British army had spread rapidly through the Boer camp, and the Veldkornets had sent word to their districts to urge more men to hurry and support them. They needed more volunteers and as the word spread, the Commandant General was gratified to see new faces arrive and begin preparations for the coming conflict, cleaning rifles, filling bandoliers and smoking their pipes. Into this mood of laid-back excitement, Jos and his sons rode with several volunteers from their district.

'Good to see you Jos,' hailed a man waving his pipe in greeting.

Jos waved his hand in acknowledgement. 'Caas, it is good to see you again. How is your Frau?'

'She is fine; we were only talking of you and Frau De Witt the other day. You can make a place here under my wagon tonight and the boys can pitch their tent here on this patch of ground if you like.'

Jos pulled up his horse, raised his hat in gratitude with as much of a smile on his face as he could ever manage and accepted the offer.

'Christiaan, Petrus, we will make camp here. Get a fire going and warm some food, we have not eaten since we left the mountain.'

'No need for that Jos, we have a fire here you can use, send one of your men to collect a little more firewood. Come, see to your pony and sit with me, tell me your news.'

Caas Van Dyke was an old friend; they had known each other ever since the great trek travelling with their parents. As youngsters, they had played together alongside wagons slowly rolling across the vast plains. They had learned to ride together, to shoot and as well as the good times, they had experienced hardship. The days spent heaving against the spokes of the great wheels as the oxen strained to haul the wagons over almost impassable mountain ranges. And there were the natives, the Zulu determined to extinguish their flame, and as not much more than children they had fought them off together. They were true Boers of the old school.

'Tie your animals up over there,' said Caas pointing to a sturdy tree, 'and pitch your tents on that ground, it will stay dry if it rains.

The men with Jos began making camp and Jos came to sit with Caas, their pipes billowing out great clouds of smoke as they caught up on the gossip and not much later Petrus came to his father carrying a mug of coffee and a plate of stew. The old man reached out to take the battered pewter plate and said to his son, 'you know Caas?'

'Yes Papa, we have seen him in church in Pretoria.'

'Ah...of course.'

'This your eldest son Jos?'

'No, this is Petrus my youngest, Christiaan is the eldest. He is here somewhere.'

'Catching up on news of the younger generation no doubt,' said Caas with a knowing smile, 'and this is Petrus. He's a fine looking boy Jos, strong, healthy. Are you a good shot *seuntjie*?'

Petrus smiled, he hadn't been called boy for quite some time.

'Sit with us a while and have a smoke. You have a pipe do you not?'

Petrus shook his head, unusually for a Boer he was not partial to smoking tobaccoo and did not possess a pipe, preferring to sit instead on the grass and listen to them talk. Invariably when the older folk got together conversation would turn to tales of the great trek and fighting the Zulus, it was his heritage and he enjoyed every minute hearing about it.

Sitting on the grass, Petrus crossed his legs, sitting quietly until his father finished his meal and Caas pulled out his tobacco.

'Here Jos, fill your pipe,' he said as Jos wiped the last of the greasy plate with some dry bread.

'Thank you my friend. Tell me what news of the British, we have been watching them for some days but something must be happening for us to be recalled so suddenly.'

'The Commendant General believes they are mustering for an attack on us. We have the Nek well protected, our men are finding good positions overlooking the road. They are making sure they have a good field of fire and are laying rocks at measured distances to help set the sights. We don't have the stores and ammunition of the British, we need to husband our resources, make every shot count.'

'Uncle Caas, what do you know about the big guns, the artillery of the British?'

Cass put his pipe in his mouth and held it tightly between his teeth, thinking how to answer.

'The field guns are a worry; we do not really know how to cope with them other than to keep our heads down when they shoot at us.'

'I hear they can kill fifty men at once.'

'Only if fifty men stand together and make a target *seuntjie*, we will not be doing that. From what I have heard it is against a massed charge that the big guns are most effective and we do not charge like the Zulu, that is not our way of fighting.'

'What should we do?'

Listening to the conversation, Jos lit his pipe. He knew very little of artillery but had heard stories and he began to worry that they might have to deal with a bombardment from the guns.

'Think about it, if fifty men stand close together and a round lands in amongst them then yes, they could all be killed but if they leave some distance between themselves then only one unlucky soul will meet his maker and if he is well hidden behind solid rocks or stout trees then he too may be spared.'

Jos sucked on his pipe, a cloud of tabacco smoke drifted above his head and he nodded slowly to himself. Cass's words were in part reasuring, there was logic in what he said and he would make sure the men from his district kept well apart when it came to the fight. He did not want to have to tell the wives of friends that they had become widows.'

'Papa, it is time for worship, the burghers are coming together for the meeting,' said Christiaan arriving back at the wagon.

'Ja, good, a few prayers will do us good. Come Caas let's hear that wonderful singing voice of yours.'

The Boer camp did not have exclusivity to musical interludes, the British had their songs too, less reverential perhaps, popular songs of the day with the wording altered to amuse. Each evening the men would sit around their campfires, smoke, play cards and the songs would ring out for a time before subsiding into laughter and backslapping. That was until the General ordered and end to the frolicking and issued orders to guard the camp, patrol the surrounding countryside and allowing the soldiers time only to eat their meals and to rest. The army had entered a time of preparation for the inevitable attack on the Boer positions.

After a day of constantly patrolling the heights Georgie and his section were glad to be riding back to camp for a few hours. His back was feeling uncomfortable, the result of too many hours in the saddle, and he was worried. He was worried because, during the past two days, the patrol had noticed a marked increase in the numbers of Boer horsemen. The enemy force was obviously increasing and he had no idea of their overall strength nor how the General proposed to deal with them.

Passing between outlying pickets Georgie led his men into camp and as they began to dismount, Major Brownlow materialized.

'Ahh…Sergeant, glad to see you back from patrol. What have you seen today, come to the headquarters tent and report; let us have a look at the map.

'Yes sir.' Private Tucker, take my horse and give her a feed.'

Georgie handed the reins to the trooper and followed his commanding officer. They made their way to the headquarters tent, saluted the officer at the entrance, and after a brief conversation with the Major, went straight to a large map lying across a table. Laing's Nek and the hill called Majuba stood out and not far away, drawn in pencil, was their camp.

'Show me what you have seen Sergeant,' said the Staff Officer.

'Well sir, they are difficult to count, always moving, ones and twos, sometimes in small groups. Mostly they keep out of sight but I have seen a lot of movement here and here.' He pointed to the ridge of hills extending either side of Laing's Nek. 'There was movement high up the side of Majuba hill, lookout posts from what I could make out sir.'

'Thank you Sergeant that confirms most of what we already know. For your information we will be going on the offensive tomorrow so you should make sure your men are ready, your horses in good condition. I will issue orders for the advance after an early breakfast. That will be all Sergeant.'

'Sir.'

Georgie saluted and marched smartly out of the tent now knowing that he would be leading his men into action the following day. The recruits had learned the craft of the Mounted Infantry but never bloodied in action he wondered how they might cope with a determined enemy. Increasing his pace, he walked over to the picket line to see that his men had finished feeding and grooming the horses. Taking a glance at the animals he winced, the men had been less than diligent in caring for their steeds leaving some still lathered from their exertions, and one of them still had a saddle on its back. Grimacing, he looked round and saw two soldiers smoking and talking at the far end of the picket line.

'Mullins, McKenzie, come here you two.'

The soldiers, none too smartly, ambled towards him making him bristle at their indiscipline.

'Sergeant,' said McKenzie, ambling up to him.

'What do you call this?' asked Georgie pointing to the saddle.

'A saddle sergeant,' he said with a grin.

'I call it slovenly and lazy. Now get it off the animals back and rub it down. If your horse is not fit then you will be in danger. How many times have I told you and you Mullins? Give these two horses a rub down before dinner.'

The men looked sullen and annoyed, McKenzie in particular seemed unreceptive to Georgie's words and did not immediately make any kind of move to carry out Georgie's order.

'I said get that saddle off your horse McKenzie.'

'When I'm ready.'

'What did you say soldier?'

'I said when I'm ready; I still have this cigarette to finish.'

He got no further, Georgie's anger boiled over and unable to contain himself any longer, punched McKenzie squarely in the face, the force squashing the offending cigarette flat into McKenzie's face and sent him staggering backwards into the picket line and slump onto his backside. McKenzie was a big man recovered quickly, jumping to his feet, and ducking back under the picket line to stand squarely in front of Georgie, his fists clenched.

'I hope you are not thinking of using those, soldier, I have wanted to give you a good hiding for some time.'

McKenzie faltered, Sergeant McNamara was a tough man, and he realised that he would he be fighting not just him, but the whole of the British army. If the sergeant decided to bring a charge, it could mean a flogging and he considered his predicament.

'You struck the first blow; I shall report you to the Major. You're a witness Mullins.'

Private Mullins looked decidedly uncomfortable; he did not want McKenzie drawing him into the confrontation and it showed on his face. McKenzie was not as popular with the men as he believed and Graham Mullins did not want to risk the wrath of the Sergeant.

'Well Mullins, you are a witness. Let's sort Sergeant McNamara out once and for all, get him reduced to the ranks and then we can really go to town on him.'

Georgie held McKenzie's gaze, a battle of wills ensuing whilst Mullins struggled to make up his mind and Georgie could see he was decidedly unhappy. The silence began to tell, Georgie's eyes pierced those of McKenzie and his resolve began to wilt and Georgie went back on the offensive, but this time it was not physical.

'I have just been told we are to attack tomorrow. Do you not realise that if your horses and equipment are in poor order your lives could be at risk.'

Many in the camp seemed to think that the Boer would turn and run at the first sight of the red coats and that a charge by the mounted force would soon have them scurrying back to their farms. Georgie had seen enough to make him wary that claim, an enemy concealed amongst the kloofs and ravines could launch an ambush at any time. He had seen Boers in action and did not believe they were up against a generation that was less than the equal of their forefathers. The men who had destroyed Dingaan and his Impi at Blood River were tough all right and a fighting spirit like that could not disappear in one generation.

'Let us forget our differences for the time being McKenzie and concentrate on what we have to do.'

'Sergeant,' said McKenzie lowering his eyes.

Mullins sighed audibly and began to rub down the two neglected horses, McKenzie began unfastening the saddle still on the horses back, and Georgie nodded with grim satisfaction.

At seven o clock the vanguard, a large contingent of Mounted Police, left the camp. Behind them, the rest of the Mounted Infantry under Major Brownlow waited as foot soldiers of the Rifles and some Blue Jacketed sailors of the Naval Contingent marched past.

'Men, we will form two squadrons for the march to Laing's Nek where we expect to encounter the enemy. I want you Captain Roberts to take half the force and ride the left flank whilst I take the rest. The plan is to halt before the Nek, out of range of the Boer sharpshooters and give them a taste of the artillery. Carry on,' said the Major.

Slowly the two forces made their way out of camp to take to higher ground on either side of the advance and from behind them came a mixed force. First came the infantry and behind them the field guns and bringing up the rear, Navy bluejackets with their rockets. The road was in a poor state of repair, hindering the main body's progress, the heavy guns churned up the muddy road and sank to their axles, but spirits were high. Each time the oxen needed help the men put their backs into digging out the gun carriages and two hours later, they were within sight of their objective.

From somewhere at the centre of the mounted squadron traversing the high ground Georgie could see the soldiers and sailors marching towards the gap between the hills and suddenly appreciated the Boer tactics. Hidden on either side of their advance, they were going to lay in wait until the army was under the overhanging escarpments and vulnerable to their guns.

The squadron halted and below him, Georgie watched as the Bluejackets passed by with their rocket tubes and behind them two of the big guns. The guns would do for the Boers, the officers said, they were of the opinion that the Boer fighters would not stand up to a bombardment and he hoped that they were right. A bugle sounded, the head of the column came to a halt, he could see staff officers riding between the different companies, giving them their orders, and then Major Brownlow rode forward to meet one of them. After a short discussion, he turned in his saddle and raised his arm, signalling his mounted force to follow him.

'Looks like it's starting Georgie boy,' said Corporal Jones in a low voice as he led his section forward. 'Wonder what sort of soldiers these Boers really are?'

'We'll soon find out,' retorted Georgie as the mounted men began to stream down to the grassy ground at either side of the road. Ahead of them Georgie could see companies of the Fifty-Eighth Rifles taking up their positions and above them, he could see with the naked eye, figures running to take up defensive positions. To his left the gunners unlimbered the artillery pieces and pushed them into position and beyond them, the Naval Brigade set up their rockets and then stiffly barked orders echoed between the hills. For a period nothing much seemed to happen, the horses seemed uninterested, grasping at as much grass as possible until each flinched at the first boom of the field guns. Shells flew high into the air, emitting a strange and frightening screech before crashing amongst the Boer positions. Georgie wondered if the opinion of one artillery officer that they would clear the Boers out of the Nek within half an hour, would be the case.

Petrus did not hear the approach of the first shell, only a brief whistle as it fell to earth and then came the shattering explosion to make his mouth dry and his heart pump with fear. More shells landed and he could not help but press his body as hard as he could to the ground and thinking 'so this is what it is like'. Then another noise came to his ears, a shrill whine as the Navy's rockets flew at them spitting fire. He saw one land no more than a hundred feet away and could not help but marvel at the fire and smoke it produced, his curiosity overcoming his fear and then, to his dismay, two of their men broke cover and ran towards their horses.

'Petrus are you alright.'

'Yes Christiaan I am fine. Is anyone hurt?'

'No, I don't think so,' retorted his brother, 'they are passing right over us. There are men with the horses over the hill, some of the horses have bolted I think.'

'I can see some of our men are running away.'

'Well we are not,' shouted his father lying alongside Christiaan. 'Remember what Caas said, keep well-spaced out and keep your head down Petrus.'

Petrus gritted his teeth and nodded to no one in particular. He was frightened but relieved to find that the shelling seemed to cause less damage than he had imagined. For twenty minutes, he felt that he was in hell and then, suddenly, there was silence. He waited, wondering why the bombardment had stopped and dared to raise his head just enough to look to the valley below. Red and blue coats were swarming towards them, a multi-coloured snake winding its way along the road with little regard to stealth and still some way off. They looked to be heading towards a ridge just out of rifle range, marching smartly as if on parade and then he saw the Mounted Brigade streaming down from higher ground. The sound of a bugle rang out and peered over in that direction to see a mass of red moving towards them.

'I think they are coming,' called Jos. 'Remember the Commandant General's words. Thus far and no further, we hold them here.'

Even as he finished speaking a wave of reinforcements joined them, taking up positions amongst them. Two stocky Militiamen slid to the ground beside Petrus and with their heads protected by a rocky outcrop, each lifted his rifle to point it towards the advancing redcoats. Petrus grinned, did likewise, squinting along the barrel of his gun at tiny white targets sitting squarely above red coats, and then, from behind those soldiers came the mounted squadron.

'Hold your fire until you are sure of your target,' his father called.

They needed no telling, their Westley Richards single-action rifles fired only single shots and took time to reload and when hunting game, each man made sure that his first shot counted. Today would be no different except that the red-coated infantry, still moving forward would substitute for wild game. Still advancing, the enemy began to reach the first of the ranging boulders and was within range of Jos's commando. Quietly he told them to allow the soldiers just a few yards more before shooting and levelling their rifles, the Boers took aim. The first shots rang out; Petrus picked a white helmet as the target for his first shot, squeezed the trigger and less than a second later saw the white helmet and its wearer disappear into the long grass. He rolled over onto his back, swung open the block, and relieved the gun of the spent cartridge. All around a methodical crackle of gunshots rang out, the commando picked their targets, and, other than a few satisfied grunts, no one spoke. Their fusillade was having its effect, the attack began to falter just as the mounted force reached the infantry and Petrus could see the officer leading the charge urge his men forward, his white gloved hand waving them on.

Out of earshot of Petrus the officer shouted his orders,' draw your swords, let's give these blighters a taste of British steel,' and not far away Georgie knew that tone of voice from countless engagements. It was the sound of an officer in search of glory and Major Brownlow was no exception. As if to prove it, the fast walk soon became the trot and then they were galloping full pelt towards the Boer positions and the ground began to rise quite steeply. This added burden caused the force to slow noticeably, the horses struggling with the incline and Georgie wondered just what they were doing. This was not the Mounted Infantry's way of fighting, this was a cavalry officer leading them, and this was a cavalry charge.

The two lines of horses and riders wheeled to the left, red, blue and black uniforms intermingled to give a clue as to the hasty creation of the mobile force. Somewhere within the second line, Georgie and his section drove their horses forward, the thundering hooves close on the heels of line in front.

'The men on foot have passed under the overhang, we cannot see them anymore,' called a man watching their approach.

'There is more to worry about,' retorted Petrus catching sight of horses trying to out flank them.

He looked again for the infantry but could not find a satisfactory target and so turned his attention to the mounted men. They were approaching rapidly and overawed by the power of the force he felt his heart in his mouth. The horses had made good progress, galloping across the open ground to the beginning of the incline and the lines had held their shape.

Amongst them, Georgie still had his doubts because although they were Mounted Infantry, their primary purpose to scout for the main body of the army. When it did come to fighting, they would skirmish and fight from the ground, a cavalry charge was alien to their discipline and training.

'Shoot at the horses,' shouted Jos as he too became alarmed at the sight of the thundering mass coming their way.

The Boer fighters needed no telling, almost to a man realising that the horses were the real danger. If they did manage to carry their riders in amongst them then all could be lost. The Boers were good at shooting, good at running away when circumstances dictated but they were no good in a close quarter encounter and seeing flashes of reflected sunlight from outstretched sabres worried them. At the top of the sloping hill the men had a stark choice and did not have long to make their decision.

'Thus far and no further,' called out Jos, with determination. 'Remember the Commandant General's words, thus far and no further.'

A muted cheer rang out from those who heard him and within seconds, the sound of rifles firing heralded their decision. Petrus had a sickly grin on his face as his beating heart came back under control his resolve stiffened in the knowledge that every man would stay and fight. He was almost right, a few faltered, broke ranks and crawled away to run back to their farms but most did not.

Those steadfast Boers that remained had a steely determination that began to manifest itself as they consolidated their positions and soon many of the first wave of the charging horses was on their knees and from his position near the ridge Jos watched events unfold. As his sharpshooters picked off the horses fell and their riders he realised that the British had made a potentially disastrous mistake. The leaders of his volunteer army had planned well, choosing positions to defend the Nek with purpose. The slope of the escarpment the British were attempting to negotiate was steep whilst the ground behind the defenders sloped more gently and was easy for their agile ponies to negotiate to reinforce the weaker sections of the line and it was beginning to tell.

On the slopes leading to the Boer positions the charge was faltering, the horses were exhausted from the climb and the accuracy of the enemy's shooting was formidable. For the first time in his military career, Georgie felt afraid, very afraid and he was beginning to believe that this time he might not return. He had never had doubts like this before, never had his nerves frayed and never had he the urge to turn and run. However, he would not run he was too much of a soldier for that and then the bullets began to whine in amongst them as the Boer sharpshooters turned their attention to Georgie's end of the line. The front rank of horses and riders were almost half way up the incline and he could see them labouring, more than one buckling as a bullet found its mark. Riders toppled lifeless to the ground or, if they were lucky, dived for cover and still they charged on but at an ever-diminishing speed.

Almost oblivious to the events nearby, Georgie watched the carnage ahead and realised that soon they would catch the front rank and be in the same predicament. A scream nearby drew his attention and turned briefly to see trooper McKenzie gripping his shoulder then a second bullet took the side of his face away and he fell lifeless from the saddle, his bravado and ill-discipline of no use to him.

On the ridge Petrus and his brother lay not far from each other, each firing their guns in a slow methodical manner to make each shot count and as Petrus watched the charge coming ever closer he thought to himself, 'They are slowing, the horses are blown, they will not make it.' He glanced at Christiaan and could see that he had come to the same conclusion and they grinned at each other.

It was true, the effort of the charge was too much for the horses, gaps had appeared in the line, and men and horses littered the ground. Still the Boers fired on them, a fusillade landed near Georgie and he felt his horse sag under him. He pulled on the reigns and tried to steer the stricken animal towards easier ground but it was of no avail, her legs buckled, she sank to the ground and in panic, leapt from the saddle, hitting the ground hard. His helmet fell from his head, his sword span off ineffectually he was dazed and bewildered and as his mind began to clear, he became acutely aware of the

sounds of battle, gunfire intermingled with the cries of
wounded men and horses.

His horse was dead, his sword gone but he still had
his rifle slung across his back, and he struggled to free it.
Twisting his body and loosening the strap, he let it slip
from his shoulder and looked for cover but there was
nothing. Only scrub and a few small boulders offered
any sanctuary but even those would not hide him from
the onslaught. His only hope of any respite was a horse's
corpse lying nearby and as quickly as he could he made
for it. A bullet whizzed close by as he dived headlong for
safety and after a few seconds he managed a brief glance
around and dared to raise his head to watch the charge's
progress. No sooner did he peer over the animal's body
than a bullet whizzed not six inches from his head
forcing him back down. Then the thunder of hooves
reached his ears, the charge had broken down and the
surviving troopers had decided there was little hope and
had turned tail.

Even as they galloped past his hiding place, the
sharpshooting Boers brought down several more of
them and lying flat, he watched the rout with dismay. A
rider less horse came careering towards him and he
seized his chance, leaping to his feet and dropping his
rifle he reached out with both hands for the trailing
reigns. Grabbing hold as best he could he tried to get a
foot into the stirrup but the force of the animals'
headlong bolt was too much for him. Caught off balance
he hung on desperately as the horse dragged him down
the grassy slope until he fell between the animals flailing
feet. Instinctively he raised his arms to cover his head,

saving his life because the horse was in no mood to avoid him. Flailing hooves caught his arm, spun him to the ground, repeatedly rolling him over until his head hit a rock and he came to rest. Above him, along the crest of the hill, came a cheer as the Boer defenders realised that they had won the day but Georgie heard none it as he laid, arms outstretched and oblivious to everything.

Chapter 10

With grim satisfaction Jos, Christiaan and Petrus
walked cautiously amongst the dead and dying soldiers
and all along the hilltop, others did the same.
Occasionally a shot rang out as someone put a horse out
of its misery and the eyes of a wounded soldier looked
up at Jos with pity in them.

'We do not shoot helpless enemies my friend. God
has smiled upon us this day and we will not offend him
by killing a helpless enemy.'

The man blinked several times before closing his eyes
and letting his head droop onto the grass. He coughed
and a thin smear of blood appeared at the corner of his
mouth.

'Here friend, have a drink of water from my canteen.'

Jos unslung the metal container from his shoulder
and crouched beside the man, lifting the vessel to his
mouth. Still with his eyes shut, the stricken soldier took
a long drink, coughed once more, and finally opened
them again.

'Th...thank you,' he managed to whisper before
drifting into unconsciousness.

Jos grunted and looked across at two soldiers who had come the closest to them; they were both dead, such a waste of life he thought. The British seemed stupid when it came to fighting, charging up a steep incline straight into their waiting guns.

'We will see how many wounded men are here and offer to let their doctors tend to them. I want a volunteer to go down the hill and meet with the British General, tell him to collect his wounded and bury his dead. Who will go?'

'I will father,' said Petrus.

'Good boy. You will need a white flag as a sign of truce. They are honourable men I think and a white flag will suffice. The rest of you gather up any guns and take their ammunition belts and if anyone needs a new pair of boots, well now is your chance.'

The Burghers needed no encouragement, although showing mercy to the fallen they had no compunction in taking anything of use, the guns being the most valuable. They had only a limited amount of ammunition, many of their guns were only ancient, single shot models, and these modern weapons would be useful. Their supply of munitions came mainly from Natal, slowly arriving with the gunrunners dodging both the British and the Zulus. If this war were to carry on for any length of time then they would need all the supplies they could get.

Leaving his comrades, Petrus made his way down the hillside past the carnage of the battle, appalled by what he saw. So many dead men, far more than he could have believed possible to kill in so short a time. The sight of dead horses, animals that would be valuable assets on the farm, saddened him, but their orders were to shoot the horses first and the soldiers second. He could see the logic in that now but at the time, he had believed they should be shooting at the men.

Picking his way over the broken ground he waved his white, a shirt taken from a corpse and made his way towards a group of uniformed men.

'I have been sent to offer you a truce, to allow you to tend to your wounded and bury your dead.'

The officer in charge took a step towards Petrus and with a face creased with worry saluted the young Boer.

'I thank you for that offer. I have called a cease-fire until further notice. Sergeant Major.'

A burly man in a red uniform marched the few steps to the officer, stamped to attention and saluted smartly. 'Sir,' he said in clipped tone.

'See to it that medical staff is sent out to tend to our wounded. Tell the surgeon major to ready his hospital and tell Major Symonds to organise a burial detail.'

'Sir.'

The Sergeant Major marched off and the officer turned to Petrus.

'Once again I thank you for your consideration. Please convey that to your commanding officer. Good day.'

The officer turned and walked towards the small knot of uniforms and it seemed that Petrus's contact with the British army was at an end and suddenly he felt very thirsty. The day's events had caught up with him and not only did he feel thirsty but very tired. He looked up towards the crest of the hill ready to begin the long walk back. Letting his rifle hang loosely across his shoulder, he held the flag of truce aloft, and set off on the return journey passing medical orderlies and wounded soldiers. It was a remarkable sight, a triumph for the Boers. They had routed the British army and inflicted very heavy losses on them at very little loss to themselves.

As he climbed, he thought about the confounded field guns, the big guns that were supposed to have beaten them. For a moment, remembered how frightened he had been and how surprised he was at their ineffectiveness. If the soldiers had aimed those guns better, he knew that the outcome could have been very different.

With weary steps, he climbed the last of the incline his white flag still flying when a fine black horse caught his eye and he decided to take a small detour to look at it. He saw a rifle lying where its owner had dropped it and then a sword and he reached down to pick them up and looked round for the owner. Perhaps there would be an ammunition bandolier to go with them, he thought as his eyes flitted across the battlefield. He saw a pair of boots sticking out from behind a boulder and decided to investigate and walking the few yards to the corpse looked down to see that the soldier had a bandolier and it was almost full. The boots were in good shape too and he wondered if he should take those as well. The man seemed to be about the same size and they were a fine pair. He placed his flag and his weapon on the ground, reached down to relieve the dead man of his ammunition belt, rolling him from side to side to ease it over his head, a head covered in dried blood and then he turned his attention to the boots.

The first one coming off easily enough but the second took extra effort, requiring the body to roll over before he could to prise it over the heel. Gripping the British army tunic, he pulled the body onto its side and then, with a push, it was lying flat on its stomach and he had room to manoeuvre the boot. Twisting it from side to side, he felt it loosen and, with one last tug, he would be the proud owner of a pair of quality British army boots. Leaning forward he pulled as hard as he could and felt his prise begin to slip off the foot but before it came completely off he felt an enormous kick in his buttocks. The combination of physical force and surprise propelled him forward, protruding roots tripping him as he went, his balance gone and he fell awkwardly. Letting out a howl of pain, he lay stunned for a moment, shaking his head in disbelief and then he struggled to get to his feet but the fall had fractured his leg.

Gripping his leg with both hands, he fell back, groaning in pain and feeling nauseous. After the exertions of the day, the excitement of battle and the climb down the hill and back he was very tired and lay for a moment with his eyes closed. The pain had temporarily excluded the British soldier from his consciousness but suddenly he remembered and tried to sit up.

He saw his gun lying not more than a few feet away and tried to reach it, dragging himself along on his elbows but it was too much for him and he collapsed face down on the ground. Georgie was in no better shape and watching the Boer making for his gun galvanized him into doing the same. He looked at the Boer's weapon, then back at the Boer, groaning in pain and struggling to move, and although his own wounds had left him weakened, he managed to reach the gun first and lift it to his shoulder.

'Who are you?' he quizzed.

'Petrus.'

'Petrus?' quizzed Georgie for no apparent reason other than he was feeling disorientated.

'Yes.'

Georgie began to feel dizzy and had to close his eyes for a moment, enough time for Petrus to draw a knife and attempt to attack him. However, the movement disturbed the broken leg, sending a shock wave through his body and he collapsed shrieking with pain.

Georgie opened his eyes to see Petrus, arm outstretched, the knife lying harmlessly beside him and closed his finger on the trigger.

'You going to kill me? Can I say a prayer first?'

'What happened today, where are our soldiers?'

'Many are dead, many more wounded. I have been to tell your officer that we will allow you to tend to your wounded without fear or harm.'

Georgie, still with the gun pointing at Petrus, looked around to see more than a few dead horses, and amongst them, wounded men calling out and suddenly his mind cleared.

'We were routed?'

'Yes, but we take no pleasure in that.'

The pain in Georgie's head abated, he could think more clearly and gradually the part of the assault he could remember filled his mind, the foolhardy charge, McKenzie falling dead beside him and then the screams of the wounded. Then a vision materialised, the black man he had killed in cold blood in that earlier conflict and then another, the Zulu he had spared. Those memories, intermingled with the fear he had felt during the charge, fear that he would not survive the encounter and gradually he came to terms with the new reality. He was still alive and yet had half expected to die and he was grateful for that.

'Petrus I do not want to kill you, I do not want to kill another human being as long as I live. Here, take your gun.'

'God will remember you for this my friend. What is your name?'

'Georgie.'

'Thank you Georgie,' said Petrus wincing in pain.

Georgie closed his eyes for a few moments more and drew a large breath before looking more closely at the Boer.

'You seem to be in pain, let me help you. Where does it hurt?'

'My leg, I think it's broken.'

Georgie walked unsteadily the few yards towards Petrus and crouched beside him.

'I can see. The shin looks un-natural. I know a little of first aid, the first thing we need to do is fasten some splints to hold it in position. Can you hang on for a while; I will see what I can find.'

Petrus nodded and managed to sit a little straighter, his face contorted in pain and Georgie patted him on the shoulder and touching his own wounded forehead went to find his missing boot. He found it near his dead horse and seeing his water bottle slipped it off the saddle and returned to Petrus.

'Here, have yourself a drink,' he said taking a deep draught himself and, feeling better, looked around for materials for a splint.

They were not far from a thicket and minutes later, he had cut and trimmed several stout twigs with his knife. Kneeling beside Petrus, he slit open the injured man's trouser leg and after taking off his shirt, he set to work.

'Here, keep your leg straight whilst I cut up my shirt. Hold these pieces of wood like this and I will bind them tight,' and as he straightened the injured leg, Petrus gritted his teeth to fight the pain. Securing the damaged leg with the makeshift splint, he tied pieces of the shirt tightly round it before standing up to admire his handiwork.

'Do you think you can stand?'

'I will try.'

'Use your gun as a crutch. Take your weight off the leg and I will help you.'

Slowly, with Georgie's help and leaning on his upturned gun Petrus managed to stand.

'Where are your lines? I will help you reach them.'

'You are a good man Georgie and I thank you,' said Petrus struggling and sucking his breath through his teeth.

Georgie did not reply, his mind was troubled, a change had come over him, and he was not sure of what it was nor how to manage it.

'Our lines are up there.'

'Put your arm over my shoulder, it doesn't look much of a climb,' said Georgie helping Petrus swing his arm over his shoulder and together they hobbled slowly up the grassy bank but before they had gone fifty yards, Boer fighters appeared and surrounded them.

'Hands up soldier,' said one.

'Shoot him now,' said another.

'Do not touch this man or you will pay for it in the afterlife,' growled Petrus.

His obvious anger had its effect; the men lowered their guns, and sheepishly took over from Georgie helping him to the Boer lines.

'What has happened?' asked an anxious Jos approaching his son. 'I expected you back hours ago. I looked with the telescope, where have you been?'

'Father, I had an accident and this man helped me. Treat him kindly, he has saved my leg.'

Jos looked at Georgie and then back at Petrus unsure of what to do with an enemy soldier.

'What exactly happened?' asked Jos, looking at the bound leg.

'An accident father, I tripped over some roots and fell awkwardly and this man helped me.'

'I thank you for that soldier, you will not be harmed, but you are our prisoner, we cannot let you go.'

Georgie hung his head, averting curious eyes and wondered what kind of a predicament he had landed himself in. the events of the past hour had moved quickly and he had not really thought that he was crossing over into the enemy line but at least he was still alive.

'Christiaan, take two men and ride to the Commandant Generals headquarters. We have more wounded men here; bring back a wagon for them, to take them to safety and get some medical attention. Go, hurry,' ordered Jos 'The rest of you go back to your positions and keep your eyes open, we don't want any surprises.'

The journey to the Transvaalers camp was difficult for the wounded, the Boer Conestoga wagon living up to its reputation as a less than comfortable mode of transport. Built without springs, it bumped and shook as it navigated uneven ground and inside its wide canvas cover, Petrus had to grit his teeth each time the solid wooden wheels lurched over uneven ground.

The only outward sign of his discomfort were beads of sweat on his forehead, he was tough, but at times, the ordeal was almost too much. Taking a deep breath, he shifted his position, allowing the pins and needles his buttocks to fade and looked out through the wagon's flapping sheet to see how Georgie was faring. He had his wrists tied together and was stumbling behind the wagon at the end of a length of rope and for the next three hours, the wagon made slow progress until eventually the drover decided that the oxen were tired and hungry and called a halt.

'I need to let the beasts graze for a few hours otherwise we will not get much further. Bring the prisoner to help me outspan the animals,' he said to one of the two escort riders.

'What do you want him to do Abe?' shouted the outrider.

'You can untie his hands; he will need both of them and keep a gun on him if you must but I do not think he will be leaving us in a hurry by the look of him.'

The guard grunted acknowledgement and left Georgie in the charge of the drover who explained how he was to unhitch the oxen and stake them out.

'Make sure the stakes are well driven in, we don't want to find any animals missing in the morning. If any *are* missing you will get the blame and we will hitch *you* to the traces.'

Georgie said nothing; he knew what to do. For more than five years, he had travelled the length and breadth of the country, hauling the great Boer wagons over mountains and through mud sometimes up to his knees. He took the hammer and stakes from the drover, found a clear, well-grassed area, and began to drive the wooden stakes deep into the earth.

'You need your own wound attending to soldier. Here let me wipe the blood off your face. I think you boys had a bad time of it today,' said the drover after tying the last of the oxen to a stake. He found a water bottle and soaked a rag before giving the rest of the water to Georgie before roughly wiping away dried blood. He was a typical Boer, tough, roughly dressed and yet he had compassion and Georgie was dismayed at how easily a bunch of farmers like him had routed the British army.

The Majors leadership disappointed him, taking them up the steepest part of the slope and why did they charge like cavalry. They were not cavalry they were Mounted Infantry, their job was to scout, take ground little by little not to charge headlong into the guns. What about the artillery, what came of the promises that they would rout the Boers in quick time? He was tired, hungry and his head was throbbing from his injury, there were too many unanswered questions and they were beginning to affect him.

It took them until noon the following day for the wounded to reach the main Boer encampment and receive attention from two volunteer German doctors from Natal. Initially Georgie did not receive any treatment, as a prisoner of war he was of low priority, but once the doctors had dealt with those in most need he was summoned him to the hospital wagon.

'So, you are English, you have a bad day yesterday I think.'

'Seems that way.'

'Let me have a look at your head, Ah, a bad cut only and some bruising. You will live my friend. Sit here and I will clean it. The cut is deep; I will need to put in some stitches. This will hurt a little but I think it is necessary.'

For several minutes the doctor worked on Georgie's cuts until, eventually he stopped and admired his handiwork. 'You will have a scar I think. You can wear it as a badge of honour, show that you have fought in battle, yes.'

Georgie's head was throbbing and he was less than amused. It had taken all his concentration not to cry out during the procedure and he was in no mood to suffer the German's jocularity.

'You can go now, come back tomorrow for me to make sure that there is no infection.'

Georgie stood up and walked out of the tent unsure of what he should do but his guard was nearby and he was soon on his way to meet the Commandant General.

'So we have another prisoner, which makes five of you. You are a sergeant I see, and what regiment?

Georgie remained silent.

'Do not be afraid, we are kindly people and have no wish to harm you but we have no facilities in which to house prisoners. Petrus De Witt has petitioned me to allow you to go with him to his father's farm and work there until this conflict is resolved. He tells me that you helped him in his time of need and deserve leniency. If you give me your word of honour that you will not try to escape, nor fight us in future, then you may go with Petrus until peace returns to our land.'

The Commandant General looked at him from under bushy eyebrows. 'Well?'

Georgie was a good soldier, had always tried to do his best, and had never questioned orders. The Twenty-Fourth of Foot had been in some difficult situations during their time in South Africa, particularly the fighting at Isandhlwana and Hlobane. They had fought natives then but these people seemed hardly any different to him, acted like him, sometimes spoke like him and he knew that he did not want to fight them, his fighting days were over, and he was never going back to the army.

'Thank you sir, I give you my word of honour.'

'Good, you may go now.'

With his long beard pressing into his chest, the Boer leader turned away to attend to more pressing business and the guard signalled for Georgie to follow him.

'Petrus, your prisoner, the Commandant General says you can have him until the war is over. Work him hard, get your money's worth,' said the guard chuckling to himself as he walked away.

'Well my friend it seems you will be spending some time on our farm. My father and brother will be here soon I think and then we will decide what to do with you. Have you worked on a farm before?'

Georgie shook his head; he had seen a bewildering turn of events and he had not really known what he was letting himself in for helping Petrus, the only certainty that he was finished with fighting.

'Can you drive a wagon?' Petrus persisted.

'No.'

'But you can ride a horse; you must be able to do that.'

'Yes I can ride a horse.'

'Well that is something. Have you eaten?'

'Not since yesterday morning.'

'You can start your chores now by getting me some dinner. Go to the canteen wagon and get us both some food. Tell them you are the prisoner of Jos De Witt and they will give you something.

'Jos De Witt?'

'My father and your master for the next few months or until this war ends.'

War, was it never ending in this country, the Xhosa and the Zulus and now the Boer. Georgie's first encounter had been against rebellious miners and Fenians in the diamond fields of Kimberly, a show of force dissuading them from actually fighting. The troopers had spent some time in Kimberley, panning for diamonds during the weeks of rest and recuperation and wished he were there again as he reached the canteen wagon.

'So you are the English prisoner,' said the cook spooning out two portions of stew and handing over several chunks of dark brown bread.

Georgie nodded and carried the pewter plates past several Boer fighters who observed him in silence and he began to feel very alone as he made his way back to the De Witt's wagon.

'Some sort of stew,' he said to Petrus, placing the plate in his hands.

'Springbok I think. It smells good don't you think?'

Georgie only half heard him as he began to eat his own meal, wolfing it down and beginning to feel better. The food warmed him, his throbbing head seemed to calm down, and he took time to look around. The camp was alive with commandos returning from the fight, he counted upwards of two hundred men, all going about their business in a calm and methodical way. He saw riders coming in from the surrounding darkness and wondered where his unit was. The last he had seen of them was during the charge and he recalled seeing more than one fall to the accurate Boer shooting. He felt sad and lonely but before he could dwell on his predicament, Jos appeared.

'Petrus you are all right,' a statement rather than a question.

'Yes father, the doctor said that my leg should heal properly and I should feel no ill effects. He said that our prisoner had done a good job with the splint and that he had probably saved me from a permanent limp.'

Jos looked at Georgie sitting with his back against a wagon wheel and lifted his hat in acknowledgement.

'I thank you for that. We owe you a debt of gratitude soldier.'

'He's called Georgie and we are to take him with us when we go home. The Commandant General has allowed two other prisoners to leave for the Orange Free State with the promise not to take any further part in hostilities and Georgie here has promised not to run away but to work for us until the war is over. He can take on my chores until I can walk again.'

Jos's brow furrowed and he reached into his pocket for his pipe and lighting it he sat on an upturned bucket. For ten minutes he said nothing until finally, he took the pipe from his mouth and knocked out the embers on the heel of his boot.

'It seems to me the Commandant General believes we are going to win this conflict. We routed the British just as we did at Bronkhorstspruit; we gave them a bloody nose alright.'

Georgie looked at the ground, embarrassed to wear the red tunic of the Infantry, embarrassed that so many of his comrades were dead, killed so easily by these unassuming farmers. How could it have happened?

Chapter 11

For once, the trail was easy for the mules the road to Pretoria flat and dry with wide expanses of open country on either side and plenty of rich pasture to feed on. It was a very different proposition to the kloofs and ravines of Zululand where the passage was both difficult and dangerous. They had left Zululand two days before after crossing Zibhebhu's territory where the threat of danger was still very real. Nkosinathi had insisted they travel only during the hours of darkness because like John Dunn, Zibhebhu would extract as much tribute from trespassers as he could.

'Riders approaching,' called Jake from the lead position.

William and Phillip heard him and following with the mules, looked up with some trepidation. They had come a long way since the start of their journey at Richards Bay and were well aware of how dangerous their foray into the northern territory of Transvaal could be.

'Who do you think they are William?'

'I don't know but we are outnumbered two to one and I don't fancy tangling with them. Let's hope they are Boers and not the English.'

'Can't see them being English, not this far from Pretoria, the garrison there has been under siege for two months,' said Phillip.

Ahead of them, Jake pulled his horse up and signalled for them to halt and to wait for the riders to approach. They sat watching, Jake, his two companions, and a little way off, Nkosinathi. When the riders were almost within shooting distance Jake visibly stiffened but when he realised they were not holding their guns in a belligerent manner he relaxed.

'Hello,' he called out and waved his hand from side to side.

The leader waved back, and Jake recognised the wide brimmed hats and hardy ponies of a Boer commando and minutes later they came to a stop in front of him.

'You with the Boers?' Jake asked.

The man pursed his lips and nodded.

'Yes, we are guarding the road into the capital. And who are you?'

'Traders, you have a man called Cornelius Haring amongst you?'

'Ja, he is the Veldkornet. Who asks?'

'Jake O'Neil, I have brought him some guns.'

'You come with us; we take you to our camp.'

At last, safely under the protection of a Boer escort, the traders and their mules followed them across the veldt towards a prominent kopje quite soon, a cluster of tents appeared, and a guard came out to meet them.

'This man is looking for Cornelius, go, and tell him the guns are here,' said the one leading the patrol and within a few minutes, a broad shouldered man with bushy grey sideburns came out to greet them.

'Jake O'Neil, my friend. You have returned as you promised. What have you brought us? Guns I hope, modern repeaters eh?'

Jake signalled to his men to lift the box from the lead mule and lower it to the ground then he took a metal implement from his saddlebag and prised open the lid. As the wooden planks came away, they revealed a pile of modern repeating rifles wrapped in greasy paper. He lifted one, took a rag from his pocket, and rubbed off the thickest of the grease before handing it to Cornelius.

The Dutchman held it lovingly, turning it in his hands, caressing it with his eyes before lifting it to his shoulder and aiming at an imaginary target.

'It feels good. How many have you brought?'

'One hundred, all as good as this one.'

'And how much are you asking?'

'I am not a greedy man,' lied Jake. 'The same price as you paid last time, five pounds each.'

'Five hundred pounds?'

'Five hundred pounds.'

'But we buy in bulk – four hundred and fifty pounds and you have a deal.'

Nkosinathi waited on a Kopje with a wide view across the Highveld for the mules to return. He had refused to go any further into the explaining to Jake that as a Zulu he was not welcome in the country of the *iBhunu*.

'They have no respect for the Blackman, they only want us to work as slaves and take our land, and I do not want to walk amongst them. I will wait here for your return.' he had said, and sitting amongst the undergrowth near the top of the hill, he chewed on a long stalk of grass.

To the casual observer he was invisible and patient, an art mastered as a boy keeping watch over his father's herd when he had spent days alone with the herd. For him it was second nature to be alone for hours on end waiting, watching and eventually he spied horses and riders in the distance and estimated that they would not reach his position for at least another two or three hours and when they finally reached the hill they stopped and looked for him.

'I wonder if he is here,' queried William.

'He will be here soon I think; he'll appear from nowhere like he always does,' said Jake chewing some tobacco.

Nkosinathi was a hundred yards away, watching, for any sign of trickery, and satisfied there was none led his horse towards them along a small ravine out of their line of sight.

'Are we really going to pay him Jake?' said William.

'We need to humour him a while longer, at least until we retrieve the rest of the guns then we can dump him. Have you mapped the whole of the trail we took through Zulu country?'

'Most of it, I didn't get much down to begin with, a few more landmarks would be useful but I can draw those during the return journey.'

'Do you think he noticed we were mapping the route Jake?' asked Phillip urging his horse alongside the other two.

'Naw, even if he did see William scribbling it is doubtful he understood what he was doing,' said Jake spitting the wedge of chewed tobacco into some bushes.

For a few minutes longer, the White men talked amongst themselves and as Nkosinathi emerged from the ravine Phillip exclaimed, 'blimey, he's here. How did you do that? You sure know how to creep up on a person.'

'You White men ride with your eyes shut. Maybe if you took more care you would see where I come from,' said Nkosinathi letting out a throaty laugh. 'If it had been one of the Paramount Chief's patrols then maybe you would all be dead. You pay me now.'

'Not yet,' said Jake. 'I'll give you your money when we reach the place where we left the box. That's what we agreed'

Nkosinathi's eyes narrowed and he looked Jake aware he was dealing with a treacherous man. 'I will take you back then you must pay me and when I show you the box.'

'That's it boy, you guide us all the way back and show us the box then you will get your money.'

After several days heading south terrain familiar to Nkosinathi came into view, the hills of his homeland and before long, they were following the river into the Ngome forest.

'You got this down on the map?' Jake whispered to William.

'Sure I have boss.'

Jake grunted with subdued pleasure. He was pleased with their trip, the money they had made and soon he would be getting his hands on the rest of the guns.

'Hey boy, where is that box? If you want paying you had better hand it over.'

'Have no fear white man your box is safe.'

'Where is it?'

'Safe, I take you to it in the morning then you pay my enough for ten cows.'

'What, you want cash?'

'Yes, the paramount chiefs are taxing us heavily and they want the Whiteman's paper. I can buy cattle from other villages with that.'

'How much?'

'Each cow is worth fifteen of your shillings.'

Jake frowned, he had anticipated a few beads as the price of Nkosinathi's services, and he was not ready for such a surprise. Fifteen pounds was a heavy price to pay even though Nkosinathi had done a good job, kept them from harm, and knocked a week of their expected journey time. On the plus side, William had at least mapped the trail and next time they ventured into Zululand, they would not need the native to guide them.

Interrupting his thoughts Nkosinathi said, 'you make camp here and tomorrow I take you to the place where you find the box and then you pay me.'

Jake nodded and looked at his two companions. 'You heard the man, let's stake out the mules, and pitch the tent. I'll get a fire going and make some coffee. I think we will soon be at the end of this trip, back to civilization where we can have some fun.'

Phillip and William grinned, began unsaddling their horses, and while they were busy Nkosinathi quietly slipped away into the forest. On foot to begin with, he led his horse into the trees and when he was far enough away, mounted, and urged the animal towards the steep sided bank that led to the cave.

His brothers had done well, screening the cave entrance and leaving few tell-tale signs that they had ever been there. Only a competent tracker would notice the broken twigs and faint impressions of African feet in the soft earth and he knew that the box was safe. He looked up at where the cave entrance should be and jumping from his horse began scrambling the last few yards towards the cave entrance. He could see it now, a dark shadow in the cliff face and parting some of the new growth squeezed into the cave and in the gloom, he saw the box. Reaching out he ran his hands over the lid, feeling for signs of tampering, but there was none and then he froze, the hairs on the back of his neck involuntarily standing on end. He was not alone and as to confirm it, a low throaty growl sprang from the darkness deep inside the cave and his is stomach knotted in fear.

Slowly, he felt for the hunting knife at his waist and then, very slowly, he began to retrace his steps towards the cave entrance, his ears alert his eyes searching the darkness. He was at a disadvantage with his silhouette visible to the predator deep inside the cave and increased his pace hoping that the animal was not hungry.

His nostrils flared uncontrollably and his heart thumped crazily in his chest as he emerged into fading daylight to see his horse where he had left it. If the beast decided to come after him the horse was too far away, but he had no choice. Turning, he ran as fast as his legs could carry him and in one movement reached for his gun and spun round to face the cave entrance. His heart was pounding so fiercely he felt his chest would burst but at least with his weapon firmly in his grasp he had a chance. Forcing himself to hold steady his eyes flitted from side to side in search of movement but there was none, not even a rustle of leaves and he began to realise the beast had stayed inside the cave. He had held his breath for two long minutes and finally he exhaled a long and measured sigh and he glanced skywards to thank the spirits of his ancestors for their protection.

Not long after first light, Jake kicked the fire's embers across the dry earth and they began to break camp.

'Where do you say this cave is Kosinathi?'

'Up ahead, along the river bank there is a cliff face and half way up there is a wide ledge. We can take one of the mules there but there isn't enough room for the horses as well.'

'That's fine; we can leave them tethered whilst we load up the mule. William bring one of the mules with you, we can leave the others here until we are finished. Okay, show us the way.'

Nkosinathi mounted his horse and led the three White men along the trail and riding in silence; each man was alone with his thoughts. For Jake it was the culmination of an ambitious and successful trip, he had money in his pocket and was looking forward to a good time whilst Nkosinathi was thinking of his own reward. With the money promised him, he could buy enough cattle to keep his people alive but there was still one last act to play out.

Reaching a narrow section of the trail as it passed between rocky outcrops he jumped from his saddle, and coaxed the horse towards a safe place.

'We leave the horses here.' He said and his companions understood.

Dismounting they tied their horses to some bushes and made ready to move on foot with the mule but it was in no mood to oblige. Baying and digging its feet in it refused to budge forcing an angry Jake to reach into his saddlebag for his bullwhip. He was not having this stupid mule deprive him of the box of guns and the whips sharp crack did the trick.

Nkosinathi was alarmed at the antics of the mule and its handler, the predatory cat could be lying in wait, and that was a worry. More than that were the three White men; he had noticed them talking in whispers after he returned to camp the previous evening and this morning they were doing it again. Their body language had changed, they were excluding him, and a sixth sense warned him to be careful.

'Here, behind these bushes, the cave. You will find your box in there. Now it is time to pay me for my work.'

'Not till we get the box. Phillip, William drag it out whilst I get Kosinathi's money ready.'

The two men pushed past Nkosinathi and began to pull at the undergrowth, exposing the mouth of the cave and they peered in.

'It's here alright Jake, time to give it to him.'

That was the signal; Jake's hand reached inside his jacket but instead of the banknotes he pulled out his pistol, at the same time William and Phillip turned their backs to the cave entrance, and levelled their own pistols. Nkosinathi was expecting some sort of confrontation but they had taken him by surprise and he was unable to bring his rifle to bear. In desperation, he gripped the barrel, swung the stock towards Jake but he was too late to stop a shot ringing out. It was enough though to unbalance Jake in his eagerness to kill Nkosinathi, his aim was wide of the mark, and the bullet missed its target. The hot lead flew inches past the left ear of Nkosinathi causing him to yelp with surprise and he dived headlong into the undergrowth to escape.

William and Phillip were at first unsighted by Jake and when they finally started shooting Nkosinathi was fast disappearing into the thick vegetation. The unexpected action that saved the Zulu caused confusion amongst his assailants. First Jake shouted for them to chase after Nkosinathi and then, before they could move, a terrible roar echoed from inside the cave. Phillip and William screamed in terror, as the Leopard emerged, disturbed by the noise of the gunshots. However, the animal was not in hunting mode, it too was terrified of the strange and distressing noise of the guns. At first it had decided to investigate the sound of voices, but then the sound of the guns had propelled it into action and unnerved it raced past the terrified men to make its escape.

'Jesus that was a close one,' exclaimed Phillip.

William remained silent, shocked by the closeness of the predator and Jake shook with fear.

'Quick, the horses come on,' shouted Jake. 'If he gets to the horses we could be stranded here.'

Jake was right, Nkosinathi was at that very moment lifting his ammunition belt from his saddle. He did not intend to ride away and slinging the bandolier over his head, he made ready to escape. From the corner of his eye, he saw Jake and William break through the undergrowth and catching full view of him, they began shooting. The bullets whined past him like mad insects, thudding into tree trunks forcing him to duck low as he ran into the trees.

'There he goes, quickly, after him,' shouted Jake and more shots rang out.

The shooting was wide of the mark; the revolvers were soon out of ammunition and forced the men to take time to reload. The time wasted helped Nkosinathi to put more distance between him and the White men and running with hunched shoulders, he made himself a difficult target.

Dodging from side to side, his blood up he felt like the Zulu warrior he was and his military training came to the fore. As he ran, he wondered what his Induna would do in a situation such as this. He could hear his voice, calm, controlling, "become invisible, be like the wind, strike the enemy where he least expects it, disappear, and like the wind, blow from a different direction".

'Think I might have hit him,' said Jake. 'He cried out just before he disappeared.'

'Yeah, reckon I got him too. He will not get far and we have his horse,' said William.

'Come on, let's load up this mule with the guns and then we'll get out of here. I don't think our Zulu friend or that darn cat will be back in a hurry,' said Jake touching his jacket pocket to make sure the roll of banknotes was still there.

'Where's the damn Mule?' said William now fully recovered from his ordeal.

'If it's gone well use the Zulu's horse come on,' said Jake beginning to trot towards the cave.

William and Phillip followed close on his heels, and after a search found the Mule munching happily on some grass. Leading it to the cave and after some exertions the managed to drag the box from the cave, and lifted it onto the animals back.

'Okay, let's get moving, the sooner we are out of here the happier I will be,' said Jake.

'Where do you reckon he's gone Jake?'

'Probably back to his village to get help. Even more reason to get moving. I do not fancy taking on a bunch of angry Zulus. Do you?'

Far from heading to his kraal, Nkosinathi was running as fast as he could towards the staked out mules and soon after Jake led his men to the mules. After a tense few minutes the three white men had strung the mules together and broken camp ready to leave for Natal.

'Come on, let's get out of here,' called Jake and from the rear of the mule train William waved to show he was ready.

Phillip led the first animals and the others followed, Jake rode on ahead to keep a lookout and rode unwittingly past the hiding place of Nkosinathi. They were making their way out of the forest towards open country and as Nkosinathi watched them pass, he realised that he had to act quickly. He pulled his knife from his belt, gritted his teeth, and pressed forward on a parallel path to the mule train.

The animals were considerably happier now that their heavy loads were gone, docile, and less irritating they made good progress. Phillip rode alongside the lead mule leaving William to bring up the rear and from time to time, he anxiously looked around. If the Zulu was still around he did not want him take him by surprise. Nevertheless, taken by surprise he was.

As Nkosinathi's' best chance presented itself he ran swiftly through the trees, his bare feet making barely a sound and he closed in on his prey. He had noticed a turn in the trail near to cover, a perfect place for an ambush, and as the lead animals disappeared round the bend he launched himself up behind William, clamping his hand tightly over the man's mouth and together they both fell to the ground. Even before they landed, Nkosinathi's knife had done its work and he left William flat on his back staring at the sky with lifeless eyes.

Darting back into the trees, he took the short cut across the bend until he was no more than a few yards behind Phillip. His bare feet, hardened from his time with the Impi, carrying him swiftly towards the unsuspecting Phillip but then disaster struck. Inadvertently he trod on a dead twig, its retort loud enough to alert Phillip who turned in his saddle and with one hand aimed his rifle at the oncoming Zulu. Nkosinathi was already leaping onto the rump of Phillip's horse and before he could shoot the gun spun from his grip and Nkosinathi drove his knife deep between his ribs.

Phillip died quickly but not before a gurgling, blood spattered scream left his lips, alerting Jake who riding twenty yards in front. He turned round, alerted by the dying man's cry, and saw two rider-less horses and then he saw Phillip lying on the ground and Nkosinathi getting to his feet. More in panic than with skill, he lifted his rifle and fired a lucky shot catching Nkosinathi in the shoulder and sending him spinning into the undergrowth.

'William, Phillip,' Jake screamed out, not yet aware that both of his partners were dead.

There was no reply but he knew that he had hit Nkosinathi and felt the best path was to finish him off.

'I will get you this time you bastard,' he said sliding from his saddle, his rifle pointing at the gap in the bushes left by Nkosinathi and in those bushes, Nkosinathi lay writhing in agony.

The bullet had hit him squarely on the shoulder, his arm felt useless, and although the pain was excruciating his mind kept racing. he knew that Jake was coming to kill him and that he must keep going, get as far away from him as he could. He shook his head, took a deep breath, and crawled away on his good hand and knees. He remembered seeing Phillips rifle fall as the two of them had hit the ground and looked around for it. With a gun he had a chance but he had very little time to find it and crawling through the undergrowth he heard Jake's cursing and then he came across Phillips body.

'Where are you Kosinathi? Come on out and let me kill you. Where are you, you bastard?'

Nkosinathi winced in pain as he passed William's body and there, not ten yards away, was the gun. Quickening the pace of his crawl, he reached it and gipping the barrel used the stock to get to his feet and staggered more than ran to put as much distance between himself and Jake as he could.

The pain in his arm had turned to a throb and he made better progress but the he caught his wounded shoulder on a low branch and could not hold back a howl of pain. Not more than fifty yards away Jake's ears pricked up, he changed direction and made for the sound's source.

Nkosinathi halted and listened but he could hear nothing, nevertheless he guessed that Jake had heard his cry and that it would be only a matter of time before he caught up with him. Beads of sweat began to roll off his brow and into his eyes, blinding him and the pain in his shoulder had returned. He blinked wildly in the hope that his vision would return and knowing he could not go on much longer, there would have to be a showdown.

He looked for a suitable place for an ambush and exhausted slumped with his back against a rocky outcrop and held the gun against his good shoulder and with the barrel resting on his knee, he waited.

He seemed to be there for hours and then abruptly Jake appeared walking slowly, cautiously. There was some cover between himself and Jake, enough for Jake not to see him immediately and steeling himself, he watched and when the showdown came, it was sudden and violent when Jake saw Nkosinathi slumped against the tree and shouted out in triumph. The sight of his injured prey invigorated Jake and he took aim for a final, telling shot but in his haste he did not notice Phillip's gun and as he squeezed his trigger, a double crack echoed through the trees.

Chapter 12

The weather was no better, the London fog had returned and Ellen was thoroughly miserable. Trying to sit up in bed, she found it a struggle and Patrick had to help her. He lifted her bodily and placed an extra pillow at her back for support and when she was comfortable, he unscrewed the top of the medicine bottle. Pouring out enough of the sweet smelling mixture to fill a spoon held steadily in his hand, he placed the bottle on the side cabinet and waited for a few seconds.

'Here, try some of dis cough mixture. The doctor says it will help, come on open wide.'

Patrick stuck the spoon unceremoniously in Ellen's open mouth and watched her swallow the medicine.

'Better.'

Ellen nodded and waited for him to remove the spoon. He reached over, kissed her on the forehead, and sat back on the chair next to her bed.

'There is news from Africa, the Times newspaper has a report of the fighting and it does not make pleasant reading.'

Ellen's eyes opened a little wider as she anticipated the meaning of his words.

'Georgie?'

'I don't know but there has been a large loss of life and there are many wounded. The newspaper says that de fifty eighth was routed and the mounted squadron decimated.'

'What about Georgie is there any news of Georgie?' Ellen demanded.

Because of her fever, her eyes appeared less alert than normal but the brain behind them was working at full speed. She sensed that Patrick was holding something back. Again, she asked about Georgie and Patrick lowered his eyes.

'What has happened, tell me Patrick,' she demanded again.

'Well notin' actually. There is a list of dead and wounded from a place called Laing's Nek and also a list of those missing in action and Georgie is on dat list.'

'Missing in action, what does it mean?'

'It means he's missing in action.'

'Patrick, tell me in English.'

'Well it doesn't say he is dead or dat he is wounded but he might be dead or...'

'Or what?'

'He could have been taken prisoner or he might have just wandered off.'

'What do you mean, wandered off?'

'Well after the fightin' at Ulundi, when we beat de Zulu's he told me dat he had had enough of fightin'.'

'So?'

'Well I got de feelin' then that he might abscond, desert.'

'Desert, do you think he really would?'

'Well he wasn't happy having to stay behind when the regiment came home. He expected to see out his service back in England, the same as I have. I am not a betting man but I would put money on him deserting.'

'Not a betting man!' Ellen perked up markedly. 'Not a betting man, ha. I tell you what Patrick, as soon as I am rid of this dreadful fever we shall go back to South Africa and look for him.'

'South Africa!'

'Yes, I am fed up of this London weather. I realise now what I am missing and as soon as I am well enough I will have a meeting with Mister Jones.'

She sniffed, closed her eyes ready to sneeze and Patrick put a rag in her hand.

'Achoo...achoo. Oh, the sooner I get better I can sign those papers for Mister Jones and the inheritance will be mine. Then we will be free Patrick, free to do whatever we wish.'

Ellen closed her eyes and slipped back into the pillows, drifting into a light sleep. The doctor had said that the fever would last no more that forty-eight hours and advised she stay in bed until it had passed and she had weathered the worst of it. Looking down at his her, Patrick could see that she was on the mend and he reached out to touch her hand. She had closed her eyes and he looked at her intently, she had never mentioned anything of any money she expected to inherit, not until today.

She opened her eyes again and saw him staring at her.

'What's the matter?'

'Er....your inheritance, you have told me you expect to inherit your husband's estate but you said it probably wouldn't amount to much.'

'Patrick, what if I tell you I am to inherit a great deal of money? I expect to have enough to go back to South Africa and look for Georgie.'

For a few seconds their eyes met and as the moment passed, he released her hand to sit back in the bedside chair, bemused. The revelation stunned him and at the mention of South Africa, his thoughts too turned to Georgie. Where was he, was he still alive? He was not even sure of that but he hoped to God that he was. He thought back to the day they first met, boy soldiers learning their trade and the campaigning, first in the Eastern Cape then Griqualand and Natal. For quite a few years they had risked their lives together and now, looking out of the rain streaked window he yearned for the warmth of Africa.

The carriage made its way along the Old Kent road, clattering over the cobles and pulling up outside the offices of Bartlett and Bartlett. For Ellen it had become a familiar journey and today she had come to meet with Frederick Jones to finalise the transfer of her father in law's estate into her name.

'Do come in er...Mrs. Jameson.'

Frederick Jones was still not used to calling Ellen by her Christian name and blushed with embarrassment.

'Come now Freddie, you can call me Ellen. Are we not good friends? I know this is business but you have helped me so much – call me Ellen.'

Freddie's blush spread and Ellen smiled at him. She had that effect on men.

The journey from the main Boer camp had taken the greater part of three days, stopping twice a day to rest and graze the Oxen. Each night they sat around the campfire, Jos and Christiaan puffing away on their pipes and talking in subdued voices about the war, the farm and religion. Georgie said little to begin with and Jos, a man of few words, had not encouraged him but Petrus, and to a lesser extent Christiaan, were eager to learn a little of the world outside their own.

'Where is it in England you come from?' had been the first question.

'I grew up in the back streets of London; we were poor, my mother and I. She was a seamstress as I remember.'

'Remember, don't you know what your mother did?' asked a slightly indignant Christiaan.

'I was orphaned at nine years of age.'

'Oh, I'm sorry. And what of your father?'

'He was killed fighting in India, he left when I was five and I never knew him.'

Christiaan withdrew a little, refilled his pipe, and did not ask further questions. Petrus was silent for a time, imagining what it must be like for one so young alone in a city like London finally saying, 'London must be a large city. Is it bigger than Pretoria?

He knew nothing of London and could only wonder if perhaps it was like Pretoria, the largest settlement he had ever known and then Jos spoke. Sitting on his upturned bucket, his pipe fully charged and glowing red he sucked in the thick white smoke and spoke in an unexpectedly gentle voice.

'You have led a lonely life?'

Georgie was surprised at the question though it invoked memories and those memories seemed to spring into life, faces, and places flashed through his head and his eyes focused on the far distance. He had been in the company of his fellow soldiers since the age of fourteen and before that had lived a charged existence with his Aunt and uncle and their two youngest children. The eldest, Billy junior, he could hardly remember, he only turned up at the rookery after he had committed a robbery somewhere. From what Ellen had told him, the police had finally caught up with him and he was spending his time in a penal colony. Then, before any other long forgotten memories surfaced, Jos spoke again in his slow, measured tone.

'We do not wish to fight the British; we simply want to be left alone to live our lives in peace but they insist upon imposing taxes upon us, expect us to conform to their rigid rules. That is not our way, we are a god-fearing people, and you will see how strong our family links are. Perhaps for a time you will be a part of our family and live a different life from the one you have so far.'

He fell silent again, sucked on his pipe, Georgie looked at him, slightly overawed, and he wondered if most Boers were like him. If they were, how was it they had so easily defeated the British assault? That question was one he could not answer, he was tired, his wound throbbed, and the journey into the Transvaal was taking its toll.

'I see you are ready to sleep, we will say a prayer in thanks for our deliverance, and you can go under the wagon until morning.'

Georgie watched in silence as the three Boer men bowed their heads and Jos murmured a prayer before banking up the fire for the night. Christiaan stood and disappeared into the darkness to see to the oxen and horses. Petrus struggled to his feet, leaning on a crutch someone had fashioned for him and began hopping towards the wagon a few feet away.

'Come on Georgie, it seems you are one of us now. You can sleep under the wagon; I will sleep here because I have to take over from my brother during the night keeping watch.

The De Witt farm was typical for the Transvaal, more than six thousand acres according to Petrus, ten square miles he said and to Georgie it seemed to stretch as far as the eye could see. Once they had crossed the slow flowing river that marked the boundary, it took another hour before the farm buildings came into view. Two of them, built from sun dried clay bricks and roofed with thatch, appearing almost red in the late afternoon sun. Georgie looked around, marvelling that one family could own so much of the rolling grasslands and as they neared the house, he saw a herd of cattle lazily munching away inside a large rustic pen looked over by two native youths.

As they drew near a woman emerged from the larger of the two buildings dressed in a white pinafore and Georgie noticed that she carried a gun. Jos raised his hat in greeting and flicked the reigns to urge the lumbering oxen on.

'Mutti,' shouted Petrus excitedly. 'My mother and here is my sister,' he said to Georgie walking alongside the wagon.

A younger woman had appeared from the doorway and Georgie could not help staring at her.

'Petrus, Christiaan, you are back safe.' she called and Petrus waved his acknowledgement but Christiaan could not wait, nudging his horse forward he went to meet his family, be the first tell them the news of the battle.

'Papa Jos you are returned safe,' said the older of the two women, 'Christiaan has told us of your victory at the Nek.' Then her face became stern and enquiring as she looked at her youngest son sitting beside his father and then at the stranger in a British army uniform.

'Yes we are safe, Petrus has a broken leg, but he will mend.'

'And who is this?' she asked pointing at Georgie.

'He is our prisoner, he has promised the Commandant General that he will stay with us and work on the farm until the war is over.'

Mutti looked a little astonished, casting her eyes over her son and then the stranger once more.

'What news of the fighting, you are back safe, what has happened, Christiaan says you beat the British?'

Jos explained to his wife that they had won a victory but not yet the war. He told her of the British attack, the field guns and their fearful power and then how their own commandos had inflicted many casualties on the British.

'We are here for only a few days to see to the farm, to take in as much of the harvest as we can but then we will return to Laing's Nek because the British have not yet gone away and the Commandant General believes they will try once more to break through to the Transvaal and Pretoria.'

'What of Petrus, surely he cannot go back.'

'No Mutti, I will not go back just yet. My leg is broken and needs time to heal, I will be of no use.'

Christiaan began unhitching the oxen and called to Georgie in a gruff voice to help.

'You can start your chores straight away, help me with these animals.'

Georgie had not understood the conversation in Afrikaans but Christiaan's clipped English jolted him and he went to his aid. The first oxen was unhitched and he led it by the nose ring towards a pen and as he did so Petrus's sister ran before him to swing open the gate. Georgie was not sure of what to do, averting her eyes to begin with, simply thanking her in a low voice as he coaxed in the animal through and slapping it on the rump let the big animal amble away. He turned back towards the gate to leave the coral to collect a second animal and his eyes met those of the girl. She dare only give him a cursory glance to begin with but a second later, they unwittingly looked into each other's eyes and Georgie felt his mouth go dry.

'Annika, don't be so familiar with the prisoner, come, we will prepare some hot food for our menfolk. I want to know all that has happened. Were any of our men killed Jos?'

'One only, a few were wounded who were sent to the field hospital and we said prayers for them. When this is over we will see how we can help their families.'

Mutti pursed her lips and nodded slowly as she digested the news, picked up her rifle and followed by her daughter, walked back into the farmhouse.

The following three days were hard for Georgie, unused to the kind of physical work a farm demanded he very soon ached all over. He had worked long hours during his military service, struggled with wagons through mud and rain with the military column but always there were many hands to help. Here he was on his own hour after hour swinging the axe to cut up logs and then working in the field harvesting mealie and wheat. It was backbreaking work, but at least there was no Sergeant Major nor upstart Lieutenant barking orders at him. Each night he would sit at the De Witt's table, head bowed as Jos blessed the food and after a good wholesome dinner, he would crawl under the wagon and fall into a deep sleep.

He kept himself to himself as much as he could, acclimatizing to this new environment, working diligently in case his hosts should decide they did not need him after all and for the first time in eight years, he was free of army discipline. That alone was a new and pleasant experience, yet his future was uncertain. But even that became a little more clear when Jos decided that his invalided son and Georgie could manage the farm without him, announcing that he and Christiaan would be returning to Laing's Nek to help with the defence of their territory.

'You take care of yourself my husband and you too Christiaan. Don't take risks I want you both back here safe.'

'We will Mutti. We will not be letting those British get close to us have no fear. I think Piet Joubert considers that we can hold them, beat them.'

She seemed reassured by her husband's words; she trusted the Commandant General and if he thought they would prevail against the British, then that was good enough for her.

This time they did not take the wagon, loading instead their tent and cooking utensils onto Petrus's horse, which allowed them to move more quickly and as they rode away, the three remaining members of the De Witt family and the prisoner stood for a long time watching them.

'Annika come, we will continue making clothes and Petrus, lay your leg up, you will be deformed if you do not rest it. Have you not seen the Bekker boy, they did not set his broken leg properly and now he walks with a limp.'

Petrus looking suitably admonished hobbled towards the rocking chair on the verandah and as he did, Annika looked at Georgie.

'Georgie I have some new clothes for you. Well perhaps not quite new, a shirt belonging to my brother I have repaired and I have cleaned and repaired an old leather jerkin to protect you against the thorn bushes.'

Annika had not spoken to him directly before, the family spoke amongst themselves mainly in Afrikaans, mostly leaving him out of their conversations.

Petrus was the only one to speak with him regularly, Jos occasionally and Christiaan only to give him orders. He turned to thank her, briefly their eyes met and he could see what a beautiful woman she was. Since first seeing her several days before he had only glanced briefly at her, not daring to look at her for long then she smiled at him and offered him the clothes. Gratefully he accepted, glad of a change from the rough serge army tunic he had worn since helping Petrus.

'Can I try it on?'

'Surely.'

He smiled back but the smile was short lived, crushed by harsh words from her mother emerging from the house with fire in her eyes.

'Go behind the shed, Annika should not be seeing a half-naked man. God will not be pleased with you parading your body before my daughter.'

'I...I'm sorry, I just want to see if it fits,' said Georgie shyly withdrawing to try on the shirt.

'It looks fine,' said Annika on his return. 'Now put on the jerkin.'

The leather Jerkin caused much less consternation as he happily slid his arm into the sleeve.

'Here, put this hat on Georgie,' said Petrus hobbling towards him with an amused look on his face.

'You will need this to make your transformation complete. We Boers are lost without our bush hats.'

It was indeed the type of large floppy bush hat favoured by the Boers and after Petrus had planted it firmly on his head, the three of them grinned with approval – he had become a Boer just like them

The recoil of the gun caught Nkosinathi by surprise, threw him backwards and the pain in his injured arm became too much for him. His eyes clouded, a dark red mist descended and he could not see, his hearing was impaired and he slipped into unconsciousness and when he finally came round it was to the sound of a man moaning. He opened his eyes, stared straight up at the clear blue sky and knew that he was still alive. Strangely, the pain in his shoulder had subsided, replaced by a dull throbbing and he felt that he could move. Slowly at first, he rolled over onto his uninjured side and for several minutes lay panting from the exertion, then he forced himself into a sitting position, and there not twenty yards away lay the mortally wounded Jake. He was living out the last few moments of his life, his lips covered in blood from deep inside his lungs, a contrast to his ashen face.

Nkosinathi could see that his adversary was no longer a threat and getting shakily to his feet, he managed to stagger the few yards to where Jake lay and for a while stood looking down at him. Jake had paused only seconds too long to celebrate his perceived triumph and had fired his last shot just too late. Nkosinathi's bullet had ripped into him even as his finger closed on the trigger, spoiling his aim and saving the Zulu's life.

From the ground, Jake looked up at Nkosinathi but his eyes did not see him, the fingers of his right hand twitched one last time and his head rolled lifeless to one side. Nkosinathi felt nothing, he had seen many men die and this one was no different nevertheless, he was in a bad way. He was feeling weak from a loss of blood, dizzy, his mouth was dry and with some effort, he managed to reach down to take Jake's water bottle from around his neck. Pulling it free he took a long draught of the refreshing liquid, and began to feel better.

For several minutes, he took stock of the situation. The three white men were dead, their animals and their guns were strewn about somewhere and it left him thinking that if he could only pull himself together they could be all his when suddenly a low, throaty growl made the hairs on the back of his neck stand on end. The smell of blood must have attracted the leopard, it had returned to the killing ground and its presence caused him to give up all thought of taking the horses and guns, a more pressing task was that of saving his own life.

Picking up Jakes gun he shuffled over to an ancient Umfomothi tree, its thick twisting branches offering at least some protection, and laying the gun in a cleft between the branches, he managed to pull himself up onto one of the lower branches. Gasping for breath, he climbed higher, wedged his body safely against the trunk, and reached for the gun.

He did not have to wait very long, a minute later the long grass parted and the leopard came into sight. Her mottled coat blended well with the shadows but Nkosinathi could see her and levelled his gun. At first, the leopard did not pick up his scent; instead, she made for Jakes corpse, paused to examine it, and repeated her low throaty growl. She circled once and then stood stock still, her eyes half closed as she analysed a new scent and opening them again looked straight up at Nkosinathi. He felt his heart begin to pound, felt dizzy and for what seemed an eternity, both he and the leopard looked at each other.

To his relief the leopard did not move nor did it appear ready to spring. Instead, the lithe, athletic predator lowered its tail and slinked off into the undergrowth leaving Nkosinathi to let out a sigh of relief and then, the baying of a panic-stricken of a mule reached his ears. For more than an hour, he waited, listened for the return of the Leopard but he heard no more and the forest was still save for returning birdsong and it was time to make his escape.

Georgie swung the axe in a long and lazy arc and for the hundredth time smashed it down to split a log clean in half. It was hard, hot work and in the heat of the day he had stripped to the waist. Although the work was physical, he was enjoying it, toiling for long hours, eating good food and sleeping soundly at night. His new life was strengthening both his body and his mind and reaching over to the pile of sawn logs he felt rather than heard her approach.

'You have worked hard Georgie; I have not seen such a pile of firewood.'

Georgie dropped the log, laid the long handled axe against the fence, and turned to face Annika. He caught an admiring look, involuntarily flexed his muscles and for a moment she looked away in embarrassment.

'I had better put on my shirt.'

'Mutti has sent me with some food for you. She says you cannot stay out here all day without some sustenance.'

Annika placed her basket she on the ground and waited in silence, a faint blush spreading across her cheeks as Georgie fastened the last of his shirt buttons.

'It looks good, cold meat, some of that wonderful bread you make.'

'I'm glad you like it,' she said thoughtfully. 'You have worked well; Mutti says we could not have managed so well without you.' Then, in a rush, 'do you like being here, away from your own people?'

Georgie looked at her in surprise. 'I have not really thought about it, I'm just glad to be still alive.'

'Yes, of course, but do you like living amongst us?'

Georgie could not understand why she was so interested in how he felt and then he realised that she liked him.

'I am very happy here Annika, you treat me well and I have never felt so free even though I am supposed to be a prisoner.'

Annika took a hesitant step forward, reached up to him, kissed him on the cheek, and for a few seconds they simply looked into each other's eyes and before Georgie could pluck up the courage to say anything Petrus appeared. He had been sorting seeds for the planting season behind the small shed and now he was hobbling towards them. His father had told him to rest his broken leg, give it chance to heal, but after a two weeks of inactivity, he was far too restless for that.

'Petrus, what are you doing, Mutti said you should not be putting any weight on that injured leg of yours,' scolded his sister.

'Aw, I cannot sit around all day, there are things to be done, and I should really be out hunting for our dinner. All we have left is biltong, no fresh meat.'

'We can manage a bit longer on biltong, no need for you to go hunting just yet Petrus.'

'Perhaps I could try a bit of hunting,' said Georgie, forcing his eyes away from Annika.

'Can you shoot straight? From what I saw of your army none of you seem to be particularly good shots.'

Georgie frowned, this was an insult after all, he was an infantryman, and an infantryman's skill lay in shooting. However, he decided not to reply and instead picked up the axe ready to split another log and Petrus began laughing.

'What's so funny?'

'You, cutting logs like that. When you first started splitting the logs for firewood you missed most of the time.'

'Watch this then.'

Georgie lifted the axe head high over his shoulder, with one fell swoop, spilt the log into two equal parts, and turned to Petrus for approval.

'Not bad soldier boy, but you are still a poor shot.'

'How do you know what kind of shot I am, you haven't seen me shoot.'

Petrus's face clouded over a little as he weighed up Georgie remark. Was he getting angry, was he spoiling for a fight? Annika saw her brother's expression change and then she looked at Georgie expecting some sort retaliation to the jibes but he was grinning and then with relief, she saw her brother's face break out into any equally broad grin.

'Stupid men, why do you always have to fight?'

'I'm not fighting,' they said in unison.

Petrus and Georgie looked at each other for a second in silence and then burst out laughing at them both uttering the same phrase at the self-same time.

'Well I am pleased to hear that. Petrus there is some food in the basket and a jug of beer. It is meant for Georgie but I'm sure he will share it with you.'

The two men looked at each other again still grinning and Annika was pleased that they were friends, not enemies. Her eyes flitted from one to the other several times and once she was satisfied that they would not fight, straightened her bonnet, and walked back towards the main house. That was the trouble with men, they were always fighting each other over something stupid, and she had presumed that they were all the same.

Petrus and Georgie watched her go and settled down against the shed wall hungrily devouring the dry bread and strips of biltong.

'Do you eat biltong in the army Georgie?'

'No, we always have bully beef.'

'What is that?'

'It's meat mixed with corn in a tin.'

'Is it good to eat?'

'If you are starving it's alright but much better to have fresh cooked beef. We get that in the base camp but not when we are on the march.'

'What do you think of biltong?'

'Horrible.'

'I think so too. I think we should improve your shooting and go out hunting for fresh game. What do you say soldier boy.'

'Hey, stop calling me soldier boy, I am not a soldier anymore, and if I can get away with it, I never will be again.'

Petrus looked sideways at Georgie and stopped chewing, slowly nodding his head in understanding. He need not fear this man, for he had seen him change in only two weeks and he knew that he could be trusted. For Georgie's part, he had never been healthier or happier and most of that was down to his new friend's sister.

The tin can flew off at an angle, the shot hitting it slightly to one side. If it had been a springbok or a gazelle, then Georgie would have made a kill.

'Georgie I take it back, you are a good shot, but I think you need to know more about setting your sights.'

'We were always told by an officer where to set our sights.'

'Well there are no officers out here to tell you what to do. You must learn because we cannot waste our bullets.

Three more and then we will go for dinner and tomorrow you can help me onto my pony. We will go hunting for some fresh meat, no more biltong.'

'Or bully beef.'

The two of them laughed and for the next few hours, Georgie returned to his tasks of splitting wood and Petrus sat nearby sorting seeds. He rested his injured leg on a pile of the split logs Georgie piled up for him and as the sun began to sink Annika called from the house to say that dinner was ready. Georgie reached for his new shirt, Petrus stuck his crutch under his arm, and slowly the two of them made their way towards the farmhouse.

'Come on you two, dinner is nearly ready,' said Annika looking straight at Georgie.

'We are going hunting for game tomorrow Mutti,' announced Petrus as he sat at the dinner table. 'It's about time we had some fresh meat.'

'You father told you not to overdo things, to rest and let the bone set properly.'

'I have, I do not put any weight on it Mutti and the pain has all gone. They told me in the camp that it is not a serious break and I could be walking on it in three to four weeks. I'm half way there already.'

'But you will struggle to get on and off your pony.'

'I will stay on it.'

'Then how will you shoot, you cannot shoot well from the animal's back.'

'I will not be the one shooting, Georgie will.'

Both Annika and her mother stopped eating and looked at Georgie.

'What will your father say? Georgie is a prisoner of war; you cannot let him have a gun. He is the enemy.'

Georgie frowned, yes, he was a prisoner, but he *had* given his word that he would not run away nor harm any of Jos's family and he certainly could not harm even one hair on Annika's head.

'I have given my word that I will not cause any trouble Frau De Witt and Petrus is right, we could do with some fresh meat. You do not know how long this war will go on for so it might be that we have to make more biltong anyway.'

'He's right Mutti,' said Annika, 'let them at least give it a try.'

Sibusiso was working out in the field when he first saw it. At first, he did not know what it was and ran to the top of the small hill a few hundred yards from the village for a better view. It appeared to be a lone horse silhouetted against the setting sun but as it neared, he could see someone was lying prostrate against the animal's neck. His brothers, Dumisani and Somopho were not far away and he ran towards them waving and shouting.

'Look, over there a horse and there is someone on it. Come let us see who it is.'

Together the three of them ran across the open ground to meet this strange object and as Somopho was the fleetest of foot, he reached the horse first. Reaching for the bridal, he halted the animal's progress and looked at the figure on its back. It was a man, lying face down and at first, he believed he was dead until his brothers caught up with him and they lowered the body to the ground.

'He has a lot of blood on his arm,' said Dumisani.

'I wonder who he was,' said Somopho leaning over the prostrate form, convinced the man was dead and then with some shock exclaimed, 'he is Nkosinathi, he is our brother.'

Dumisani leaned forward to look more closely at the the face, recognition dawning and he called out Nkosinathi's name several times. 'Nkosinathi, Nkosinathi, what has happened to you my brother. Speak to us, do not go to your ancestors yet, – SPEAK,' he almost shouted.

Tears welled up in Sibusiso's eyes and involuntarily he reached down to touch Nkosinathi's wounded shoulder and from his stupefied state Nkosinathi heard his name, his lips moved as if to say something and then the fingers of one hand clenched and unclenched as if it were a signal.

The cool refreshing water ran down Nkosinathi's face, his sister wiped his brow, cleaning his wound and applying a healing compound. Later, after regained consciousness, she made him eat some maize porridge and as she used her fingers to place small amounts of the food in his mouth he had simply looked her and remained silent. Eventually his strength returned, the wound began to heal and his father came to squat beside him.

'You have been asleep for two days my son.'

'Uh...Father.'

'You are safe now. Your sister has cleaned your wound, bound it with the leaves of the cancer bush and already it is healing. You are a lucky man Nkosinathi, you have been shot but the bullet has passed straight through and the Isangoma says that you will soon be well again.'

Nkosinathi closed his eyes recounting the time Jake shot him, the three dead white men, the leopard, and he let out a sigh of relief that he had survived the ordeal alive. He clenched his fists, tested his body, and tried to rise from the mat but he was still weak from loss of blood, and lay back wondering how the village was coping.

'How are things with you father, have John Dunn's men been back since I left?'

'No they have not bothered us for some time. Do not worry about them. Your sister will bring you food and you will regain your strength fully. Rest a while and we will talk of John Dunn later.'

Nkosinathi was a strong healthy man, it was not long before the food, and potions had him well along the road to recovery. Daily his sister cleaned the wound and applied the potion and within a week, he was strong enough to stand and exercise his arm, one evening he came to sit by his father's fire and for a time, he listened to tales of woe, truths that encouraged him to take a fateful decision.

'Father I must leave, there is something I must do, something that will save the village. I will go as the sun rises in the morning and I will return as soon as I can.'

Chapter 13

Majuba, the name was on everyone's lips, another African disaster for the British public to despair over and Patrick was no different. He folded his newspaper made it more manageable to read and scanned the despatches from the battlefield. Ever since the Crimea the British press had insisted upon their own correspondents accompanying the army and now they had managed to lay bare the full extent of the army's reverse. How could a bunch of farmers so easily defeat a modern British army that possessed field guns, the new-fangled Gatling guns, and repeating rifles with antiquated, single shot weapons?

He turned over the folded newspaper to finish the article and horrified at the losses, paused to look up from the breakfast table. a waiter was serving people at a nearby table, they were chattering, laughing, oblivious to the disaster unfolding in Africa. He had discovered many things since leaving the army and one was that the British Public did not understand what it was like to fight. He did and as he picked up his teacup, he cast his mind back to a few of the desperate battles he had fought.

'What's the matter Patrick, you look as if you have seen a ghost.'

'You could say that, ghosts of fallen comrades. Have you seen the paper, the rumours we heard yesterday are true, there has been another defeat at the hands of those rebellious Boers, many of our lads have been killed. They say that a good many of the Boer were killed and wounded too, but they said that about the fight at Laing's Nek didn't they?'

Ellen did not reply as she stood patiently behind her seat waiting for Patrick to move her chair for her and once she was seated, he passed her the newspaper.

'Here, look, it says that the Boers were taken by surprise when Colley led the troops to the top of this hill called Majuba and he should have overcome the Boers. What has happened to the army, why were they defeated when it seems they had the advantage? It looks to me as big a disaster as Isandhlwana.'

As Patrick ranted on Ellen read the headlines and a part of the article and then a waiter appeared to take her order.

'The usual madam, scrambled eggs?'

'Yes, and some of that wonderful toast you do.'

'Would madam prefer tea or coffee this morning?'

'Tea, what about you Patrick, do you want some more tea?'

'Er...yes, bring me another pot waiter.'

Ellen stared at the newspaper, her eyes focused on the middle distance, her mind on Southern Africa. Every time she read about the fighting, she could not help but think of Georgie. It had been a month since they had read the first reports of the rout at Laing's Nek and now here she was reading of a second defeat and heavy casualties. There was no list of the dead and wounded, simply rough estimates that made harrowing reading.

'Patrick, what do you thing has happened to Georgie, will he be still alive?'

Patrick stared out of the window and blowing through puffed up cheeks tried to think of an answer and for a minute, he said nothing. Finally he turned back to look at Ellen.

'I told you before, I'm not a betting man but the casualty reports of battle at Laing's Nek make no mention of Georgie other than he is one of several missing in action. I've read everything I can in the newspapers and there is nothing, nothing other than that first report of him missing, and since I am not a betting man I would put money on him being alive. I reckon he's done what he said he would do, desert or at least he was taken prisoner.'

Ellen smiled at Patrick's contradictions, his opinion making her feel a little better. What was she to do though? She had become a wealthy woman, Freddie had told her to expect her inheritance to total well over a million pounds, and there was the property in Belgravia. She was receiving a handsome income from the estate whilst it was being wound up and today she was to meet with Freddie to sign the papers that would start the transfer of Edward Jameson's estate into her name.

'I have been thinking Patrick; I am inheriting a lot of money and we can easily afford to go back to South Africa. I want to go there and find Georgie.'

Ellen did not easily cry, her upbringing had made sure of that, but even so, a lone tear appeared at the corner of her eye and ran down her cheek. Patrick looked at her and for once, held his Irish blarney in check.

Petrus could stand unaided, the fracture in his leg was healing well, and as he looked out across the veldt, his heart missed a beat. Several horses and riders were heading their way. He counted maybe ten of them, but could not tell whether they were friend or foe.

'Annika, Annika bring me my gun, hurry, riders approaching.'

His sister heard his call, reached for Petrus's hunting rifle, and at the same time grabbed her own.

'Here Petrus,' she said emerging from the house. 'What is it?'

Petrus took the gun and pointed towards riders engulfed in a thin cloud of dust kicked up by their horse's hooves. Annika's gaze followed his pointing finger and she squinted trying to make them out, but like her brother, she could not tell at such a distance.

'I will tell Mutti, she is collecting eggs round the back amongst the straw bales. What about Georgie, I think he is somewhere in the field cutting maize. I will go and fetch him.'

Petrus thought for a moment, trying to decide whether he should enlist the help of Georgie. If they were enemy soldiers, he might change his mind about remaining on the farm and side with them. But he was too late, Annika had already run round the side of the house and was shouting for her mother as she raced to the field to find Georgie who was gathering in part of the mealie crop with two native labourers.

'Georgie come quick, there are men coming. We might need your help.'

'Why, who are they?'

'We cannot tell but we need to be ready in case there is trouble.'

Together the two of them ran back to the house and found Petrus and Mutti standing by the doorway looking out across open country.

'I think they are our people, they are riding Boer ponies, and I can see their hats. They are not British soldiers.'

'Oh good,' said Annika leaning her rifle against the house wall. 'Is it Papa and Christiaan?'

'I think it is, and the others look like the men from the district. I wonder why they are all coming home.'

'Maybe it is over already,' said Mutti.

Annika and Petrus looked at her, their faces breaking into wide grins. Of course, that must be it; there could be no other reason and standing a little way apart, Georgie could not help but feel happy for them. He had come to admire these tough, resilient people for their hard work and honesty. he could see riders quite plainly and they were indeed Boers and Jos and Christiaan were riding at the head of the group.

'Mutti, Annika,' called out Jos when the men were within earshot, 'prepare some food and drink for these men, they have earned it. It is over; we have won a great victory at Majuba, many of the enemy were killed, even their commander,' said Jos climbing from his pony.

Standing squarely before his family, he dusted off his jacket and with a stern yet kindly his face, he stepped forward, briefly embracing his family.

'The British are bloodied and in disarray. We threw them back at Majuba hill. They took it during the night, a night when we did not deploy our pickets so we were surprised and angry to see them there at the top of the hill in the morning. We were worried that they had taken their field guns right to the top. If they had, they would have commanded the terrain for miles around but our scouts reported only small arms fire so the Commandant General asked us to attack them. We struck camp and went towards the hill and at about seven o clock we started climbing taking care to remain hidden as much as possible. The Commandant General told us to join Stephanus who was to lead an assault along a different path from the main attack and once the attack began, we picked them off one by one. When we finally reached the summit, we killed many more of them and after what must have been no more than an hour they broke and ran. We heard later that their commander was dead.'

'Papa, you say there will be peace, how do you know, what kind of peace?' said Annika. 'We had peace and peace treaties with the British before and they turned out to be worthless. Why should it be any different this time?'

'I don't know that things will turn out any better this time but we have inflicted heavy losses on them and we suffered only light casualties. Joubert thinks they will not want to pour any more resources into this war because for them there is very little to gain. He has sent messengers with letters to try to find out their intentions and to offer peace.'

'Well I hope you are right. Annika, come,' said her mother

The women went into the house whilst the men of the commando attended to their ponies, lit their pipes, and sat about relaxing. From the sidelines Georgie listened, troubled by the news. He had experienced the Boer fighting qualities and it came as no real surprise that they had held off the British army again, but a rout was a shock. His thoughts were for the young soldiers fresh from England and he was glad he was out of it.

'So, pilgrim your army seems to be stuck at the Nek. I am sorry so many of those young boys died,' said Jos lighting his pipe for a second time. 'I suppose you are free to go now if you wish, you are no threat to us if you go back to your friends.'

Just then, Annika and Mutti walked out of the house with baskets of bread and cold meats for the men and Annika noticed Georgie's expression of despondency.

'What is the matter Georgie, you look sad, is it because you have lost your friends. What have you been saying to him Papa?'

Georgie and Jos looked at her, surprised at her concern and, as a blush spread across his daughter's face, Jos knew then that she was sweet on this Englishman.

'I was telling him that he is free to go. There is no need to keep him prisoner any longer.'

Annika looked at Georgie, her blushes spreading and he looked into her eyes, seeing something he had seen before, and he felt his stomach turn over. Unsure of quite what to do he said to Jos.

'I...I gave my word that I would not try to escape and that I would only leave once I had permission.'

'And are you leaving?'

'Mister De Witt, I do not want to leave, there is nothing for me in the army. I am due to be discharged in a little over six months anyway but after that I could well be in the same position as I am now, penniless and adrift in a strange country.'

'You think this is a strange country?'

'No, I didn't mean that. I have few if any friends outside the army. Even if I went back to England, there is no one there for me except perhaps Patrick and Ellen. I don't even know where they are now.'

'Patrick and Ellen?' queried Annika.

Ellen is my cousin and Patrick was my friend in the army. He went home with the regiment after the Zulu war. His time was almost up and I don't know even if he is still in the army.'

'Annika, called Christiaan, 'are you going to feed us?'

Annika looked straight into Georgie's eyes commanding him to stay and then she turned towards her brother and having witnessed her look her father frowned and sucked on his pipe.

'So, you have nowhere to go. Perhaps you don't need to leave at once. We have to plant for next year, you could earn your keep.'

Georgie tried hard not to let his feelings show but inside he was jumping for joy. It looked like he was gaining his freedom had now he had found somewhere to live.

'I would like very much to stay here; it will give me time to decide what I can do. I will need a job of some sort soon enough I expect.'

Jos tapped out the remains of his pipe, and pursed his lips as he contemplated what he had just offered. He did need help on the farm because although he could see that Petrus was recovering well, he would still be unable to carry out the heavier tasks, then there was his favourite child, and she was troubling him.

Before he had time to dwell, Georgie returned to the job of stacking the logs he had cut and the burghers of Jos's commando mounted their ponies. 'Jos, we are leaving, thank you for the food. God bless you and your family. We will see you again when we have the service of thanksgiving?'

'Oh yes, but let us not count our chickens just yet. The British might just be stupid enough to carry this fight on.' He paused, and with a smile said, 'but I doubt it,' said Jos who began walking towards the house, and said quietly to Christiaan, who had joined him, 'the Englishman likes it here. Technically, he should remain a prisoner of war until our leaders sign the peace treaty. What do you think?'

'He has as worked hard father and he has been no trouble,' said Annika speaking first. 'He has earned his keep, he has done the work Petrus, and I find too strenuous.'

'But he is not of us, he is not a follower of God and it will be an extra mouth to feed in winter.'

'He has told me he does not want to return to the army and he did save my leg, I for one think he should stay even if it is only for a short time,' added Petrus overhearing them.

Annika looked at her brother, pleased that he had spoken up for the handsome Englishman. Christiaan was the only one who had not yet spoken and he waited until everyone had finished speaking.

'He is our enemy whichever way you look at it. I think he should go. We only allowed him to stay whilst we were away and unable to work the land. I say he goes, and as soon as possible.'

'I think maybe he is right,' said Mutti joining in.

'No,' said Annika, 'he is all alone in the world, at least let him stay until he is able to make his own way.'

'What do you mean daughter.'

'He has nothing, let him earn some money to afford at least a pony and then he can ride to wherever he pleases.'

Annika's mother listed to her daughter and wondered why she would stick her neck out for an enemy. Admittedly, he was handsome, polite, and hardworking, not the sort of conduct she would have expected from a British soldier. She had heard that wherever the British army went, there was trouble, drunkenness, and fighting and she did not want any of that here, but the look on her daughter's face caused her to hesitate and turning to her husband said, 'Let him stay a while longer Papa, until we have planted the next crop as Annika says.'

'What do you say,' Jos asked each family member.

Petrus and Annika said let him stay, their mother agreed but Christiaan was less amenable to the idea.

'He should go. We do not want our friends and neighbours saying we are harbouring an enemy. If he were black, there would be no question of him staying unless it was as a servant. Perhaps he should stay as just that a servant and pay him nothing.'

Jos was a little shocked at his son's outburst but he could understand his feelings and maybe he was right. They had had their say, he had listened, and he knew that whatever decision he made they would adhere to.

'I have made a decision. He can stay for now, help with the work and when this is finally over, we will see.'

'Oh thank you Papa,' said Annika a little too enthusiastically.

Petrus smiled at his sister, he liked Georgie too, and he wanted him to stay, Christiaan was the only one who seemed less than happy.

Chapter 14

The horses were long gone, disappeared into the forest with the mules and Nkosinathi knew that they would probably not have survived. He pulled up his horse and looked up at the cave, more accessible now the brushwood had been disturbed but it was not his destination. He rode past the cave for a few hundred yards looking for the outcrop that signposted the place where he had killed Jake.

During the time spent with the White men, he had learned many things and most of all the power of the paper they carried and it was the paper he was looking for and although it had rained a lot the trail was still visible. The deep impressions made by the mules had not disappeared, he was finding it easy to retrace his steps, and looking ahead, he saw the marker.

The rock shape was familiar and as he edged his horse towards it, the memory of his last visit made him touch his shoulder a reminder of how lucky he was. The bullet had ripped through the soft tissue near his armpit, missing the bone by no more than a hair's width and clenching his fist round the reigns, nudged his horse forward to search the ground. It had all happened so fast that he could not remember exactly where he had killed Jake; he needed a hoof or a footprint as a guide.

Pulling up his horse he sat for a few minutes listening to the sounds of the forest, listening for the birdsong for it was the birds that first gave warning of danger. There was nothing, he froze, strained his ears and then he heard the distinct sound of a dry twig breaking and his nostrils twitched. The sound had come from the place where he expected he might find Jake and his partners and he began to worry that someone else had found them first and in a mood of mild panic he slipping from his saddle. Landing softly on the ground he lifted his rifle off his shoulder to hold it at the ready and led his horse into some dense vegetation near the riverbank. Finding a gap, he led the horse into a small clearing, tethered the animal to a branch leaving it munching on some grass, and continued on foot.

Carefully backtracking, he picked up the trail, sure, that he would soon come across signs of the struggle with Jake and his partners. Stopping for a moment, he listened and hearing nothing, moved on keeping his wits about him. The forest was still, a few birds circling overhead the only sign of life and then he stopped dead in his tracks. His senses had picked up something unusual, intangible at first and then and then he heard a faint sound of human voices.

His eyes scanned the donga, the foliage, the boulders for a sign of life and the dodging behind a tree; he stood still for a few minutes trying to judge the whereabouts of the owners of those voices. They seemed to be no more than fifty yards away, through an impassable thicket and he decided to circle through the trees for a look. Holding his gun at the ready, he moved silently picking his way carefully towards the voices and finally a glimpse of movement caught his eye. He was close enough, any further risked detection, and spotting a rock fall surrounded by bush and he decided to hide there and wait.

The voices were louder now, more than one man he was sure, maybe as many as half a dozen and he could see their shadows slowly moving in his direction. Carefully he parted the bushes; just enough to see the trail and the first of them appeared on horseback causing him to catch his breath. A mild panic overtook him as he recognised Rabanina, the leader of John Dunn's border patrol and withdrawing into the foliage he prayed to his ancestors that they pass by and leave him undiscovered.

However, they did not, instead of continuing the riders halted and Nkosinathi closed his eyes tight to listen to their every movement. If they discovered him and it came to a fight then he wanted to be ready, to know their every position.

'Look another mule.' He heard one say.

Then Rabanina added, 'one of you remove the tack. It is strange that we should find three dead mules so close together and each one killed by a wildcat. They look to have been dead for a while so I think we will take a look round and see if we can find out what has happened.'

Rabanina gave his orders and the men of the patrol began to spread out to search the forest. Nkosinathi withdrew further into his hiding place, a minute later two of them passed close by, and then he began to wonder if they might find his horse. And Jake, what if they found his body? If they did, his plan could end in failure.

For several minutes the tension was acute, beads of sweat rolled down his forehead, and then, as the patrol drifted away, all became quiet again and sure that they had passed he parted the bushes. Through the gap, he could see just enough see that they were heading towards the river away from where the fight with Jake had taken place and his heart leaped. It was unlikely they would come across any of the White men's bodies on the path they were taking. They were heading in the wrong direction and once they were some way off, he decided to risk moving from his hiding place. Slowly he emerged and stole away looking for the rocky outcrop he used as a landmark, and then, as if by magic it appeared through the trees.

Picking up his pace, he had almost reached the marker when he heard the sound of a horse's hooves rapidly approaching and dived instinctively into some tall grass. It was one of Rabanina's men probably sent to check the area and he was making his way back to the patrol. Nkosinathi parted the grass and to his horror saw that the man was heading straight towards the rocky outcrop and it could only be a matter of seconds before he came across Jake's remains.

The pace of the horses hooves slowed and the rider brought his horse to a halt not twenty yards from Nkosinathi, whistling softly through his teeth. Daring to raise his head, Nkosinathi watched the man climb from his saddle, bend over something on the ground and he knew what it was.

The situation was precarious; the man had discovered Jakes remains and the patrol no more than a loud hail away. It was now or never, if he did not act he could lose everything. Leaving his rifle where it lay, he drew his hunting knife and launched himself like a big cat. The stalks of tall grass parted and he bounded forwards, covering the ground towards the man in seconds, cupping his hand over his victim's mouth, and driving the blade deep into his body. The man stiffened in shock and for more than a minute tried to struggle free but he was too late, the knife had done its work and finally he succumbed, slipping lifelessly from Nkosinathi's grasp.

Nkosinathi glanced around to be sure that no one else had witnessed the disturbance and then looked down to see that it was Jake all right, but not the Jake he had left behind. Scavengers had done their work, gnawing at the face and leaving only a solitary eye to stare at him and grinning lipless teeth that seemed to sneer at him. Shuddering in disgust, he pulled at the torn clothing still clinging to the corpse finally revealing the soft leather pouch.

Somopho saw the thin wisps of smoke rising in the distance, faint against the clear blue sky and excitedly he called to his brothers. They were almost home, the circular Kraal with its Beehive huts soon coming into view. Sibusiso and Lindani were further back, coaxing the animals forward, using their sticks to move them on but Nkosinathi was not with them. He was worried the patrol of John Dunn might find them and was moving between vantage points keeping a good lookout.

Stopping beside a small stream, he dismounted and satisfied they were safe enough, let the horse drink and rest a while. He let the strap of his gun slide off shoulder and squatted beside his horse cupping his hands and scooping up some water. Wiping the last few drops from his lips, he felt in the leather pouch hanging from his waist, pulling out some biltong to chew. The moon had completed almost a cycle since he had retrieved Jake's ill-gotten gains and he and his brothers had made the trek north. They had gone first to the small trading post run by a half breed named Jacob where he bought cartridges, knives and goods to trade, then they went north.

In this part of Zululand, the strife was less acute, some of the clans had grown rich in cattle, and it was to these kraals that they carried the White man's goods. Standing up he ran his hand over his horse's neck, felt its chest, and checked the animal's health. Satisfied he remounted her and sitting high in the saddle, he too saw the wisps of smoke.

'You have done well my son,' said a proud but frail looking Mondli waiting by the entrance to the kraal. 'I have watched your approach since the sun was over the mountains and my heart is glad you have returned safely and with such rich reward. We will select an animal and feast to celebrate your homecoming.'

'Father, we must keep the herd secret for as long as we can. John Dunn's tax collectors will notice that the herd has increased and they will report to their chief.'

'You think there might be trouble?'

'There *will* be trouble father. If Dunn's men come looking and find these animals they will want to know how we came by them. We should separate them from the main herd; graze them in small numbers out of sight, and only to bring them here during the night for protection from predators.'

'That sounds a good idea; talk to your brother Dumisani, tell him to organize the boys and young men to oversee the herd.'

'Perhaps you should tell him father, he is the eldest son and will not take kindly to me telling him.'

'It shall be as you say Nkosinathi; I will tell him when we feast.'

The fire crackled like it had not done in years, the great slab of blackening beef turned slowly on the spit and illuminated by the flickering light of the fire, the young men and women of the village began to dance, dance in the old ways. Dumisani led the young men swaying back and forth, stamping their feet in unison and when they had finally stopped, he found his brother.

'Nkosinathi, it is a good day for us, you have done well increasing the herd, but father has told me to disperse them during the day. That will be hard for us; surely, we will find it easier to keep the herd as one.'

'It must be as our father says; the herd must appear smaller than it is in case John Dunn's men return and discover we have so many animals. They will want their share, that could mean all of them and our efforts will have been in vain.'

Dumisani looked a little glum, it was his responsibility to look after the herd with the boys of the kraal, but he knew that to disperse the herd was going to be difficult. He loved his brother, all his brothers, and his half-brothers, but he resented their father's favouring of Nkosinathi. True he had somehow found the white man's money to buy the cattle, hunted game when they had been near starvation but had not he, Dumisani, served the King, had he not respected and served his father too.

'We should drink some more beer together brother; celebrate our blessing while we can for tomorrow may bring a reversal of fortune,' said Nkosinathi trying to soothe his brothers feelings.

'I do not see why they would take more cattle, we have paid this year's tax, what we have left is our own. Why should we worry about John Dunn's tax collectors until next year?'

Nkosinathi looked at Dumisani not understanding his thinking but he did not wish to argue. He had been through a lot recently, he was tired, and his wound had taken its toll.

The light footsteps on the hard earth took Georgie by surprise as he swung the axe, methodically splitting the never-ending supply of logs.

'Good news that the war is over Georgie,' said Annika. 'A rider has arrived with news. The war is over there is to be an armistice.'

Georgie stopped his swing in mid arc and lay down the axe. The three months since he had helped Petrus on the slopes of Laing's Nek seemed to have passed in no time and now news of an end to hostilities had reached the farm. Good news indeed for Petrus, Annika and their mother but for him it could lead only to uncertainty.

'Oh...yes, good that there will be no more killing.'

'No and you will be free I suppose, free to go,' she said hesitantly

'I suppose, but I will but we have to wait for your father to return before I know my fate.'

He felt sad, a turning point in his life had arrived, and he was not at all sure what to do about it. He was a prisoner of war, still technically a soldier in the British army and the news of an end to the fighting left him in limbo. He was half a world away from the life he knew and if Jos did tell him to leave, he did not know where he would go or what he would do. He had neither friends, nor money but the one thing he did know was that he did not want to return to the army and then he looked at Annika.

'You are very beautiful Annika. I shall be sad to leave here mostly because of you,' he blurted out.

'Who says you are leaving, I'm sure Father will let you stay until the harvest is in at least and I for one do not want you to go.'

She looked at the ground for a few seconds and then, raising her head, she looked straight at him.

'I...I should perhaps go back to the house.'

'No don't go yet Annika, I like your company and if it is true the war is over then we are enemies no longer.'

'You were never my enemy Georgie. You saved my brother from becoming a cripple at least, you are not an enemy.'

'Thank you for that, I am not sure what to say, but I like it here and I like seeing you. I don't know what it is I...'

Annika could stand his hesitation no longer, took a step forward, and planted a kiss on his lips. Taken aback for an instant Georgie soon recovered feeling her softness, breathing in her aroma and such a happiness engulfed him that he could not stop himself laughing aloud. It was infectious and before long Annika joined in they were both almost crying with laughter until a shout from the house stopped them dead.

'Annika, what is that noise, are you alright.'

'Coming Mutti, there is nothing wrong. It is Georgie, he is happy the war is over.'

She reached out to him with both hands and he responded amused that she should blame him for the commotion. She looked at him and gave him a knowing smile before she turned to walk back to the house and it finally dawned upon him that he was in love.

A day later, Jos and Christiaan were back, Mutti saw them coming and called to her children to come and wait by the verandah for them.

'It is over Mutti, perhaps we can get on with the farming now,' said Jos dismounting.

'We have hot food ready. See to your ponies and we can have a celebration meal.'

Jos nodded and turned his pony towards the corral whilst Christiaan became engaged in conversation with his brother who wanted to know about the battle of Majuba Hill and as Christiaan took his horse to the water trough Petrus hobbled across the yard towards the field where Georgie was working.

'The war is over my friend, we have won and the British are suing for peace.'

Georgie looked up from his work. 'It was expected I think.'

'Ja,' said Petrus a little subdued for he could see the hurt in Georgie's eyes. 'You have lost a lot of comrades.'

'Yes, I expect so. It all seems so wasteful, white man fighting white man.'

'It is more than that my friend, they want to change our way of life, tax us until we have nothing left. You would fight for that I think.'

Georgie did not want to argue with Petrus about the merits or otherwise of the war, he was too busy wondering what the future held for him. He had lived on the De Witt's farm for several months experiencing a different life to that of the army and he had met Annika, but all that might change.

The evening meal was a subdued affair after Jos offered up prayers for their deliverance. For a time everyone ate in silence until Christiaan said, 'there is talk of self-rule. We will not have to live under the British crown.'

'Do not be too sure son; the British Empire is large and powerful. I was talking with some of the Burghers and they think that the British will not go away, we should simply agree a truce on the best possible terms and get on with our lives.'

'But Papa we have defeated them haven't we?'

'Yes Petrus but they have far more resources than we have and if they have a mind to they will come back with a larger force and next time we may not endure.'

There was silence for a few minutes, Mutti and Annika cleared the dinner plates, and the decamped to the verandah to smoke and watch the sun go down.

'You have not said much,' said Jos to Georgie, sitting in his usual place with his legs hanging over the verandah.

'No sir, I do not know what to say.'

'I am not surprised the way we beat you,' said an aggressive sounding Christiaan.

'Now Christiaan, he was our prisoner but now he is our guest. Treat him as one if you please.'

Christiaan fell silent but his eyes flashed a warning and before Georgie could react, Petrus spoke.

'He has worked hard Papa and we have talked a lot about the war, our comrades. Georgie has lost many of his friends and that is not a good thing. He says he does not want to leave us just yet, says he has nothing, and knows no one other than the army and he does not want to go back there.'

'Is this true?'

'Yes sir, I don't know what I would do if I left. I like it here; I have never had a real family, I was orphaned. My uncle and aunt took me in but that only lasted two years until the peeler caught me.'

'What is the Peeler?' asked Jos striking a match.

'Police, I was a pickpocket in London and I was caught.'

'A pickpocket, a thief!' Jos exclaimed, drawing on his pipe.

'Yes, it was all we could do to live.'

The men fell quiet for a time, Jos and Christiaan smoked their pipes, Petrus looked out across the veldt and Georgie looked at his feet, unsure of whether or not he had offended the old man.

'A pickpocket, and how old were you?' asked Jos, his pipe aglow.

'I was caught when I was thirteen, nearly fourteen. The Peeler let a recruiting sergeant enlist me in the army and he said I should really be fourteen.'

'I think maybe you have an interesting story to tell. What is London Like?'

'Well...' said Georgie, and for more than half an hour he recounted his life in London, roaming the streets in search of victims, told them of his uncle and aunt, his cousins and in particular Ellen. He spoke briefly of his time in the army, the campaigns, the war against the Zulus, of his friend Patrick, and when he finished, Jos tapped out his pipe's embers a thoughtful look on his face.

'So you want to stay a while, you have nowhere to go and no possessions.'

Georgie looked back at the grey bearded sage, feeling that perhaps Jos was mapping out his destiny.

'Petrus is he a good shot?'

'Not bad Papa, but not as good as us.'

'Could he perhaps go with you on the hunt?'

'Of course, He needs to learn something of the land if he is to survive out here; we have talked about that already.'

'Good, then he will accompany you, he can borrow Annika's gun and we will pay for his services in cartridges which he can use to kill game and then sell the skins to buy a pony.'

'Oh Papa, what a good idea and you will help him will you not Petrus?' asked Annika, from inside the doorway.

'Annika, you should not be listening,' said her father in mock annoyance.

Petrus smiled in mild amusement but Christiaan frowned it was not an outcome he welcomed. If that was what his father wanted then he must obey. Nevertheless, it was becoming ever more difficult for him to hide his disgust at having one of the enemy in their midst.

Below the blue cloudless sky the air was still and in the distance, a small unconcerned herd of springbok grazed and Petrus cautiously led the way towards them.

'They are far enough away not to see us but we must go very carefully if we are to get within range. Look there are some bushes over there, we might get close enough if we use them for cover. Thank goodness the air is still, it will give us chance to get closer before they pick up our scent,' whispered Petrus nudging his pony with his knees.

The pony knew exactly what to do, trotting forward
to the place Petrus wanted it to and a few yards behind
him followed Georgie. Once in amongst the vegetation
they dismounted, concealed themselves and their ponies
amongst the thicket and then Petrus swung his rifle
from his shoulder. Crouching low, he made his way
through the vegetation towards their prey and after a
few yards signalled to Georgie to lay on the soft earth
and together they lifted their guns to their shoulders.

'Take aim,' whispered Petrus. 'Shoot when I count to
three, we must fire at exactly the same time because
these boys are quick.'

Setting the sights on their rifles the hunters took
careful aim.

'One two, three,' whispered Petrus as loud as he dare
and immediately there was a double bang.

Each gun fired within a millisecond of the other, and
several hundred yards away two springboks fell to the
ground. There was no chance of a second shot, the
remaining animals immediately stampeded into the long
grass and out of range.

'Good shooting Georgie, come on let us collect the
carcasses before any scavengers pick up the scent,' said
Petrus running for his horse and two minutes later the
two of them examined their kills.

'Look, I hit mine squarely between the eyes, yours
you hit in the chest. Better to make a clean head shot
and kill the animal outright, a chest shot might only
wound and you could finish up without any supper.'

Georgie looked at the two dead animals, the shooting
by Petrus mightily impressing him. No wonder the

Boers had decimated the British ranks; if they could all shoot like this then there was little wonder so many of his comrades had fallen. He looked at his own kill and thought that if this had been a regimental shooting competition he could well have won it yet the shot Petrus had just made was far more accurate.

'Should be worth a bit Georgie, another twenty or so like that might buy you a horse and the next twenty maybe buy your saddle. Come on let us ride for home.'

Another forty animals, thought Georgie mounting his pony, at this rate he could have his own horse in not much more than a month – and then what? He did not have time to contemplate; storm clouds were gathering in the distance and heading their way.

The rains came an hour before they managed to return to the farm and find shelter. Thunder echoed across the distant hills, lightening flashed through the dark clouds and before long, they could hardly see where they were going in the downpour.

'We cannot stay out in this much longer,' Petrus shouted through the rain. 'There looks to be shelter over there.'

Through the bush, he had seen a place of shelter, thick overhanging vegetation against a low cliff with enough room for them. Petrus reached the overhang first, dismounted and pulled his animal after him. Georgie followed suit and soon they were both wedged in the meagre shelter away from the worst of the storm. It was a miserable time and both men shivered as they waited for the rains to stop but eventually it did, just as abruptly as it had started.

'I think the worst has passed, the rain is easing now,' said Petrus, water dripping off the brim of his hat and soaking his clothes.

Georgie fared little better, his boots squelched as he walked and it was a sorry pair that returned home late in the evening.

'Mutti, they are back,' said Annika opening the door, her face lighting up with a smile. 'You have been successful I see.'

'Yes sister, Georgie made his first kill. He's not a bad shot but he needs to improve if he is to sell undamaged skins to the traders in Pretoria.'

'You can skin the animal yourself. Do you know how to?'

Georgie looked at Petrus and shook his head.

'You have a lot to learn soldier boy.'

Georgie's kill hung from the rafters of the outbuilding overnight to bleed and then, under the watchful eyes of Petrus and Annika, he began the task of skinning it and after a difficult hour of painstaking work he stood back to admire his handiwork.

'Not bad, you need to lay it out and scrape all the fat off, flesh it, then we will soak it in the salt water barrel.'

'Is that all?'

'We need to dry it off,' said Annika. 'We have a stretching frame out back where you can leave it to dry for a few days then you must scrape the hair off. There is still a lot to do, you must take its brain out for me to boil up, it will give you the oil you need to soften the skin.'

Georgie looked at her, a frown on his forehead; he did have a lot to learn, army life had taught him very little about the outside world. Scratching the stubble on his chin, he wondered where to start and Annika smiled, amused at his awkwardness.

'It is Caas and Abraham, Annika go and tell Mutti,' said Petrus spotting two riders coming towards the farm. He looked at Georgie, could see he was capable of managing on his own, and went to stand by the open door to greet the new arrivals.

Caas, the older of the two men and a comrade in the commando pulled up his pony alongside the barn and leaned over to speak to Petrus.

'Petrus, good news it is over, the British have agreed to leave us alone. No more fighting, God has looked after us.'

Petrus pursed his lips and nodded his head, pleased at such news and then he squeezed the muscle of his injured leg to remind him of the price he had paid for this peace. The broken leg had healed well and apart from lingering pain he was as good as new and quietly he thanked Georgie's quick thinking for saving him.

For more than a month Georgie and Petrus hunted game in the vast open grasslands and Georgie revelled in this new life. Hunting became second nature to him and before long, he had accumulated enough hides to sell at the market in Pretoria. The British garrison was still in place, in need of the Boer farmers produce, and from the south traders were returning.

'I think you will get a horse for those skins Georgie,' said Jos one morning. 'We have planted next year's crop and we don't need your help any longer. Go with Petrus to Pretoria trade the skins for a good horse and you can be free.'

Jos's words were not unexpected, but even so they still they came as a shock and he felt sadness knowing he would have to leave. He had enjoyed his time living on the farm, a different life to that of a soldier and he had made a good friend in Petrus. Then there was Annika, and when she learned that he would be leaving she sought him out.

'You are leaving Georgie,' more a statement than a question. 'You must come and see us again, you must.'

Georgie stopped scraping the hair from the hide he was working on, lay down his knife and standing tall over her looked into her eyes. Then he took a step towards her and without thinking, wrapped his arms around her, felt the press of her strong soft body and for the first time they kissed. How long they held the embrace they did not know, but when finally relaxed their grip it was to stand in silence until Georgie finally spoke.

'I have wanted to do that for a long time,'

'I have as well Georgie but if Papa finds out I will be in trouble.'

'I understand, your father is very strict but I can't let it end, I want you.'

Without a word, she took hold of his hand and led him towards the cornfield a sea of tall, golden plants swaying in the breeze, parting them as she went and after twenty yards, she turned to face him.

Chapter 15

The oxen strained at their yokes as the wagon trundled slowly across the veldt and Petrus strained his eyes. Looking through the haze, he picked out faint outlines of buildings, the Dutch church standing tallest. Ahead of them Christiaan had halted his pony and he too was gazing across to the settlement.

'Look, over there Georgie – Pretoria. We will stop up ahead for the night. Christiaan has signalled that he has found a stream.'

Sitting beside Petrus on the wagon Georgie tugged the brim of his bush hat to shield his eyes and searched for the town. He was excited at the prospect of acquiring a horse of his own tempered only by the fact that he was a deserter and if anyone from the British garrison recognized him that could be the end of it. He was wearing the jacket Annika had made for him and apart from the brown military corduroy trousers and the military issue boots; he looked as much a Boer farmers as the other two.

'Petrus I am worried that I might be recognised. There will be Soldiers from the fort in the town I'm sure.'

'You will have to stay in the wagon then. Christiaan and I can do all the talking if anyone comes too close. Will you trust me to trade the skins for a horse if I have to?'

'Of course, you know as much about horseflesh as anyone and you will be probably be dealing with your own people.'

A wry smile creased Petrus's face as he flicked his long whip across the back of the lead Oxen.

'Maybe I should deal with the Burghers anyway; they drive a hard bargain and would run rings round you I think.'

Georgie's face relaxed and he forced a smile but inside his stomach felt knotted. For the past few months, he had lived a carefree a life, helping on the farm and now that he had declared his love for Annika, the last thing he wanted to do was to spend the next few years in a military prison.

They broke camp early and two hours later met a wagon coming towards them. A man and his wife stone faced and gaunt sitting together on the driver's seat and behind them three dirty young faces peered out of the cover. The children looked thin and undernourished and Georgie felt a sudden sadness.

'Who are they?' he asked.

'They are British, they are leaving because we have regained our country and they know they are not welcome anymore. Perhaps they are heading back to Natal or the Cape.'

Normally involved in purely military matters and usually on the winning side, it came as a shock to Georgie to see his own kind defeated like this. He watched them pass and began to wonder how the Boers might treat him if they found out he was an Englishman for although Petrus and Christiaan knew him well enough others would not.

Finally, arriving at the outskirts of the town they passed whitewashed wooden buildings and came across open ground with a row of Boer wagons. Georgie counted at least twelve of them surrounded by townspeople and as they got nearer, he heard Pretorians arguing and bartering as they searched for bargains.

Goods on offer were mostly produce, crops grown on outlying farms but one of the wagons took Georgie's eye. A crowd of people were looking intently at his offerings and he quizzed Petrus.

'Who is that?'

'An English trader named Thompson, he has a store at the far end of town, and it seems strange that he should be selling from a wagon.'

'Perhaps he is leaving too. Maybe he is selling everything and heading to Natal as well.'

'If he is then we should go and see him before everything goes. He sells the rolls of cloth Mutti asked me to buy for her and if I return empty handed I will be in trouble.'

Just then Christiaan rode up to them, he had gone on ahead to look for a suitable place for them to set out their stall.

'Go to the end of this row, there is still a stand free. When we stop there Englishman you can and start unloading our tent while we outspan the oxen.'

Georgie did not reply, instead, when the wagon came to a halt, he began unloading, angry that Christiaan should keep calling him Englishman, the last thing he wanted was to draw attention to himself. Reaching for the heavy canvas tent, he rolled it over the tailboard but to move it further was more than one man could manage and he looked round to Christiaan for help. Christiaan was not more than twenty yards away talking to a Boer and Georgie could see by his manner that he was in no mood to help him. The canvas was awkward and heavy but he was determined that the arrogant Christiaan would not get the better of him and with some effort he managed to roll the tent across the hard ground and still Christiaan still did not move until his brother called out indignantly.

'Is this how you help us, leave Georgie here to do all the work?'

'I did not see him.'

Petrus did not pursue the argument; he knew Christiaan well enough, he had grown up with Christiaan and he knew that he felt himself superior but at least he had goaded him into action.

'Well soldier boy it looks as if most of the British have already left. My friend tells me that even our own people who sympathised with the enemy are going, hounded out by those who took up the fight. Looks like you British have had your day in the Transvaal,' said a gloating Christiaan.

Georgie looked at him and saw the hostility in his eyes. It was obvious that Christiaan still saw him as the enemy and that it was pointless antagonizing him.

'Get hold of that corner and pull, that's right, lay it flat and then go and get the pole,' said Christiaan enjoying giving orders and knew Georgie could not retaliate nor refuse.

Inwardly Georgie grumbled to himself, he had erected more tents in his time than Christiaan had eaten hot dinners *and* he had experienced the sharp tongues of drill sergeants. He could manage Christiaan, he would bide his time and one day even the score he thought as he began knocking in the tent pegs with more gusto than they deserved.

'Here, Georgie you can give me a hand. My brother is giving you a hard time is he?'

'Er...yes I suppose he is. It's not a problem Petrus; I know that he wants me to leave.'

'Yes he does, it's not our way to turn someone away but Christiaan hates the British and to have you around only makes him worse. Papa has spoken to him and told him to show you some respect but here in Pretoria it seems that he can do as he likes.'

'The best thing is for me to get hold of a horse and head south I think.'

'Head south, where to?'

'I haven't told you about the time I was in Kimberly?'

'No, when was that?'

'Well, shortly after the regiment arrived at the Cape we were sent to Kimberly to stop a rebellion. Militant miners and Fenians were trying to take over the diamond fields so we crossed the Great Karoo to stop them.'

'The Great Karoo, I have heard of that, a desert plateau isn't it.'

'Yes.'

'That must have been hard.'

'It was.'

'And Fenians, what are they.'

'Irishmen, who hate Britain, want to regain Ireland from the British Queen.'

'I can sympathise with that, isn't that why we have been fighting, to stop the British Government dictating to us.'

Georgie sensed that he had better change the subject; he had no interest in Britain's intentions to take over the Transvaal. He was a simple soldier; the politics were of no import to him.

'I should start looking for a horse.'

'Yes, but first tell me about Kimberly.'

'We are not going to fall out are we?'

Petrus smiled, although he had felt a surge of nationalism it had passed and he had become more interested in Georgie's experiences in Kimberly. Apart from his brief visits to Pretoria and his time at Laing's Nek, he had not seen the world outside their farm and Georgie's stories intrigued him.

'No Georgie, you are my friend and from what I have seen you are my sister's friend too.'

For several seconds Georgie's mind stopped thinking about Kimberly or a horse, and then reality resurfaced in the form of Christiaan.

'Have you two finished talking, we must start and sell some of our produce before it goes off.'

Petrus and Georgie ended their conversation and set about readying the wagon. Buyers were appearing, two soldiers amongst them, and they slowly made their way towards the De Witt's wagon. One was a Sergeant as Georgie had been the other a Lieutenant and Georgie wondered how he might handle the situation should they come too close.

'Good morning,' said the Lieutenant, his eyes on a pile of maize. 'How much are you asking for this lot?'

'All of it?' asked Christiaan.

'No, just the price of a sack full, I work for the garrison quartermaster and as we do not expect to be leaving soon we will need provisions. If I know the price first then I will decide how much we might take.'

Christiaan was a little slow when it came to business and he was not good with figures but his younger brother was different. 'If you buy just sack full of mealie it is ten shillings a bag but if you take all we have then it is eight shillings a bag.'

Christiaan's eyes flashed at his brother's bold intervention but remained silent. Their father had said that they should try to get five shillings a sack for the mealie and here was Petrus doubling the price.

'I tell you what,' said the officer, 'If you make it seven shillings then I will take half of what you have.'

'You will take it now?'

'No, I want you to deliver it to the fort and I will pay you there.'

'I am not sure that is a good idea, we will need to span the oxen to move the wagon. And what will we do with the rest of our produce? We must stay here to meet other buyers.'

'It is a case of take it or leave it I think,' said the soldier appearing uncooperative.

Petrus gave nothing away guessing that underneath the bravado the army would be desperate for anything they could get. To feed a garrison and keep them happy was neither an easy nor cheap but a pause had descended. Georgie felt that he should help Petrus and in a quirky Afrikaans accent, said, 'I think you should show them the vegetables as well.'

He looked Petrus in the eye, turned and walked towards the front of the wagon before anyone realised what he was doing but Petrus was sharp enough, and understood they needed a few words in private.

'They want the lot Petrus, stick to your guns, tell them it's all or nothing and you will throw in some of these,' he said, pointing to the sacks of potatoes, 'or maybe some of the eggs. I have seen this piece of theatre many times. They will buy the lot you just watch.'

'We have some potatoes and several dozen eggs. I will give you a sack of potatoes and two dozen eggs if you take the entire load of mealie at a price of seven shillings a sack and we will deliver by this afternoon,' said Petrus returning to his visitors. His voice was calm, confident and he looked the young officer in the eye to re-enforce his credibility.

'Very well, Sergeant, count the sacks and write out the requisition for the goods. Mister erm....'

'De Witt.'

'Mister De Witt, you will need this requisition order when you reach the fort. Ask for the quartermaster and he will show you what to do and pay you.'

The Lieutenant saluted and began to wander away whilst the Sergeant rested the order book on the step of the driving position and he began to write.

'Forty two sacks I make it,' he said to Georgie.

Georgie nodded, not speaking just in case his accent was not good enough and the soldier guessed his identity. The Sergeant wrote slowly in sweeping copperplate with his pencil and when he had finished, tore the page from his notebook and gave it to Petrus. Turning his head a few degrees, he looked at Georgie.

'You know, you look very much like a fellow soldier I used to know. Ever been to King Williams Town?'

'Er, no...'

'Funny, I could have sworn you were Georgie McNamara but then again I heard he was killed at Laing's Nek. Bad business that. Sorry to have bothered you,' he said giving Georgie a knowing wink.

Georgie's stomach did a summersault; his mouth dried instantly but as soon as the shock wore off could not help but smile to himself. He remembered now, his name was Albert Thomas, one of the lucky ones like himself who had left the camp at Isandhlwana with Lord Chelmsford's column on that fateful day and his look had said that he would not give him away.

'We'll see you gentlemen at the fort this afternoon.'

The Sergeant walked towards the officer who was now inspecting what was on offer in another wagon, leaving the De Witt's to organize their delivery.

'He knew you didn't he,' said Petrus.

'Yes, I'm pretty sure he did. We served together during the Zulu war. He's a good soldier and I just hope he keeps quiet.'

'Time we had a look round to see who will take the hides and when we have our money from the army, we will do a little buying ourselves.'

For the next few hours, Georgie and Petrus walked around the settlement talking to traders looking for a buyer for the hides. Petrus did most of the talking, eventually finding an Englishman who was ready to leave Pretoria for Natal. He had run a small trading post on the road to Rustenburg trading tobacco and imported Indian cloth but now, like many others, he was leaving.

'There is no future for me here; even my best customers are shunning me because I am English. I will be leaving in a day or two with the last of the tobacco but if you fellas want to trade then let's see what you have.'

'We have our wagon on Kerkstraat, said Petrus, 'You can see the hides.'

The man thoughtfully rubbed the stubble on his chin. 'Have a look here and see what you want to trade for, it is mostly tobacco and a few implements. Hides are interesting though, I know a man in Bloemfontein who deals in hides and Ostrich feathers. He might well buy them off me.'

Petrus looked over the tobacco and wondered how much he should take for the Englishman's wagon was full of it, so much so that it would last Jos a thousand years.

'Have you any rolls of cloth?'

'Yes, just two. Here look.'

The trader rolled back a canvas cover near the front of his wagon and revealed two rolls of the Indian cloth dyed in the light khaki colour favoured by the Boers.

'I will take some tobacco and the cloth.'

'Good,' the man's eyes lit up, 'I had better have a look at your hides, and maybe we can do a deal.'

'There is one thing more; my friend here has hides to trade as well. He needs a horse and a gun.'

The man looked at Georgie. He had not taken a great deal of notice of him whilst Petrus was talking but now he gave him his full attention.

'A horse and a gun, well that could be a little difficult. Let me have a look at the hides first and maybe, if you have enough of them, I can rustle up a horse. I still have plenty of contacts and with so many leaving; there will be one for sale somewhere. Take me to your wagon.'

Georgie felt a lot happier as they walked back along Kerkstraat, past a market in full swing, the clatter of trade ringing in his ears. The Burghers of the town were stocking up and with so many farmers in town, there was a good choice of produce at reasonable prices.

'Ah, little brother, you are back and who is this?' asked Christiaan turning from his conversation with two Burghers.

'He is an English trader and has come to look at the hides.'

'Huh, an Englishman, and what is he still doing here?'

The English trader was surrounded by Boers, his recent enemies, and was not about to become involved in an argument about the rights and wrongs of the recent conflict. He was not a stupid man; the writing was on the wall and knew it was time to leave.

'Don't worry I am leaving just as soon as I wind up my business.'

Christiaan shrugged his shoulders, turned back to his conversation, leaving Petrus to arrange any deal he in the offing.

'Come, I will show you what we have.'

He led Georgie and the trader to the back of their wagon, lifted the sheet, and exposed the hides. The Englishman reached out to feel the quality.

'Not bad, I think we can do something. Tell you what...'

Petrus and the trader argued for almost twenty minutes, discussed the merits and values of their own goods and in the end, they had a deal.

'Well that is settled and what about you mister er... You don't sound like a Boer.'

Georgie remained silent, if this man suspected he was not a Boer then others would too.

'Your hides look good enough to me and I am sure I can find you a horse. Apart from the tobacco, I have nothing left, so give me a few hours and I will try to trade the tobacco for a horse. How's about you come to my wagon tomorrow late on and we can finish our business.'

First thing the following morning the well-rested oxen were back in their traces and Petrus's long whip snaked out to urge them on towards the fort.

'So this is where they were holed up,' said Christiaan as the wagon came to a halt and he dismounted. Tying the reigns to a wagon wheel, he walked towards a guard standing by the entrance and Georgie and Petrus watched from the driving platform. Minutes later Christiaan returned, accompanied by the same Sergeant whom they had met the previous day.

'If you off load you wagon there,' he said pointing to a clear area next to the entrance gate. 'I will arrange for some soldiers to come and carry the sacks into the fort. I will need to check each one off and sign the requisition as delivered and then you can go and see the quartermaster to get paid.'

The Sergeant strode back towards the fort leaving the three of them to unload the wagon and within ten minutes, returned with four soldiers. Georgie stiffened, although confident Sergeant Thomas would not give him away these Privates were a different proposition. If any of them had had been in the camp at Newcastle at the same time as he was then they might recognise him and cause an incident. It would be best if he kept out of sight until they had completed the transfer and so, as the soldiers began moving the sacks, he kept to the blind side of the wagon, his wide brimmed had tilted to obscure his face.

'Right, here's your paperwork for the quartermaster. One of you follow me and I will take you to his office, the rest of you stay with the wagon and make sure you come no closer to the gate as the guards are on full alert even now.'

Christiaan said nothing, a faint sneer creasing his face the only outward sign that he was still fighting the war and from his position near the wagon wheel, Georgie watched. He was relieved that the morning's work had gone off without incident and then to his surprise, the Sergeant walked straight up to him.

'What happened out there, why are you with these Boers?' he said in a low voice.

Georgie took a deep breath.

'I was wounded on the charge up the hill, passed out and when I came round Petrus was standing over me. My position was hopeless and he took me prisoner. I was supposed to be going home before this last lot started and I thought my best chance was to surrender and hope they would not be too hard on me.'

'Were they, too hard on you?'

'No, some wanted to shoot me but their commanding officer asked me to give my word I would not escape and said I should take Petrus's place on their farm until he was well enough to take over again.'

'Hmm...well enough?

'He had a broken leg; I helped him back to his lines.'

'You are not alone you know, deserting, there have been many of late. Young lads who could not take it, disillusioned by the defeats we have suffered. Can't say I blame them but this is an army and you don't do that.'

'I know, I've wondered if I was doing the right thing but I've served my country, risked my life and after the past three months on their farm I want to start anew.'

Sergeant Thomas looked Georgie in the eye, a cross between reproach and kindliness, saluted and marched away with the bearing of a soldier. Georgie watched him go and felt more than a little guilt.

Unaware of the scene so recently played out, Christiaan announced that he would go to collect the payment for the mealie and as he did Petrus moved closer to Georgie. He had noticed the Sergeant speaking with him and by the tone of the conversation wondered if Georgie was in trouble.

'So, it seems the Sergeant knows. Will he keep quiet?'

Georgie nodded, not wanting to dwell on the subject, just relived that he did not have to face a Courts Martial.

The oxen had an easy time of it, pulling the empty wagon back towards the town and Petrus hardly needed to use his bullwhip. Sitting with one leg dangling over the side of the driver's seat he occasionally flicked the reigns whilst Georgie sat beside him thinking of the horse he hoped to acquire. Christiaan had left them as soon as they began the short journey, riding ahead to meet with fellow burghers and to seek out the last of the provisions they were to bring back with them.

'This Kimberly, you say you have been there, what is it like?' said Petrus suddenly.

Georgie smiled in mild surprise. He had known Petrus long enough to understand a little of his character, his inquisitiveness. Boer society was closed and insular, their huge farms isolated and the children grew up knowing very little of the outside world. Almost since the beginning of his captivity, Petrus had questioned him about the wider world.

'There is a place called the Big Hole, a hole in the ground as wide as from here to that tree and almost as deep, dug by men searching for the diamonds. I have seen it but I looked for diamonds elsewhere, in the river and along the river bank.'

How do you find diamonds in water?'

'With a sieve, a circular implement with an iron mesh. You scrape it along the riverbed and let the water wash away the silt. If you are lucky you are left with a diamond.'

'Did you find diamonds?'

'Only one, a very small one and when we sold it to the dealer we had to share it five ways. There was not a lot for each of us, enough to pay for our beer before the army moved on.'

'Papa says that diamonds and gold are of the devil and we should have nothing to do with any of it.'

'What if you find enough to make you rich, you will be able to buy your own farm.'

Petrus sat with his eyes fixed on the lead oxen digesting Georgie's words, when suddenly he jerked his head towards Georgie.'

'Can you really find so much wealth from those little stones?'

'Oh yes, why do men spend so much time and energy looking for them. They only do that because they want to become rich.'

'I would not want to be rich, I would have to live in Pretoria, and I could not hunt every day.'

Georgie laughed slapped his thigh and pushed the bush hat to the back of his head.

'If you were rich you could buy the best hunting lands and you could even build a fancy house. You could afford to buy one of those new German guns and a string of fine ponies?'

'Hmm...I cannot see Papa and Mutti letting me do that, they like us to live in the old ways with little need for money. We hunt and we farm, we have all we need.'

He fell silent; Georgie folded his arms and sat back as the wagon bumped along and his thoughts turned to a horse and a gun.

Chapter 16

The journey back to the De Witt farm was not easy the rain incessant during the night left the trail muddy and difficult to negotiate. The storm clouds were gathering even as they made their final preparations to leave and Georgie had managed to trade the last of his skins for a waterproof cape. During his time in South Africa, he had experienced many a downpour, surviving in wet or damp clothing for days on end and acquiring a cape seemed a good idea. He was also the proud owner of a sturdy looking Basotho Pony, and he had a gun. The trader had found him one, said that it was almost brand new and from its condition Georgie believed him.

'You will be leaving soon Georgie?' said Petrus flicking the reigns to urge the oxen on. Then quite unexpectedly, he said, 'I want to come with you.'

Georgie looked at Petrus in astonishment. It had not occurred to him that he might ever want to leave the farm.

'Why, are you not happy?'

'Yes but I have seen nothing of the world. Meeting you and hearing about what you have seen and done has made me curios. You have seen London; they say it is the greatest city in the world.'

'For some maybe it is, but I lived there a long time ago, I have forgotten most of it and what I can remember doesn't make me want to go back there.'

'The rain is stopping, time to rest the oxen.'

Georgie looked at Petrus and wondered why he had changed the subject so abruptly. Maybe he was afraid to ask to come with him, but before he could raise the subject again Petrus said, 'I will make a fire and heat water for the coffee. We can go a few more miles before dark. How is your pony Georgie?'

'She's fine; I will move her into the long grass for a while.'

Not the long grass, there is danger in the long grass. Do you not know about the horse flies? Have you not heard of rinderpest? We don't want your pony to die here in the Transvaal soldier boy do we?

'Better that you should be miles away from here when that happens,' said Christiaan overhearing their conversation.

To Georgie it was obvious Christiaan did not like him and his attitude seemed to have hardened since they had been in Pretoria. Georgie turned to his tormentor, tipped his hat back on his head, and spoke in a direct voice.

'You won't have to worry about me much longer so keep your hair on.'

'What did you say?'

It was becoming clear that Christiaan wanted to pick a fight, his face had reddened, and he began clenching his fists.

'What is the matter with you brother, the war is over, Georgie will leave soon. Why are you so angry with him?'

Christiaan had no answer, his hatred stemming simply from an inbuilt prejudice fuelled by stories of Boer persecution; the constant battle for survival and the Great Trek and he believed they were God's chosen people. To him, Georgie was certainly not one of them but his brother's words stayed his hand, he blinked relaxed his clenched fists and with some embarrassment began to take the saddle from his pony. Relieved that the altercation was going no further, Georgie let out a sigh and wondered where it might end.

Sweeping windblown leaves from the verandah, Annika was the first to see them, calling out to her mother working inside the house but she did not hear her daughter's call.

'Mutti, they are back she called again and this time her mother did hear and came to the doorway.

'Go tell Papa, he's with the ponies.'

Annika picked up her skirts and ran towards the corral calling out to her father. Jos heard her and let go of the hoof he was inspecting and slowly walked to the gate. There was no point rushing, it would be some time before his sons reached the house, and a smoke would be a good way to celebrate their homecoming.

'I wonder what they have bought,' said Annika excitedly standing with her parents to watch the wagon.

'I hope they have the cloth I told Christiaan to purchase, we are in need of some new clothes.'

Annika waved her arm in greeting hoping that Georgie was still with them. She could not see him at first, he was not with Petrus driving the wagon, and Christiaan was on his pony several yards in front. Her eyes searched back and forth and she began to believe that he was not with her brothers. She need not have worried; Georgie was riding his new pony at the rear of the wagon and once he came into view, he responded with a wave of his hat.

'Look, there is Annika, and your mother he said riding up alongside Petrus.

'I see them. It will not be long my friend.'

'No, and are you still sure you want to come with me to Kimberly?' quizzed Georgie.

'Oh yes, I have thought of nothing else all day.'

'What will your father say, does he not need you to help on the farm.'

'Yes he does and I expect he will not be very pleased but there is something telling me that I must do this. It's as if God is saying to me, Petrus; you must go into the wider world and explore it before you grow old.'

Georgie's eyebrows rose a little. He had learned how religious the Boers were but even so, this statement surprised him. Perhaps that was the problem; Petrus had been isolated for so long and steeped in their religious fervour that he really believed God put each thought into his head and pursing his lips in thought rode in silence for the last hundred yards.

Petrus and Georgie were glad to be back, Petrus because it was home and Georgie because he would see Annika. However, Christiaan was the first to arrive, spurring his steed into a steady trot, wanting to be the first to bring news of Pretoria and by the time Petrus brought the oxen to a halt Christiaan had fully informed his family.

'You have done well Christiaan; it seems there were bargains to be had from the *rooineks*,' said Jos.

'Yes, the English don't want to be here anymore and I say good riddance to them,' retorted Christiaan looking towards Georgie.

Georgie did hear his tormentor as he walked towards the house and as he came up to Jos he put his hand in his shirt and pulled out a small package wrapped in greaseproof paper.

'Here, this is for you,' he said calmly handing it to Jos.

'What is it?'

'A new pipe, I got it from the trader when I took possession of my new gun. You have been kind to me and I want to show my appreciation.'

Jos held it up the simple briar pipe to inspect and nodded his head.

'It is a good pipe. I thank you for it Englishman. Now what about some dinner, you boys deserve it'

After blessing the food, the conversation turned to Pretoria and the consequences of the rebellion, Jos wanted to know everything. 'Christiaan tells me that the English are leaving in droves. We are getting our country back.'

'It looks that way father, the traders were selling everything they could not carry and we were able to trade eggs and potatoes for anything we wanted. It is a good job we had so much to trade.'

'And you pilgrim, you traded your skins for a pony see It looks a fine animal. I will take a closer look in the morning.'

'You will need to be up early Papa, he is leaving first thing.'

Georgie did not react to Christiaan's provocation and finishing his dinner in silence, he looked up and met Annika's gaze.

'You are leaving so soon,' said Mutti, breaking the tension.

'Er...yes, I had not planned to leave tomorrow but it seems you son cannot wait for me to go.'

Each of them turned towards Christiaan who was wearing a smirk on his face and secure in the belief that his family agreed with his point of view.

'Maybe it is best if I go sooner rather than later. I will gather my belongings and leave at first light. Does that please you Christiaan?' he said looking straight at his adversary.

'Yes, the sooner the better Englishman.'

'No,' cried Annika, 'that is no way to treat our guest. Where is your compassion brother?'

'She is right son, he is our guest now not a prisoner of war. We would never have got the harvest in or been able to plant the next crop without him.'

'He is our enemy; all the British are our enemies. They have tried to take our lands, dictate to us how we should live and tried to make us pay taxes to keep their army and magistrates. No papa, the sooner he goes the better.'

Georgie's instinct was to get up and leave there and then but Annika was looking straight at him and he knew that he could not.

'I don't want Georgie to leave, not like this,' she said

'It's alright Annika, Christiaan could be right, I was a British soldier, I was the enemy and now the fighting is over perhaps it is time for me to go.'

'No.'

'Christiaan you have upset your sister with your harsh words. Georgie we will need another pair of hands in the spring, perhaps you can visit us again and work here for a while.'

'Thank you Jos, I am not sure what I will do, but I have a mind to head for Kimberley and try my luck in diamond fields.'

'Papa,' said Petrus a little nervously. 'Papa, I am going with Georgie to the diamond fields.'

'What! You are going against all we stand for. Symbols of the ungodly are not for us. Why would you mix with the Uitlanders, why would you want to be like them and worship the God Mammon?'

'It's not like that Papa, I want to see something of the world. I have grown up on the farm, have never been further than Pretoria but Georgie has seen London and Cape Town, big cities of the world and I have seen nothing.'

'You cannot leave, how will we run the farm without you?'

'Papa you can hire more blacks, I will come back in the spring to tend the crops and bring in the harvest. You will come as well Georgie,' he said as more of a command than a question.

Georgie looked at Annika and nodded, 'yes, if you want me to.'

Everyone fell silent as the shock of Petrus's words slowly sank in, each of them with their own thoughts. Jos and his wife worried about the farm, too large for them to manage in their advancing years, for Christiaan it was revulsion at his younger brother leaving with the Englishman and for Annika, to lose both her favourite brother and Georgie had come as a shock.

'I need to go and look at my pony, I think she is lame,' said a sulky Christiaan rising from the table and crossing the room and with his jaw set firm, disappeared into the dark night. Jos began filling his new pipe, his face set in stone, the prospect of such change concerning him greatly.

'Petrus are you sure you want to do this?' said Mutti, her brow furrowing.

'You don't need to go tomorrow,' said Jos, 'Christiaan has been a little hasty. I think the fighting has made him this way, give him time and he will not be your enemy Georgie, and you Petrus, this is so sudden, we cannot let you leave for a day or two.'

'No Papa, I have things to do before I leave, there are jobs to finish, and one last hunt maybe.'

Jos sucked on his pipe and nodded slowly, content enough that he would have a little more time with his son and that they would finish the planting and from across the table Annika's eyes held Georgie's.

'You will come on a hunt Georgie, see if we can find some fresh meat and some skins for Annika to work with,' said Petrus trying to lighten the atmosphere.

'I can think of nothing better.'

'What will you do, how will you live when you get to Kimberly?' asked Jos who had been mulling over the problem.

'Georgie has been in Kimberly Papa, he knows what to do. We will live off the country until we get there and then we look for diamonds.'

'Is it so easy?'

Petrus and Georgie left early for one last hunt, their breath turning white in the cold air as they trotted out onto the veldt. It was a chance for Georgie to get to know his new steed, to try out his new rifle and for Petrus a last look at the land in which he had grown up and after almost two hours he halted and stood high in his stirrups.

'Look, over there Georgie, the donga leading towards that hill. That is where we will go today a place I have not hunted since I was a boy.

'Is the hunting different up there?'

'This time of year the grass is sweet and the herds like to go there. The other side of the hill leads towards a river and almost certainly we will find game,' he said pulling his bush hat firmly down onto his head and sitting back in the saddle. 'How is your pony?'

'Good, she's easy to ride and I can feel she has some strength in her.'

'Just what we need for the trek to the diamond fields eh, and your gun, we will see how good your gun is soon I think.'

Petrus knew every Kloof and donga for miles, and decided that they should take the trail up onto a plateau that was a favourite grazing land of the Impala and Gazelle. He wanted to experience its splendour before he left home and knew that it would be a good testing ground for his friend's new gun. The plateau nestled in amongst the surrounding hills like an enormous Amphitheatre and as they reached the crest of the hill overlooking its flat grasslands, they halted. Petrus sat motionless, his eyes fixed while Georgie, struck by the beauty of the place could not help but look in everywhere at once.

'This place is beautiful Petrus.'

'Yes it is beautiful; I came here only a few times when I was younger. I wanted to see it again before we leave for Kimberly and I want to hunt Impala. Let's go over there and have a look.

They rode slowly down the sloping hillside onto the flat grasslands, past a fast flowing stream and towards a thicket.

'Keel your eyes open for lions, there are one or two prides somewhere round here if I remember. If you see any stay still and we will try to avoid them.'

Georgie blinked, they had not come near any large predators during their previous hunts, a few giraffes and rhinos were normally their only companions but lions were different. He touched his rifle barrel and then he patted the sturdy Basotho Pony for reassurance for they would be his salvation should they be confronted by lions. Petrus watched him and smiled, amused by his obvious discomfort.

'Don't worry; they will keep away from us as long as we don't disturb them. If they have eaten then all they will want to do is sleep and if they are hunting we will soon know.'

Reassured, Georgie followed Petrus towards cover and the two of them settled down to wait and almost within minutes some Game appeared to graze just out of gunshot range.

'Look, Impala,' whispered Petrus, 'if we can get close enough to them and make a kill then there is no point in staying here.'

Taking his rifle, he cautiously led Georgie towards the grazing animals and lay down to judge wind and cover.

'We are lucky, the wind is blowing our way, and they seem to be getting closer. Set your sights and wait.'

For most of the day they waited, the Impala were oblivious to them and came very slowly towards them but then everything changed. First one then another lifted its head and then the panic set in. The lions had decided to hunt and like the two men had crept slowly towards the impala and now the grazing animals had sensed them.

'This is not good, get ready in case a lion sees us. Let's hope they bring one of those impala down and start feeding before they see us.'

The hairs on Georgie's neck stood up and he felt fear like he had never felt before but Petrus remained calm and that gave him strength. He held his gun ready and watched as the Impala dodged towards them and then he saw the first lion, A large male with a magnificent mane closing in on a fleeing animal and as its prey dodged from side to side to avoid the fangs it stumbled and the lion was on it instantly.

Georgie lost sight of the kill as the two animals thrashed about in the long grass and then he saw two more lions. They had given up on the chase and were heading for an easy meal when Petrus turned and hissed at him to run for it back to their ponies.

'With luck they won't bother us now but to be safe we will head for that high ground over there.'

The high ground was a mile away and all the time they rode towards it they watched out for danger lurking in the long grass. The ride was hectic but the Lions were not interested and so it was with great relief that Georgie finally pulled up his pony.

'Phew, that was close,' he said.

'No, we were safe enough but we have lost our chance of a kill, we will wait here and try again.'

Georgie reached for his water bottle, his mouth was so dry he could hardly feel his tongue and again, they waited until a small herd of Gazelle came into view.

'Looks like I will have to forget the Impala,' said Petrus eyeing them, and after an hour's patient wait, the unwitting Gazelles wandered within range of the hunter's guns. Setting their sights for maximum range, they took careful aim and when the hunters finally returned home, Annika rushed out to meet them running her hand over one of the carcasses.

'These will make fine shirts Georgie, the animals are young and supple,' she said. 'When you come back next year they will be waiting for you. You will come back?'

'I will, and will you be waiting for me?' he said feeling his heart thump.

'Yes Georgie, I will be waiting for you.'

The two ponies stood side-by-side waiting patiently for their riders. The small group standing with heads bowed, Petrus and Christiaan to one side, Mutti and Annika together with Georgie facing Jos who was reading a passage from the bible

'But the Lord is faithful. He will establish you and guard you against the evil one.' He looked up, closed the bible, and said. 'It is a rite of passage that you undertake my son. May God be with you and keep you safe, Amen,' he said pulling out his pipe. 'The tobacco you brought from Pretoria is good, but before I smoke let us eat a final meal together.'

The group began to break up; Mutti was the first to go into the house followed by Christiaan and his brother leaving Georgie and Annika to stand awkwardly with Jos.

'You will be coming back pilgrim, for the spring planting?'

'Er...yes sir, that is my intention.'

'And you daughter, what do you say.'

'Say papa?'

'Yes, do you wish for Georgie to return next year?'

Annika's face turned a shade of pink and she looked at the floor in embarrassment.

'Well daughter, what do you say? It has become plain to me that you two have formed an attraction.'

Annika looked up, her eyes proud and defiant, her secret revealed.

'Yes Papa, I want very much for Georgie to return.'

'I don't think your mother realises yet what is happening. Perhaps when you Georgie and Petrus return with your diamonds the two of you can tell her,' said Jos with stern, yet kindly eyes.

Chapter 17

Many months had passed since Nkosinathi and his brothers' triumphant returned to the kraal. They had driving the cattle before them, arriving home late one afternoon to a warm welcome and in a short space of time, the villager's health had vastly improved. Mondli looked happier than he had for a long time and Nkosinathi returned to hunting game to supplement their diet.

He sometimes traded skins for the White man's goods with traders passing but they were less frequent than before. The cost of crossing John Dunn's land had become prohibitive, many had found new routes to the north, and Nkosinathi was finding it hard to trade for cartridges. He needed to find some and heard from one trader of a place in the Transvaal close to the border with Zululand where he might get some and he had decided to go there. It would be a long journey across dangerous country and he would be gone for many days and so, later that day, he announced his intentions.

'My brothers, I will be gone for many days, look after the herd and beware of John Dunn's men. Keep the cattle well-hidden from them and do not antagonize them if they seek tribute. We do not want to bring down the wrath of the Chief John Dunn upon us.'

'Have no fear, we will take care,' said Dumisani. 'Mondli grows old; the responsibility for the kraal rests on my shoulders. I will see to it that the herd is well looked after, as for John Dunn, I have no fear of him brother.'

Nkosinathi's head rotated backwards slightly and he breathed heavily through his nose, a sign that he was not all together happy with Dumisani's answer.

The ever-cheerful Sibusiso did not notice Nkosinathi's displeasure and wished him luck on his journey 'Take care brother and may the spirits of our ancestors guide you.'

'Thank you, I will watch out have no fear,' said Nkosinathi walking towards his horse.

'And you, Nkosinathi, have no fear that we can look after the herd and the kraal. We can handle the men of John Dunn who come to take our grain and our cattle. Mondli has made me the one in charge, he can no longer lead but I can,' said Dumisani and as Nkosinathi mounted his horse, he could not help wondering.

Nudging his horse forward with a gentle pressure of his knees he rode slowly through the kraal and out onto the plain. His journey would take him west through John Dunn's territory and then north into the lands of Hlubi, to the settlement of Amersfoort. A challenging yet familiar route, one he had taken with Jake and his gunrunners many months before.

Nkosinathi's horse carried him across open veldt for two days, until finally he came upon the Qudeni Forest. It was the place where he had first encountered Jake, where he had killed him. Picking up the old trail, he soon came across the small stream and followed it deep into the forest. Finding a small clearing, he paused to rest a while and climbing down from the saddle, led the animal to the water's edge, leaving it to drink as he listened to the sounds of the forest. In the distance, he heard birdcalls and shielding his eyes from the sunlight, scanned the lace like shadows spread across the valley floor and seeing no immediate danger, decided to remain where he was for the night.

He dare not risk a fire in case John Dunn's men were in the vicinity but equally he knew that he must be alert for the predators of the night and decided he would sleep in a tree. It would be safe enough for him but the last thing he wanted was for a leopard to take his horse. Removing the saddle, he reached into the leather bag slung across it and took out a stick of dried meat to chew. The light was beginning to fade, his defences seemed secure enough, and so, fastening the horse securely he climbed into the branches of a stout tree. He had a good view of the trail able to see equally well in both directions and with his gun lying across the branch he settled down to catch up on some sleep.

At first, he did not know what had woken him, only that his horse was agitated and as he peered through the gloom, he heard a throaty and suddenly he was wide-awake straining his ears and reaching for his gun. He had no idea of how long he had slept but now adrenalin was coursing through his body and there was little chance of any more sleep this night. There was more noise, this time from further away, the squeal of a hog and a crashing of vegetation as the predator made its kill and then silence returned. For perhaps an hour, he lay in the tree; relieved that the predator had found a meal elsewhere and then the dawn began appear and he dropped to the ground.

Saddling is his horse he took time to chew on some more of the dried meat and after scouting a few yards along the trail mounted up knowing that he was close to the area where he had finished off William and Phillip. Coming across their remains he was shocked, two human beings reduced to nothing more than piles of white bones and torn clothing discarded by the scavengers. Nkosinathi did not want to dwell, only to pass this place of death as quickly as he could and even his horse seemed to sense the phantoms that lurked. Not much further on, he passed the small cave half way up the slope, a dark shadow amongst the vegetation kindling memories of his encounter. His mind filled with the thought of spirits haunting the place encouraging him to urge his steed on, and late in the afternoon, he reached the edge of the forest. The canopy thinned out; bush veldt replacing the trees and he realised that soon his cover would be gone.

Stopping by a stream to rest his horse, he took stock listening and looking along the banks of the stream. Nothing moved and then his eye caught a ripple in the water and focusing his eyes, peered beneath the surface.

Silver shapes drifted slowly in the current, several large fish not more than ten feet away and holding his breath, he stepped back from the water's edge. Glancing round, he caught sight of a young tree with long straight branches and cautiously pulled out his hunting knife to cut away a slender branch. Sharpening the end to make a primitive spear, he felt a swell of nostalgia taking him back to his days as a cadet learning. This was not the first time he had speared a fish for his dinner.

Keeping to the shadows, he peered into the water seeing the fish huddled together and lifting the spear, held it ready above his shoulder. Just as he had done all those years ago as a Cadet, he crept along the bank side and reaching the fish, he took aim. With one silky movement, he stabbed into the water, retracting the spear with a yelp of delight. His catch twisted and turned in an effort to break free, its thrashing causing it to slide down the shaft and drop onto the ground and Nkosinathi picked it up by its tail to smash its head twice against a rock. Picking it up his hunger pangs stirred and he could not resist cooking it there and then. He was hungry, fatigued and for once, he let his guard slip.

The diminutive native stopped and scoured the landscape as he had done regularly for several days. He was of the Khoisan, diminutive, with a magnificent head of tight curly hair and the ability of an expert tracker. His job was to search out the tracks of humans in the great wilderness for his master Rabanina the leader of the border patrol. For several days, the patrol had travelled inland from the coast, looking for trespassers, smugglers, and legitimate traders.

The tracker stood still his eyes focusing on the trees in the distance.

'Boss, someone there,' he said pointing.

Rabanina looked towards the forest two or three miles away but could see nothing.

'Where, what can you see Jolu?'

'There boss, smoke from a campfire.'

Rabanina strained his eyes, finally picking out a very faint wisp of smoke drifting above the trees but the night was closing in and soon the smoke was lost from view. Even Jolu lost sight of it and for a minute or more; the two men looked towards the forest until finally, Rabanina turned towards his men.

'Put that campfire out. There is someone at the edge of the forest. We will rest here for tonight and tomorrow but I think we will hunt them down.'

The fish was good-sized and with enough flesh on it for more than one meal, but Nkosinathi was ravenous. Pulling the parcel from the fire, he cut the grass cords securing the wrapping of leaves and sitting back against a tree trunk; he stuffed the hot white flesh into his mouth and renewed his strength

Rubbing his hands on the grass, he removed the fish grease and pondered the next part of his journey. Tomorrow, when he ventured out onto the open veldt the chances of anyone seeing him would be greater and he would need to be vigilant. The fire flared up and he opened his eyes, a feeling of alarm spreading over him in the realization that the glow would be visible from a long way. Jumping to his feet up he quickly raked the burning wood from the heart of the fire and beat out the flames leaving only smouldering twigs before regaining his position against the tree. A few feet away, his horse snorted and then all was quiet again and Nkosinathi relaxed.

The diminutive Khoisan tracker did not sleep much spending his time constantly searching for signs. He was aware that someone was at the edge of the forest and his prodigious inquisitiveness was leading him to investigate further. Slipping away from the men of the patrol, he made his way up the gully to the crest of a small hill to search the moonlit landscape. At first, he saw nothing and then from the corner of his eye he caught a glimpse of a faint orange glow and then it was gone. He looked into the black night with its twinkling silver stars picking out the one that would serve as a pointer and clicking his tongue against the roof of his mouth uttered a word of encouragement in his strange Khoisan language and trotted towards the forest.

Once the moon had risen, it was bright enough for him to move quickly and reaching the edge of the forest he stood and listened. There was nothing, and so he slowly he made his way between the first of the trees, creeping forward towards the place where he expected to find the camp fire. After maybe a hundred yards he stopped again to listen, all was quiet, and then he heard a horse snort.

That same sound made Nkosinathi turn his head and reach for his gun, had the horse sensed danger? It might be nothing, perhaps he feared the return of the leopard, he did not know but all the same, he stood up to listen. There was no sound and he searched the darkness with his eyes but still there was nothing. Perhaps he was imagining things and squatted again, his mind turning over the possibilities and then he suddenly froze. The campfire, what if someone had seen the campfire, what if someone was looking for him? Again, he rose to his feet and creeping a few yards into the thicket searched the darkness and in the darkness Jolu took one-step at a time, slowly, inching his way towards the sound of the horse. The forest was becoming more dense offering good cover and expertly he moved ever closer stopping every few yards to listen. The sound of dry leaves rustling broke the silence, someone or something was moving, a warning to him. Slowly he crouched to his haunches to make himself as indistinguishable as possible from his surroundings and listened again. That faint rustling sound had stopped, unusual for a group of men and horses and he was sure that whoever was there must be alone and he decided then to return to Rabanina and report his suspicions.

Even before first light Nkosinathi was wide-awake in the branches, he was well fed and after a fitful sleep he felt refreshed. He had scouted the immediate area around his camp when he felt danger threaten and satisfied he could do no more he obliterate the remains of the fire and climbed into the tree and now he was ready to leave and led his horse to the edge of the forest. A steep kloof cut into the hillside caught his attention, it would afford cover and mounting the horse he steered towards it and no more than two miles away, Rabanina's men were also breaking camp.

'Hmm...you are right Jolu, just one man, a native and he is riding a horse. Not often you see that.'

Rabanina lowered his telescope and slammed it shut, pursing his lips in thought.

'You men,' he said to the patrol already mounted and waiting, 'we will follow this native at a safe distance until we can be sure of catching him. Jolu follow him and report to me as often as you can. When you think we are in a position to surprise him, let me know and we will take him.'

Jolu clicked his tongue in response and trotted off in front of Rabanina. Although small in stature he was tireless, could run all day at a steady pace and by taking paths unsuited to the horses would easily keep up. After a few hundred yards, the party slowed to a steady walking pace, leaving Jolu to go on ahead to find the likely trail of the lone horseman and trotting up the sloping ground he came to a natural break in the ridge. He peered into the valley below saw that the landscape was streaked with shallow sided kloofs, the only vegetation odd clumps of trees and thickets, not an easy place to conceal yourself. But of Nkosinathi, there was no sign and so he retraced his steps, to signalled to the patrol the direction he was heading in search of their quarry.

Nkosinathi was unaware of the patrol, his attention focused solely on the path he was taking. The valley side was steep, littered with loose rock and boulders and together the man and his horse had cautiously to pick their way. For most of the morning, they headed along the valley until finally a landmark Nkosinathi recognized appeared in the distance, a clump of tall trees standing alone, a place where he would find water a place to rest.

A small stream trickled between the trees and as the horse lowered its long neck to drink, Nkosinathi climbed the ridge to scour the countryside. There was nothing save a small group of Nguni goats on a nearby hill and a few birds. Transferring his gaze towards the route he had just taken, he spent a few minutes examining the scene. He saw some birds rise into the air and wondered what had disturbed them. Perhaps he could shoot one, his biltong and mealie cakes were long gone, he had nothing to eat and lifted his rifle to his shoulder. Traversing it slowly from side to side, he searched for a target until suddenly he dropped to the ground in mild shock. Wriggling forward he peered through the long grass, his eyes focused on the birds and then on the ground below them and in shock he dropped to the ground. He was still a long way off but it was a man and he was following the same trail.

Jolu concentrated hard on the ground in front of him, it was stony and the trail kept disappearing. His quarry was moving around a lot and he had to look hard to find the hoof tracks. He had run towards the forest, made his way to the place where he had entered the night before, and fully expected to pick up his quarry's trail and after a search, he came across fresh horse tracks. At first he made good progress following tracks left in the soft earth but once out in open country the rock strewn ground made it more difficult and he had to move more slowly.

Nkosinathi sucked in his breath, his fears of the previous night now seemed well founded and by the way, the man was moving he must be a tracker working for one of John Dunn's patrols. It was the one situation he feared the most. Casting caution aside, he slung his gun over his shoulder, raced to his horse and leapfrogged into the saddle to set it at a steady trot along the valley.

Jolu picked up the trail again and stood for a moment to look along the likely path traced out by the hoof marks, taking in the shape and directions of the kloofs. He not only followed tracks but could discern much about his quarry from them. He had not been on Nkosinathi's trail long enough, nor seen enough of his movements to make a complete judgement but he was sure the man he was tracking was not white and for the rest of the day the Khoisan tracker followed Nkosinathi traversing the valleys and escarpments.

By the end of the afternoon he was not much more than a mile behind his quarry and stopped following, instead climbing to the highest point on the ridge to look for Rabanina and the rest of the patrol. He had a good idea where his quarry was heading and felt it time to inform Rabanina; leave it to him to decide what to do next. His eyes roamed the countryside, finally making

out the patrol traversing the ridge and he set off at a
steady trot, finding the patrol making camp for the
night.

'You are back little man,' said Rabanina. 'What have
you found?'

'Native man, on horseback, heading that way. He is
maybe half a day ahead of you and going towards the
land of Hlubi.'

'Hlubi, I wonder if he is one of the old chief's spies. It
does not sound as if he is trading. Has he got pack
animals with him?'

'No boss, just a horse.'

Rabanina thought for a moment or two, wondering
who this stranger might be because it was unusual for a
native to be in possession of a horse. They had
confiscated almost all of the native horses on the pretext
of taking them as the white queen's taxes. He lifted his
hat and rubbed his fingers in his tight black hair
deciding what course of action to take.

'Can you pick up his tracks easily?'

'Yes boss.'

'Good then grab something to eat and get some rest. I
want you after him at first light. Find somewhere to
signal to me because we will be right behind you. We'll
soon find out what this one is about.'

Nkosinathi searched for a safe place to spend the night
he was hungry and tired and he knew he must allow his
horse some rest. The tracker would probably not be able
to follow his trail in the dark but if he had guessed right,
the man was a competent tracker and he would need to

leave early, before dawn but first he needed to find a safe place.

He slid from the saddle, let his horse drink from a stream and surveyed the scene. He was not aware of any immediate danger knelt beside the horse to take a drink himself. It was not much more than a trickle but it was enough and after he found a few berries to help suppress his hunger he sat with his back to a large rock, lay his gun across his knees and fell into a fitful asleep.

Chapter 18

The two riders approached the killing ground that was Laing's Nek in silence, both alone with their thoughts. Neither had stepped foot on the emotion laden ground where they had witnessed such slaughter for more than half a year. For Georgie the memories were particularly painful, the thought of so many of his comrades falling to the accurate Boer fire weighing on his mind. Petrus saw things differently, his emotions tied up with the fight to free their lands of the British yoke and shielding his eyes against the setting sun he looked at Georgie, and decided to remain silent until they had passed through the Nek.

'We should think about setting up the tent for the night,' he finally said when the pass was behind them.

'Yes, the tent.'

'Are you all right?'

'Yes, just feeling sad, feeling for those boys that will not be going home.'

Petrus was not one to gloat, although his people had won a victory he understood how Georgie was feeling.

'It's over now, its a shame but what is done is done. We need to think about tomorrow and Newcastle, we need to replenish our stores if we are going to make it to Kimberly.'

Georgie nodded agreement, shook off the melancholy that was beginning to grip him and began to worry about entering the settlement. he might be recognised but they did need to restock their stores for the ride across the Orange Free State. The town had an army depot, soldiers, ones that might recognise him but it was a risk he had to take. In his favour was his appearance, changed significantly during his captivity. Gone was the red tunic with its three white stripes, replaced by the leather jerkin Annika had made for him and he wore a Boer's style bush hat and sporting an excuse for a Boer beard he felt had a chance of remaining anonymous.

'At this rate we should be in Newcastle by the day after tomorrow said Petrus pulling up his horse. 'This looks a good place to spend the night. Look a stream, let's water the horses and then we can get a fire going. That reminds me we will need to buy some warm clothing, it can get pretty cold up on the High veldt, even at this time of year. I have heard stories of cold winds coming from nowhere and killing sheep and cattle.'

Georgie grunted, he was well aware of conditions on the High veldt. The first campaign he had taken part in was to cross the great Karoo, he had experienced those cold winds, when temperatures could change in an instant. During his days as an ordinary foot soldier, struggling to get the wagons up the steep rocky inclines, he had spent many a night out in the open shivering instead of sleeping. He remembered heaving on the wheels of the wagons stuck in the mud, the crack of the drover's whips and the frantic braying of the mules, sounds he did not want to ever hear again if he could help it and then his mind turned to the time they had spent in Kimberly, the reason for his return. The General had decided to show the rebellious miners who was in charge and used the excuse of resting his army for a month to intimidate them.

He wondered where Dickie Henderson was now, Dickie's desertion ultimately inspiring him to make this trek. They had found the diamond only days before the order came for the army to return to the Cape but Dickie was having none of it. For a month they had rested, enjoyed the warm sunshine as they sifted the sludge from the riverbed and after finding that solitary diamond they had sold it to buy a copious amount of beer and Dickie had waxed lyrical about life as a miner. He said he might make his fortune if only he could find enough diamonds and when the army moved out, he had deserted.

Until the final battle at Ulundi, he had been a good and loyal soldier never considering that he might leave the army. He had fought hard, killed his share of Zulu warriors but the bloodletting had eventually sickened him. He remembered the look in the last Zulu's eyes when he had spared him, a look that had left a lasting impression. He could have easily killed the man, shot him or run him through with his sword but he had not. He could see the respectful thankful eyes now and he would never forget that face as long as he lived.

'What are you thinking Georgie, you have gone very quiet?'

'Oh, just wondering why I am here. I would never have believed my life could change so quickly. Yesterday I was a soldier and today I am a budding prospector.'

'Ha ha,' laughed Petrus. 'You sound as if you have had a revelation.'

'Maybe I have.'

Nkosinathi was under no illusions, for more than two days he had caught odd glimpses of the man following him. Never much more than a mile away and relentless in his pursuit, he was beginning to wear Nkosinathi down. After making his way through numerous valleys and climbing steep sided ravines, he had reached the highest point of his journey. He could see the hills of Natal in the distance and it would not be long before he left the lands of John Dunn and he hoped then that he might lose his pursuers.

He was still unaware of Rabanina and his men but experience told him there would be a patrol somewhere and although he had not seen them they were closer than he knew. On the advice of Jolu, Rabanina had taken the patrol on a different route, along an ancient bridle path that would allow them to outflank the lone horseman. Jolu had guessed with some accuracy where his quarry was heading and Rabanina had seen the logic. He might have called off the pursuit under normal circumstances there being little prospect of profit in it but there was something about this native on horseback.

'Senzile, take two men and ride to the ridge over there, you know what to do,' he said to one of the

Xhosa's. 'We will be ready to catch this Zulu quite soon I think.'

The patrol consisted mainly of Xhosa, John Dunn had insisted on not using many Zulu, reasoning that they had ties with the people of whom he was demanding tribute. The Xhosa were no friends of the Zulu and took pleasure in destroying the kraals and stealing their cattle and it had proved a wise decision.

'You men follow me, Jolu says this kloof runs into the one where our friend is and if we can get there first we will have him. If he turns back Senzile will cut off his escape.'

Rabanina kicked at his horse's flanks and set it onto a fast trot and together with the rest of his patrol, headed towards the junction between the two valleys and not far away Nkosinathi looked up at the sky. The sun was past its zenith, the air warm and still and he twisted in his saddle wondering where his pursuer was. He had not seen anyone else during the chase; just the one following and he began to feel uneasy. Several times, he had obliterated his tracks as he crossed hard ground and once he had ridden along the bed of a stream but each time the tracker had reappeared, no closer yet no farther away and now, he could see the valley's end. The ravine was changing shape, opening out, becoming flatter and he thought that he was likely to make better time.

Reaching for the ostrich shell water bottle slung over his saddle he drained the last of the precious liquid and looked back along the track. After carefully surveying the landscape he noticed a glint of light high up the escarpment and let the water bottle slip from his grasp.

He touched his gun for reassurance and his eyes searched the ridge for movement, within seconds spotting something. He guessed that It must be the patrol and nudged his horse towards some trees to a rest a while and for him to take stock of the situation.

He would be invisible to those above for a time but the tracker would close on him if he stayed too long. Slipping to the ground, he took a few steps forward and peered through the branches and there they were, two of them, just visible over the crest of the ridge on horseback and picking their way slowly over the uneven ground.

So his worst fears were realised, a party of John Dunn's men were after him, and not far away either. He searched the ridge again and with a feeling of anxiety, he turned back to mount his horse, his instinct telling him he was heading into a trap.

The steep sided valley lay ahead of them, sloping markedly as it joined a second valley, growing on its slopes were many trees and thickets, ideal for Rabanina's plan, and there he halted his men.

'I want you Senzile and Jama to ride to the ridge and conceal yourselves, keep a sharp lookout in case he doesn't come this way. I want to know as soon as possible if he decides to take another trail. The rest of you come with me.'

The patrol split up, the two men riding up towards the ridge to keep a lookout whilst Rabanina led the others along the side of the ravine to a place of concealment overlooking the valley floor and there they waited and a long way down in the valley Jolu diligently followed Nkosinathi's tracks. All save the little Khoisan were feeling the heat of the day, impatient to get it over with and return to the Dunn estate.

On the ridge Senzile and Jama sat motionless scanning the valley, of Nkosinathi there was no sign and they were beginning to believe that perhaps there was no one there after all. Jama patted his horse, lifted his water bottle to his lips and looked again for their quarry.

'There is no one down there, maybe we should tr further along, up there maybe.' Senzile followed his companions gaze towards an outcrop and nodded agreement. 'We will have a better view from there.' said Jama and the two riders set off to pick their way towards the vantage point while out of sight Nkosinathi wondered where his antagonists might be.

He searched the ridge again but Senzile, Jama had dropped out of sight, and he began to wonder. As a cadets learning the ways of a Zulu warrior he had practised pincer movements and using that same tactic when they had defeated the British army at the hill of the cow's stomach. Was that what was happening here, were they trying to pen him in between two forces?

A line of trees and thickets ran diagonally down from the opposite side of the valley, good cover, a place to hide but he knew that if he crossed over he would expose himself. If he kept going though, he might make his way out of the valley towards open ground and once there he could let his horse run free and try to lose them. He looked up to where he thought the men on the ridge might be and seeing no sign decided that it was now or never and clicking his tongue against the roof of his mouth, directed his horse into a steady trot. He looked up at the ridge, at the clusters of cover along the valley sides and feeling confident enough, kicked at the horses flanks and galloped towards some trees.

Breathing heavily, more with excitement than exertion as he reached cover, Nkosinathi reigned in his horse and looked back towards the ridge but still, there was no sign of the patrol. After resting for a few minutes and feeling a little more confident, he made rapid progress through the trees towards the end of valley where it opened out, joining a second and it and struck him that this was where they could be lying in wait for him.

It seemed obvious, the men on the ridge were there to cut off his retreat, the main body would be concealed somewhere nearby and slowing his horse he wondered what he should do. If they were lying in ambush he would have to run a gauntlet and hope he could keep out of the line of sight of their guns or he could turn back but the tracker was somewhere down the trail and he would not escape his eyes. No, it was better to go on and perhaps disappear into one of the gullies up ahead.

'I am a warrior and warriors fear nothing. They will not catch me,' he murmured to himself, kicking his horse into the gallop.

Indeed the trees did hide him but the ground was dry and hard and the horse's hooves thundered out a presence and in the still warm air of the African afternoon, the sound a galloping horse reached Rabanina's ears.

'Listen, hear that. He is coming, get ready.'

The men stirred into life, each one reaching for his rifle and as they did so, a horse, surprised by the sudden movement emitted a whinny, the faint echo loud enough to alert Nkosinathi. His ears pricked up his nostrils flared and his heart thumped in his chest as the realisation dawned that the trap was about to be sprung and only yards away Rabanina was signalling to his men.

'There boss, in the trees.'

Rabanina's eyes focused on the shadow moving swiftly through the trees and then, as it broke cover, he caught a glimpse of the rider and recoiled in recognition. Releasing his rifle's safety catch he, roared with anger and charged after the fleeing Nkosinathi.

Nkosinathi heard the expletive, managed a brief sideways glance and saw several riders appear no more than twenty yards away, but he was going at full pelt and they were not yet at the gallop. Increased his lead he encouraged his horse to follow a gully and managed to disappear from his pursuer's sight.

'Over there, he's gone that way,' shouted one of the Xhosa who had seen Nkosinathi's horse run into the gully but bunched as they were, they lost time negotiating the narrow approach and Nkosinathi increased his lead. Reaching the end of the gully his horse picked its way skilfully across the rock-strewn ground and very soon, he was in amongst thicket and trees looking furtively for a route through. It was clear he had run into an area of heavy vegetation and that would give him good cover but was proving difficult for the horse to negotiate.

Shouting reached his ears as Rabanina and his men closed the gap but they too would have some difficulty crossing the uneven ground and then they started shooting. Rabanina was angry, he had recognised the man they were chasing as his one-time tracker and he wanted to know what he was doing here on the border.

Bullets whizzed past Nkosinathi, too close for comfort, rekindling memories of those terrible final days of the war. The flight from Ulundi had been desperate, with mounted men at their heels, the broken Zulu army had run for their lives and he remembered how desperate he felt. A soldier on horseback had cornered him and feeling exhausted he had turned to face his death. However, the soldier, about to shoot him, had unexpectedly lifted his gun and allowed him to escape, as if the spirits of his ancestors had saved him. Then a gap opened up in the thicket and he felt as if those same guiding spirits had returned. Wheeling his horse round he forced it between the closely packed thorn bushes and as they closed behind him he knew he had a chance.

With little time to think, other than to urge the horse on, he galloped from the trees and across open ground. Behind him, the sound of men shouting reached his ears and he glanced round but of his pursuers, there was no sign. He was breathing heavily with the strain; the shouting becoming a blur yet something told him he was leaving them behind.

Unknown to him each of Rabanina's men believed he knew the path to follow but they were all wrong and before they could regroup Nkosinathi had crossed the open ground and guided his horse into undulating country and easily found a gully that would hide him from their line of sight. He guided his horse along the gully as fast as he dared, eventually reaching a stream running diagonally across his path and there he looked up at the sun to gauge the direction he must take. Kicking his horse forward he crossed the stream and for a few yards let it run along the river bank before turning round to navigate back the way he had come for fifty or so yards and then he persuaded his horse to take the plunge.

It was a ploy he had learned with the cadets, double back, leave a confusing, indeterminate trail and then go where you needed to. It would buy him time he hoped; give him a chance to reach the land of the Hlubi where he would be safe. it was unlikely the men immediately following him would be able to pick up the trail but it was inevitable that the tracker would eventually unravel the puzzle.

He had cut it fine; Rabanina had discovered the gap in the thicket, was even now emerging from the trees and had found his tracks.

'Down here, look fresh hoof prints. Follow me and keep your guns at the ready because I do not want this man to live to see the sun go down.'

The riders galloped down into the gully, following the tracks, clear enough even for a novice tracker. On they came, their confidence increasing by the minute until they reached the stream.

'Here,' shouted one of them, 'he has crossed over and is heading south.'

The others splashed across the stream and once again they were on Nkosinathi's trail but not for long. The false trail was good, it was baffling and before long Rabanina had to split his force to cover more ground but their efforts were in vain, his only recourse to await the appearance of Jolu.

'Find some high ground and look for him. You get up there and you two, over there, that kopje, see what you can.'

The men moved to higher ground to carry on the search and Rabanina sat pensively in his saddle. He needed Jolu more than ever now; he was so close and the little Khoisan would have little trouble picking up the trail but he was still a long way back. He felt for the revolver stuck into his trouser waistband, caressed the warm metal and vowed that the Zulu would pay for outsmarting him. What was his name? He thought for a few moments, Nkosinathi, that was it, from the village of Mondli on the edge of the Ulundi plain near the White Mfolozi. He would make a detour on their way back.

'Rabanina, we see him.'

Rabanina snapped out of his thoughts, nudged his horse forwards and joined his men on the higher ground.

'There,' said the man pointing towards the distant rider.

Rabanina held his palm flat shielding his eyes, watching, calculating, and felt they could still catch him before he left the lands of John Dunn. Perhaps his horse would tire or become lame. Between him and his men were seven horses, all in good condition and once Jolu was back on his trail he felt it highly likely they would catch Nkosinathi.

'Dunga, stay here and wait for the others. We will follow him; lay an easy trail for you to follow. We will catch this man.'

The two men rode in silence. It was more than a day since they had ridden between the towering hills, a day since they had relived that terrible morning. Georgie had wondered what had driven the General to believe they could scale them at the charge. It was obviously a good defensive position and would be very hard to take but the glory-seeking officer seemed not to care. He sucked in his breath and put the thoughts to the back of his mind.

'We should be there in a few hours Petrus. I remember this road well, another twenty miles I think.'

Petrus smiled and looked south, towards Newcastle, excited that he was really starting his adventure. He had lived on the farm all his life, venturing only as far as Pretoria and Middleburg and now he was about to experience the outside world.

'What is Newcastle like is it bigger than Pretoria?'

'Just a bit. If the army is still there in force then it will be. We didn't see much of the townspeople when we passed through so I can't tell you much else.' said Georgie, beginning to wonder if there would still be a large military presence. The thought that he might be running the risk of being recognised as a deserter occupied him until late in the afternoon when the settlement's single story white washed buildings began to appear.

'The trading post, look over there Georgie, De Klerq's trading post, a Boer. Perhaps he can help us.'

A black painted sign hung over the verandah and beneath it dog lay watching as the two men climbed from their saddles. It had been a long day, breaking camp at four 'o' clock, followed by a ride of twelve hours and stopping only once to rest the horses. Patting his horse's neck in appreciation Georgie placed his hands in the small of his back and leaned backwards to shake off the stiffness as Petrus did the same and began to dust off his jacket.

'What about sleeping in a proper bed tonight Petrus? My back has had enough of sleeping on the ground.'

'You are getting soft my friend. What will we pay with, we need what little money we have for supplies and there is no guarantee Herr De Klerq will trade for any of the skins we have left.'

'He will I'm sure.'

Mister De Klerq was a small man, not robust at all like the Boers Georgie had met up in the Transvaal and more than that, he was a busy man. He wore a long white apron and stood with his hands spread flat on his counter top as they entered and his eyes narrowing as he weighed up the two strangers

'Gentlemen, what brings you to my humble abode?'

Petrus had thought to speak in the Afrikaner language, let the storekeeper know they were of the same clan but De Klerq's manner and speech was more of the English and came as a shock.

'We need some supplies, we have a long journey ahead of us,' said Georgie taking the initiative.

The man's eyes lit up, the prospect of selling goods to these men cheering him. Since the army had come to town, he had made a lot of money but now, with the war over, business was slow and his profits had declined.

'I am running low on a few things, what is it you want?'

'Coffee, salt, and some dried or tinned food?'

'I don't have tinned food; everything I had has gone to the army.'

'Are they still here in town?'

'Yes, there is a military camp out on the Ladysmith road. They have been leaving town for weeks but a lot of them are still around. Why do you ask, are you expecting trouble? There have been a few Boers from the Transvaal come here but there has not been any disturbance if that is what you think.'

'No, er...no, I just wondered?'

'Where are you boys from anyway?'

'Transvaal,' said Petrus.

'Well it looks as if you will be keeping your Transvaal after all,' said the man.

There was silence for a few seconds, Petrus embarrassed to be a lone Transvaaler in, what was, hostile country and beside him Georgie was feeling uncomfortable thinking of the army.

'You haven't heard? There has been an *Indaba* between the British and the Transvaalers, the Transvaal is to remain independent. No matter, that is all in the past now, what can I get you?'

'Well first we want to know if we can trade skins.'

'Possibly, let me have a look at them.'

'Petrus go and bring in a couple of skins for the man to have a look at whilst I see what he has in his store.'

Petrus nodded and walked towards the door while Georgie began to look at the goods on offer. There were piles of wooden boxes; rolls of cloth filled a shelf and smoked hams hung from the ceiling and the thought of some decent food made him wonder if De Klerq had any beer on the premises. He had not had a drink in the six months or more spent living amongst an abstemious Boer population and then Petrus interrupted his thoughts, returning with a bundle of skins.

'Here, look at these,' he said laying them on the counter top.

'Not bad,' said De Klerq, pursing his lips and looking them over and feeling their texture, 'I think we might be able to do a deal.'

Nkosinathi was leading Rabanina and his men a merry dance, keeping well ahead of them and laying false trails but he had not covered as much ground as he might and now the little Khoisan had caught up with Rabanina.

'How far ahead Jolu?'

'An hour, maybe two.'

Rabanina looked across the veldt, searched the kloofs running towards the distant escarpment, and wondered where his quarry might be. He looked back at his men, signs of weariness showing on their faces.

'This is no time for rest; we will keep going until we catch him. We are close to the land of Hlubi and I don't want to upset the Induna by crossing the border, but if we have to then we will and once we have this elusive Zulu there will be a bonus for you.'

He looked at his each of his men, their fatigue forgotten, replaced by white toothed grins at the thought of a bonus. They were aware the man they were chasing was resourceful, elusive and able hide his trail but Jolu was back, a no more expert tracker in the whole of Zululand.

Ahead of them Nkosinathi had reached a small hill and halted his horse at its summit to scan the open country. Turning in his saddle he looked back expecting his pursuers to be nowhere in sight, but in the distance he saw a line of horses and riders. Shocked and dismayed at how close they were he kicked his horse into a fast trot to try to open the gap. He took a second look and then his horse stumbled, let out a loud snort and pulled up short. Alarmed, he slid off the saddle and ran his hand over the horses legs looking for a sign of distress. She was lame and would not be able keep up the blistering pace she had managed for so long and his heart sank.

'Beautiful one you have done well but you cannot fail me now. See if you can walk without me riding you,' he murmured.

Pulling the reigns taught he hoped that she might be able to walk a little but she did not move, resisting as he tugged.

'Come on girl; see if you can walk just a little way.'

This time she did, following on behind him, slowly at first, she gradually increased her pace. Nkosinathi dare not ride her for risk of permanent damage and dragging her along behind him he wondered how he might escape his pursuers then a familiar sound attracted his attention, the unmistakeable sound of running water.

He was feeling vulnerable, his stomach was turning at the thought of Dunn's men catching him and an involuntary sob passed his lips, the nadir of his resistance. Then a new resolve took hold, this new element, the river was playing on his mind and he knew what he needed to do.

'Come on girl, come on, there is some nice cool water to sooth your leg,' he said under his breath as they followed a path to the river's edge. The bushes were tall enough to obscure a rider less horse and using them as a screen Nkosinathi retraced his path, a dangerous strategy, but he knew what he was doing.

Two hours later, Jolu stopped near the riverbank and held up his hand as his eyes examined the ground for fresh tracks.

'What is it Jolu, why have you stopped?'

'He has dismounted and taken his horse towards the river. He will be trying to lay a false trail I think.'

Rabanina snorted in disgust, they had wasted many hours unravelling Nkosinathi's false trails and he did not want any more delay.

'Has he crossed the river?'

'I will go and see.'

The little man plunged into the water and splashed his way across. It was plausible that their quarry had crossed over and as soon as he reached the far bank, he began looking for fresh tracks. There were none and he waved to Rabanina to indicate that he would move along the bank to search, find where Nkosinathi had emerged from the water and for more than an hour, the little man searched. Occasionally he stepped back into the river to test its depth, finding the water shallow enough for a horse to negotiate then he would walk a little way inland, crouching to examine the earth. Eventually he stood up straight looking pensively along the water's course and then he crossed back over to the watching Rabanina.

'Boss, I cannot see any tracks. I think he is still in the river, the water is shallow and the bed is mostly sand, easy for a horse.'

'But he will not be able to travel as fast as on the bank side. Come on we will move faster if we follow the riverbank. We have him now.'

Luckily, Nkosinathi's tracks were invisible under the water and did not betray the fact that his horse was lame. If they knew that then Rabanina might have the foresight to search in both directions simultaneously. The confusion of Nkosinathi's own tracks and the uneven ground had left Jolu believing that nothing was wrong and that his quarry was simply using the river as cover for as long as he could and would re-emerge onto the bank-side at some time. That was indeed the case but Nkosinathi was heading in the opposite direction back into the lands of John Dunn, a possibility that had not yet crossed Rabanina or Jolu's minds.

After more than a mile of walking through the water, a stroke of luck presented itself and Nkosinathi gratefully embraced it. A fork in the river, confronted by a natural obstacle, the flow had split into two on either side of an expanse of rock rising no more than a foot above the surrounding landscape. He quickly decided on which route to take and for a further half mile traversed the new tributary until the going became too difficult for the horse. The rock seemed to spread for miles and he knew that his tracks would be almost impossible to see if he were careful, and so, leading the horse from the water, he crossed the hard rock plateau and into the surrounding bush.

Chapter 19

The Central hotel was a long wooden building painted the ubiquitous white; an English run establishment De Klerq had said offered beds for weary travellers. The bar was half-full when Georgie and Petrus walked in and through the haze of smoke and chatter, Georgie noticed there were two military men in officer's uniforms, a worry. He might still be recognised but on this occasion, neither of them paid any attention.

Tired though they were from their journey they had bartered with resolve. They had managed to exchange their skins for several sacks of foodstuffs, a few necessities and at De Klerq's suggestion, parted with two of the skins for cash to spend on a decent meal and a bed for the night and now Georgie was in sight of his first drink for many months.

'Two beers.'

The man behind the bar turned and picked two bottles off a low shelf and set them on the bar in front of him.

'India Pale Ale, I haven't had a taste of that for months,' said Georgie licking his lips in anticipation and beside him, Petrus looked on with trepidation, confused, his Calvinist upbringing discouraging the consumption of alcohol. The elders frowned upon the practice, Uitlanders and soldiers were well known to fall victim to its curse, even some of his own kind succumbed, but if a Burgher were found drunk in the street, his peers would ostracise him publicly and he had no wish to find himself in such a position.

'What's the matter Petrus?'

'I cannot drink this.'

'Of course you can. Listen we are not going to get drunk, just one or two and then we will see if we can get a hot dinner and a bed for the night.'

'Papa would be very annoyed if I were to drink alcohol, it's against our religion.'

'Well, it's not against my religion, in fact quite the opposite. If you really want to see what the outside world has to offer then you will be taking a drink sooner or later Petrus.'

Georgie smiled at his friend's naivety and called to the innkeeper.

'Would you have any hot food and a bed for the night?'

'Yes we have. Food today is game stew and there are beds out back in the bunkhouse. One shilling and sixpence for the stew, three shillings a night for the bed, oh and the beer is one shilling and ten pence ha'penny a bottle.'

'We'll take them,' said Georgie reaching into his pocket for some coins. 'Can we bed the horses somewhere?'

'Yes, out back by the bunkhouse is a trough and if you want feed for them that will be three pence each for the hay.

The innkeeper placed the bottles of ale on the counter top and called to his wife working in the small kitchen for two dinners.

'I will give you a nod when your dinner is ready gentlemen. In the meantime make yourselves at home.'

Georgie grinned and lifted his beer bottle in salute before leading Petrus to a table to sit and watch the clientèle until their first decent meal in days was ready.

'How are you feeling Petrus?' said Georgie finishing his dinner.

The young Boer's cheeks were red, he had a silly grin on his face, and as Georgie drained the last of his beer, he looked at him with some amusement. He remembered the first time he had become drunk in the company of fellow soldiers, how he had become sleepy and found it difficult walking.

'You feeling better after that,' he said pointing to Petrus's empty plate.

Petrus simply grinned back, smiling, remaining silent until a hiccup shook him back to life.

'Yes,' he managed to say.

'Come on; let's take a look at the horses and then a good night's sleep. We should be heading up into the Drakensberg soon and then it's a hard ride to the diamond fields. I can't wait to dig up a few diamonds, what do you say to that?'

Petrus looked back across the table through bleary eyes and did not answer.

Nkosinathi shivered, the night air had become cold and damp and his time spent walking in the cold waters of the stream had not helped. He had not eaten for many hours, his body was weary from the constant bursts of adrenaline and he needed to sleep.

The ground was devoid of good cover, only grass and boulders to hide him and his horse but several hundred yards away there was a thicket. He led his horse towards it, across softer earth, away from the hard ground that had been so useful in concealing his tracks.

Soft moss covered the ground and there was grass for his horse and for a while, he could relax but well before the dawn, in the silvery glow of the full moon Nkosinathi opened his eyes with a start. A thin white mist was spreading silently across the ground like ghostly fingers trying to hold him in its grip. Shivering he looked up at the still visible stars and then towards the horizon where a greyness signalled the dawn.

The mist made him invisible, only his horse's head and chest rising above the white cloud was visible, but it was enough for the little Khoisan. Blessed with a sixth sense inherent in his kind, Jolu had called upon the spirits to guide him when Nkosinathi's tracks had disappeared. Try as he might he could not find them again but the moonlight had been kind, he had spent all night searching and now they had reappeared. Faint yet clear enough for him to follow he had reached the riverbank and was staring at the ghostly apparition He had felt that he could go no further, the spirits did seem to want to guide him any longer and he decided he must rest until the sun returned. Looking round for a suitable place above the mist, he started in fright as across the river a detached horse's head appeared.

For a few seconds the Khoisan believed a spirit was watching him and his heart beat so fast he thought it might burst. The creature of the underworld was still a long way off, but even so he felt the hairs on the back of his neck rise up. Then the ghostly form moved, the head turned to look straight at him and and he felt his mouth turn dry. What was he was looking at? Confused and fearful he retraced his steps to secrete himself in a tangle of thorn bushes and await the rising of the sun.

Georgie opened his eyes and, after several seconds, stretched his arms above his head, releasing the stiffness from his muscles and from the next bunk; Petrus's snoring told him that he was still fast asleep. Reaching to the chair by his bed he picked his hat up from the top of the pile of clothes carefully took aim and with a deft flick of his wrist, spun the wide brimmed hat expertly towards the sleeping Boer.

'Wh...what! Oh!' exclaimed Petrus pushing the hat away and pressing the palms of his hand hard onto his face. 'Oh...and again, 'oh...'

'What's the matter Petrus how is your head this morning?'

Georgie felt mischievous; the feeling Petrus was experiencing was not new to him and he was glad that today he felt no ill effects. Lying back for a minute or two he listened to Petrus moaning.

'Want some breakfast? How about some bacon and coffee?'

'I don't think I can eat anything.'

'Come on, let's get up, we need to be on the road as soon as we can.'

Jumping out of bed he pulled on his clothes and with braces hanging loose, began to wash his face and neck from a basin of cold water.

'Come on Petrus, I know you Boers are not ones for washing much but it will make you feel better. I will fill some buckets for the horses while you pull yourself together.'

Petrus took a deep breath, climbed from the bed and began to wash. The cold-water was anathema to him, all the time he had lived at home he had never washed more than once a week and the experience on top of a hangover was less than pleasant but at least it brought him round.

'You know the road Georgie; you know how to get us to Kimberly from here?' he said joining his friend by the horses.

'I have travelled the road before, yes, look, over there, those hills, keep those on our right and follow the road to Dundee and then Ladysmith. We can resupply in Ladysmith if we need to before we tackle the passes up the escarpment to the Highveld.'

'Have you been into the Drakensberg?'

'No, but I have travelled the Great Karoo, it was just as difficult. I hear that once we get onto the Highveld and into the Free State, the going will be easier.'

'I have heard stories of our people making the trek. It was hard.'

'We are travelling light compared to those people and there are no Natives to worry about these days.'

The light began to spread; the sun's orange glow announced its imminent arrival and Nkosinathi knew he had delayed too long. He was cold and shivered as he saddled his horse, rubbing his arms to improve his circulation and then he slid his hand over the horse's forelocks. She seemed easier today and he wondered if he might try to ride her again. First though, he needed to get away from the river and the blinding, swirling mist and pulling his horse along behind him, he made for higher ground before deciding on which way he should go.

The mist extended only a few hundred yards in front of him and he as the ground rose he could see in the distance the Drakensberg escarpment. From his days with the smugglers knew that he should head towards those mountains, find a road and turn north, maybe his journey would be easier. He patted her neck and looked down at her hooves; she had walked well enough so far and putting his foot in the stirrup, he gingerly climbed into the saddle. Softly he talked to her, coaxed her forward and was relieved to find that she could carry his weight. By mid-day, they had travelled almost eight miles, the sun had warmed him and he had found some berries to eat but it was hard going. From time to time, he had stopped to look over his horse, running his hands down her legs, feeling for any sign of weakness but could find none. She seemed to be walking as if she had no discomfort and he was as sure as he could be that he had lost his pursuers. If he took it steady then maybe the two of them could reach the road north and leave the country of John Dunn.

The water in the coffee pot began to boil, emitting a cloud of steam and Georgie carefully lifted it from the fire, put in some of the coffee beans and let it brew.

'Coffee is ready Petrus,' he called out.

Petrus was twenty yards away lying flat on some raised ground, his eyes scanning the veldt for any sign of game and after a quick look around, he stood up and made his way back to the campfire.

'See anything?'

'Some wildebeest but they are too far away.'

Georgie lifted the coffee pot and filled the two enamel mugs, taking his own to sit back against a tree. Feeling in his jacket pocket, he pulled out a hard biscuit to dip into the hot liquid and Petrus did the same, joining him against the tree where the two of them quietly ate what was their dinner.

'Another two days or so and we will be heading up there Petrus,' said Georgie pointing towards the Drakensberg that had grown larger every day.

'I have heard tales of those mountains since I was a boy. The old men told me about hunting there, the steep valleys and clear water. I hear it is not so good for farming though, only few Boers up there.'

'Still quite a few I think, once you get across the Free State towards Kimberly. You would think any man who is so close to the diamond fields would not bother with farming.'

'Our way is not the way of the Uitlanders, we don't worship gold like you do, we love the country and the freedom it gives us.'

'But you are still coming to Kimberly with me.'

'Yes, I do not deny it but I look to see other men and other places. I did not think much about the outside world, but since the fighting and seeing other men from far away, I have become fascinated to see other places for myself. To come with you is an opportunity for me.'

Georgie smiled at his new friend, Petrus was still a simple farmer but he seemed to have an ambition that was lacking in his fellow Boers. They were forever moving as far from civilization as they could, shunning new ideas and wealth yet Petrus seemed to be heading in the opposite direction and Georgie was glad to have him along. Drinking from his mug, he let his eyes wander away from the splendour of the far mountains, let them come to rest no more than a few yards in front of him on a single blade of grass. He had not thought much about his predicament for a while but the proximity of the army at Newcastle and the realisation that Petrus was going against many of the things his people believed in had made him wonder. He was a deserter and as such could be court marshalled and probably shot if they caught him but weighed against that was a sense of freedom he had never known.

The army had changed mightily in the few short years he had been a soldier, changes that had left him feeling disillusioned. He had served his country and almost completed his service but a chance to escape had presented itself and he had taken it.

'What are you thinking about Georgie, I can see something is bothering you.'

'Oh...no, just thinking about the days ahead, wondering how rich I will be a year from now.'

Petrus frowned and drank the last of his coffee.

'You might be poorer in a year than you are now. Have you thought about that?'

'No, and I do not want to. I am going to see to my horse before I turn in, what about you.'

'Yes I will make sure she is happy for the night.'

The sun was almost touching the horizon when the two men dampened the fire and climbed into the small tent knowing that the next few days would be arduous.

Two hundred yards away the long grass parted and a black face appeared. Nkosinathi was ravenous, he had seen the smoke from the camp fire and had crept towards it. He saw two white men and hoped that they would be friendly enough to him, hoped that they would give him some food. Stepping boldly from cover he pulled his horse towards the smouldering camp-fire.

'I come to trade,' he said in his deep resonant voice, and from within the tent there was a scramble as Georgie and Petrus hurriedly dived out to confront him.

'Who are you, where did you spring from?' said Georgie to the figure sat cross-legged near the dying embers.

'I am Nkosinathi, son of Mondli of the Magwaza.'

'And what do you want?'

'Food, I have not eaten for three days and I am hungry.'

'Why haven't you eaten, what have you been doing,' asked Petrus, more inclined to shoot than talk.

'I have made a long and dangerous journey and there are many men chasing me.'

In the dying light Nkosinathi looked drawn and haggard, and Georgie at least felt some sympathy for him, yet even he was wary.

'Are you alone, have you a horse?'

'Yes I am alone and my horse is over there. I will fetch her.'

'You speak English.'

'Yes, I work with white men as a guide for many moons and learn to speak like them.'

'Well I'll be dammed. Go fetch your horse boy and we will rustle up some food for you,' said Georgie eliciting a frown from Petrus

Nkosinathi was thankful; it showed in his eyes, even a white man could see that and as he stood up he looked Georgie in the eye and in that instant a memory stirred inside the Englishman, something deep, something painful and it puzzled him.

'You have a gun,' said Petrus when Nkosinathi returned.

'Yes.'

'But you didn't carry it when you crept up on us.'

'No.'

'Why not?'

'If a native carries a gun in the shadows then he runs the risk of being killed and I do not want you to kill me.'

Petrus nodded, it was a reasonable assumption and he admired the man's bravery. He for one would not be without his gun no matter what the situation.

'Here, some biltong and cold beans. That will have to do for now,' said Georgie handing an open tin of beans and some dried meat to their visitor.

Nkosinathi took the offering in both hands, devouring the food like a hungry Hyena and demonstrating the depth of his plight. Petrus and Georgie looked at each other and began to relax, believing the Zulu's story.

'These men, who are they, why are they after you?'

'And where are they?' chirped in Petrus.

'They are the border patrol of John Dunn. They look for smugglers and traders crossing his land to take their share of the goods and to make them pay money.'

'John Dunn eh...I have seen him. When Cetshwayo was defeated, the authorities divided his Kingdom and John Dunn got the biggest part. He is a white chief, is that right?'

'Yes, he is the chief over my father's kraal and he takes everything we have.'

'So why are you being chased?'

'I am my father's son and I kill game to feed the village but I need more cartridges and can only get them from the Whiteman's trading post to the north.'

'So you crossed John Dunn's land and his men thought you were a smuggler?' said Petrus.

'Yes.'

Georgie looked at Nkosinathi a little closer, his features seemed familiar and yet he knew no Zulus.

Perhaps he had killed too many during the war and they were beginning to all look alike and then he wondered if this man been a part of the Zulu army, tall and muscular he was the right age.

'Were you ever one of Cetshwayo's warriors?'

Nkosinathi's eyes flashed, memories returned and at the same time, Georgie thought about the warrior he was about to kill.

'Did you fight at Ulundi?'

Nkosinathi seemed not to hear him until eventually he finished eating and his eyes met Georgie once more. The white man was looking straight at him, recognition flickering in his eyes and in only a few seconds Nkosinathi re-lived the last desperate moments of the battle at Ulundi. the British square, the warriors of the uVe falling around him and the sound of their bugles. Then the square of red and white had parted and mounted men had poured out to overwhelm them and with their spirit broken the Zulu army had fled. Fearless warriors running from a hopeless situation as fast as they could and he had followed. Although fit and strong, the exertions of the long marches, lack of sleep and food had eventually worn him down to the point where he could run no more and he had turned to face his executioner, a soldier in a red coat pointing his gun at him.

However, he had lived, the horse soldier in the red jacket was ready to kill him but he did not pull the trigger. Instead, he raised the barrel of his gun, given him what was almost a salute before letting him go and for the second time he was looking into those eyes.

'You remember don't you?'

'Yes, you spared my life and now you have saved it again.'

'I hardly think a tin of beans has saved your life,' said Georgie with some embarrassment.

'You know this man Georgie?'

'I think so. We last met on the battlefield of Ulundi did we not?'

'Yes.'

'Let's make some more coffee. Do you want some more biltong?'

Nkosinathi grinned and nodded his head and Georgie reached down to heap some dry twigs on the embers.

'I think I would like another cup of coffee to help me over the shock,' he said putting the still half-full pot back on the fire while Nkosinathi sat happily chewing on a piece of biltong and a puzzled Petrus looked on. He had not fully grasping the situation, did not understand the camaraderie that seemed to lie between Georgie and the black stranger, a situation that went completely against his natural instinct. The natives were inferior, why would a British soldier be so friendly and accommodating to a Zulu once a sworn enemy?

'What happened to you after I let you go?'

Nkosinathi recounted all he could of that fateful day, how he had stumbled along half dead to escape the horse soldiers and although Georgie had spared him, he had enough common sense to realise that another of the enemy might not be so generous.

'It was the end of our King, the end of our way of life. The new chiefs are greedy and cruel, bleed the people dry and that is why I wander the land today.'

'Will you go back to your kraal?'

'I cannot, they know who my father is, they will go there and wait for my return and if I do they will kill me.'

Nkosinathi looked sad, gazing into the fire as it came back to life and after a brief silence Georgie asked, 'so, what will you do now?'

'I do not know. I will trade the few skins I have left for cartridges, go to live in forests until I feel safe again.'

'What's your name, I never asked your name.'

'Nkosinathi.'

'Well Sonathi I am Georgie and this is Petrus. How would you like to tag along with us, we are heading for the diamond diggings in Kimberly and we could do with another pair of strong hands to help us.'

Petrus swung his head towards Georgie, shocked that he should invite a native along but resisted the temptation to complain.

'Well, Koson...'

'Nkosinathi.'

'That's a hell of a name boy; I think we'll just call you Koso if you don't mind.'

Nkosinathi swallowed some of the biltong and grinned, he did not mind, he did not mind at all.

Chapter 20

From a farmer's point of view the countryside was shocking with not a sign of vegetation anywhere on the desolate red brown landscape. Petrus pulled up his horse and pushed his hat back on his head as he took in the scene finally emitting a low whistle.

'God in heaven's name what is all this?'

'Well boys, we made it, look at that lot,' said Georgie enthusiastically.

'Look at what? It looks to me like the devil's work.'

'No Petrus, not the devil. Men have dug the hole with their bare hands and some have grown rich on what they dug up.'

He had dreamed of a moment like this for a long time, often wondering what would have happened to him if he had stayed with Dickie Henderson. The time spent here with the army of the Vaal as a young private had been enlightening and one or two of the older men had seen the possibilities. For them, life as diamond prospectors was far more appealing than soldiering and they had deserted to go in search of their fortunes. It seemed a lifetime since he had cast his eye over this place the so called "Big Hole", a vast area of diggings, mine dumps and miners shacks something had changed though, this was mining on a scale he had not seen before. Diggings cluttered the terrain almost as far as he could see as men fought to uncover the wealth hidden in the red earth and he could not wait to join them.

'Well Petrus, what do you think?'

'It is hell on earth that's what I think. In the bible, Jeremiah tells of Gods displeasure with idolatry, worshipping other gods and I think the god of money is here. This place looks like Gods destruction of the towns of Judah. What do we do now?'

With the back of his hand, Georgie rubbed the sweat from his brow and wondered. He had not expected such a change; his previous experience of the place an inadequate preparation for his foray into diamond mining.

'Er...I think the first thing is to ride into town and see what's going on. I..Er, think we might have to purchase a claim off someone or maybe the authorities.'

'Buy a claim! With what?'

England's south coast slipped slowly past as Ellen, leant on the ship's rail and followed its contours with mixed feelings. She had seen and learned a lot during her time spent in London, she had become a very rich woman and she had Patrick, her, a rough ex-soldier. At times though, he could be tender and caring and as she gazed across the water he came to stand beside her, wrapping his arm around her waist and pulling her to him. She liked that, he was a strong man and he made her feel safe.

'I wonder if we will ever see England again.'

'What makes you say that Ellen?'

'We are going half way round the world and who knows what we will find.'

'We will find Georgie, that's what.'

He looked at her and smiled, encouraging her to believe that she was right even though he had his reservations. Her new found wealth gave her a freedom to do almost anything she desired and he wondered if returning to South Africa in search of Georgie really was a wise decision.

He had served for ten long years, most of that time alongside Georgie and they had become best friends as well as comrades in arms. He had read the newspaper reports, all of them, searching for any scrap of news that might indicate Georgie's fate but all he found was a brief paragraph reporting on prisoners of war and his name was on the list. That was a year ago and since then he had heard nothing and was about to say so when Ellen thumped the rail.

'You said he talked of deserting, wanting to look for diamonds. I know Georgie better than anyone Patrick, we will find him,' she said with conviction.

He had fought many battles in South Africa and he feared the worst because even if Georgie had survived the fighting he could have easily died of wounds or disease. But to her credit, Ellen's belief that he was still alive never faltered, she was adamant that he was still alive and that she was going to find him and he admired her for that. She had been so confident when they had decided to take the steamer but he knew of the dangers his friend would have faced during the fighting and the potential consequences if he had deserted. Just because the army had said that there was no record of him either alive or dead it signified nothing. Perhaps she was right, perhaps Georgie was still alive.

The big Hole was vast, with a perimeter of a mile, getting on three hundred feet deep and criss crossed by rickety, fragile looking bridges that separated the claims. Surrounding the diggings, dirty white tents were springing up daily almost as flowers after a desert storm. Thousands of men, white, black, every hue in between with picks and shovels swarmed over the diggings and Georgie could not even begin to count their numbers.

'I never see anything like this, I did not know so many men lived on the earth,' said Petrus in astonishment.

Georgie might have laughed at the simple Boer except that he was a little overawed himself, astonished at how much the place had grown and he was feeling unsure of how to proceed.

'I think we had better head for town, see if we can find somewhere to pitch the tent, water the horses.'

'Which way to the town, I cannot see any buildings other than that shack over there,' said Petrus pointing towards a corrugated affair with hastily painted wording above the doorway. Georgie followed his gaze towards the shack seemingly an important element in the mining operation judging by the number of men congregated around it and he was curious for a closer look.

'The Barnato Diamond Mining Company, I wonder who they are.'

Petrus and Nkosinathi had no idea,   the noise and the red dust rising slowly from the huge man made crater was beyond their comprehension and they did not reply. The door to the shack opened and from the dark interior a man dressed in a grey woollen suit and bowler hat appeared, stood silhouetted in the doorway for a few seconds before he stepped outside and Georgie decided to hail him.

'Say mister, how does a fella get hold of a claim to work down there?'

'With difficulty my friend. Claims are bought and sold but you have to be in the know and you will need a deal of money. Why are you men looking to invest?'

Invest, what did he mean?

'Er...we were looking to do a little prospecting for diamonds, find a small claim maybe.'

The man compressed his lips and his eyes became a little vacant, he had seen more than enough *rooineks* in Kimberly and like so many before, he expected them to leave town disappointed and broke.

'I can't help you I'm afraid gentlemen. The native might find work as a labourer, there is a shortage of black labour this year but you two, I do not know. Maybe you could make a living killing a few wild animals for meat; there is always a demand for meat. There is a market in town most days, in the square. Saturday is a busy day and it's still only Thursday.

A dry smile appeared on his face and he turned to walk away, leaving Georgie, Petrus and Nkosinathi to gawk after him.

'You any good at hunting, Zulu?' asked Petrus

Nkosinathi had not followed the conversation too well but he understood and grinned, his strong white teeth lighting up his face as he said. 'I kill many *insephe*.'

'Springbok eh, I guess you can. I hear you boys are handy with your spears but what about your gun?'

'I can shoot but I have no cartridges.'

Georgie twisted in his saddle and looked at his two companions. They had lived on small game crossing the Drakensberg, and if the Zulu could shoot then the three of them might be able to make a living until they could find a claim to work.

'How about it boys, shall we do a little hunting?'

Petrus chewed his bottom lip and nodded confidently, considering for a moment where he thought they might find the best game. They had crossed the mountain range, then the Highveld and he reckoned that about ten or fifteen miles back, in amongst the long grass they would find springbok, blesbok, and maybe some wildebeest. Hunting was second nature to him and having seen the chaos of the mines he preferred to make his living from hunting. He looked at the mine, just a hole in the ground, bigger than anything he had ever seen and listened to the metallic clatter of thousands of picks and shovels chipping away as the miners searched for the precious diamonds.

Surrounding the perimeter of the excavation was a wooden structure supporting hundreds of ropes. These descended into the depths to bring, buckets and leather bags full of spoil to the surface, each rope hauled by black labourers or a donkey attached to a treadmill. Once at the surface the labourers tipped the shale into waiting carts their melodious singing adding to the cacophony from below.

'I think hunting is more in my line Georgie.'

'What about you Koso, do you fancy trying your hand at mining?'

Nkosinathi grinned, his black face lustrous in the sunlight. 'I do anything.'

'Good, then let's have a ride into the bush and see what we can find. We are hunters today and maybe we'll be miners tomorrow.'

Nkosinathi just grinned, his ears found it hard to take in the noise but his eyes had picked out Zulu, Xhosa and men from many tribes and it was good to hear familiar chants.

Petrus was an experienced hunter and after making camp, he led the way towards the open plain early the following morning. First, they crossed several miles of scrubland before reaching low hills with the promise of good grazing. Georgie was right behind him, Nkosinathi brought up the rear, and leaving the flat bushland, they spread out. They rode in silence, each alert for signs of game and the Zulu was the first to spot their prey. Cupping his hands over his mouth, he made the sound of a Nightjar alerting Petrus who turned his head to see Nkosinathi pointing towards several black dots in the distance and for more than an hour they circled downwind of a small group of blesbok.

Nkosinathi was in his element as he closed with the blesbok, their distinctive white faces and curved horns familiar from his days hunting up near the Tugela River. Petrus watched his movement and realised he was a natural hunter, feeling a sudden respect for him and nudging his horse slowly towards Nkosinathi he handed him a cartridge.

'You will not have time to shoot anymore, make it count.'

Nkosinathi grinned, held out his hand to take the small brass cylinder and slipped it into the rifle breach. They were ready and dismounted, tied the reins of their animals to some bushes and began to creep towards the blesbok. Petrus whispered that he would take the first shot, it would alert the animals and Georgie and Nkosinathi must shoot as soon after his shot as they could.

The sun was well past its zenith, the air was still and the blesbok were unaware of the hunters until a big male, the leader of the group, lifted his head and sniffed the air. Something had alerted him, he was nervous, both Petrus and Nkosinathi understood. Bringing their rifles to bear they prepared to take aim and Georgie followed suit. They were at extreme range and Petrus knew there was a good chance they might miss but he had to try. Then the animals panicked, the male deciding that it was time to leave. Bounding across the ground, he believed that he was leading the herd away from the danger but whatever it was that had spooked him it was not the men. He came straight at the hunters secreted in the long grass, Petrus took his shot the bullet finding its mark in the bull's chest, and for a few yards, it stumbled on before crumpling to the ground and then two more shots rang out and a second animal crashed to the ground.

'Well it looks like you two are the regular hunters in this outfit,' said Georgie with a frown. He had always considered himself a good shot but he had missed his target and was feeling a little envious of the other two.

'We will take them back to town? asked Petrus.

'I reckon so, Saturday is supposed to be a big market day and maybe we can sell this meat and trade the skins. Let's find a camp site close to town and maybe we'll find buyers tomorrow morning.'

Saturday was a day off for the miners and the road into Kimberly was busy as the hunters made their way into town. Passing whitewashed buildings, they made their way towards the town square where the discordant noise of men shouting and the trader's bells met their ears. It was an astonishing panorama of Boer wagons laden with fresh produce, the oxen sat lazily beside them and in the centre of the square traders had set up stalls with piles of blankets, cooking utensils and all manner of items useful to the miners. The bars and hotels were already doing a roaring trade and from the brothels, girls in brightly coloured dresses and with blackened teeth beckoned them in.

'Blimey, will you look at that lot. The man told us it would be busy. Have you ever seen anything like it Petrus?'

'I have seen plenty of markets Georgie but not like this,' said Petrus slipping his hat to the back of his head and beside him Nkosinathi appeared wide-eyed.

'I think we should find a pitch over there, look some men are already selling game I can see springbok and wildebeest,' said Georgie. 'Stay here and I will have a stroll round to see if I can find out the prices to charge.'

Petrus nodded, it was a good idea and took Georgie's reigns as he dismounted and disappeared into the crowd towards the butchers' stalls.

He noticed some stalls thinly distributed with meat and at one, a rowdy miner was arguing with a trader attempting to reduce his price. He was having none of it and stood his ground and Georgie reasoned that meat must be in short supply today.

'How much for the big one?' he heard a man call out and point to a side of wildebeest.

'Ten pounds,' said the butcher.

'And those chickens, how much for those chickens?'

'I will do the chickens at two shillings and sixpence each.'

'How much for the lot?'

'Six chickens at two shillings and sixpence is...let me see,' said the butcher, a twinkle in his eye.

'No, not two shillings and sixpence each, tell me, how much if I buy all of them?'

'And the wildebeest?'

'Yes, and the wildebeest.'

'Ten guineas for the lot.'

The buyer smiled, and pleased at the reduction dug his hand into his pocket for the money.

'Do you want me to cut the beast up for you?'

'Yes, I'll call two of my labourers over to carry it back to camp.'

The labourers appeared and between them they carried off the carcass and chickens leaving Georgie to watch and wonder. He had seen Petrus expertly skin an animal and cut up the meat for biltong but they had nowhere here to perform the task. It was hardly a good idea to butcher their animals on the ground. Then he had an idea.

'Say mister.'

'What?' said the butcher not looking up from his work.

'How much would you charge to skin and cut up an animal like that.'

'Eh....'

The man stopped what he was doing to look at Georgie, his eyes narrowing.

'Myself and by friends are new in town and we have two blesbok to sell but we have nowhere to butcher them properly.'

'Ten shillings each and if you wait until I sell the rest of my stock I will sell them for you for a small consideration.'

'It's a deal, I will be back shortly.'

It day turned out more successful than they could have hoped. The butcher was as good as his word, skinning and selling the blesbok, and after they had found ready buyers for the skins, they were more than five pounds richer. To celebrate their good fortune, the two white men found a bathhouse.

'Oh this is good,' said Georgie laying back in the large galvanized tub, and closing his eyes. He was feeling content, they had made enough money to survive in this town for a time, found a way at least of making a living but he wanted more. Diamonds were the main aim, enough to make him rich, enough for him to return to the De Witt's farm and marry Annika.

Suddenly he sat up, splashing warm water across the floor, causing Petrus to give him a puzzled look. He knew that he was in love with Annika but had never considered marrying her. He could do with a drink.

'Say Petrus, how do you fancy a drink? Let's find a decent place to eat and have a few beers.'

Petrus nodded his head slowly, still wary of the effects of alcohol but after his first ever bath, he was ready for anything. Bathing was not a common attribute of the Boers, normally he would either dunk himself in a river or throw a bucket of cold water over himself, but this was different and he was enjoying it.

They found Nkosinathi squatting against a wall near the bathhouse, his job to keep an eye on the horses. He had spent his time swirling the end of a stick nonchalantly in the red dust, making patterns and watching the world go by and thinking. Since the war he had spent a lot of time amongst the white men, learned of their customs but he had never seen such a cosmopolitan multitude that passed him by today. He heard many different tongues, English, Afrikaans, yet others he did not recognise, and then there were the Native labourers. Some of them were dressed as the white men, loose fitting woollen trousers and cotton shirts while others wore tribal attire and he took pleasure in noting their clans but then his companions appeared. Jumping to his feet he shook his head in disbelief.

'You are not Petrus!'

Georgie laughed and Petrus looked a little sheepishly at the Zulu. He had debated for some time whether to shave off his beard. The Burghers wore their beards as a badge to show the world that they were Boers and proud of it but Georgie had persuaded him that the heavy work they soon hoped to undertake would be more difficult with the bushy growth covering the bottom half of his face.

'It will be hot during the day Petrus, did you see the miners, everyone looked uncomfortable in the heat and a beard will only make things worse for you.'

Petrus had looked long and hard into the small broken mirror in the bathhouse, his only concession to vanity, and had finally agreed.

'Alright, I shave it off but once we finish here I grow it again,' he had said rather grumpily.

'When we finish here I too will grow a beard. Let's hope we will be rich men when that happens,' said Georgie stroking his chin aware more than a disguise of some sort might help the army to forget about him.

'Koso, do you want something to eat? Petrus and I are going to find a canteen and have a good feed. Want to come along?'

Nkosinathi threw his stick away and followed the two White men as they strode across the street towards the canteen. It was a two-story affair built of wood and called 'The Star of the West' and was full of half-drunk miners. There were black ones and as well as white enjoying a little respite from their toil and Georgie had to push his way through to reach the bar.

'What's on the menu today?'

'Anything you like off the board,' said the bar tender pointing to a blackboard above the bar. 'Now gentlemen what can I get you to drink?'

'Three beers and three plates of your mutton stew I think. Yes three plates of mutton stew.'

The man slid the first of the tankards across the counter top. 'That will be a shilling each for the beer and one shilling and sixpence each for the dinner, seven shillings and sixpence please. You can sit over there and I will send the food across in a few minutes.'

Clutching their tankards the three of them sat at a small table near a window overlooking the street and Petrus leaned back on his chair to take in the bar's surroundings. Men congregated around the bar, waiters in long white aprons rushed past with tankards of beer and plates of steaming food and he felt his stomach cry out. Nkosinathi seemed more interested in his beer and had no such desire to observe, instead he lifted his tankard to his lips.

Georgie watched them both and grinned, drinking beer was not new to him, it was a soldier's duty to drink. He and his comrades had consumed gallons of the stuff in their free time and he knew what it could do to the inexperienced. From their stop in Newcastle he knew Petrus was not used to drinking beer and he suspected that Nkosinathi was more used to the weaker native home brews and thought he should keep an eye on them both.

Lifting his tankard, he drained half of its volume, delighted at washing away as his thirst. Nearby two natives began shouting at each other drunk and slurring their words. It was obvious an argument had developed and he watched with interest as one of the men rose to his feet, a big man, bigger than Nkosinathi and bent on violence. However, the drink had made him incapable of controlling his posture and he staggering backwards to fall flat on the floor. The incident caused uproar, white miners, none to sober themselves, laughed and taunted the native group with cries of 'get out you drunks' and 'learn to hold your liquor' and as the commotion subsided, his companions hauled the drunken native to his feet. By the white miner's reaction, it seemed to Georgie that it was a common occurrence and as if to confirm his thoughts the waiter arrived with their food muttering 'Stupid blacks, all they can do is drink themselves into oblivion.'

Nkosinathi was the first to begin eating, devouring his food like a wild animal.

'Hey steady on, you will give yourself indigestion.'

'And don't get yourself in a state like those men if you want to stay with us,' added Petrus.

Nkosinathi halted the progress of his fork half way between plate and mouth, his eyes bright and joyful.

'Not worry boss, I have seen what the White man's drink can do. I not get like that but I am hungry.'

Georgie laughed, he liked Nkosinathi and he was hungry too.

The miners were a rowdy lot, laughter, loud voices and the clink of their glasses filling the room and above it all, a haze of tobacco smoke hanging like a fog. Peering through the haze, Georgie spotted a card school in progress. Army life had taught him the finer points of card games, playing against the men of his platoon to supplement his meagre pay and he looked on with interest. One man in particularly drew his attention, a flamboyant character in a top hat and wearing a silk waistcoat. He had a cigar clenched between his teeth and exaggerated the movement of his lips as he carried on his conversation, adding to the impression that he was a man in charge. Intrigued, Georgie could not help the urge to see how well he played.

'Do you want another beer Petrus?

Petrus declined, placing the flat of his hand over his tankard but Nkosinathi had a look in his eye that said he did.

'One more Koso, only one more, we don't want you drunk and disorderly, not yet anyway, we have to find a claim to work and I don't want any trouble. When we do find some diamonds and get rich, then that will be the time to get drunk.

'You seem confident.'

'Petrus, if there is one thing I learned in the army it is to believe you will win.'

Petrus grunted, the Boer community had never believed they would win so decisively against an organized and better-equipped foe yet they had. Maybe mining for diamonds required more than belief and maybe more than hard work, perhaps some luck was needed too.

'Let's have a look round, see if we can strike up a conversation with a miner or two, see what we can find out about getting hold of a claim. Last time I was here it seemed easy enough but even then we were swindled. Better keep our wits about us Petrus.'

'I think this place is full of swindlers Georgie. Perhaps we should consider joining their ranks.'

Georgie was surprised at Petrus's words, so out of character for him to think about swindling and it startled him.

'Why do you say that?'

'I have been watching and listening, some of these men would steal the shirts off a friend's back given the chance.'

Georgie knew enough about human nature to agree, but what had made Petrus say such a thing he wondered?

'I fancy a walk over to that card game, see what's going on. Maybe we can judge for ourselves how honest and trustworthy they are around here. There is nothing like a high stakes card game for exposing a man's soul, especially if there's drink involved. Koso, go and keep an eye on the horses while me and Petrus take a look around.'

'What about another beer boss?'

'I'll buy you a beer later, first we need to find a claim to work and when we have done that then I will buy you a beer my friend.'

Nkosinathi grinned, unfazed by the refusal. Georgie had saved his life, he was a good man and until he felt safe enough to return home, he would do as he asked.

'Come on Petrus, let's have a look round.'

Nkosinathi left to tend to the horses and the two White men sauntered across the room. It was crowded with miners and traders of many different nationalities and ethnicities and amongst them were a number of Boers. Their beards and clay pipes the giveaway and it took Petrus by surprise to see his own kind drinking and gambling as much as the Britishers. He had grown up to believe they were ungodly pursuits, against the creed of the Dopper and it seemed that his desire to experience the world was turning up unexpected challenges.

Petrus had no time to dwell, the card school was in full swing and Georgie was eager to take a look. He pushed through a group and joined several men come to see what was happening. Apart from one man there was nothing that made this card school particularly outstanding except for a man in the top hat and brightly coloured waistcoat.

'The Duke is making mincemeat of those poor unfortunates. It is amazing how he seems to always win,' said one of the onlookers.

'Always, he must be a clever man,' said another.

'A real Duke?' asked Georgie.

'Naw, they call him the Duke of Kimberly because he acts as if he owns the place. He's not a real Duke...I don't think.'

Georgie watched the Duke make ready to deal, his cigar held tight between his teeth and shuffling the pack with precision. First he fanned them out on the table, slid the two halves back together and then shuffled at a speed that almost defied belief.

Georgie smiled to himself, he had seen the same performance many times. He remembered his early days as a thief and pickpocket when men like this set up small tables in the street, accosted passers-by to try their hand at various games of trickery. He remembered how he had watched the shenanigans, once for two hours, trying to see how the man worked his trick. He never did find out but he could hear the man again, 'find the knave and I will pay you back double your wager.'

It seemed to work; intriguing some passers-by enough to placed bets of sixpence or a shilling and it seemed simple enough to win. One of the three cards lying face down on the table was the knave and all they had to do was turn it up. But they rarely did and yet when it was his turn, the man always deftly turned up the knave. The punters, poor souls, often became desperate, placing all they had on the table, convinced they were about to redeem their losses and more but they never did. Yes, he remembered those days well, and his name, what was it, ah yes, "the Gypsy".

'Come on my laads, place your bets, let us see that cash of yours, let us see if you can take mine away from me.'

"The Gypsy", Georgie remembered him, his strong East End accent barking out his patter and this man was just the same, a swindler and Georgie's instinct told him to be careful of the Duke.

The game was getting underway and a silence descended on the players as they concentrated on their hands and then the play started in earnest. The Duke won the first game and the next two, the pile of coins and notes in front of him steadily increased but the next game was different. With his face expressionless, The Duke lost the game, and one happy gambler scooped his winnings but Georgie remembered the Gypsy. Let the losers win, let them think they have a chance and they will stay longer and that way he would clean them out completely. Stroking his chin Georgie began to wonder how the man with his flamboyant behaviour and incessant patter could be so successful and it seemed to him that he must be cheating.

'He is a clever man alright. I never saw anyone with such luck,' said Petrus as they walked towards the horses.

'It's not luck Petrus, he's cheating and I want to find out how.'

'You going to play against him?'

'Maybe, I need to know how he does it first. I have seen his type before; we'll come back tomorrow and take a closer look.'

Darkness was descending as the hunters pitched their tent and settled down by the fire. The blackened coffee pot had seen some service during the past few weeks and as Georgie watched it boil, he spoke to Petrus.

'What do you think about selling the pack horses and the ponies?'

'Why, what do you mean?'

'Well firstly they are your horses, but we don't need them anymore, not unless we decide to stay as hunters forget mining but if we do find a claim to buy we will need some money.'

Petrus fell silent as Georgie's words sank, making him think. His pony was his life, he had ridden ponies since he could walk and had never been without one but there was some logic in Georgie's words.

'How much are they worth in this part of the world do you think?'

'I don't really know fifteen or twenty pounds apiece maybe.'

'How much do we need for a claim?'

'That's a hard one. I was speaking to a couple of miners in the canteen whilst we watched the card game and they told me that there are very few claims for sale these days and they cost hundreds of pounds.'

'And we don't have hundreds of pounds.'

'No we don't.'

'So we stay as hunters and sell the meat.'

'Well not exactly, it seems that a lot of claim holders are prepared to split their claims into four parts to sell or rent out to raise some money.'

'How much will one of those cost?'

'Maybe two, three hundred pounds.'

Petrus let out a low whistle and Nkosinathi got to his feet as the water in the pot began to boil.

'I make the coffee.'

'Yes, good boy Koso, I think we need a hot drink right now.'

'Why don't we try to sell the pack horses and keep the ponies for now in case we have to hunt for game?'

Nkosinathi looked up from making the coffee, a puzzled look on his face. 'I not sell my horse.'

Georgie let out a sigh, things were not as easy as he had thought and he could feel resistance to his plan.

'Alright, we'll keep the ponies and Koso's horse for now but if we get the chance to buy a claim we should sell them.'

The other two looked at each other and then at Georgie, nodding agreement and Georgie could not help grinning at them.

Saturday was a day of rest for the miners and they would be in town in strength according to the locals so today might be a good chance to sell the animals said Georgie. Petrus and Nkosinathi agreed, their feelings mixed, but if they were going to succeed then it seemed inevitable they should sell their mount.

Petrus was beginning to enjoy his time in Kimberly and he led the way. He had seen what money could buy, realised that some of the more enlightened of his people were happy to indulge in the pleasures of the mining town and although It was against his upbringing he liked it, liked the noise and colour, the excitement and decided that he was not about to give it up.

The primitive dirt road was filling up with ox wagons lumbering over the uneven ground, miners and groups of black labourers on foot were heading towards Kimberly. Saturday was the the one day they could indulge themselves, and when Georgie, Petrus and Nkosinathi reached they found the market square buzzing with excitement. Boer wagons lined the street the vendors shouting at the tops of their voices and colourfully dressed natives were everywhere.

Nkosinathi stared wide-eyed at the scene, he had seen the white man's market in Pretoria when he was with the gunrunners but that was nothing compared to this. In the Orange Free State native labourers were under few restrictions, the atmosphere was relaxed and carefree. Some Zulus were poking at a pile of vegetables on a Boer wagon he could not help but laugh as the owner of the stall tried to shoo them away and then one looked up, recognizing a fellow Zulu and called out a greeting.

'*Sanibonani.*'

'*Unjani,*' replied Nkosinathi, 'I am well,' and as he rode past each of the group waved him a greeting.

'You've made some friends already,' said Georgie.

'Yes, they are of my father's clan.'

Georgie understood; Nkosinathi would have family just like anyone else although he had never spoken of them.

'Do you miss your family?'

'Oh yes, but I cannot go home yet.'

Before Georgie could probe any deeper, Petrus called a halt at the edge of the square and dismounted, pulling his packhorse closer.

'Well this is as good a place as anywhere to try and sell the horses. What do you think?'

'As good as anywhere,' said Georgie joining him and before he had even dismounted Petrus, eager to show his skill as an auctioneer, began encouraging a crowd to form.

'Horses for sale, horses for sale, 'he shouted at the top of his voice and then, in his native afrikans, '*Perde te koop, Perde te koop.*'

It seemed to work, heads turned, several men wandered over to see what was going on and before many minutes had passed a crowd had gathered.

'How much do you want for these animals?' asked a man in the middle of the small crowd

'Whatever you want to pay mister.'

'Well,' said the man, his eyes lighting up, 'how about a five pounds.'

'That is a very generous offer my friend and I would take five pounds but I think there are some here who would pay me more. How about you sir,' he said to an onlooker, 'What will you give me for this fine animal?' He patted the pack horse on its back and then, running his hands up its neck he took hold of the animal's lips and pulled them apart to expose its teeth. 'Look how healthy she is, a fine animal and she will be a credit to whoever buys her.'

The man held up his hand to show that he was not interested but in amongst the crowd another offered six pounds and then another voice called out seven and before long the bidding had reached twenty two pounds.

'Twenty two pounds I am bid. Come on my friends you can do better than that. Who will give me twenty three?'

But there was no answer, twenty two pounds was the final bid, generous thought Georgie, but hoped for more as he looked over the crowd but no further bids were forthcoming.

'Why thank you sir, if you will give me the money you can take this fine animal right now.'

Without ceremony the man dug into his pocket and pulled out a wad of notes, peeling off several to hand to Petrus and the young Burgher shook the man's hand to seal the deal.

'That was easy enough,' he said out of the corner of his mouth to Georgie. Lets try the other one while we have a crowd.'

Petrus was soon back in his stride, '*Perde te koop,* Horse for sale.' The crowd had swollen to well over a hundred onlookers and the bidding was brisk, this time reaching the handsome sum of twenty five pounds leaving the three of them overjoyed as the crowd dispersed and they counted their spoils.

Chapter 21

The morning was chilly, a light mist covering the ground, as the three future prospectors saddled up. It would be another hour before the sun warmed them through but by then they would be in Kimberly.

'What do you think of it,' Georgie asked Nkosinathi as they entered the main square already bustling with people. Nkosinathi did not answer directly because he a strange sight that had caught his attention and he was transfixed by it. Finally, he pointed towards a life size wooden effigy of an American Indian chief standing sentinel like outside one of the bars.

'He looks like a Zulu but he is the wrong colour. I have never seen a man that colour.'

'Ha ha,' laughed Georgie. 'Someone is using it to entice customers to drink in his bar. I must say it is a strange thing to see here.'

Georgie knew a little of American Indians and learned from soldiers newly arrived from England that the American Wild West was popular in England. Some had brought penny dreadfuls with them, he had read them from cover to cover, marvelling at the colourful stories of that country, and it occurred to him that South Africa was not so different.

'Never mind, he's not real and there is no chance of meeting a real Red Indian out here.'

Petrus looked on, taken by the figure almost as much as Nkosinathi. He had never heard of America and if this was their native, then he guessed they would have just as much trouble with their indigenous people as the burghers did with theirs.

'We going to the same bar as yesterday Georgie?'

'I think so, I want to see if the Duke is holding court, I want to see if I can figure out how he is cheating and then we'll play him at his own game if we can. We need more money for a claim and maybe we can win it at the card tables.'

Petrus pursed his lips, unhappy that they were to rely upon gambling, an occupation he had been warned against many times. Then he saw a sign above a single story office further along the street.

'Look *Diamant Koopers,* that could be a good place to find a claim for sale. What do you think?'

'Why not, a diamond dealer will know what's happening in and around the mine. Yes let's see if he is open for business.'

They turned their ponies towards the corrugated shack serving as the diamond buyer's office and found several men lounging about on the verandah. They were a surly looking bunch watching them in silence as they dismounted.

'Hello, any of you know where we can get hold of a claim?'

A tall man in a grey, crumpled suit leaning against the doorframe lazily changed his posture.

'What you lookin' for?'

'A claim in the Big Hole, do you know of any for sale?'

'I might, come inside and let's talk.'

'Petrus, you come with me. Koso look after the horses while we're gone.'

Nkosinathi nodded his head and took the reins from his two companions as they dismounted and made their way up some rickety steps and followed the man into the gloomy interior. Georgie could not see much until his eyes adjusted and he could see that the sparsely furnished interior contained nothing but a rickety looking table, three chairs and in one corner an iron safe.

'Take a seat gentlemen, tell me exactly what it is you are lookin' for.' said the man seating himself at his table. 'As you will have noticed I deal in diamonds and as such have many contacts in the industry.'

Georgie and Petrus declined the offer to sit. 'We're looking to purchase a claim to work,' said Georgie.

The man exhaled with some exaggeration, leaned forward clasping his hands and rested his elbows on the table.

'How much can you pay?'

Georgie was about to speak when Petrus butted in.

'I think we would like to know what people are asking first. We might not have enough for what is on offer. You tell us what the claims are going for.'

Petrus's face showed no emotion, his natural Boer astuteness coming to the fore, quelling the diamond miner's enthusiasm. The man had seen plenty of *rooineks* pass through Kimberly in his time and had made a profit out of their ignorance but something told him that these two were different and that he should watch his step. He cleared his throat.

'Well, unless you have around ten thousand pounds to spare you will not buy a full claim.' He watched their eyes, ten thousand pounds was definitely out of reach judging by their reaction. 'I see disappointment in your faces boys. Thousands of pounds too much is it? There is another way. Some of the less productive claims or ones subject to landslip can be had for as little as one hundred and fifty pounds. If you don't have that kind of money you could think about the Koffyfontein mine, claims there go for as little as thirty pounds but you will be lucky to find any diamonds. The Big Hole is the best and I know one or two claim holders that are in need of some quick money, gambling debts and all that, and maybe they would be willing to split their claims, sell a half share or maybe a quarter. What do you say, might cost two to three hundred pounds? Does that sound more like a proposition?'

'Yes it does. Thank you for that mister...?'

'Liebermann, Jacob Liebermann. If I can be of further assistance let me know. If, when, you find your diamonds be sure to come and see me, I will give a good price.'

'Thank you mister Liebermann,' said Georgie, 'we'll bear that in mind. In the meantime, we would appreciate you talking to your friends; maybe we can manage a part share.'

'I'll see what I can do.'

'Thank you, er...good day,' said Georgie opening the door.

'What do you think Georgie?' asked Petrus as they walked towards their Nkosinathi.

'Sounds possible but we are still short of money, even at two hundred pounds is too much, and don't forget we will need some equipment and from what I have seen we will have others to pay for transporting the spoil.'

'What do you mean?'

'I spoke to a couple of miners and they told me that the blue ground is so deep and hard that it has to be hauled up to the surface, carted away and left for weeks to dry out before it can be worked for the diamonds.'

Petrus fell silent; he had not fully appreciated the effort in working the mine, expecting only to dig and find a diamond to make them rich.

'Come on let's have a drink and see what the Duke of Kimberly is up to,' said Georgie slapping him on the back.

Sat in his usual seat, dressed in his waistcoat, his top hat perched on his head and a large cigar stuck out from the side of his mouth the Duke was busily shuffling cards.

'My deal gentlemen, let's see if this time you can take some of this money from me,' he said, expertly shuffling the deck.

Stopping the shuffle, he cut the pack, spread two fans face down on the table, and then, in one slick move, re-combined them before starting to deal.

The cards slid effortlessly across the table towards each player who carefully lifted them to discover his hand. Georgie had played this same game with his army comrades on many occasions and had become a competent player. He knew how to read a man's expression and one by one he looked at the players on either side of the Duke. Two of them looked to be novices, their eyes giving away the strength of their hands but the third player appear different. And so it proved, after several rounds only he and the Duke were still in the game and then, surprisingly, the Duke folded his cards and conceded defeat.

'Your luck seems to be running out Duke.'

'Temporarily my friend, only temporarily.'

The Duke relit his cigar, sat back in his chair and for once was quiet as he waited for the cards to be dealt, lifting them one by one as they slid towards him.

'My, my, this is a surprise,' he said pushing several coins into the centre of the table.

The weaker players read his low stake as a poor hand and recklessly bet more than they should but, although the Duke's hand was not very good and they beat him their fellow player's hand beat theirs. It was a disastrous round and their confidence was overdone, their conceit trapping them and leaving them penniless. Their faces dropped as the cards turned and with very little money left, they had no alternative but to leave the table.

'Sorry to see you fellas go, better luck next Sunday. Now we have two spare seats here, who will join us?'

For some the lure of the table proved too strong and their alcohol consumption had left them feeling relaxed and over confident, just as the Duke hoped.

'Glad to have you with us boys, let's see what you can win,' said The Duke weighing up the two men stepping forward.

The first was a big man, tall and broad shouldered who nodded a brief greeting as he pulled up a chair. The second was less forthcoming, scruffily dressed as if he had just left the diggings and he sat opposite the Duke. The big man was poker-faced, thoughtful, and Georgie guessed that he was no mug and was intrigued to see how he would cope with the Duke's cheating ways.

Adding to the sense of theatre, a sudden flash of lightening followed by crash of thunder heralded an imminent storm and within minutes, heavy rain rattled the tin roof of the canteen. The player's eyes looked up, attracted by the sound of the rain but the Duke was unmoved, shuffling the cards until his opponents were ready and almost as soon as the storm had begun, it abated. The dark clouds moved on, bright African sunshine penetrated the windows and from the sidelines, Georgie and Petrus watched the game develop.

'What's the matter with you?' Petrus asked Nkosinathi, staring intently into his tankard.

'I see someone in the here. He is looking at me.'

Petrus gave him a puzzled look. Could it be that some native superstition that had taken hold of him he wondered? Georgie became distracted and turned to look at them, wondering what was going on. The Zulu was moving his head from side to side, his eyes wide as he peered into his tankard and it amused Georgie, then he suddenly looked up.

'He has gone, he was a spirit but I don't know if he was friendly or not.'

'Friendly, definitely friendly,' said Georgie.

'How do you know?'

'Have we not been fortunate since we came here? We have sold the wild game and the packhorses and soon we will be able to buy a claim and find diamonds. Your spirit is friendly and is looking over us.'

Inwardly Georgie admonished himself for pretending to know the nature of the spirit but he could not help a soldier's dark humour.

'Should I drink?'

'Of course you can. Any spirit in there is friendly I'm sure, a good spirit and one that will look after you.'

With some hesitation, Nkosinathi lifted his tankard and managed to drink, a feat he could not have undertaken had the spirit in his beer been evil. Petrus looked at Georgie and grinned, Georgie winked at him and smiled, they had both realised that the atmospherics of the storm had exaggerated Nkosinathi's own image and his reflection was in fact the spirit.

Georgie turned away grinning with amusement but his joviality lasted only a few brief seconds. The Duke was reaching across the table to pick up the deck of cards and the big man was leaning back in his chair with a frown on his face. Had he missed something?

It was the scruffy miner's turn to deal and after stacking the cards and began to slide his opponent's cards towards them. The big man picked his up one by one and held them close, studying his hand and then he pushed several notes into the middle of the table. Georgie watched, thought that he perhaps had a good hand by the way he placed his bet but equally he could well have signalled that to the other players.

If they suspected he did have a good hand they might fold and he would not win much but in the event they did not. They had good hands too, one of them took the pot and Georgie watched the big man's face darken. The Duke appeared impassive his body language giving nothing away as the dealer won.

The Duke's money was reducing but not as fast as the Big man's and he began to appear more and more agitated and Georgie watched the drama unfold. The Duke began to win and the others experienced mixed fortunes until the big man lost the last of his money.

'You're cheating, you have marked the deck. I want my money back,' he growled with anger.

'Sorry friend but I am not cheating. This is not a marked deck, here check it out.'

'I don't believe you,' said the man getting unsteadily to his feet.

'Steady on friend, we don't want any trouble.'

'Well trouble you are going to get,' said the disgruntled miner pushing his chair away and suddenly the Duke became aware of how inflammatory the situation was becoming and deciding on drastic action, nodded to two thickset men sat at the next table. But not before the miner, blinded by hate and drink, had taken hold of his waistcoat. His intention was to drag the Duke from his chair but he got no further, a sand filled leather club crashing against the back of his head and knocking him senseless to the floor.

'Get him out of here; we don't want his type in here,' said a shaken Duke straightening the collar of his silk shirt. 'Seems to me gentlemen there is a place here for a lucky player. Who wants to join us?'

Nobody moved for a moment or two, Petrus put his hand on Georgie's arm and whispered. 'Are you going to try your hand? The Duke seems to be losing quite a lot. Perhaps it is a fair game after all.'

'Don't bet on it Petrus. No, not yet, I think he is up to something and I want to see what it is.'

Suddenly a voice called out from the crowd, a man stepped forward and the game was back in progress.

'Well boys it's my deal again and this time I am going blind.'

A dangerous strategy, but not unknown at the gaming tables of Kimberly. The word spread and a murmur of excitement percolated through the canteen. Several men came to join onlookers seeking entertainment and partially blocked Georgie's view. He moved to one side, pushing a drunk away and regained his position, sensing that something significant was in the air.

'Get me a coffee and make it black,' the Duke called to one of his thugs as he slowly began stacking the cards in contrast to his earlier distractions.

'Where's my coffee?'

'Here Duke,' said a waiter placing a cup at his side.

'Thank you, now perhaps we can start. Ready boys?' he said to the players.

The gamblers indicated that they were and the Duke began to deal. Georgie noticed quite soon that he was dealing slower than he had done on previous occasions and that puzzled him.

One by one, the players added to the ante and picked up their cards, the Duke lit another cigar and, as the betting opened he watched his opponent's eyes. The newcomer went first, pushing his bet towards the pot, the others two following suit, but as the Duke was playing blind he needed only match half the bet.

Georgie guessed each player had a decent hand by the way they played, and after four rounds of betting, the pile of notes and coins at the centre of the table had grown considerably. Then doubts began to creep into players' minds, one ran out of money and could not continue laying down his cards with a sigh, then the newcomer lost confidence in his hand and folded.

'Just me and you.'

The scruffy miner's eyes showed little emotion. He had won several times, had a large pile of cash in front of him and the pot looked inviting. It was the Duke's turn and he pushed some money towards the centre of the table.

'I'll raise you.'

His opponent looked at the cash and weighed the situation up finally saying, 'I will see you.'

'Bravo,' said the Duke with an unnervingly confident look and as his opponent's cheek twitched under the pressure, the Duke's face exhibited the faintest of smiles. At that moment Georgie knew he was going to win, he was cheating but he still did not know how and it infuriated him.

At the table, the miner began to reveal his cards, his confidence returning. The cards were red, picture cards and Georgie strained to see what they were. He had the King and queen of hearts but the knave was a diamond, a run and a decent enough hand but it could have been better. Now what did the Duke have?

The room was hushed, the gamblers were playing for high stakes and whoever won would be a relatively rich man. The tension rose, the word spread and the circle of onlookers grew in size to observe with baited breath. The Duke lifted his first card, an ace, the ace of clubs, and then he turned his second card, the three of clubs and the tension in the room increased. The silence was overpowering as, slowly and with some theatrical indulgence, he turned over his third and final card to reveal the deuce of clubs. He had a running flush, a very good hand, a winning hand.

The loser's head dropped, a few supporters of the Duke roared approval and as he raked in his winnings, Georgie noticed he was extra careful to avoid knocking the coffee cup.

'Bad luck Tom, you played well but I guess I was luckier than you. Tell you what; come back next week and I'll give you the chance to win your money back.'

The man's face creased with anxiety as the reality of his predicament dawned. He had lost everything on the turn of a card and Georgie felt some sympathy; he had experienced that same feeling of loss when he had seen his army pay vanish. It was all about winning and the

Duke had won handsomely, almost one hundred pounds he reckoned.

'Some game Georgie.'

Georgie emerged from his thoughts and looked at Petrus. 'Well I guess you understand now what can happen in a high stakes game. Win or lose a fortune on the turn of a card.'

Chapter 22

Since before daybreak Nkosinathi had foraged for kindling and had just started the fire when his companions emerged from the tent.

'Good boy Koso, just what we need to start the day a good mug of coffee. How's your head Petrus?'

Petrus did not answer, simply rubbed his face hard, finally saying, 'British beer is strong; I don't remember much about coming back here last night.'

'I bet you don't remember singing either do you?'

'I was singing?'

'Yes, you must have sung every hymn in the Calvinist hymn book on the way back. Even Koso here was trying to join in.'

Nkosinathi grinned, the memory of Petrus's antics still fresh in his mind.

'Oh...what will my father think?'

'He won't know and we are not going to tell him, so don't worry. We need to worry more about getting hold of a claim. I reckon we ought to pay a visit to our friend the diamond dealer, see what he has to say. It would not surprise me to find a few miners wanting to sell after losing their money yesterday to the likes of the Duke. Come on, we will have some coffee and beans and take a ride over to see mister Liebermann.'

The diamond dealer's cabin looked much as it did the last time they visited, a rusting corrugated tin roof atop shabby paintwork peeling in the sun, the one difference the lack of hangers lounging on the verandah. Today there was only one and as they approached, he turned and said something through the open doorway and a moment later Lieberman appeared at the doorway.

'Hello boys, back again,' he said touching his hat in greeting and forcing smile,.

'We are still looking for a claim to buy, anything turned up.'

Lieberman pulled his hat forward to shield his eyes, rubbed the stubble on his chin and waved them into his office. Mounting the steps onto the verandah, Petrus and Georgie glanced at the lone hanger on and Georgie touched his hat in greeting. The man did not reciprocate, appearing morose, distant and rubbing the back of his head and it was then recognition dawned. He was the miner who had lost heavily to the Duke and Georgie guessed he was rubbing his head because he was still sore from the blow dished out by the Dukes henchmen.

'Close the door gentlemen will you and pull up a seat.'

'We'll remain standing if you don't mind.'

The man paused and feeling the initiative slipping away, he produced a box of cigars from his table draw.

'Can I offer you one?'

'No thanks mister.' Georgie pursed his lips. 'After our conversation a couple of days ago I wonder have you found anything that might interest us.'

The man bit off the end his cigar and spat it towards the corner of the room before lighting it and leaning forward to speak in a hushed voice.

'There has been a development, the miner out there,' he pointed to the door, 'the big man you saw with the black eye.'

Georgie nodded.

'He has had a run of bad luck, gambling debts, lost most of his money and doesn't have enough to pay the wagon drivers to haul his spoil to the drying grounds. That means he can't do any more digging until he can find some more money. He came to me first thing this morning and asked if I knew of anyone who would be interested in buying his claim.'

'How much does he want?'

'He is asking eight hundred.'

'We don't have that amount, what about a part share,' asked Petrus.

'That's what I want to talk to you about. If you are willing to come up with, say two hundred pounds I might be able to talk him into selling a quarter share in his claim. What do you say?'

'We need to talk about it, see how much we can raise. How about we come back tomorrow?'

'Fine by me, I will talk to him and see what he says about splitting his claim.'

'Eight hundred pounds for the claim is a bit beyond us,' said Petrus as they walked back to the horses. 'even two hundred is too much for just a share.'

Georgie bit his bottom lip, deep in thought and simply nodded his reply.

'We could go hunting again; sell the meat in the market.'

'Petrus it will take us months to raise the sort of money they are asking – I have a better idea. Koso, we are going to buy a few supplies in the market square, why don't you have a look round and met us back here.'

Nkosinathi grinned, pleased to wander the town for a while, meet some of his own kind and catch up on gossip. Leaving him the two White men went looking for supplies and he walked slowly past some wagons spread along the roadside. From the square, the sound of the trader's bells reached his ears and he decided to take a closer look. A man shouted for him to buy some shiny knives as he passed a stall and beyond him he could see a group of natives gathered round a table piled high with rolls of colourful cloth.

Sauntering over to take a closer look he saw that there were at least a dozen of them, arguing and laughing, tall proud Zulu men, and then he saw a familiar face. Khulekani he was sure of it.

'*Sawubona* Khulekani.'

The man turned and looked at him in surprise at first expressionless and then a wide grin spread across his face and his eyes sparkled with joy. '*Mehlo madala!*

'Yes old friend it has been a long time.'

'You are working in the mine Nkosinathi?'

'Not yet, maybe soon.'

'I am alone Nkosinathi, I came here to find work. The homelands are desolate, our cattle are gone, eaten during the famine and our crops are destroyed.' His eyes suddenly became dull, inward looking and he stared at the ground.

'I know, it has happened in my village also. We cannot live under the new chief's yoke.'

Both men fell silent, reflective and then Nkosinathi slapped his friend across his shoulder as they had done during their days in the Zulu army.

'We should not be sad old friend, we should look to the future, to the future when I find a diamond.'

He let out a deep belly laugh and Khulekani grinned, his morose thoughts evaporating as the two of them renewed their friendship, a friendship forged as cadets and then as soldiers of the uVe regiment

The two of them had grown up in separate villages, coming together as military cadets and then as warriors when the King formed a new regiment. For a few hectic and traumatic months, they had campaigned together across vast tracts of country, fighting the invading British in a war in which they were inevitably defeated and they had not seen each other since.

'How is it in the Kingdom of Mgitshwa?'

'It is hard, we are constantly attacked from the north, food is scarce in the dry season and that is why I come here. And you Nkosinathi, why are you here?'

'The same, it is not safe for me in the village of my father, not for a long time I think.'

The two ex-soldiers of King Cetshwayo talked for a long time, Nkosinathi catching up on news from home and Khulekani enquiring about finding work.

'I do not know yet how to find work Khulekani; I have been here only a short time. The white men I serve are themselves looking for work.'

'You are serving White men!' exclaimed Khulekani.

'Yes, they are kind to me and I have no one else. They saved me from the dogs of John Dunn, brought me here to look for the "*idayimane*".

'I know of these small stones, they say a man can live in comfort for the rest of his life if he finds only even one, maybe I can find one here.'

Nkosinathi laughed again, they swapped stories, and for the first time Nkosinathi heard of the King's return

'Will the lands be as they were before.'

'They say not. Chief Zibhebhu is contesting his right to rule and there is civil war.'

Nkosinathi did not know what to make of Khulekani's news. He had heard stories of the King crossing the great seas to see the great white queen and if it were true civil war had erupted then he wondered what might happen to his village. He had not thought much of the kraal, his father and his siblings or of his mother. He had not been there for a long time and wondered how his brothers were coping and for some reason Nozipho his favourite sister, came into his mind.

'What is the matter Nkosinathi, you have gone very quiet?'

'Oh...nothing...I was just remembering my little
sister, the one put to death to placate the evil spirits
that had brought fire to destroyed the village'

'Nozipho, the one betrothed to Manelesi?'

Nkosinathi slowly turned his head to look at his
friend and a frown creased his forehead. Manelesi, a
friend, a comrade killed at the battle of Isandhlwana, he
had almost forgotten him and then he remembered how
together they had carried his body. His burial as a
warrior carried on his war shield to the fast flowing river
where they had sent him to the spirit world.

'Manelesi, the bravest of the brave, I have not
thought about him in a long time. Khulekani you have
brought me great joy with your presence but now I feel
nothing but sadness.'

'Do not be sad great warrior for both live.'

Nkosinathi's jaw dropped and he looked deep into
Khulekani's eyes for confirmation.

'They are living at the church of the Missionary from
the far north.'

'The far north?'

'The one they call the 'God Talker', the one that lives
at the far side of the Buffalo, the Christian mission with
a white church.'

'I have heard of that place but I have never been
there.'

'I have, only this many days ago,' said Khulekani,
holding up the fingers of both hands.

'How, I do not understand.'

'I came with others I met on my journey, crossing
the Buffalo and stopping at the mission to rest. A

woman with a scarred face brought us clean water to drink and then a man with only one arm came out to see us. He brought food, asked questions, questions about Zululand and the new Kingdoms and I answered him. He looked at me very closely and then he said "do you remember the uVe" and it was then that I recognized him, it was Manelesi. He told me the story of how the missionary and Nozipho, your sister came to rescue him from the river. We thought he was dead, killed by the British, but he is not dead and then Nozipho came to sit beside him. They are Christians and they are married.'

'Nozipho my little sister lives?'

'Yes Nkosinathi and Manelesi the bravest of the brave, he lives too.'

A tear rolled down Nkosinathi's cheek and he rubbed it away in embarrassment. 'They are alive.'

'Yes.'

'I am so happy. Thank you Khulekani, one day I will go to the mission and see them and for this, I will help you,' he said with emotion. 'I must go now but we will meet again old friend.'

Nkosinathi walked back to the horses with a spring in his step to find Georgie and Petrus already there. They had bought provisions to see them through the next few days and waved as he approached.

'We are going to the canteen for a while Koso,' said Petrus, 'look after the horses while we are gone.'

Petrus had acquired a taste for beer and as they entered the bar, he looked forward to quenching his thirst. They passed the card tables taking everything in, noticing first the card game in progress dominated by the Duke. He was at in his usual chair, a cigar protruding from his mouth like a phallic symbol and Georgie wondered.

'You want a beer Georgie? This heat makes me thirsty.'

'No, I'll give it a miss for now. Maybe a ginger beer - that's all.'

Petrus turned to look at Georgie, puzzled that he should decline a drink. 'Are you ill?'

'No, and do not ask too many questions.'

Petrus frowned, not really understanding as he turned towards the barman. However, although he was puzzled; he was not stupid and guessed Georgie was up to something.

'Do you want to tell me what is going on?'

'Not right now Petrus let me have a look at the Duke first.'

The Duke was holding court as usual and called out to a passing waiter, 'fetch me a black coffee,' and sat back as a player began to deal.

There were five of them including the Duke, and it looked as if they were playing for high stakes. usually bets were no more than a pound but today they were playing for double that and after three rounds of betting the pile of money in the centre of the table had grown considerably.

'He's asked for a black coffee.'

I know, I heard him. so what?'

'He's cheating and I think I know how. Listen, I'm going to join the table when someone drops out and use our stake to gamble with.'

Petrus did not like the sound of that and turned towards his friend. 'Isn't that a bit dangerous?'

'Yes, but you are going to help me. Now listen...'

As the game progressed, the Duke did not seem to win many hands yet he seemed unperturbed. Then a player threw his cards down in disgust and stood up.

'That's it for me, I'm cleaned out.'

'You will have to find another diamond then,' said one of his acquaintances.

The man was unimpressed, picked his hat up from the floor beside his chair and walked away.

'Say, is there room for another player?' asked Georgie.

The Duke stretched out his arm and turned his palm to invite Georgie to the empty chair and Georgie accepted.

'What's your name stranger?'

'Georgie.'

'Well Georgie let me introduce you,' said the Duke going round the table. He knew all but one of the men by name and the one he did not introduced himself as Matt and as Georgie sat down it was Matt's turn to deal.

Georgie picked up his cards, studied them and decided that an ace a four and a six was not worth much of a gamble and declining to bet, sat the game out. It gave him time to study the other players and try to understand a little of their strategy. He watched their eyes for clues as to how good a hand they had. Two gave nothing away but the others twitched and blinked almost imperceptibly on occasion, a small indication as to the strength of their hands and as if to confirm his observations, both players eventually folded.

'I'll raise you,' said the Duke, putting his money on the pile.

His remaining opponent matched the stake and the betting passed back to the Duke. for a few moments he studied his cards, took a long drag on his cigar and through the cloud of tobacco smoke said, 'I'll see you,' and placed more notes on the pile at the centre of the table.

The other player nodded and slowly turned over his cards to reveal an eight a nine and a ten– a run.

'Not bad Jerry but I think this beats it,' said the Duke laying out a ten a nave and a queen.

A murmur rose from several onlookers but at the table, there was silence as the Duke scooped the pot.

'Ah, put it there,' said the Duke to the waiter as his black coffee arrived. 'Any of you gentlemen want a drink while the waiter is here.'

'I'll have a ginger beer,' said Georgie.

'A ginger beer,' scoffed the Duke, 'I would have thought you were a whiskey drinker.'

'I used to be but I got the shakes,' said Georgie holding out his hand, twisting it rapidly from side to side.

Two of the players laughed but the Duke did not, drawing on his cigar and eyeing Georgie suspiciously.

'Well let's get on with the game shall we, your deal I believe.'

Suddenly Petrus appeared at the Dukes shoulder and began to cough violently holding his chest and letting his head droop. Everyone turned to look, the Duke turned sideways and forced to avoid Petrus, grasped the table to steady himself. With all eyes now on the commotion, Georgie took his chance, cut the pack twice to break the cards sequence and then came a crash as Petrus's hand slid along the table, knocking the Duke's coffee over.

'What the hell are you doing you oaf. Get away from here. Throw him out boys,' he called to two henchmen sitting not far away. 'Give him a good hiding; teach him not to try that again.'

Two burly men rose from their seats to grab hold of the hapless Petrus's arms to throw him from the building and inwardly Georgie groaned. He had not expected quite such a violent reaction and he worried for Petrus's safety but if they were going to find the money for the share of a claim, he could think of no other way.

'Waiter, bring me another coffee.'

'Just a minute,' said Georgie in a calm voice. 'In some circles a cup of black coffee is seen as an aid to cheating.'

'What do you mean,' growled an angry Duke turning on him.

'Well, I've seen enough men win unfairly at cards and the reflection of the cards in your cup of coffee could be seen as an unfair advantage. How's about you forgetting the coffee. You let the last one go cold I noticed.'

'Is this true,' said Jerry, his face clouding in anger. 'Have you been cheating Duke because if you have we'll run you out of town.'

There was a murmur from several onlookers and the Duke looked decidedly uncomfortable. 'Calm down boys, I'm not cheating, here look.'

He picked up the fresh cup and swallowed its contents in double quick time, scalding his mouth in the process, not daring show his discomfort. 'Waiter, take the cup away, I'll not be accused of cheating,' he said regaining some of his composure. 'Are you going to deal or what?'

Georgie said nothing, showed little emotion and began to deal satisfied that he had spiked the Dukes guns. He had finally understood how the Duke was cheating, memorising the card sequence and noting their reflections as he dealt but now Georgie had disrupted the sequence and that gave him a good chance of winning.

The two thugs had dragged Petrus into the alleyway next to the bar out of sight of any witnesses and when they threw him against a wall, Petrus knew he was in for a beating. Instinctively he held his forearms up to protect his face and braced himself as one of the thugs snarled at him, 'right you little bugger this is where your lights go out.'

but he expected blow did not land, instead Petrus heard a scuffle, a thudding noise and daring to open his eyes he saw Nkosinathi standing astride two prostrate forms.

'Thank the Lord.'

Nkosinathi grinned, his strong white teeth his most prominent feature in the shade of the alley and to Petrus, a blessing to see.

'You are one heck of a fighter Koso, thank you.'

'Georgie tell me to keep an eye on you, he expect trouble.'

Well we certainly got some. He's in there on his own, let's go and see what's happening.

As Petrus and Nkosinathi entered the bar Georgie was sitting with his back to them but the Duke caught them full on and his sharp intake of breath alerted Georgie. He followed the duke's gaze and grinned at his friends and then he looked into the Duke's eyes. The once confident air of the ringmaster had evaporated as a the realisation dawned that his advantage was severely eroded and it was all he could to do to chew on his cigar.

Georgie noticed defensiveness in the Duke's air and looked again at the source of his discomfort, a smile of satisfaction on his face at seeing Petrus and Nkosinathi in good health. He turned back and scrutinised the other players, to see their reactions, but apart from the one called Jerry, they seemed oblivious to the situation.

'Jerry is the player to beat,' Georgie thought looking back at his cards.

He had already played three games, so far won nothing so if he did not start winning soon his stake would disappear, and with it all hope of owning a claim. He considered his hand, a nine high straight, decent enough, but he would need to be reasonably sure it would win if he were to gamble on it.

The betting started with Jerry followed by a much-subdued Duke and then the next player folded. The one called Matt was next, he hesitated, his eyes flitting over his cards, and although he had seemed a confident player, his hesitation gave him away. In the event, he matched the betting and Georgie followed.

Jerry pursed his lips and decided to fold and then again, it was the turn of the Duke. Georgie watched his eyes, non-committal and yet still a hint of arrogance in them and Georgie wondered if it was simply bluff. The next player, probably influenced by the Duke's posturing, folded and the betting returned to Matt who matched the betting.

Georgie's mind raced as he turned over possibilities and probabilities. He was playing against the Duke, a cheat whom he had effectively stymied, but, still a dangerous opponent and then there was Matt. He was convinced the man had a half-decent hand and wondered if it was worth risking a wager.

'I'll raise you,' he heard himself saying and with steely eyes looked at the Duke. It worked, the Duke decided to fold and now all he had to contend with was Matt.

Matt hesitated for a fraction of a second and Georgie began to wonder if he really did have a decent hand and did not have to wait long to find out.

'I'll see you he said,' pushing more money forward.

Georgie laid his cards face up for everyone to see, at the same time watched Matt's eyes, and saw a flash of defeat in them. He knew then that he had won.

'Beat's me,' said a gloomy Matt showing a pair of aces before slumping back in his chair.

'So you've finally taken a gamble,' grunted the Duke, his eyes showing signs of menace.

'Beginners luck,' said Georgie nonchalantly reaching out to claim the pot. It was a decent amount, covered all his losses from the previous games and now he could concentrate on winning some more.

As the three of them walked towards their mounts Petrus was full of admiration for Georgie.

'How the heck did you do that Georgie? I have never seen anything like it; you must have taken all their money off them. The Duke looked angry when we left, he is a dangerous man, we should be wary of him.'

'I know, even though I spiked his guns and the other players were not so good, I won't be as lucky next time.'

'There will be a next time?'

'Probably not for now, we have what we want, enough to buy a half stake in the claim and tomorrow we will go and see the Jew.'

they reached the ponies and as they rode out of town, Nkosinathi listened to the conversation. He did not understand the Whiteman's cards but he was pleased that he had contributed to their success.

'Thank you for your timely intervention Koso; if you hadn't arrived when you did I would be in a sorry state by now.'

'It was nothing, I enjoyed it; I have not had the pleasure of hitting a Whiteman for some time.'

There was a silence for several seconds until the powerful Blackman let out a great belly laugh, infecting first Petrus and then Georgie and all three of them roared with laughter.

Chapter 23

They were lucky, the miner was at the end of his tether having gambled away all his profits and run up debts he could not pay, he was ready to give up.

'How much can you raise,' asked Lieberman speaking in a hushed voice and leaning forward across the table.

'Why, has the price gone up,' queried Georgie.

'No quite the contrary. Mister Briggs wants out completely, and he has asked me to see what I can get for the whole claim.

'He wanted eight hundred, right.'

'Yes he did.'

'For the whole of the claim I understand. We haven't got that much money; we came here today to see about buying a part of it.'

'I know but Mister Briggs is prepared to drop his price to get rid of the lot. How much will you offer him?'

Georgie pushed his hat back on his head and looked at Petrus for inspiration but the Boer had nothing to say, only puzzled eyes communicating his thoughts.

'Give us a minute mister Lieberman; we'll need to talk this through.'

'Sure, take your time.'

Georgie and Petrus came out of the shack and stood out of earshot of the Jew.

'Well it's not going to cost eight hundred but what can we raise. Let's count everything we have and see.'

'I have some money in my saddle bag; Mutti gave it to me before we left. It's not much, about ten pounds; she said it was in case I got into trouble.'

'Well you are in trouble, go and get it,' said Georgie with a grin.

The cloud of tobacco smoke rose from Jacob Lieberman's cheroot and hung over him like a Genie escaping from a lamp, disturbed only when the office door swung open.

'Back again boys, what have you to tell me?' he said drumming his fingers gently on the table top.

'Well, we don't have eight hundred; in fact we have nowhere near that amount. We can offer four hundred for a half share.'

'I told you Briggs wants to sell the lot and quickly. Can you borrow more?'

'Nope,' said Georgie firmly, 'that's our offer.'

'Well you are in luck gentlemen because Mister Briggs will take four hundred for the whole of the claim.'

Georgie turned towards Petrus and looked him in the eye. They had agreed that no matter what the Jew said they would not react. Georgie had stressed they were still gambling and must not cede any advantage if they could help it, yet inside both were jumping for joy.

'Are you happy with that Petrus?'

'Yes, it cleans us out but I am happy enough.'

'Good, then that is settled. I have a contract already drawn up. It just needs the amount you will pay and your signatures filling in and we can conclude the deal.

As they left the shack, Nkosinathi knew something had happened by the look on the faces of both Georgie and Petrus as they approached the horses.

'We have a claim to work Koso. Let's go and have a look at it,' said Georgie examining the claim paper for its exact location and in his office Jacob Lieberman tore up the agreement signed only a few hours earlier. Tom Briggs was a desperate man and when the Jew had offered him two hundred pounds for his claim and he had gratefully accepted.

The first week was hard for them, backbreaking relentless slog digging and hacking at the blue shale thrown up by the volcanic pipe. Georgie and Petrus soon discovered muscles they did not know they had. A month later their bodies had acclimatized, they settled into their new regime spending their days working the hard earth and alongside them Nkosinathi was indefatigable, his lithe, strong body adapting to the labour with ease and watching the White men struggle to begin with, had suggested they might employ Khulekani.

'Just another load and we can finish for today,' said Georgie wiping his brow.

During the weeks spent digging they had removed tons of potentially diamond bearing rock from the volcanic pipe and paid men with wagons to take it to the dumping ground to weather and the day had arrived when they could break it and really search for diamonds.

'We have done well; the two blacks have proved their worth. We will soon be able to work the rock I think.'

'I've been waiting for this day ever since we started. I had a look at our rock pile a couple of hours ago and I think it's weathered enough in places to begin crushing.'

'Sounds good to me Georgie, I can't wait for that first diamond.'

Georgie laughed, he felt the same. After all the hard work of extracting the shale they still had to crush the rock down to expose any diamonds but that first find would make all the hard work worth it.

'Yes, tomorrow, we'll start breaking the rock. Koso and Khule can take the sledge hammers to begin crushing whilst we finish off this section and then we can start sieving for diamonds.'

Early the following day, Nkosinathi and Khulekani began the equally backbreaking task of crushing the spoil piled up on waste ground away from the diggings. They were not alone, ten thousand labourers worked nearby, methodically swinging their hammers to the sounds of African singing.

'You have done well Koso; we have plenty to go at here.' said Georgie as he and Petrus arrived from the diggings to inspect the crushed ore.

Nkosinathi grinned, stopped swinging his hammer and rested his hands on its vertical shaft before reaching into his trouser pocket.

'Is this why we have come here?' he said producing what looked like a small piece of opaque glass.'

Georgie took it from him and turned it over in his hand, and after examining the article, he let out a whoop of joy.

'We found one, we found one,' he kept saying and then Petrus took hold of it in his own hand.

'So this is a diamond? It doesn't look like a diamond, more like any other piece of stone.'

'It's a raw diamond, they cut and polish them to make them shine but this how it starts and this little beauty is worth money.'

The diamond buyer's offices, clustered just off the main square were handling millions of pounds worth of diamonds each year and into the office of Barnato Brothers walked Georgie and Petrus. The dim interior and the lack of the noise from the street created an air of wonder for the two novice miners and Georgie began to feel a little unsure.

'Yes, can I help you,' asked a man from behind the mesh screen.

'I have some diamonds to sell,'

'Let me have a look, pass them through here.'

Georgie took the diamonds from his pocket and slid them through the small opening in the screen to the man who placed them on a small set of scales. He then placed a topless, peaked cap on his head and lifted a magnifying glass to his eye, rotating the diamonds one by one between his fingers under the glare of an oil lamp.

'The quality is not so great but I think we can do business. This is one and a quarter carats and this one here is just under a carat but I think the smaller one will cut better. I can offer you twenty five shillings for the smaller one and twenty eight shillings and sixpence for the larger one.'

'Is that the best you can do, we have heard that Mosenthal and sons are offering good prices,' said Georgie remembering the name on one of the buyers offices.

The man picked up the diamonds and examined them once more and not wanting to lose the deal said, 'I will give you fifty eight shillings and six pence for the two, that's my best offer. You know the diamond trade is not what it was.'

Georgie looked at Petrus and he nodded. 'Alright, we will sell at that price.'

Twice more that week they made the trip to the office of the Barnato Brothers and twice more they came away with a handful of cash.

'Georgie this is hard work, there is a company offering to haul our spoil and crush it in a great machine they have brought to the mine. Don't you think we would be better off letting them do the hard work? I know Koso and Khule are doing a good job but I hear this machine can do the work of ten men.'

'What will it cost?'

'I don't know but I can find out. Here let me get two more beers and we can talk about it,' said Petrus waving to draw the waiter's attention.

Georgie rubbed his chin and his mind turned over the proposition. They had been moderately successful, discovering a diamond almost every day, small diamonds and not as valuable as he would like but the idea of crushing ore much quicker appealed to him.

'Tell you what Petrus; we'll give it a try.'

Petrus smiled, dug in his pocket for some coins to pay the waiter and picking up his glass he took a long drink.

'Ah, that's better,' he said wiping his mouth on the sleeve of his jacket. 'Between you and me I've heard this machine spits out diamonds. I was taking to a man who said he was using it and his profits had trebled. It's a good idea Georgie, it will allow the blacks to work on the pipe with us and we can shift twice as much.'

Georgie laughed, 'twice as much? Those two can shift half as much again as we do. Let's do it.'

Georgie was beginning to understand business and realised that they could make better use of their resources where it mattered but there was a problem, could they afford it? He addressed the question for the rest of the day, working out costs involved and how many diamonds they would need to recover to pay for the crusher. It was a daunting task for one not experienced in business but ever resourceful, Georgie rose to the task and for the next two months, they worked the new system, gradually beginning to the fruits of their endeavours. They were recovering a lot more diamonds, the amount of shale dug from the volcanic spout increased dramatically and the crushing machine saved a lot of back breaking work.

'How much did we make today,' asked Petrus as Georgie rode up to their camp.

'Seventeen pounds and thirteen shillings.'

'Wow, that's a lot. We must have a lot of money in the bank by now Georgie?'

'Yes, I reckon we have almost a thousand pounds saved, not bad for a pair of amateurs, eh!'

Petrus smiled and nodded his head, he had wanted to see the outside world and in the last six months he had experienced more than his fair share.

'I like the idea of making money, though Papa would not approve. Our religion forbids the worship of money but I can see the benefit of it. We could buy another claim Georgie and expand our operation.'

'Slow down Petrus, you're getting carried away. Yes we have enough for another claim but that means more labourers and more headaches. Do we want that so soon, maybe next year?'

'It was only an Idea.'

'And a good one, but I have spoken with a few old hands and they say they have seen men with big ideas come and go. The Blue shale where the diamonds are can disappear just as easily as it appears and leave you with nothing. We seem to have a decent enough claim here but to buy another would be folly right now.'

Petrus pursed his lips and slowly nodded his agreement, picked up his shovel and went back to helping the two natives leaving Georgie to stand hands on his hips, looking out over the mine. It was a bee hive on a grand scale, thousands of men hacking away at the rock, a cacophony rising from the depths proclaiming man's pursuit of enrichment and here he was in the thick of it.

Chapter 24

The mail steamer's progress was slow but steady and having first called in at Cape Town it was making its way north up the coast of the Eastern Cape towards the port of Durban. Patrick said going straight to Durban would cut several weeks off the journey. If they had landed at Cape Town it would mean a long and arduous journey overland to Georgie's last known whereabouts.

He still had contacts from his army days and looked up as many as he could, to seek information about events leading up to the last days of the rebellion.

'It was a sorry state of affairs, I saw them charge the Boers but from where I was it looked an impossible task,' said Alwen Jones, late of the twenty fourth of foot. 'We were pinned down by some very accurate fire, lost some good men and expected the withdrawal but then the mounted men came thundering past attacking like the cavalry, and up the steepest part of the hill would you believe. I don't know who gave the order but it was pure stupidity'

'Was Georgie with them?'

'I expect so, I met him briefly in camp in the sergeant's mess and I know he was attached to the mounted Infantry.'

'So what do you think happened to him, his regiment told me they never found his body and he is listed as missing?'

'Some of the lads deserted you know.'

'Oh...and you think...maybe?'

'Maybe, I don't know, but I tell you what those poor bastards were in a hell of a difficult position, horses shot from under them and nowhere to hide. If you wanted to live then surrender and desert was certainly an option.'

Patrick had left the pub only a little wiser and still wondering if Georgie could still alive and if he was, where in heavens' name could he be? He and Georgie had been through a lot together, he knew his friend was no quitter, quite the opposite in fact and would quite happily take the fight to his enemy but then he remembered their parting conversation.

'Bloody hell, I have to stay behind and train the new boys, no going home for me yet and you, you lucky bastard, sailing home next week.'

'It's only another six months Georgie, six months and you will be back in Blighty. Don't worry the time will soon pass.'

But six months later Georgie was still in South Africa, and with trouble brewing up in the Transvaal he had little prospect of returning to England. On the train back to London, Patrick could not help but wonder what had gone through his mind. He himself had seen plenty of action during his time in the army but the newspaper reports of the fighting and the losses had left him sickened. He guessed the moral of the soldiers would be low and the thought of desertion would occur to some. A man could easily lose himself in such a vast country so if that was what Georgie had ended up doing, where should they look.

He remembered then, a member of his own platoon disappearing. When they had left Kimberly one of the platoon, Dickie Henderson, a man with a growing obsession for diamonds, had deserted. The army had spent a month in Kimberly recuperating after the hard slog across the Great Karoo and with little to keep them occupied; the men had decided to do a little prospecting. They had little idea of how to go about prospecting but after some experimentation and several conversations in bars they finally managed to find one tiny diamond. Dickie had become very excited, affected by the experience and when the order came to leave Kimberly, he disappeared.

Patrick wondered if Dickie ever did make it rich and then he made the connection, coming like a bolt out of the blue. It seemed so obvious, and he wondered why he did not think of it before. Of course, Georgie was following Dickie Henderson's footsteps, diamonds, what was it Georgie had said when it was all over.

'I've had enough of killing,' and then he had said 'remember Dickie Henderson?'

That was it, he *was* following Dickie's example and Kimberly was the place to start looking.

Ellen gripped the side of the boat so hard her knuckles turned white. She was afraid, would never have attempted the landing if it were not for Patrick's persuasive tone and his strong arms holding her tightly. He had warned her of the dangers but had reassured her that the seamen knew what they were doing.

'Just close her eyes if it becomes too much of an ordeal. I will look after you don't you worry,' he had said as they were lowered into the whaler for the last part of the journey and that moment her eyes were shut tight and her heart was beating madly.

As the six tough sailors rowed hard towards the shore she could hear the roar of the surf, feel the whaler heave as a wave swept under them. Her experience of the sea was limited solely to three voyages on the mail steamers between England and the Cape but Durban was different. The ship could not cross the bar and had to anchor off in deep water, the only way to land by small boat and at that moment the whaler was at the most perilous part of the crossing.

'Hang on we are nearly there,' said Patrick in Ellen's ear, his words almost drowned out by the roar of the sea.

If it were possible, Ellen's grip tightened even more on the gunnel, she closed her eyes even tighter, and then, with one final heave the boat was into calmer water.

'There, we're safe now, you can relax dear girl.'

Ellen sensed the change in boat's motion, opened one eye, then the other and took a deep breath. The temperature had changed markedly, the smell of the sea replaced by African fragrances drifting off the land and at last, she felt safe.

'That was horrible Patrick.'

'I know, it's not the first time I've done it but I hope it's the last.'

Relaxing her grip, Ellen leaned into Patrick and he held her close as the seamen pulled on the oars to bring the boat alongside the small jetty. A seaman jumped ashore and made fast, another joined him and held out a hand to assist the passengers ashore and standing above them, the white agent of the shipping line was giving orders to several half-naked black men unloading mailbags and luggage.

'Welcome to Durban Mrs...er,' he looked at his manifest, 'Donovan, and this must be Mr Donovan.'

'I am sor,' said Patrick stepping ashore, the handle of a Gladstone bag held tightly in his hand.

'I have arranged transport for you to the hotel and I have reserved a room for as long as you wish to stay. The letter from London states that you will be travelling from here to the Orange Free State and my instructions from the company are that, as you are first class passengers, to help with the arrangements. Perhaps if you settle in and rest a while we could meet at my office in the morning and discuss your requirements.'

'Thank you, it sounds as if everything is taken care of. Your name?'

'Jackson sir, Peter Jackson.'

'Well Mr Jackson, now that I am firmly back on dry land I would like a cup of tea,' said Ellen.

Ellen stretched out her arms and yawned before rubbing the sleep from her eyes. Judging by the sun streaming in through the net curtains they had slept late and and she wondered what time it was.

'Patrick.' There was no answer, she reached out to feel for him but his side of the bed was empty.

'Patrick,' she called again, but still there was no answer.

Sitting up in bed she stretched, yawned again and decided to get up. A porcelain jug with a bowl sat on the small table near the window and from it she splashed water over her face to wake herself up. After the ordeal of the landing, she had become very tired and during her first night on dry land had slept soundly and she felt refreshed. Her trunk was lying open at the foot of the bed and she decided comfortable clothes, a short jacket and matching skirt, designed primarily for horse riding, were her best option.

She dressed and was just putting a final addition to her hair when she heard a noise and turning round she saw the door open. Patrick's head peered into the room and he smiled when he saw her.

'Ah...you are awake I see and you look lovely my dear.'

'Why thank you sir, and where have you been this fine morning?'

Patrick entered the room, put the Gladstone bag he was carrying on a chair and walked across the room to Ellen and planted a large kiss her on her lips.

'I went fer a stroll along the water front, had a look round. It's strange being back you know, I have lots of memories of this part of the world so I have.'

'We both have Patrick. Now, what about breakfast, have you eaten?'

'No, I thought I would wait until you surfaced and now that you have I could murder a plate of kippers.'

Ellen was hungry and though they were not exactly her favourite breakfast dish, she could even eat Kippers but to her joy and Patrick's annoyance, they were not on the menu.

'Well I certainly feel better for that Patrick,' said Ellen finishing her omelette. 'What do you think we should do?'

Patrick scratched the side of his chin and pondered for a few seconds.

'It's a long way from here to Kimberly, could take us up to six weeks if we travel like the army does, in those slow moving Burgher wagons.'

'What else can we do? There are just the two of us and you are carrying a lot of money in that bag. Isn't there a better way?'

'Of course.'

'What then?'

'Well we ought to see our friend mister Jackson as soon as we can. He will know the set up here I am sure and we can ask him to hire faster transport for us and I need to get hold of a gun.'

'A gun?'

'Yes a gun, we don't know who or what we might encounter. This is a dangerous country, if we get mixed up with the wrong crowd and with all this money...' His voice tailed off and he looked at the valise, he knew that if word got out that they were carrying so much, they would be in danger.

'I see what you mean, perhaps you should get me one too, just a little one.'

'I will. If you have finished breakfast then we should find Mister Jackson and see what he has to offer,' said Patrick getting to his feet.

Picking up the valise he walked round the table, helped Ellen to her feet and together they left for the agent's office.

The office was a pleasant looking affair overlooking the waterfront, and there they found Peter Jackson sitting in the shade smoking a cigar.

'Good morning, I trust you had a pleasant night. What can I do for you?'

'Mister Jackson we are in need of some transport to Kimberly.'

The agent, although appearing to be simply a feeble pen pusher, was in fact an astute and capable organizer. It was a necessary qualification for a shipping agent covering almost all of the east coast, from Port Elizabeth to Delgoa Bay.

'As you are a woman missus Donovan, I think horseback is out of the question but the next best thing is a train ride to Pietermaritzburg and from there you can travel overland by stagecoach. I will telegraph a friend of mine, a mister Graham Forrest who runs a regular coach service to Bloemfontein, he will send someone to meet the train and collect your baggage.

From Bloemfontein you will easily find someone to take you to Kimberly because many of the supplies for the mines pass through there.'

'I have another request Mister Jackson; we are in need of a hand gun or rather two hand guns. I served as a soldier out here for more than a few years and I know the dangers. Can you help in that department?'

'I have anticipated that little problem Mister Donovan,' he said opening his desk drawer. 'You are not the first to make' such a request. 'Here, he said passing a revolver across the desk and then he pulled out a box of cartridges. 'That will be eight pounds and three shillings. I will try to obtain another more suited for a woman by tonight. Might I ask you to call back after five o clock? You can pay me then, I expect the smaller gun will be the same price,' he said, his eyes narrowing slightly at the prospect of a little extra remuneration.

'Thank you for your help mister Jackson. I will return later as you suggest, and the train?'

'There are two each day, might I suggest you take the early train tomorrow at ten o clock. I will let mister Forest know of your arrival so you may be met from the train.'

The ridges and koppies of the high veldt gave way to the wide-open grassy plains as the stagecoach made its way towards Bloemfontein and opposite Ellen and Patrick sat two men. Both were dressed in cheap woollen suits and with three-day stubble, their chins they had a tough look about them. They had joined the coach the previous morning and after a brief introduction sat in silence for most of the way but at least Patrick had learned they were in the mining industry and heading for Kimberley.

'We should be there soon, we stop at the way station for the night,' said the older of the two men.

'Say mister, you seem to keep a goodly embrace on that valise of yours. Must be something special in there,' added the other.

'Books, I am carrying books for an acquaintance who works in the diamond fields.'

'Sure you ain't got whiskey in there mister?'

'No I haven't,' said Patrick more than a little annoyed, his hand unwittingly touching the valise.

'Looks like we are almost at the way station,' said the older man glancing out of the open window.

'Where?' asked Ellen eager to leave the coach and the stranger's company.

'You can't see from your side, come here and sit by me and I'll show you.'

Ellen politely declined; preferring instead to look from her side of the coach at the boring landscape she had watched all day and beside her Patrick felt his hackles rising. He had seen men like these before and they always seemed to spell trouble and keeping a firm grip on the valise, leaned back in his seat to await their arrival at the way station.

The first Ellen saw of their resting place for the night were the horses congregated in the corral awaiting their turn to haul the coach and then, in a cloud of dust, the coach pulled up outside two small white buildings.

A tall thin man in a checked shirt was waiting for them, leaning on the rail of the verandah and as the driver tied the reigns to his seat he spoke.

'Afternoon Bill, you made good time, I didn't expect you for another hour, Agnes is cooking up some dinner for your passengers, four I think, an' one of them a woman.'

'That's right,' said the driver sliding his whip into the tube by his side and as he climbed from his seat the coach door opened, the two "miners" emerged, stretched and made grunting noises before walking towards the main building.

'I don't like those two Patrick. They are up to something,' said Ellen as Patrick helped her to the ground.

'I thought you were sleeping.'

'Resting my eyes and having the occasional peep at our two friends. They are becoming a little too interested in the bag and I overheard them last night when we finished dinner. I went to take some air for a few minutes and came across them smoking and talking and I am sure they are planning something.'

'What did you overhear, why didn't you tell me sooner.'

'Because I did not realise what they were up to. It was only when the older one, Brad, made that comment about the bag that it dawned on me.'

'What.'

'Leave it for now Patrick, we'll talk about it later,' she whispered as the station boss and two natives began unhitching the horses.

'Food will be ready soon, I will get the boys to bring your luggage to your rooms in the bunk house and you can freshen up. I hope you like springbok and corn because that's all we have.'

The dinner was passable and the two "miners" wolfed there food down in a very short time before leaving to smoke outside.

'Remind me never to complain about army cooks again,' said Patrick under his breath.

Ellen chuckled, the meat was tough but in general the food was not so bad and once they had eaten, they decided to take a stroll outside and away from their travelling companions.

'We should be in Bloemfontein by tomorrow afternoon according to the driver,' said Patrick rolling two cigarettes and passing one to Ellen. 'What was it you wanted to tell me about those two?' he said lighting her cigarette.

'Last night when we stopped in Boshof I overheard them talking. I went out for a breath of fresh air after dinner and saw them leaning against the coach having a smoke. I heard them say something like "we can get rid of them just before Kimberly. I did not know what they meant but I'm beginning to think it is us they want to get rid of Patrick. I'm sure they are going to try something tonight.'

'We need to turn the tables. It is those two who need to be got rid of.'

'What do you mean?'

'If they try something and leave us here then they can take the money and disappear. But what if we thwart their plans? Leave it to me, I will sort them out.'

'Be careful Patrick, there are two of them and they might have a knife or a gun.'

'If I make a mess of it then you barricade yourself in the room and scream for help.'

'You big Irish fool, just be careful.'

Patrick finished his cigarette, dropped on the ground and extinguished it with a twisting movement of his toe. For a moment stood stock-still in the moonlight and listened. It reminded him night sorties with the mounted Infantry and then he saw the faint glow of a cheroot thirty or so yards away. Straining his eyes he made out the shape of a man and beyond him he could see the dark shadows of horses, but of the second man, there was no sign. Deciding to act, he told Ellen to go inside and he set off as if he were out for an after dinner stroll, approaching within a few yards of the man.

'You keep a tight hold of that bag of yours mister, I think I would like to look inside.'

'Why would you want to look inside my bag.'

'Well it maybe you are carrying more than books. If you are then maybe, my partner and me could help keep that bag safe. Kimberley is a dangerous place for the likes of you.'

Patrick recognized the man as Brad, the older of the two, his companion missing and he sensed danger. Brad was setting him up he was sure and glancing briefly first to his left and then to his right, he caught sight of a movement. The absent stranger was behind the coach and creeping towards him and as he came close, Patrick spun round to see the blade of a long knife glinting in the moonlight.

No words only a grunt came from the man as he thrust forward with his knife aimed at Patrick's midriff and in a few furious seconds Patrick sidestepped, swung the Gladstone bag full in the face of his assailant and threw him off balance. Then the second man made his move.

From no more than a few feet away, he lunged at Patrick with his own knife and if it were not for Patrick's fighting instinct, he might have pressed his advantage home but Patrick was made of sterner stuff. The knife was nothing compared to Zulu assegais and in double quick time he had jumped out of the way and swung the bag a second time. He missed, the man had time to turn and come at him again and as his blade scythed viciously from side to side, Patrick retreated and warily the two men faced each other.

'It's all up for you, just pass me the bag and we will let you go.'

'And then what?'

'You stay here and catch the next coach in a couple of days. No harm done and your bag will be safe with us. Clive, take the bag off him while I cover you.'

by now Clive had recovered from the blow Patrick had inflicted upon him and was getting to his feet. Patrick didn't wait for him to regain his posture and took a step towards him, knocking him down again but in the process, stumbled over a rock. Reaching out for support he found none, fell to his knees and Brad managed to grab him around the neck. His sole intention was to stick his knife between Patrick's ribs and Patrick realised then that he was in trouble. Twisting his body to break the man's hold, he gained some advantage but Brad stabbed at him with the knife a second time, ripping the sleeve of his jacket.

It was a close thing but in the gloom, Brad did not press home his advantage and Patrick was able to reach out and grab hold of his wrist. Slamming his boot against Brad's shin, he used the Gladstone bag as a shield and with his free hand, smashed his clenched fist into the man's face. Then he felt an arm about his neck and the sharp prick of a blade at his throat.

'Kill him while you have chance, kill him and let's get that bag.'

'Not so fast.'

'What.

'Touch him and you are a dead man,' said a woman's voice.

Both Clive and Brad looked towards the sound of the voice and from the shadows Ellen emerged, her arm out stretched, her gun pointing straight at Clive's temple.

'You can't take both of us missus,' said a defiant Brad holding a handkerchief to his bleeding face. 'Kill him Clive and I will take her out.'

The gun did not make a very loud noise when it went off, small calibre, a woman's gun, but the scream of pain from Brad was loud enough, enough to panic Clive and send him scurrying into the darkness.

To Ellen, the town of Bloemfontein was the prettiest she had seen in South Africa, surrounded as it was by green and fertile countryside and flowers everywhere. Nevertheless, the events of the past twenty-four hours were still a distraction as she reached for the coach's open door. Patrick helped her with one hand, clutched the Gladstone bag with the other and led her, without a backwards glance, towards the wooden building. Behind them the driver helped the injured Bradley Smith down from the driving seat and of his accomplice, there was no sign.

'I'll get you for this,' Brad called defiantly after them. 'If I ever come across you again it will be a very different result.'

'What will happen to him Patrick?' asked Ellen as they reached the door of the way station.

'I don't know, depends on the police chief I suppose. He should be thrown into prison for the night and presented to the magistrate in the morning but I can't see how they can try him successfully without witnesses and we are the only ones and we're not stopping.'

'So?'

'So they might let him go and if he is heading for Kimberly then we need to be careful. He suspected I was carrying valuables in the valise and now he is sure I am. He'll try again if he gets the chance.'

'How much further is it to Kimberly Patrick, how much longer have we to stay on this dreadful stagecoach?'

Patrick was slightly amused by her tantrum but looking blankly at her, he did not feeling much like laughing. 'It's not the coach, it's the roads, they are mostly dirt tracks and when the rains come they wash away the surface. As for Kimberly I think it's about a hundred miles, three or four days at the rate we are going.'

'Three or four more days!'

Chapter 25

Patrick looked out across the dry, featureless landscape, the dry riverbeds and the orange coloured soil wondering if they really were on the right road to find Georgie. Sitting opposite him her eyes firmly fixed on the horizon; Ellen was thinking much the same thing. The coach lurched over a rut in the road snapping them out of their thought and as their eyes met each seemed to know the others thoughts.

'We should be there soon I think,' said Patrick looking at his pocket watch. 'The driver said he usually got into Kimberley between four and six depending upon the road and it's gone three.'

'I hope so, I'm getting a little fed up of this coach. What do you think our chances are of finding Georgie?'

'Well, if he's in Kimberley pretty good but there is no guarantee he is there. We don't even know if he is still alive.'

'Don't say that. He is alive I'm sure of it.'

Patrick realised he had said the wrong thing and sat back in his seat, not wanting to upset Ellen and for the next hour they sat in silence watching the flat, barren landscape go past.

The final miles were uneventful, but then signs of civilization began to appear, tents at first, the outlying miner's camps and then the odd shack until they approached the mining town proper. As the coach entered the town, it slowed and Ellen and Patrick took in their new surroundings. The miner's had pitched tents on any available ground and hastily erected wooden buildings until finally, builders erected more permanent structures near the town centre. On his seat the driver spoke soothingly to his team of horses and the coach came to a halt outside the 'The Star of the West'.

'This is your final stop,' he called out, 'I'll get your trunk down and leave you here. It's a little primitive but as good as you'll get out here.'

'Thank you driver, it can't be any worse than some of the stops we've endured,' said Patrick emerging into the sunlight.

'Not much of a place is it,' said Ellen as Patrick took her hand.

'No, but it's a mining town. I don't suppose they cater much for a woman here.'

'Well maybe not. Let's get settled in and then we can really start looking for Georgie.

After so many years of excavation, retrieving diamonds from the Big Hole had become a risky business. The removal of the volcanic spout holding the diamonds had grown to a deep and its steep side were liable to collapse without warning.

'The mine inspector has reported a crack opening up on the west side, says its safe enough for now but he will watch it.'

'We haven't had a collapse for a month, I guess one is due. Good job it's on the far side,' said Georgie.

'Good job,' agreed Petrus. 'Koso, we are going to try blasting with dynamite, loosen the rock more and we shouldn't have to work so hard.'

'I have seen them blasting, it is as you say, quicker and easier but I have seen men die.'

'Georgie was a soldier and he knows about dynamite, he says it is safe enough if the charges are kept small and it should improve our diamond haul.'

'We have found many diamonds and you are becoming rich Whiteman, what about me? I have worked as hard; I have been here since the beginning.'

'You are a native; you can't expect the same as a Whiteman.'

Nkosinathi's eyes flashed, a dark cloud passing over them and he looked at Georgie. 'What do you say?'

'I say you have earned a third share in everything we have Koso. Don't mind Petrus, he is used to natives working for nothing but you are a good friend and I will not let you down. What do you say Petrus?'

At first Georgie's comment threw Petrus; the way of things was that the black man did all the work whilst the white man took all the profit. He had grown up like that, expected it but Georgie had made him think.

'I'm sorry Koso, you have been with us from the start and you did save me from the Duke's thugs, maybe I owe you.'

For the first time in his life, Petrus saw that a black man could be his equal and reached out to shake Nkosinathi's hand, to seal their friendship.

'That's settled then, it's Saturday tomorrow, let's go into town and get hold of some dynamite and on Monday we will start blasting.'

The Star of the West was as busy as it always was on a weekend, miners, traders and labourers out to relax, out to have a good time after their backbreaking work. Nearby, Boer wagons rumbled into town to sell produce their owners announcing their wares in loud voices and amongst them rode Georgie, Petrus and Nkosinathi with Khulekani following on foot.

Georgie and Petrus had not visited the Star since that fateful day, wary of the Duke and his thugs spending their time working their claim. They had not touched a drop of alcohol in more than a month bit today was different. Their labours had produced a profit, they had money in their pockets and had decided to enjoy themselves.

Petrus was first through the door; his eyes on the bar, his mouth dry with expectancy and following behind him Georgie looked more at the gaming tables. The Duke was still here, his brightly coloured waistcoat making him stand out and Georgie told himself to be careful.

'Koso, the man in the bright waistcoat is dangerous, the two thugs you disposed of last time were his men. Keep your eyes peeled for trouble.'

Nkosinathi, chewing on a Dagga leaf narrowed his eyes. 'Not worry, I see him and I see the two I knocked out.'

Georgie's attention shifted from the Duke to his henchmen standing in a darkened corner, ready should their boss need their services. The room was crowded, too many witnesses to cause any trouble thought Georgie, the most dangerous time would come when they left.

Duke looked up as they passed and recognised Georgie, the one who had rumbled his routine and made it difficult for him to work the reflection trick anymore. It had cost him money, gamblers were wary of him for a time and he had suffered at the card table. His eyes fixed on Georgie for a few seconds, revenge on his mind. Georgie shrugged off the look and followed Petrus to the bar and as Petrus turned from the bar with the drinks he noticed Nkosinathi was missing.

'Where's Koso?'

Georgie looked round, as surprised as Petrus. 'I don't know, he was here a minute ago.'

'Well it looks like we will have to share his beer. Let's find some space.'

Threading their way through a throng of drunk and noisy men they found some space near a window and from the darkened corner the Duke's henchmen watched.

'Are you going to gamble at cards again?'

'I don't know, it's a bit risky I think, maybe a card school without the Duke, eh.'

'There's one over there look,' said Petrus moving his beer glass in that direction.

The temptation was there for sure but Georgie resisted, that was until he had drunk more beer and a seat became vacant.

'Mind if I join you?' he said holding the back of the vacant chair.

'No, sit down,' said one of the players.

Unlike the Duke's table, it was not a high stakes game and Georgie managed to win a moderate amount but in doing so his concentration was absolute and he did not notice the Duke summon one of his henchmen and whisper something in his ear. Petrus was in conversation with a miner and he too missed the cameo played out not far away but another pair of eyes did.

'Thank you gentlemen, I hope you don't mind me taking your money off you. I'll be back sometime and you can win it back,' said Georgie collecting his winnings and getting up from the table.

'Don't worry we will,' said one of the players. 'I know you stymied the Duke a while back, stopped him cheating so much. That was good; it's saved us all a lot more than you have won tonight.'

Georgie smiled, it seemed he had become a minor celebrity but that could bring unwelcome attention and he was not so sure that he liked the idea. Pocketing his winnings he glanced across at the Duke who was staring straight at him and the hairs on the back of his neck began to stand up. He had faced danger many times as a soldier, miles from camp with only his small section of mounted infantryman and surrounded by hostile forces.

In those circumstances, he had developed a sixth sense and it was telling him right now to be careful.

'We should get out of here; the Duke is up to something I'm sure.' he said joining Petrus. 'Where's Koso, has he not turned up yet?'

'No, I haven't seen him since we came in here.'

Georgie stroked the stubble on his chin and searched the room for his erstwhile companion, looking at every black face but Nkosinathi was not one of them.

'Maybe he is with Khule and the horses. Come on let's go.'

The Duke, dealing the cards, watched from the corner of his eye as and with a nod of his head tacitly ordered his henchmen to follow them. They needed no persuading to exact retribution from the two white men and as they headed for the doorway, two rough looking men, eager for easy money, joined them.

Georgie's warning had seen Nkosinathi return to Khulekani; help him move the horses out of sight in case of trouble.

'You have seen danger?'

'Maybe, the White men are in the lion's den and I know it is better to be in a tree than the den. Come we will take the horses behind that building and you will guard them. Have you a knife?'

Khulekani grinned, 'this knife has release the spirits of many white soldiers and a few more will not be a problem.'

'Not unless you have to my friend. Killing a Whiteman here is not the same as in battle. Stay quiet, stay out of sight that is the best thing to do. If I need you

I will call,' he said untying the two ponies and leading Khulekani into the shadows.

'Wait here, I will go and watch,' he said, silently retracing his steps to wait for Georgie and Petrus.

An hour later they emerged from the Star of the West looking around, aware that they might be followed. But the Duke's men were savvy, keeping out of sight until their prey emerged into the street. Two followed on their heels and two more headed for a second exit and from his seat The Duke kept a wary eye on proceedings.

He watched his thugs push through a crowd of drinkers satisfied that this time they would exact retribution and smiled to himself as one powerful looking individual stood aside to allow them free passage. Returning to his cards he did not notice that same man follow his thugs.

In the street Petrus had come to a halt, realising that the ponies were no longer tethered to the rail he looked round frantically and called out to Georgie. 'Where are the horses?' he exclaimed and then from across the street, he saw Nkosinathi beckoning him 'There Georgie look across the street, Koso.'

Georgie saw Nkosinathi and realised immediately what he had done. 'I told him to expect trouble and it looks like he's moved the our mounts.'

Nkosinathi waved a warning and Georgie looked round to see two men swinging sjamboks coming towards them and obviously intent on doing them harm.

'Aw shit! Come on, run,' shouted Georgie running across the street towards Nkosinathi and might have escaped unscathed except that two more thugs had outflanked them. They had left unseen by another door and were already closing in on them.

'Three against four and they are armed, not good odds,' said Georgie coming to a halt and beside him, Petrus had also stopped running and was weighing up their adversaries. Then things began to move quickly, Nkosinathi joined them, the thugs joined forces and began to close in.

'Where's Khule?'

'With the horses, have no fear Jiji he will come if we are in trouble.'

'Trouble is right. What do you want?' Georgie called out, 'money, here you can have all I have.'

'Oh yes we will have your money but first there is a score to settle,' said the leader smacking the sjambok into the palm of his hand.

'Come on boys, we can settle this amicably.'

'Very amicably,' said the man lurching forward and striking out at Petrus the signal for the rest of them to attack and with a menacing sneer on their faces each thug menacingly swung his sjambok.

Georgie sidestepped the first onslaught but as he turned from his attacker, a second sjambok slammed into his back and letting out out a yelp of pain withdrew several feet and out of range. Beside him Nkosinathi fared better, catching hold of one of the weapons as it swung past his head and wrenching it from its owner's hand. Standing shoulder to shoulder with Georgie he swung the weapon at their attackers making them pause and in that lull he suddenly found Khulekani at his side, his hunting knife in his hand.

'So you want to play dirty do you?' said one of the thugs producing an equally fearsome weapon.

'They are going to kill us,' growled Petrus, fear raising his belly.

'I don't think so,' boomed a voice from the shadows. 'There will be no killing here.'

Taken by surprise, the four thugs paused and turned to see a revolver pointing straight at them from a only a few feet away a strong enough incentive for them to stem their attack.

'I have six shots in this gun and there are only four of you. Now, that means I can afford to miss twice, or, and think about this, I take out only two of you and leave the other two outnumbered two to one. Those are the kinds of odd you scum understand. Right!, said the man behind the gun, his voice calm, steady and frightening.

Nobody moved, the four thugs seemed to get the message and then their leader stepped away from Georgie, a sure sign he was not prepared to call this new arrival's bluff.

'Okay, move away,' said the man with the gun edging his way between the two sets of belligerents. 'Go on, bugger off before I put a bullet in someone. Move!' he shouted.

It worked; one by one the thuggish louts let their weapons fall to their side before trudging back towards the Star of the West leaving Georgie to let out a sigh of relief.

'Thank you stranger, you saved our bacon.'

'I'm no stranger ye waster.'

'What?'

'Sergeant McNamara you are a disgrace, look at ye, scruffy, dirty and the kind of stubble on yer chin only an adolescent would be proud of.'

Georgie was dumbfounded and exhausted from the fight it took him a few seconds to comprehend what he was hearing. The voice was familiar, very familiar, and then he looked at the stranger, his eyes, grey, piercing, familiar and then he recognised the red beard.

'Bugger me, Patrick, where did you spring from?'

'I'll tell you over a drink Georgie boy. You and your friends need to watch your backs.'

'How did you know we were in trouble?'

'I was in the bar lookin' around, thinking I might catch sight of you if you really were here in Kimberly or maybe ask a few questions.'

'Why?' Georgie asked a little perplexed.

'I have another surprise for you, Ellen is here with me. It was her idea to come lookin' fer ye.'

'Where is she?'

'In there,' said Patrick, pointing with his thumb over his shoulder in the direction of the Star of the West.

'She cannot stay there, neither of you can, not now we have ruffled the Dukes feathers.'

'So it was the one in the top hat holding court at the card table that started all this was it?'

'Yes, he thinks he really is a Duke but he is just a low life card sharp.'

'I know, we arrived two days ago and I have spent a lot of time in the bar, getting my bearings, weighing the place up and I have seen him cheating. Tell you what Georgie he would not last long in the Sergeant's mess. I think that maybe the best form of defence is attack. What do you think?'

Georgie had no idea what Patrick had in mind but he was well aware of his friend's capabilities and retrieving his hat he dusted it off on his thigh and said, 'Petrus let me introduce Sergeant Patrick Donovan of the Twenty Fourth Regiment of Foot.'

'Ex Sergeant,' said Patrick extending his hand.

Petrus reciprocated and Georgie proceeded to tell him briefly of their relationship before turning to Nkosinathi.

'Patrick I want you to meet Koso, a good friend but he wasn't always so. Koso and Khule here were at Ulundi. They are friends now, help with the digging.'

'Digging?'

'Yes, we are working our own claim.'

'Have you found any diamonds?'

'Yes, lots but not enough to retire on quite yet.'

Georgie had expected to see neither Patrick nor Ellen ever again and could not believe the turn of events as he swung his pickaxe. After the fracas with the Duke's thugs, they had decided that it was too dangerous for them to remain the Star of the West and had found the private house a well-connected Burger who was very happy to rent it to Patrick and Ellen.

As he swung the pick, he re-lived his meeting with Ellen surprised at how good she looked dressed in expensive clothes and with her hair tied back. The urchin he had know had grown to become a striking and confident woman and he had listened intently as she told of what had happened since her husband's death.

'After Clarence died I was advised to go back to England. It was hard to begin with but once my lawyer had tied up all the loose ends life took a turn for the better.'

'So Clarence left you some money.'

'Something like that. It's a little more complicated and I will tell you the full story one day but for now I am simply overjoyed at finding you.'

'Not as overjoyed as I am. If Patrick here hadn't turned up when he did you might never have found me alive.'

'I've been thinking about that Georgie. This Duke fella sound like trouble, employing thugs to do his dirty work. If he has a mind to come after us we could be in real danger .'

'Yes, but at least we are reasonably safe in the miner's encampment. We tend to look after each other and if there is trouble it's snuffed out pretty quick but you could have a problem.'

'I wonder if I should take Ellen and leave town, go to Bloemfontein or somewhere a bit safer.'

'I think it might be a good idea Patrick. I would never forgive myself if anything happened to you two.'

Leaning on his shovel Georgie lifted his hat and wiped the sweat from his forehead with his forearm. Patrick and Ellen had decided to leave Kimberly in a few days and he knew that it was the right thing to do, the Duke had a long reach and they had made an enemy of him.

He had agreed with Patrick and Ellen that they should head for Bloemfontein and stay there for a while, until the dust settled.

Sighing deeply he lifted his shovel and returned to his digging but before he plunged the implement into the earth he took a look around him, Nkosinathi was a few yards away loading the bucket and above he could see Petrus and Khulekani ready to begin hauling the load of shale up to the rim. Apart from the Duke he was feeling content enough and turned back to his job. They had worked the claim hard, invested in new equipment and with the greatly increased rate the crushing machines afforded they were filtering large amounts of the lode-stock and were becoming rich.

Turning back to his work, Georgie noticed the bird life, sparse as it was round the diggings was none existent and then he heard a mule braying in the distance. The atmosphere seemed unnatural, it was a hot day, unusually still, and a sixth sense began to nag at him and he stood still listening. That was when he felt the first tremor, almost imperceptible but quickly turning into something alarming and then suddenly, there was a loud crack. A sound feared throughout the diggings, the sound of rock splitting and without further warning a shear face detached itself and came crashing down on men working below.

'Look out,' he shouted, and then looking to his own safety turned to run but he was too late, loose rock and dust crashed down with a thunderous roar and engulfed him.

Not far away Nkosinathi had been more fortunate, Georgie's warning giving him just enough time to dive out of the way of the deluge and as the the rumble of the rock fall died away it was replaced by shouts and screams of stricken men and he looked for Georgie. At first he could see no sign until he saw a hand protruding from the morass, the fingers clenching and unclenching and he called out his name.

'Jiji!' he shouted diving forward and with his bare hands he began frantically pulling away boulders and great shards of rock to expose first an arm and then Georgie's head and chest and finally he was able to pull him coughing and spluttering free from his tomb.

'You are still alive Jiji.'

'Only just I think,' said Georgie gasping for breath.

'Here, some water to wash the dust from your eyes,' said Nkosinathi producing a leather bucket half full of brackish water.

'Phew, that was close,' said Georgie splashing the water over his face. 'I couldn't have got out of there alone. You saved my life Koso.'

'Then we are even Jiji.'

'Georgie focused on the bright brown eyes looking down at him and nodded his head. 'Yes Koso we are even.'

It took a full half an hour for Petrus and Khulekani to reach the floor of the mine and clamber over the debris to Georgie and Nkosinathi.

'Are you all right, you look terrible Georgie covered in all that dust.'

'Yes I'm fine now but if it hadn't been for Koso here I was a dead man.'

Petrus looked at Nkosinathi who returned his gaze, the gaze of a proud Zulu warrior and a new and lasting respect filled Petrus's eyes. The native had saved him from a serious beating and now he had saved Georgie's life. It was a turning point, brought up to believe the Blackman was inferior he could see plainly that was not the case.

'Well done Koso, you are a good man, god will smile on you.'

Nkosinathi's face broke out into a huge grin. For a Whiteman to praise him was indeed and honour but beside him Georgie was in more sombre mood.

'I think we are finished here. Look at all that, it will take months to clear away. It is not as if we can process the rock, it's not blue ground, just rock and stone. There will be no diamonds in there.'

Petrus and the two natives looked at the mess, a once productive, it claim lay in ruins.

'What are we going to do?'

'I don't know Petrus but as soon as we've helped find more survivors I will need a drink – to celebrate my resurrection!'

Less than a mile away Patrick felt the ground shake. He was talking to the owner of a hardware store when he and heard the rumble and as the side of the Big Hole detached itself he gave the storekeeper an enquiring look.

'They've had a rock fall; we're getting more and more. Hope no one's been killed.'

Patrick spun round to look towards the Big Hole and as sound died away, he saw a cloud of dust rise from the mine.

'Georgie!' he exclaimed and without another word ran towards the Star of the West and Ellen to tell her the news.

'What of Georgie, is he alright?'

'I don't know but they say miners have been killed in these rock falls.'

'Not Georgie!' exclaimed Ellen.

Patrick grabbed her arm and led her from the building. She felt sick, they had come all this way to find Georgie and to lose him so soon did not seem fair but she had little time to dwell. Rushing past were men on foot and riders, pouring from the town and towards the mine. Patrick looked past them and could see the majority of the rescue seemed to be taking place to the left, the side where Georgie's claim lay.

'What has happened, has anyone been injured,' he asked the first man he came to.

'I think so, they've dug a few out but some of them look dead.'

He pointed to a group of miners and to Patrick's horror; he saw several bodies lying on the ground. He could not tell who they were and it would do no good speculating. Then he saw a group digging frantically, saw several men pulled free and alive and his hopes rose.

'What is it Patrick, what can you see.'

'They are digging them out.'

'Can you see Georgie?'

'No but I can see his Zulu friend.'

Sure enough, Nkosinathi, tall and muscular, stood out from the crowd, his arms working like a steam engines pistons as he pulled rocks from the pile and then to his delight he saw Georgie and Petrus. They two were helping with the rescue, shovelling loose earth left by the boulders Nkosinathi was removing.

'He's there, he's safe. Look,' said Patrick pointing and gripping Ellen's dress he held her tight as she peered over the edge. They had stood back from the rescue, waited until the miners had cleared most of the rubble. The dead were already on their way to the morgue in town and the men were coming up from the floor of the mine talking in subdued voices. They had witnessed a tragedy, worked until they dropped and it was time for a well-earned rest.

Georgie and his friends were amongst the last to reach the surface and stood for a while looking down forlornly at what once one their path to riches and it was there Patrick and Ellen found them and Ellen could not help throwing her arms around her cousin.

'Thank God you are safe,' said Patrick. 'Is that where you were working, was that your claim?'

'Yes Patrick, I'm afraid it is – was. Looks like our days as diamond miners are about over.'

'I'm sorry.'

'Don't be. It was fun while it lasted, we have made some money and there is a rumour going round that the De Beers brothers are buying up the spoiled claims. I heard they are going to try to mine from underground, dig tunnels. Maybe we can salvage something.'

'What will you do now?'

'I have no plans – except..." his voice tailed off, thought of Annika rekindled, a perfect time to return to the farmstead. He thought about her for short periods during each day but now he just couldn't get her out of his mind. 'Petrus what do you think about selling up, if we can get a buyer, and heading back up into the Transvaal?'

A week later, many miles to the north, the three riders reached a fork in the road. Ahead lay Newcastle and the Transvaal and to the east the narrow track that led towards Zululand. Khulekani had remained behind in Kimberly and now it was time for Nkosinathi to leave them and begin his dangerous journey across the lands of John Dunn.

'Goodbye my friend, it has been good knowing you.'

'And you also Jiji. You have shown me many things and made me rich enough to buy more cattle and all the cartridges I need to feed my people.'

'A noble thing indeed and I wish you luck, take care of yourself.'

Saluting their black friend, Georgie and Petrus headed towards the Transvaal and Nkosinathi turned his horse eastwards, towards home.

'Well my friend, we are not exactly millionaires are we, but at least we did make some money,' said Georgie as Nkosinathi rode away, giving a final wave as he disappeared over the brow of a hill and into the long grass.

'Yes, and I saw a bit of the outside world.'

'And what did you think of it?'

'Not much, it is as Papa said, the Uitlanders are greedy and have no God.'

'Well you seemed to enjoy yourself doing some of the bad things. You are happy to have a pocket full of cash and you certainly like a drink.'

Petrus blushed and looked away. It was true he had enjoyed his time away from home and he had acquired a taste of beer, but still he was glad to be going home.

'What will you do with the money? You could buy your own farm maybe.'

'Maybe and what will you do with yours?'

'I wondered about farming. I've only ever been a soldier.'

'And a miner.'

'And a miner,' laughed Georgie. 'I probably have enough to live on for a year or two but then what?'

'You are coming home with me for a time; perhaps we can teach you some more about farming.'

Georgie rubbed the side of his face and wondered, what did the future hold for him? One thing was for sure, he would see Annika and that could be a defining moment. Of Ellen and Patrick he was more sure, they would meet again as planned, they had spoken of the future what they might do and when Ellen learned that Georgie was determined to return to the Transvaal with Petrus she had made her feelings clear.

'Patrick, we can't let him disappear again for years on end. We will go to the Transvaal, at least for a while. I have money; we can live as we want, so why not find a nice place there. We could see Georgie regularly couldn't we?'

'The only place you could safely stay would be in Pretoria or Newcastle. I don't know where I will be after I have spent some time at the farm.' said Georgie, pausing as Annika's likeness clouded his thoughts.

'I quite like the idea of spending some time up there,' said Patrick, 'it will give us all time to decide what to do. I haven't done much since I left the army Georgie; I have just looked after Ellen.'

Ellen smiled. 'And you have done a good job of looking after me. That's what you will be doing for a while longer if I have my way.'

Chapter 26

Georgie and Petrus broke camp early, ready to pass through the Nek and enter the final part of their journey. Petrus rolled up his sleeping mat and began to dismantle the small tent, gratefully accepting the mug of steaming coffee Georgie handed him.

'Looks like you will soon be home Petrus, only a few more miles eh?'

'Yes, it will be good to see Mutti and Papa and my brother and sister. I have missed them more than I expected.'

'I suppose you must have,' said Georgie taking a sip of his own steaming hot brew.

'And you, have you missed Annika?'

Georgie almost scolded his lips as the shock of Petrus's comment drove home.'

'Er...yes I suppose I have.'

'Suppose, come on Georgie I have seen you two together. There is something between you isn't there. This is why you are coming home with me, mm?'

'Petrus, I'm not so sure it was a good idea taking you with me to Kimberly. You wouldn't have asked such a question a year ago.'

'Was it that long since we left?'

'It must be.'

'You have not answered my question.'

'And I'm not going to. Saddle your pony and let's get going,' said Georgie dispensing with his morning coffee, over the small fire and dampening it down.

Mutti was hanging out the washing when she first saw the two riders. They were still many hundreds of yards away and she had to squint to try to recognise them.

'Annika, fetch the gun, riders approaching,' she called towards the open door of the farmhouse.

'Where Mutti, where are they.'

Her mother pointed towards the track coming from the south, across the hills, a track only those with local knowledge might use.

'I see them.'

'Just keep an eye on them until we know who they are. Your father will be back soon, a gunshot will warn him if it's trouble.'

'You are expecting trouble?'

'Not really but there have been some bad words said about your brother, some of the Burghers disagree vehemently with his point of view and I know he has been in a fight. Maybe someone is coming to seek revenge.'

'Oh Mutti, don't be silly.'

'Better safe than sorry, there is something about those two. Why would the take the hunter's trail?'

Annika raised her hand to shield her eyes from the sun and tried to make out the riders and then she felt her heart miss a beat. They were both wearing leather jackets, the kind she had made for her brother and Georgie. Could it be? She gripped the clothes rail to steady herself, to concentrate on the lead rider a well-built man, easy in the saddle and she was sure that it was Petrus, and the rider following, was it was Georgie?

'It's Petrus and Georgie, they have come home,' she called out.

Mutti, with the gun held ready, strained her older eyes trying to seek out familiar features and suddenly she knew her youngest had returned.

'Go and fetch your father, fetch the baby.'

Annika did as she was told, first running into the field where her father was supervising his native labourers, and then back to the house, her chest heaving from her exertions and by the time the riders were within hailing distance, the welcoming committee had assembled. Papa and Mutti stood together by the washing line whilst Annika and her baby waited on the verandah.

'Papa, Mutti,' said Petrus jumping from his saddle and walking towards them, a huge grin on his face, 'we have come back to help with the harvest.

'Oh Petrus, you really have come back to us, I am so happy,' said his mother.

Papa remained silent, acknowledging his son with only a cursory nod of his head, his attention more on Georgie.

'I have brought Georgie back with me for a few days. We found diamonds, I have seen many things,' said Petrus full of enthusiasm.

'And you have brought him, the one we sheltered and took in as part of our family.'

'Yes father, we have been partners since we left, shared everything.'

'Everything except him!' he snapped pointing towards Annika.

Georgie had dismounted and was tying his pony to the rail when he saw the look on Jos's face, a look that he did not understand and then he looked towards Annika.

'What is it Papa?' asked Petrus as confused as Georgie at Jos's manner.

'Annika, she has had a baby boy not two weeks ago and she is not married. She has brought shame on our house.'

At that moment, the baby cried out and Georgie looked at Annika in disbelief. She had forsaken him and found another, dashing his hopes and longings in an instant.

'You,' snapped Papa, 'you Englishman, in the eyes of God you have brought shame upon us.'

Georgie was bewildered, what was he talking about, what had he done, who was the father of the baby in Annika's arms?

'I...I do not understand.'

'You Englishman have fathered my daughter's baby out of wedlock and brought shame on this household.'

It was true he and Annika had made love, but only a single time, frantic, hurried love and he could not believe the child could be his. He looked at Annika and began to walk towards her, their eyes locked together and he knew then that the baby really was his. He had a son by the one woman he wanted, and the mixture of conflicting feelings inside his breast made him feel unusually weak.

'Annika is it true? I...I had no idea.'

'Yes Georgie it is true Hans is our baby.'

'You have chosen his name already?'

'Why of course. I did not know if I would ever see you again.'

'I have thought of nothing else ever since I left. I always planned to come back for you. I love you know.'

'Oh Petrus, I feel the same but I have offended my father and Christiaan wants to kill you. I don't know what to do.'

For what seemed an eternity the two of them stood looking at each other until finally Annika spoke. 'Don't you want to see your son?'

Georgie exhaled a great lungful of air as the reality of the situation dawned and his eyes began to shine with the pleasure of a new father.

'Here, look,' said Annika pulling back the soft blanket to show the baby's face. 'He looks like you Georgie.'

'Does he?'

'Of course he does,' she said smiling, and Georgie could not help but gaze at the infant for a minute or two longer, and then he looked at Papa Jos scowling, Mutti with a neutral look on her face and Petrus simply looking bewildered. He looked at each in turn, made up his mind in an instant and turned back to Annika.

'The lad needs a proper father. Will you marry me Annika?'

'Yes,' she said, her voice barely audible and tears in her eyes.

'Right, that's settled then. Mister De Wit,' he said addressing Jos. 'Mister De Wit, I would like to ask your permission to marry your daughter.'

Jos De Wit remained silent, his face deadpan, but by his side his wife seemed pleased and that gave Georgie the encouragement he needed.

'Mister De Wit I spent most of the past year searching for my fortune. I know that your way is to spurn the quest for wealth but you came here many years ago and simply claimed the land you farm. I had nothing; if I am to make my way in life, care for a wife and bring up a family then I need some form of income. Although I am not a rich man and not yet, a good farmer, I believe I will have enough money from the diamonds to buy a farm hereabouts and it is my intention to live on it and bring up Hans as a good Christian. Sir, do I have your permission.'

Still Jos said nothing, instead he filled his pipe and the tension was almost unbearable but if Georgie had learned one thing living amongst the Boers, it was that you could not rush them. Finally, Jos said 'I will think about it. For now you are not welcome in my house – you can sleep in the barn with the horses.' With that, he walked back to his native labourers and left his family to pick up the pieces.

Annika took a step towards Georgie holding young Hans close to her chest and looked at her mother.

'Mutti, he will come round? Georgie has already asked me to marry him and I have accepted. Please make him give permission.'

'Well this is a shock. Georgie you are not doing this to salve your conscience are you?'

'No, I truly love Annika and want to marry her. I did not know about Hans, how could I?'

'He will agree,' said Petrus 'but you will have trouble with Christiaan I think.'

'He is not here, he is in Pretoria stirring up the Burghers,' said Annika. 'If Papa gives permission before Christiaan returns then maybe all will be well with him.'

The room in Hendrik De Klerq's house was small but not too small to accommodate Hendrik, six Burghers of the town and at the far end of the rustic table a morose looking Christiaan. Unhappy with the state of affairs as a result of the inconclusive peace, they had gathered in secret to plot against the British.

'Gentlemen let us say a prayer before we start,' said De Klerq and each of the assembly bowed his head. 'Dear God, guide us through these difficult times, help us create the state we desire, give us the freedom that is rightly ours and banish the Uitlanders from the Transvaal –Amen.'

'Amen.'

'As chairman of this committee I take it upon myself to read out a list of demands we will make when we are in a position of strength. Have no fear that in a year or two from now we will have gathered together the vast majority of the Boer nation to our cause.'

'Can you be sure of that Hennie, we are still under the protectorate of the British Crown and if they suspect we are plotting to kick them out of the Transvaal they will surely send in more troops.'

'Not after the hiding we gave them three years ago,' added Christiaan.

'Yes, maybe we did beat them but we haven't got rid of them. The Volksraad cannot pass laws without gaining the consent of the British government. The natives are allowed to own property and live amongst us and we are in debt up to our eyes.'

'All the more reason to plan for a future uprising and get rid of them for good,' growled Petrus thumping the table.

'I think maybe it is time for a smoke my friends, we don't want to get too carried away. It's early days, we don't want to be discovered and stopped before we are strong,' said De Klerq casting a sideways glance at Christiaan.

He would need to speak with some of the Burghers about Christiaan he was becoming too much of a hot head and likely, in some unguarded moment, to give away their secret – the last thing they needed.

'Have we heard if Paul Kruger has returned from London yet Hennie?' asked one of the men.

'No I have heard nothing. The convention should have taken place a month ago and I suppose Oom Paul will want to tell the Volksraad in person the outcome of the negotiations.'

'Do you think he will succeed with our demands?'

'Yes, mostly I believe. The war cost the British a lot of money and I have it on good authority that they sued for peace because of the spiralling costs. They have what they want, suzerainty over us, and control of foreign policy and they probably think we are happy with this state of affairs.'

'But we are not,' said Christiaan.

'No Christiaan we are not and we will work to make sure we regain our freedom but let's wait and see what Oom Paul brings us.'

The stagecoach had made good progress over the hard, dry veldt and inside its only passengers sat opposite one another. Patrick was dozing; his eyes heavy with the boredom whilst opposite Ellen looked out of the window opening.

'I had forgotten how dusty it is here Patrick,' she said suddenly, shaking him from his slumber. 'I cannot wait to find a decent hotel and clean up. We have been on the road for a week and I am becoming weary of travelling.'

'I can understand but we are nearly at Newcastle. We can stop there; rest a while before we carry on up to Pretoria.'

'What about Georgie, what arrangement did you make with him?'

'He gave me the address of the De Wit farm and said he intended stoppin' there for a while, help with the harvest and that we should call there or get a message to him when we get settled.'

'Well I hope we get settled soon.'

Patrick smiled at her, for someone not used to arduous journeying she had borne up remarkably well.

'I think we are just about there, you shouldn't have to wait much longer my dear,' he said leaning back in his seat.

For the next hour they sat in silence, the coach clattering and bumping over the uneven ground and then they heard the driver whistle through his teeth. Patrick leaned out of his window to see the cause of the driver's vocalization and no more than a few hundred yards away, he saw the way station, an old wooden structure that had seen better days. The coach began to slow and within minutes came to a stop alongside the main building and after helping Ellen to the ground Patrick saw a man emerge from a shuttered doorway.

The man who seemed to be the owner of the place, speaking as he did to the driver and after calling to two of his native servants left them with the driver to unhitch the horses and unload the passenger's trunk.

'Do you have a dining room,' Patrick asked

'We do, it's not exactly the finest dining you will ever taste but it will fill your belly.'

Ellen was less than impressed by the accommodation. but after such a gruelling journey, she was happy to sleep anywhere so long as it was in a bed and in the morning they would look for a decent hotel .

Patrick rose early the following morning and, after a brief discussion with the proprietor, managed to hire a buggy for them to have a look for somewhere a little more comfortable in the town itself.

'You know Patrick I feel that I have come home. I know I have complained about the dust and the poor state of some of the places we have been but we have found Georgie and that does make me very happy.'

'I'm glad about dat, the boy means a lot to me too. We covered some ground together you know, campaigning and the like. We got into some scrapes I can tell ye,' he said in a broad Irish brogue.

'Well Patrick, I think I want to have a good luck round here see what it's like. I know it's not London or Cape Town. Maybe like you I have had experiences that have changed me. Helping in the hospital during the war made me realise how far I have come since my childhood. Those days with Georgie stealing silk handkerchiefs seem such a long time ago, my life has moved on and it's time I settled down.'

'To be sure you've become very philosophical all of a sudden Ellen my girl.'

'That's a big word,' she said and burst out laughing.

'Here comes out transport, it looks a little more comfortable than the coach,' said Patrick as one of the station workers drove up to them.

'Boss says to give you this,' said the native boy and jumping from the seat handed the reigns to Patrick.

'Tell your boss I will send someone back with it in a day or two, when we have found somewhere to stay.

It was no more than two miles into Newcastle and as Patrick flicked the reigns and the horse began to move, he took a sideways glance at Ellen. He had never seen her so happy and wondered if it might be the time to ask her to marry him.

'Ellen.'

She turned her head and smiled at him.

'Ellen, will you marry me?'

She held her smile but behind it her eyes changed and Patrick's heart sank but he persisted.

'You seem so happy and I know you love me, what do you say, say yes.'

Her smile faded, he knew she was going to refuse him and as the feeling of dejection came over him, he could not help but lower his eyes. It was now or never, he felt that he had never had so good a chance of winning her but if she spurned his advances while in such a happy mood then she would never say yes. It was a shock, it made his chest tighten, and his heart thump and his head swirled as disappointment engulfed him. He had felt for a long time that they were made for each other but she was rejecting him.

'Patrick,' she said gripping his arm, 'I will marry you but not yet. I have something to tell you.'

He looked up, into her eyes, inquisitive, not knowing what to expect.

'Patrick the love of my life I am a wealthy woman.'

'I know dat.'

'But you have no idea how wealthy,' she said in a trembling voice and for a few seconds their eyes bored into each other's brains. 'Patrick when Clarence's father died I expected just enough to survive on as an independent woman. The old man was a bastard, threatening to cut me off completely except for a hundred pounds a year. But when his sons drowned, I became the sole beneficiary to his estate and more than that, the clever solicitor I employed made sure I inherited his sons estates as well. There were no other beneficiaries just me.'

'So how much was it?'

'I can't tell you, not yet. It's into millions that's all I will say.'

Patrick's eyes widened, he could not imagine such a sum of money and for a what seemed an eternity he stared at her. 'How does that affect us, what has it got to do with you not agreeing to marry me?' he was finally able to say.

'I have agreed to marry you, but not yet. Don't you see, if we get married you will have control and I don't want that, not yet.'

Patrick was bewildered and sat back holding the reigns oblivious to his surroundings.

'Don't look so glum, it will work out, just give me time. It's not easy being a millionairess when you grew up in the gutter you know.'

Georgie ate alone in the stable, his back against the wall and staring through the open door at the wide expanse of the De Wit farm. It had come as a shock finding out that he was a father of such a healthy, beautiful boy and it made him feel proud but the question of marring Annika was weighing him down. In Boer society, the head of the family was all-powerful, he had already learned that, and to go against Jos's decision would be folly. Sighing, he pushed his half-eaten dinner to one side, stood up and walked to the open doorway with his mind in turmoil. He had hoped to return a rich man, sweep Annika off her feet and marry her anyway but the question of her giving birth out of wedlock had created an obstacle and he wasn't sure of how to overcome it and for ten minutes, he stood pondering until the sound of footsteps, heavy footsteps, disturbed his thoughts.

'Englishman I have come to a decision. I have spoken with my wife and daughter and they have convinced me that the right thing to do is to allow you to ask for my daughter's hand. I must say I am not happy but it seems the best solution.'

Jos did then what he always did when a problem weighed upon him, he took out his pipe and began to fill it.

'Petrus has also spoken for you, he says you are a good man. He told me of his time amongst the Uitlanders and says that you found many small diamonds and that you have enough to buy a farm.'

'I might have, depends on what the asking price is. I have considered farming, Annika knows how to farm and I am not afraid of hard work. It seems the best solution.'

'It does and it is in keeping with our tradition. The boy will have to be brought up in our religion; I do not want him godless like the rest of your kind.'

'We are not godless; we just don't worship as often as you do.'

'Come, we will smoke on the verandah. Tomorrow Christiaan will return and I will tell him of my decision.

Georgie nodded and followed Jos towards the house, relieved for the time being but Christiaan was another matter, a dangerous man and he knew that he would have a fight on his hands when the elder brother returned.

Sleep did not come easy and when the dawn finally broke, Georgie was wide-awake and brushing the straw from his hair, rose from his makeshift bed.

'Good morning,' said a soft female voice as he splashed the water over his face from the trough.

'Annika, hello, your father told me I can ask for your hand in marriage.'

'I know and I hope you haven't changed your mind.'

Wiping the water from his eyes he marvelled at how beautiful she looked and could imagine that any man would want her as his wife, but she was his.

'You look lovely, how is Hans this morning?'

'He is well, I gave him a feed not an hour ago and he is sleeping. I saw you come to the trough and thought it a good time to meet.'

'I'm glad you did. I don't know quite what to do.'

'Papa has accepted you but Christiaan could be a problem.'

'What of your mother, what does she think?'

'She knows that you work hard and she wants me married as soon as possible to avoid the shame I have brought upon the family.'

'Are you happy to marry me?'

'Oh yes Georgie, of course I am.'

'Did Petrus tell you about the diamonds, the money we made in Kimberly?'

'Yes, he said that you have enough to buy a farm. is that what you will do?'

'A farm for us, you teach me the ways of farming and I will work hard for you and Hans.'

Her eyes gleamed, she was happy that her son was to have a proper father and happy that she could make a life for them on their own farm and happy also that she was truly in love.

'Petrus told me about your friend from England, the Irishman.'

'And Ellen no doubt.'

'Yes, who is she; he said she is your cousin.'

Georgie smiled, things did not seem half so bad as they had only a few hours before. He almost had a wife and child and his best friend, favourite cousin had come to Africa to find him, and for the first time in many years, he had a family that was not the army.

Nkosinathi had family, lots of them. In his extended family were Mondli his father and Themba his mother but as a rich man, Mondli had married three more wives who had produced many children and he had many half brothers and sisters and his life growing up in the kraal had been a happy one. However, times had changed; the King was dead, the Kingdom broken up and the kraals reduced to near starvation.

Since his appointment John Dunn, the one-time friend of the Zulus had changed. Since his elevation to Chief, he had demanded exorbitant taxes in cattle and mealie and left the kraals in a desperate situation and returning home almost two months earlier, he had found Mondli's people in crisis and had immediately set out hunting game to help feed them.

'My son, it is good to have you back. Your gun feeds us well; we will regain our strength and plant more crops. We will rise again,' said Mondli cutting a piece of blackened meat from the the carcass of Nkosinathi's latest kill.

'Yes father, we will.'

'Tell me about your travels. You left almost a year ago to buy cartridges and did not come back. I worried that a wild animal had taken you.'

'Ha, wild animals, yes wild animals but more the two legged kind.'

'How so?'

'The men of John Dunn who patrol the land, men who show little mercy, men who take everything they can. They hunted me like a wild animal but I am a Zulu warrior and they could not catch me.'

He leaned towards the fire and with his knife cut a piece of meat from the dwindling carcass, and as he chewed, he remembered those difficult times.

'Those men of John Dunn, you must be careful my son, they are dangerous.'

'I know father, I will be careful. I will hunt near the forest for a few days, for the black pigs; they are tasty are they not.'

Mondli laughed for the first time in many months and for once went to his sleeping mat with a happy heart.

The horses picked their way silently through the long grass, stopping well before the crest of the low hill. Two of the riders dismounted and looked towards Rabanina who silently swept his arm across his chest. It was his signal for them run into the tall grass and in the moonlight, he watched as the tall stems swayed back and forth in their wakes and for many minutes sat motionless in his saddle until the swaying grass heralded the return of the scouts.

'Oh masterful one, the kraal sleeps; there is no one on guard. They sleep, the fires are out and the cattle stand in the coral.'

'How many cattle?'

The man opened and closed his hands four times indicating the number.

'Not many, I expected at least twice that number. They must be hiding part of the herd, we will find the hiding place but first, we will search for the one known as Nkosinathi and kill him. Should any of them resist then you know what to do. We will go now to the kraal.' he said nudging his horse forwards.

The Zulu had outwitted him, made a fool of him and silently Rabanina swore revenge, no one got the better of him and lived. Ahead of him in the moonlight the scout had stopped and raised his arm, the signal to dismount and leave the horses and after tying his reigns to a tree Rabanina signalled his men to follow him and the group, slipping silently to the ground, unslung their rifles and spread out.

Rabanina was first reach the crest of the hill and there he lay flat on his stomach scrutinising the valley below. A wall of interlaced thorn bushes protected the kraal and past it, silhouetted in the moonlight, were the tops of the beehive huts. It was a peaceful scene, but he knew it would not last. Scanning the open ground towards the village, he looked for movement but there was none, no sentinel safeguarding the sleeping villagers and he knew their task would be easy.

Standing up Rabanina signalled his band of marauders to follow him and swiftly they set off towards the kraal no more than two hundred yards away. Within minutes the first of his men had pulled down the gate and the rest streamed in to search amongst the beehive huts. They had their orders to guard the tunnel like entrances to the huts in case anyone tried to make his escape and await their leader's orders.

Rabanina knew the layout of the kraal, knew the location of the headman's hut, and it was to there he strode.

'Mondli, leader of the village, come from your slumber and meet the representative of John Dunn, your lord and master,' he shouted, awakening the whole kraal.

At first, there was little response but as the people began to peer out from their huts to see what was going on, screams and shouts filled the air as they realised their predicament. The intruders were not gentle, digging rifle butts into the bodies of those inquisitive enough to look out, kicking them, and then Rabanina spoke again.

'I have come here to collect for John Dunn what is due to him, taxes, Royal cattle that do not belong here. Come Mondli, show yourself.'

Mondli was old and tired, weak from months of semi starvation and yet it was a proud chieftain who emerged to face Rabanina.

'What is it you want coming here in the middle of the night; we have paid our tributes to the lord and master of the land. We have nothing left to give.'

'Nkosinathi, your son, where is he?'

'Nkosinathi?'

'Yes old man your son, where is he, which hut is he in?'

'He is not here; he left more than a year ago and has not returned.'

'You lie,' said Rabanina angrily hitting Mondli across the face with the back of his hand.

Mondli stepped back as the force of the blow almost knocked him over. 'I tell the truth on the spirits of my forefathers, Nkosinathi is not here.'

Rabanina looked the old man in the eye and was unsure that he was telling the truth and his anger welled to the surface.

'Search the village,' he shouted to his men. 'The first to bring me the renegade will be well rewarded.'

Whooping with joy, his men began to drag anyone they could find from the huts but Nkosinathi was not amongst them. Dumisani and Somopho, Nkosinathi's brothers resembled him enough for closer inspection. Rabanina walked towards them, pointing his rifle at Dumisani, aggression that was not wasted. Dumisani's eyes widened in fear as he looked at the small black orifice and Rabanina pressed home his advantage.

'You, brother of Nkosinathi, where is he?'

'I don't know.'

'You, tell me where your brother is,' said Rabanina turning towards Somopho.

The terrified native looked at the ground, unable to speak until he felt the rifle barrel smack against his naked shoulder and grimacing with pain he looked up, and Rabanina hit him again.

'Tell me or you will die.'

Something happened to Somopho at that moment, an inner strength maybe, perhaps it was the life force of a Zulu warrior, but at that moment, he did not fear death and looking at Rabanina, he lifted himself to his full height, scowled with disdain at this man who had wrecked their lives and was looking to kill his brother.

'You think I will not kill you. I will kill you and I will kill everyone in this kraal until I find he whom I seek.'

Dumisani could see he would do as he said and could bear his oppression no longer. He did not fear for himself but did for the rest of the villagers and he felt forced to relent.

'He left to find a trading post in the north, to buy cartridges to hunt. It is as my father says, he has been gone more than a year, he has never returned. Look, we are starving, we have barely enough cattle to feed ourselves and you take most of the maize. Take what you want and leave us alone.'

At that moment, Rabanina's lieutenant arrived and whispered something in his ear. Rabanina looked thoughtful for a moment. 'You are hiding cattle that belong to the White Queen, cattle John Dunn should take care of until they are called for. Where are they?'

Dumisani had decided that they must tell where the cattle were for this man of John Dunn's was angry and he feared that his men might kill them all.

'If you will leave us alone I will show you.'

By mid-afternoon, Rabanina's men had rounded up the cattle hidden in the forest and were slowly herding the animals towards the kraal. At the entrance, Mondli, sat in silence with some of the elders and watched them approach. He knew in his heart of hearts that to lose so many of the herd spelled doom for his people, without those cattle and without Nkosinathi bringing meat they could not survive another winter.

As the first of the cows came to a halt, grazing the lush grass surrounding the kraal Mondli rose to his feet. It was as if knew his destiny had arrived for he was not only the leader of his people but their guardian and he believed he had failed. The good times, when the King ruled over them and food was plentiful were no more. Since their defeat by the British and the partitioning of the Kingdom, corruption and greed had taken over, old scores were being settled and life was difficult but Rabanina had no feelings of compassion. His search for Nkosinathi had proved in vain and he had decided to exact retribution from the whole village.

'Mondli, you have hidden cattle that rightfully belong to the Royal herd and for this you must pay. I will take those that are rightfully the White Queens' and half of your herd in punishment. What's more, we have found a grain store you have not declared and I will take all that is stored there.'

'You leave us to starve; you take more than we can give? How is that the deed of good and compassionate ruler? Is that not the way of a tyrant?'

'Mondli, you have cheated John Dunn of his rightful taxes and you must pay. You have hidden away the one called Nkosinathi and for that you must pay.'

Mondli snapped, it was too much for him to bear and as fast as his old and pained body could carry him he lunged at his tormentor, gripping him around the throat and despite his advanced years, began to throttle Rabanina. His grip was firm but still not enough for the younger man to break and to draw his knife, plunging into Mondli's heart.

'Do not dare to attack me old man,' he said, as Mondli sank to his knees, his lips red with blood.

Somopho saw his father fall and rushed to his aid but he was too late and before he could retaliate, two of Rabanina's men gripped his arms and threw him to the ground.

'Come, leave them,' said Rabanina striding towards his horse. 'Gather the men, set fire to the huts and let's take these cattle home,' he said and within minutes the the raiders had left a scene of panic inside the kraal.

The Zulus fought to stem the flames, rescue anything of value and as the men and boys beat the burning thatch the women and smaller children brought water from the stream in anything they could find.

'What do we do now?' asked a forlorn and exhausted Dumisani as the last of the fires were extinguished

'I do not know brother; we have nothing left save the crops in the fields. At least they did not take those.'

'We are weak from lack of food, we are finished,' he said sinking to his knees.

'We need Nkosinathi more than ever but it was he they came for not the cattle. If he had been here we might have been spared and our father still alive.'

'But we cannot deny Nkosinathi; he is the one to keep us together.'

'And where is he now?'

Nkosinathi was still several miles away; walking his horse with the pigs he had shot hanging from its sides. It had taken him almost three days to reach the forest hunt and return, skirting the few kraals along the way and almost home again his spirits were rising. Looking between the low-lying hills to the south, he searched for the wisps of smoke rising from the cooking fires but could see none. At first, he guessed that he was still too far away but then, slowly, the cold hand of fear gripped his heart and he coaxed his horse on as fast as she could go for the last few miles, and when the village finally came into view, his heart sank.

A scene of devastation met his eyes, the fires were out but the half-burned huts stood like giant deformed insects, blackened and broken. The roofs were almost gone and ashes replaced half of the surrounding protective wall of thorns. He could see figures walking about and as he drew nearer, he began to recognise faces he knew well.

'Mandible, what has happened?' he asked the first person he reached.

With sad eyes, the man looked up. 'John Dunn's men came looking for you and when they could not find you they took everything and burned the kraal. Mondli's dead, their leader killed him.'

Nkosinathi stiffened with shock as the dagger of despair plunged into his heart and he let out a great roar of rage.

'Rabanina, son of John Dunn you have done this. You have done this and I swear on the spirit of Mondli that you will die for it,' cursed Nkosinathi.

Chapter 27

The underground movement was still small, just a few hotheads with a hatred of any foreigners in the Transvaal, their common denominator. Christiaan had joined them soon after it became clear that they were not wholly free of the British, becoming one of the main agitators and Hendrik De Klerq and his friends had several times to intervene as the young hot head became embroiled in arguments. They were working in secret and did not want the authorities involved. If Christiaan were to be arrested for brawling they could be exposed and there might be serious repercussions for the movement.

'Christiaan, I thought you were going back to your farm, you are still here in Pretoria.'

'Yes, I wanted to meet with Anders Van Buren, he has contacts in Natal and can bring weapons in for us.'

'I know Anders, he did bring in guns during the rebellion but they cost a lot of money and we do not have much. Wait; wait until we have more support before you go chasing after guns and anyway it will be a committee decision not yours.'

Christiaan's eyes flashed for a second until reason overtook his emotions and he nodded his head in agreement.

'I know Hennie, but I am eager to rid us of the Uitlanders.'

'You might like to know that Oom Paul is back from Europe. I think he got most of what we wanted so perhaps we have been too hasty. The British have relinquished many of their powers and reduced out national debt. We have won many concessions.'

'That still doesn't solve the problem of the Uitlanders.'

'I think the Volksraad will be able to take care of them. There are not so many, a few laws to restrict their activities should be enough.'

'We should still make plans to get rid of these newcomers; they are not welcome in our land.'

'We will Christiaan; we are meeting at my house again tonight. That is what I have come to tell you, we need to be ready to ferment an uprising to throw these Uitlanders out of the Transvaal.

Georgie was sitting with Annika and their baby on the verandah when he saw Jos come out of the house with a grim expression on his face followed by Petrus and Mutti.

'Georgie, we have been discussing you and Annika, your proposal of marriage. It puts me in a difficult position; you are not of the Dopper. You are one of the Roman faith and I cannot in my heart condone the marriage of my daughter to a Roman Catholic.'

Georgie felt cold, his stomach turned at this news. He had always known his faith was something of a problem in this devout Protestant household but it had never occurred to him that it would prevent him marrying Annika.

'Don't look so despondent,' said Mutti stepping forward to stand by her husband. 'There is a way out of this. It is true that we cannot allow our daughter to marry a Roman Catholic but if you were to convert to the Calvinist faith then we would reconsider.'

Jos looked uncomfortable, fidgeting, examining the wooden floor in minute detail and then Petrus spoke.

'Georgie it is true my father cannot accept a Catholic into the family and what he wants to say is that if you agree to...'

'Convert to our religion,' said Jos, finding his voice again, 'then I will agree to your marrying my daughter.'

Georgie looked Jos in the eye, his mind in a whirl; he had been a Catholic ever since he could remember. Was it such a big step to take, after all? He had not attended mass since he was a boy and apart from church services in the Army, he had not practised the religion. He turned to look at Annika and then at Hans and his mind was made up.

'Yes I am willing to be converted.'

'Good, but first you must, study the five points of Calvinism, they are central to our faith. You will travel to Pretoria, to the Kerk, and meet Reverend Fraans Lemmer who will teach you the ways of the Doppers. We are the chosen people of God and you must understand our ways. Petrus will write a letter of introduction and when he is satisfied that you will make a good Dopper then you can marry Annika.'

'Thank you Jos, I will not let you down,' said Georgie catching a glimpse of Annika from the corner of his eye as she cradled Hans in her arms.

'When should I leave for Pretoria?'

'First thing in the morning and do not come back here until Reverend Lemmer is satisfied with your bible studies.'

The new day was dry and hot, Ellen had taken to wearing trousers again, and sitting astride her pony on the outskirts of Newcastle, she gazed out across the veldt.

'Patrick, I have been wondering, Georgie said the De Wit's farm is not far from Pretoria didn't he?'

'Yes about twenty miles away I think.'

'Wouldn't we be better living there for a while, until we decide what we are going to do?'

'It's Boer country you know, they don't like us very much.'

'Oh don't be silly, the war ended years ago, they will be glad of our money I expect.'

'I'm not sure we can support their economy on our own but it would be easier to see Georgie if we move there.'

'Good, that's settled then,' said Ellen digging her heels into the pony's flanks, giving Patrick little chance to argue.

'Wait for me,' he shouted after her and at a steady trot, they rode on for a mile or so before coming to a halt beside a stream.

'You know Georgie might want to stay in the Transvaal Ellen. If you are thinking of settling in Natal or the Cape, then there is still a large army presence there and de lad is a deserter. If they catch him, it will be prison for a few years. If I was in his shoes I would stay put up here.'

'Could he really go to prison?'

'Aye, he could. De army don't take kindly to deserters.'

'I have never been to the Transvaal, what's it like?'

'Neither have I, this is as far as I ever got with the army,' said Patrick feeling in his saddlebag for the food they had brought with them. 'Let's have out picnic and we can talk about it.

Georgie had no more than a few minutes to say his goodbyes and considering Jos's generosity he did not linger.

'Are you happy with my father's arrangements?'

'More than happy Annika, all I have to do is spend a few weeks studying to become a Dopper and then we can be married. It's what I want, I have some money from the diamonds, enough to buy some land and then you can teach me the ways of a farmer.'

'You know plenty already, you have worked here long enough to understand a bit about the land and I will work with you. When Hans grows a bit bigger he can help and maybe he will have some brothers.'

'Ha, you are getting ahead of yourself, isn't it a bit early to be thinking of brothers?'

'I want a big family, many sons and a few daughters.'

'Steady on, you will kill me with work the way you are talking.'

Annika smiled, happy that Georgie was to become one of them, happy that he would pursue the way of life she had always known and when he was ready to leave she touched his arm, the only sign of affection she dare show under the watchful eyes of her family.

'Good luck,' said Petrus as Georgie's pony passed by. 'May God be with you and study hard.'

'Are we swapping places,' jibed Georgie, embarrassing Petrus.

'No, I enjoyed my time in Kimberly but I am home now and I will not be drinking any more of that beer, not for a while anyway.'

Georgie saluted him and nudged his horse towards the distant hills, a new adventure about to begin though he was not so sure he would enjoy it.

The town of Pretoria was much as he remembered, the wide square lined with ox wagons full of produce, people passing the time of day as they inspected the goods on offer and then he noticed a face he recognized. It was Christiaan, he was talking animatedly to two other men and did not notice Georgie riding past. There could be trouble he feared if he met Christiaan, and he vowed to avoid him whilst he was in town and how long that might be, he did not know.

Nudging his horse forwards, he negotiated people and wagons and passed within twenty feet of Christiaan who at that moment chose to turn around. At first, he did not even look at Georgie but then some sixth sense seemed to make him stare straight at him.

'You, Englishman, what are you doing here,' he called out already striding towards Georgie.

Georgie smelled trouble and ignored Christiaan but he was not giving up so easily. 'You, what are you doing here?

Again, Georgie tried to ignore him but it was becoming increasingly evident that he could not avoid a confrontation.

'I have come to meet with the Reverend Lemmer,'

'Fraans Lemmer, what does an Uitlander want with Fraans Lemmer?'

'I have to learn the ways of the Dopper.'

'You, a Dopper?'

'Yes, your father says I must if I am to marry Annika.'

'Marry Annika!' Christiaan scowled. 'You are the father, I knew it, rapist. 'This man is a rapist,' he called out to his companions.

'Listen, I'm no rapist. I've come here to study your religion so that I can marry your sister.'

Georgie felt that it was a reasonable statement but Christiaan had other ideas and became incandescent with rage. Lunging at Georgie he took him by surprise and such was the force of Christiaan's attack that he lost his balance and fell from his horse. If it had, it only been Christiaan he had to deal with then he might have escaped injury, but Christiaan's friends joined in and together overwhelmed Georgie. Pinning him to the ground they fell upon him and proceeded to knock him senseless.

'This man raped my sister,' said Christiaan to some onlookers, 'We take him to the elders to answer for his crime,' and together with his accomplices, Christiaan dragged the still senseless Georgie towards the house of Hendrik De Klerq.

'What is this?' asked a surprised Hendrik as his door flew open.

'This Uitlander raped my sister and I want him tried and punished.'

'What proof do you have?'

'My sister had a baby not a month ago and it can only be him,' he said pointing to the figure lying on the floor.

Georgie groaned as he began to come round and his captors asked for some rope to bind his arms, none too gently hauling him into a chair and tying him securely.

'There, that will keep you still while the court convenes,' said Christiaan.

'Wh...what, what are you doing?'

'Quiet prisoner,' barked one of the Burghers hitting Georgie across the face with the back of his hand. 'You are to be tried for the offence of rape.'

'I haven't raped anyone. Christiaan, what are you doing, let me go.'

'It is out of my hands now. The charges have been laid and you must face them.'

'Georgie's head was swimming, the pain from the beating coupled with the accusation had left him unable retaliate and slumping his head forward he tried to think. It was becoming obvious that they were holding a kangaroo court and he felt for his safety.

'You, George McNamara stand accused of raping this man's sister. How do you plead?'

Georgie felt trapped, hopeless and heard himself say 'not guilty you bastards.'

'A profanity, add that to the charges,' he heard a voice say and at that moment he knew that he was doomed. What of Annika, what of Hans, would he ever see them again?

'What is the evidence, who can offer evidence against this man?'

Georgie opened his eyes and lifted his head to find his captors had secured him to a chair at one end of a long table. Facing him was a Burgher not much older than he was, and on either side sat Christiaan and his two friends.

'I do,' said Christiaan. This man is a deserter from the British army and a scoundrel. He lived on our farm for over a year and when he left my sister was pregnant with his child.'

'Is this true?'

'Mm...yes but I didn't rape her. We are to be married.'

'Liar,' screeched Christiaan, 'you are a rapist and should hang.'

'I don't think hanging is appropriate Christiaan, fifty lashes I say. Do you all agree?'

'And run him out of town,' added Christiaan raising his hand. 'What about you two?' he challenged the men sitting opposite and slowly they raised their hands in agreement.

'Take him out and lash him to the wagon wheel while I fetch the whip,' said Hendrik getting to his feet.

Christiaan and the others began to release Georgie from the chair and dragged him outside. Although battered and bruised, his hands tied, Georgie's fighting spirit was alive and well and he was having none of it. Kicking out with a foot, he managed to disable one of his captors and with his forearm knocked another to the ground but it wasn't enough, he was outnumbered and very soon subdued and manhandled towards the wagon.

'Tie him securely, his feet as well, we don't want him trying that again,' said Christiaan.

'Tear his shirt off,' said Hendrik returning with the whip, 'I want to see what I am whipping.'

'Here,' said one of the men stuffing a large twig between Georgie's teeth, 'bite on that.'

Georgie did bite and as hard as he could as the first of the lashes seared across his exposed flesh. The pain was almost unbearable but Georgie was made of sterner stuff than these Boers realised. Thinking hard of Annika he told himself to hang on but it was too much and he lapsed into unconsciousness.

'That will do,' said Hendrik, 'we don't want to kill him. Fetch his pony.'

One of the men hurried to the small building that served as a stable and brought out the still saddled Boer pony and together they hoisted Georgie onto its back. Lying him flat against the animal's neck they secured him with rope and Christiaan took great pleasure in leading the horse towards the road out of Pretoria.

'Good riddance Uitlander and don't come back,' he snarled as he struck the horses rump, sending it galloping out onto the veldt with Georgie, oblivious to his plight, spread-eagled across it's back.

It was not the first time some unfortunate had received such punishment, after the rebellion, several Britishers had suffered the same fate and was no surprise to several passers-by as the pony galloped by and for half a mile or more the animal kept up its pace, eventually slowing to walking speed. Lying flat across its back Georgie finally stirred and groaning with pain, he tried to open his eyes. He was helpless in his bonds, the pain in his back was overwhelming and as the horse eventually came to a halt on the deserted road he wondered how he could free himself before slipping back into unconsciousness.

How long he lay there, he did not know but as he began to come round, he heard a human voice.

'Begorrah, what has happened to him,' it said and then he felt his bonds loosen and cut free, he was unable to help himself, sliding inexorably to the ground.

'It's Georgie, shrieked a woman's voice, 'look at him, oh dear God what has happened?'

Georgie groaned and incapable of helping himself lay where he landed until he felt strong hands lift him to a sitting position and felt cool water dribbling into his mouth.

'What de hell has happened to you Georgie, who did this to ye?'

Georgie hardly heard the words, oblivious to the fact that it was Patrick and Ellen who had found him. They had bought a buggy and horse in Newcastle, were on their way to Pretoria to see him and it was fortuitous indeed that they were the ones to find him.

'Here Georgie boy, let me clean those wounds. Ellen, the tin of Vaseline is in the valise pocket; pass it to me so I can seal these cuts. Oh Georgie you'll have these scars for the rest of your life, never in all my time at Her Majesty's Service have I seen such a whipping.'

Patrick lay Georgie onto his stomach and taking one of his own shirts he tore it into strips and began to clean the wounds as well as he could.

'Who's that, groaned Georgie coming round a little more. 'Jesus my back hurts. Bastards.'

'He will recover, I'm sure of that now darlin' girl so don't you worry about Georgie here; he's as tough as dey come.'

'Georgie, can you hear me,' said Ellen leaning over him. 'It's me Ellen, what happened.'

Georgie turned his head and half opened his eyes, managing a weak smile when he realised who was talking to him.

'I think we had better get him onto the buggy, find somewhere to sleep tonight and make Georgie as comfortable as we can,' Ellen said to Patrick.

Georgie was a dead weight but Patrick was an unusually strong man and with some twisting and turning he managed to deposit his friend into the buggy with his feet hanging over the back.

'Are you comfortable enough?' he said to his patient and Georgie managed at least a nod of his head. 'Good, I'll tie your horse to the back and we'll head for Pretoria.'

Georgie's luck had turned as soon as Patrick and Ellen had found him and it was still running in his favour as they pulled up outside a lodging house. A man and his wife originating from the Cape ran the establishment and were friendly enough towards Uitlanders like themselves.

'The Burghers did this did they? It is not the first time, they hate us and want rid of us so they can have the Transvaal to themselves. Bring him in here and you can have the larger room at the front of the house. There is water and some hay out back for your horses. That will be two pounds and eight shillings for the night – in advance.'

Patrick dug into his pocket, retrieved a note and some coins and counted them into the man's hand.

'What about some food?'

'That's included; my wife is making it now. I thought you all looked a bit worn out and told her to prepare something.'

Georgie lay face down on top of the bed, still in his trousers and Patrick's spare shirt and for most of the night he slept well enough. The pain still racked his body but it was bearable and as he lay there, he recounted his ordeal. How, he wondered, would tell Annika that her brother had done this to him.

'Are you awake?' whispered a voice.

'Yes.'

'Can I come in?'

'Yes.'

The bedroom door slowly opened to reveal an anxious looking Ellen.

'How are you feeling?'

'Not so good but I think I will live.'

'I'm not surprised, you were pretty beat up when we found you. Patrick is going to find us a proper hotel for you to rest.'

'Tell him to be careful, I don't want those Burghers to know I'm back in town.'

In the event they did not look for a hotel or lodging house, Patrick had realised that Georgie might still be in danger and decided that they would remain where they were, several miles out of town and in the hands of a sympathetic innkeeper and a day later Ellen pushed open Georgie's bedroom door

'I've brought you some tea, how are you feeling?'

Georgie was sat hunched over in a chair by the window and he turned his head. 'I'm a lot better today; the pain is a lot less than it was, so long as I don't move quickly.'

'Good, Patrick wonders if you can ride the buggy.'

'Why?'

'He's found an isolated farmhouse we can rent for as long as we want and he thinks maybe it's time to move on.'

'Sounds good, here let me see if I can stand unaided,' he said gripping the sides of his chair. Slowly and grimacing in pain Georgie rose unsteadily to his feet and grinned at his cousin. 'Not too bad eh... I think I might manage a ride in the buggy.'

'Good, drink your tea and I'll fetch Patrick, he's just outside.'

Ellen left the room, returning in less than a minute.

'So you think you can make it?' said the big Irishman.

'I think so.'

'I'll load our trunk and we'll leave straight away. I've been and had a look at the place, it's a couple of miles away and isolated enough to keep prying eyes away until you are yourself again to be sure.'

Georgie managed a smile, the first one in some time and with Ellen's help, managed to climb into the back of the buggy unaided.

Chapter 28

Nkosinathi's dead father sat, as he had in life, with his blanket across his shoulders and his eyes closed as if he were merely asleep. The wound to his chest invisible, covered as it was by his blanket and the blood wiped from his lips left the impression that he would once again rise to his feet. It was a forlorn notion and not one that Nkosinathi believed in yet as he looked down at the old man he felt that he would open his eyes, offer him his snuff horn and they would talk as they had done many times before. However, it was not to be, Rabanina had taken Mondli's life and he, Nkosinathi, would take that of Rabanina. For an elderly Zulu to die was not unusual, not a condition to become emotional about but the manner of Mondli's dying had cut deep into Nkosinathi's heart, like a butcher's knife, and unleashed a thirst for revenge.

'Oh father of our kraal go to the spirits of your father and his father before him, take your place in the world beyond and watch over us and give me the strength to seek out the one who has done this.'

Taking a deep breath, his nostrils flaring, Nkosinathi stood to his full height and uttered a silent oath against

Rabanina before turning to walk towards the small knot of men preparing the grave.

'He is ready; the womenfolk have prepared food for his journey, laid out his warrior shield and assegai for him to ward off any evil spirits he might meet. You are our chief now Dumisani, tell us what we should do and we will obey.'

Dumisani looked up from supervising the task of digging the grave and turned to his brother.

'It shall be as tradition dictates; a servant shall accompany Mondli to the other world. You,' he said pointing to a young man of no more than sixteen years of age, 'you shall go with Mondli, carry his shield through the next world.'

The boy, for in reality he was no more than that, shook with fear, his eyes widening as the weight of Dumisani's words sank in and his head drooped. He was surprised for he was never Mondli's servant, a grandson through his second wife and felt that it was not his place to die with the old chief but Dumisani, the new leader, had decreed it.

'It shall be as you say oh chief,' said the youth fatalistically and he began to walk towards the graveside.

'You and you fetch the body and you bring his shield,' ordered Dumisani to three of the men who had dug the grave. 'We will bury him as a chief should be buried, with a warrior's possessions and a servant to attend his needs.'

Nkosinathi looked at his brother, at the open grave and at the sad looking youth and wondered if perhaps it was time to break with tradition.

'My brother, we have suffered much since our King was taken from us, since the White man's army defeated us and since John Dunn made rule of these lands. We have lost most of the herd, had our crops taken and left to starve, would it not be better that he lives,' he said pointing to the youth. 'Would not another pair of strong hands to work the fields, care for what herd we have left be a better way. I am sure Mondli would approve, but you are our chief and we must obey you.'

Dumisani's eyes met those of Nkosinathi and he knew that he had spoken with purpose. Although Nkosinathi was stronger in many ways, Mondli's favourite and the one who had kept the kraal alive through difficult times he did not feel any jealousy nor animosity to him, only respect and the love of a sibling.

'You speak wisely brother, we need all the help we can get and to sacrifice one so useful would be folly. Perhaps another should accompany Mondli.'

'It will be as you say but we are desperate and I might not return from my quest.'

'Quest?'

'To avenge our father, to kill the one they call Rabanina.'

'You are going to the camp of John Dunn? You will not survive, they will catch you and kill you and then when they discover who you are they will come here and kill us all.'

'Be brave my brother, trust in me, I will never betray
our kraal, our people but I must avenge the death of
Mondli. I must leave to hunt down the one who killed
our father but I will be careful, I will not let them know
that I am the one.'

The brothers looked deep into each other's eyes, one
afraid, one ready to follow his destiny and finally the
spell was broken as Mondli's body arrived at the
graveside. The youth sank to his knees in expectation;
his head bent forward, his eyes closed in anticipation.

Strangulation was the normal method of execution
for one to go with his chief into the afterlife and his
mouth became dry at the thought. Then a hand gripped
his shoulder and Dumisani spoke.

'You are to be spared; the spirit of Mondli asks that
you be spared but that you will forever dedicate yourself
to the well-being of the kraal. Stand aside and let us
send Mondli home to his ancestors.'

The youth stood, his eyes avoiding everyone and
quickly he moved out of the way, as they lowered body,
still in the sitting position, into the grave. Dumisani,
looking on, clapped his hands, and after carefully
placing items useful for Mondli's last journey about the
corpse, the men began to pile the soil back into the hole,
covering the body and building up a small mound of
stones to keep the wild animals away.

'I am Dumisani, your new leader, Mondli is no more,
he has gone to take his place amongst his ancestors and
to celebrate we will feast in his memory. Go; take an
animal from the herd.'

'You have a great responsibility brother,' said Nkosinathi standing at his shoulder. 'I will help you all I can but I must avenge our father's death. First I will hunt the wild animals to feed the village then I will seek out the evil one – it is my destiny.'

'Be careful or John Dunn's men will kill you and return here to wreak vengeance upon us, destroy us.'

'I have told you brother, if no one knows it is I who kills Rabanina you will be safe. Trust me; I will make sure they do not come here.'

Chapter 29

The door to Georgie's bedroom creaked, alerting him, and he turned on the bed to see Ellen peering into the room.

'How are you feeling, can you manage some broth, I made it myself. I looked in earlier but you were sleeping.'

'I am feeling much better thank you, the pain has almost gone, more of an itch now.'

'Patrick has been to town and seen a doctor, asked for something to rub on your wounds. We used the last of our Vaseline yesterday and he thought we should get hold of something else to help you heal.'

Georgie twisted in the bed, explored his body and a smile came to his face. 'I think I am on the mend. If it wasn't for you two finding me I don't know what would have happened.'

'Who is Christiaan, you kept mumbling something about Christiaan when we got you here but since then you haven't mentioned him.'

Georgie's smile evaporated as quickly as it had appeared and his face became serious.

'How long have I been here?'

'We found you four days ago.'

'Four days, I should have been back at the De Witt's place by now, Annika will be wondering what has happened.'

'Annika?'

Pursing his lips he carefully slid his legs over the side of the bed and pushed himself into a sitting position.

'Careful, shall I help you?' queried Ellen.

'I think I can manage. Here pass me the broth,' he said holding out his hands and soon he was wolfing down the warm food and feeling his strength return.

'Phew, that's better. You make a mean stew cousin, where did you learn to do that?'

'You mean you have forgotten how we lived, forgotten the stews mother used to make.'

Georgie's smile returned as memories came flooding back, growing up with Ellen, when food was hard to come by, when somehow Aunt Jane produced the self-same broth.

'Yes I remember, hard times eh?'

'Hard times Georgie boy. Who is Annika?'

Ellen was intrigued, unaware that there was a woman in her cousin's life.

'Er... Petrus's sister, the mother of my son.'

It was a bombshell and Ellen's jaw dropped.

'You have a son?'

Georgie took a deep breath and let out a long slow sigh.

'I suppose I should tell you everything.'

Ellen said nothing, her eyes firmly on Georgie's and after what seemed an interminable pause he began to tell her about Annika and Hans, about his impending wedding and finally he told her about Christiaan.

'Annika's brother did this to you? He doesn't sound a very nice man. What will you tell Annika?'

'I have no idea right now. It's all been so sudden and the way I feel at the moment there isn't a lot I can do.'

'Perhaps not, but let me tell you not to worry about it. You have some money from your diamonds and I know you are a hard worker. You will manage I am sure and if you can't...'

Her voice trailed off, her eyes turned away from Georgie and he knew she was hiding something from him.

'I've told you my secret now what's yours?' he said startling her.

Ellen knew that one day she would tell Georgie of her good fortune and had been waiting for the right time and perhaps this was it.

She looked at Georgie and was about to say something when there was a tap on the door.

'Is that you Patrick?'

'Aye.'

'Well come in,' said Georgie.

'How are you feeling? You look well and I see you have eaten. That's a good sign,' said Patrick standing squarely in the doorway.

'I'm feeling a lot better, the pain is just about gone and it only hurts if I move too much. Have we any beer, I feel like getting up and having a beer?'

'Dat's more loike the Georgie I know. Yes I have a few bottles of India Pale Ale and it will be a pleasure to share them with ye, come on and let's sit a while on the verandah.'

'Your good health,' said Patrick handing Georgie a bottle as he made his way tentatively out onto the verandah.

'And you Patrick.'

'Are you ready to tell me what happened?'

Georgie drained half the bottle, wiped his mouth on his sleeve and took a deep breath. 'I reckon so.'

'Who did it?'

'Yes,' said Ellen appearing at the doorway, 'what happened, look what this Christiaan did to you?'

'Sit down and I will tell you. You ask about Christiaan, well he is my prospective brother in law.'

'What!' exclaimed Patrick.

'Yes, I am about to be married and he will be my brother in law. It started at Majuba, when the Boer sharp shooters pinned us down. Our leadership was as bad as I have ever seen it, our lads were being picked off and yet they still ordered the charge up that bloody hill. It was murder, young lads fresh out of Blighty with no idea of how to fight, and the General leading us into that hell. I tell you Patrick it was no wonder I deserted.'

Patrick looked at the floor having mixed feelings. He had known men desert for all manner of reasons but had never believed that Georgie could ever do such a thing but he seemed to have good reason.

'I heard it was a bad do, I suppose it was all too much for you.'

'Aye it was. After fighting Zulus and then the Boers I was sick of the killing.'

'This Christiaan, how did you come to meet him? He must be a Boer with a name like that.'

'He is Petrus's brother. You must have heard Petrus mention his name.'

'Can't say that I do.'

'Well he's Petrus and Annika's brother but he's not like them.'

They made me a prisoner of war after I helped Petrus back to his lines. When they signed the peace, I decided to stay put and I spent the next two years working on their farm and it was then that Petrus and I decided to go and search for diamonds.'

'And what about his sister,' added Ellen.

'Annika, she's beautiful and we have a son.'

Patrick looked at Ellen. 'A son, did you know that Ellen?'

'Yes he told me only a short while ago.'

'So is that why you are getting married?' asked Ellen slowly.

'Partly, I want to marry her, I am in love with her.'

'You seem particularly friendly with Petrus, what has he to say about his brother?'

'He doesn't know. Petrus and I are good friends I only have a problem with Christiaan. He hates all Uitlanders, all newcomers, and I think he is part of some secret movement agitating for another fight.'

'To finish what they started,' added Patrick.

'Maybe, it's a dangerous game though.'

'So what are you going to do cousin? *Are* you going to marry this Annika?'

'Yes of course, but first I have a score to settle.'

'You must be careful Georgie, you cannot afford to alienate her family, I know, I have been through that,' said a thoughtful looking Ellen.

'Clarence's family?'

'Yes. Patrick knows a little of what happened but I haven't told him the whole story.'

Patrick glanced at Ellen.

'It's my turn to tell I think,' she said sitting on a chair, composing herself. 'When Clarence was killed his commanding officer offered me some advice, gave me all Clarence's back pay, his horses, saddles and the like and after selling them I took the mail steamer back to London...'

Leaving out only one small detail she went on to describe her trials and tribulations at the hands of Clarence's father, about Freddie, the lawyer and the sinking of the ferry.

'So both brothers drowned and you became the sole heir to a fortune,' said Georgie with some wonderment.

'Yes, and with Freddie's help I inherited the lot.'

'How much?' asked Georgie.

Ellen looked at them both and felt she had kept her second secret for too long, felt she must tell and when she did, both of them whistled through their teeth.

'Listen, I am supposed to go to the Kerk for some instruction, learn the ways of the Boer before I can marry Annika,' said Georgie. 'I can't stay here much longer.'

'What if those men see you again?'

'I hadn't thought too much about that, maybe I should forget it, just go back to the farm and see if Jos will let me marry Annika anyway.'

'Whatever you do we are coming with you, you need someone to look after you,' said Patrick.

'I'll go to the Kerk tomorrow and see the Reverend Lemmer, see what he has to say and maybe he can help.'

'Like I say, we are coming with you.'

The Reverend Lemmer was a kindly, tough man, one who had endured the hardships of the great trek, fought off the native tribesmen and built a new life in the Transvaal. He was devout and truly believed the Doppers were God's chosen people and when Georgie came with his story; he relished the task of converting him.

'So Jos wants you to become a member of our church so that you can marry his daughter does he. You say Annika has had your baby and you want to marry her. In god's eyes you have sinned, you must repent your sins, and if you can do that and learn the scripture, I will allow you into our church. But you must want to join our church.'

'I do sir, I understand very well what I am doing and I hope to become a good member of your church.'

'The Reverend Lemmer grunted and looked Georgie over with a kindly eye.

'Well we had better get started then had we not.'

It was a daunting task but Georgie set to it with a will, grateful now for those Sunday teachings his mother had taken him to as a child. The scriptures were not so different from those of the Catholic Church and after a week of instruction, he felt he had made some progress and then, one day, the Reverend Lemmer asked, 'Read me the passage from Isaiah and this time tell me what it means to you.'

Clearing his throat and in a strong, confident voice began to read.

'*He grew up before him like a tender shoot, and like a root out of dry ground. He had no beauty or majesty to attract us to him, nothing in his appearance that we should desire him...*'

When he had finished he looked up at the kindly old Boer.

'What do you believe that tells us?'

After a short pause he said, 'it is about Christ's suffering, he will appear as an ordinary man with no special powers, no riches and he will suffer for all mankind.'

The Reverend Lemmer nodded solemnly. 'It tells us that worldly goods are not so important. The word of God is central to our lives and we should pray every day for our salvation. You have studied well my friend, although you still have a lot to learn, and I believe you will become a good Dopper. I know Annika will help you; she is a good servant of God, so let us pray for your salvation, for your future wife and your son.'

Together the two men bowed their heads to pray in silence, the Reverend Dopper for salvation and Georgie for release from his wearisome task and when he opened his eyes it seemed that God had answered his prayers.

'I have decided that you have learned as much as you can in such a short time. You must study the bible every day from now on to understand more fully the word of God and so it only leaves me to ask you to make a confession of your faith. Answer the following questions

'Do you acknowledge the doctrine of our church, which you have learned, heard, and confessed, to be the true and complete doctrine of salvation, conforming to the Sacred Scriptures? Do you promise, by the grace of God, to continue steadfastly in the profession of this doctrine and to live and die in accordance therewith?...

Relieved to have his freedom once more, Georgie saddled his pony and looked forward to a future with Annika and their son and inside the church the Reverend Lemmer was busy writing a letter for Jos.

'Give my regards to Jos,' said the minister handing Georgie the letter. 'Tell him to come here to the Kerk and pray and you bring your son for his baptism.'

'I will sir, and thank you,' said Georgie stuffing the letter inside his shirt before he bid farewell to the minister.

He was about to mount when from across the street Christiaan and his friends appeared and he hoped they would not recognise him, but he was mistaken.

'So, Englishman you are back in town. It seems we did not whip you severely enough, perhaps you need another dose of our medicine,' snarled Christiaan staring straight at him.

Georgie's heart sank, there were too many of them for him to fight alone and he glanced furtively around for help. None was forthcoming, the men were beginning to close in on him, and it seemed there was little chance of escape, but the thought of suffering at their hands a second time was too much. Holding tightly onto the reigns, he kicked out at his horse's buttock and forced the alarmed beast to swing its body across the path of the oncoming men. It forced them back, blocked off the attack long enough for him to leap into the saddle and unceremoniously he kicked at his pony's flanks. The pony responded and took off down the street leaving Christiaan and his friends cursing after him.

'Damnation,' said an infuriated Hendrik De Klerq. 'Get the horses, we will follow him. Someone must have helped him and that is where he will be heading I am sure.'

Christiaan was the first to react, finding a horse tethered to a rail he expertly leapt into the saddle shouting to Hendrik, 'I will follow him catch me up, this time we will make sure he never returns.'

Hendrik De Klerq's reply was lost in the clatter of hooves as Christiaan spurred on his horse. Behind him, the others looked for horses, unwilling to steal them as Christiaan had just done.

'Are you sure it is a good idea Hendrik?' said one, his face betraying a reluctance to carry on the pursuit. 'Christiaan will kill him this time; I don't want to be a party to murder.'

'Ah...you are weak; if we are to rid ourselves of these Uitlanders we cannot afford to be weak. Come, we have no time to lose.'

For several miles, Georgie's sturdy Boer pony galloped on, until finally the small farmhouse came into view. His heart was still trying to burst out of his chest and when his adrenalin rush finally subsided, he pulled the animal up and sat for a few minutes to watch the trail but could see no one. He had expected his path and Christiaan's would cross again sometime but the force of the onslaught had surprised him and it seemed that Christiaan would stop at nothing to destroy him.

Less than half a mile away Christiaan was closer than Georgie realised, crossing unfamiliar country and wondered just where Georgie was heading. Pulling up his horse for a moment, he twisted in the saddle to look for Hendrik and the others and with still no sign of them, he decided to find a vantage point and wait.

Guiding his horse up onto higher ground, he waited amongst some trees and watched Georgie's progress. He would have preferred it if Hendrik and the others were here but he could not afford to lose sight of his quarry and as he watched Georgie he saw him turn off the trail. There was a risk he might lose sight of him and wondered should he follow or wait for Hendrik and then he saw it. A house tucked between two koppies, a small stone built structure and with a thatched roof and he knew that he had found the hideout.

Climbing from the saddle, he led his horse towards a solitary tree and watched as Georgie reached the house and dismounting. So, he thought, this is where you have been hiding and this is where we will finish you Englishman. He looked back along the trail and with relief saw Hendrik and his fellow nationalists not far away and he lifted is bush hat and waved to them.

'There he is,' said Hendrik nudging his horse towards Christiaan and within ten minutes reached Christiaan.

'He's over there in the *opstal*.'

'It's the Booysens homestead, the old man died six months ago,' said the rider next to Hendrik.

'So it will be deserted except for the Englishman.'

'I haven't seen anyone else since I have been here. I think it is deserted, he is alone.'

'Did he have a gun; did any of you see a gun?'

Each shook his head and Hendrik's face lit up with a grin. 'This will be easy, we will kill him and bury his body, no one will ever know.'

'I...I...I'm not sure we should kill him Hendrik, killing someone is too much.'

'Shut up Johannes, we'll never be rid of his kind if we are not strong. You don't have to pull the trigger.'

The man called Johannes looked at the ground, not prepared to argue with the stronger character but he felt unhappy.

'I have been looking at the house Hendrik, the roof is in a poor state of repair, the thatch is almost gone to that side, see,' said Christiaan pointing. 'I reckon we should smoke him out, shoot him as he makes a run for it.'

Hendrik stoked his chin in thought, his eyes narrowing. 'Yes, that's a good idea. Who will volunteer to start the fire? What about you Christiaan?'

'I'll do it; we need a torch for me to throw onto the roof, what have we got?'

For several minutes, the men scavenged the local vicinity for combustible materials, eventually putting together a long handled torch bound with dry grass and wrapped with a piece of oiled cotton cut from a waterproof cape.

'That should do it, no warning eh, just ride up to the house and throw the torch, then we'll wait until he is forced to run. You two cover this side whilst I take the doorway and after you have thrown the torch, you ride on to cover the far side Christiaan.'

Johannes and the fourth man set off to take up their positions while Hendrik and Christiaan worked on lighting the torch and once it started burning Christiaan rode towards the house and Hendrik ran to cover the doorway.

Georgie saw them coming by pure chance. He had looked out of the window at the very moment Christiaan's friends had joined him and from that moment had looked to his defences. He was unarmed apart from a hunting knife and would have little chance in a fight. The only thing he could think of was to barricade himself in until nightfall and perhaps then make his escape.

The first Patrick knew of any trouble was the column of smoke rising from the direction of the house and immediately he slapped the reigns across the horses back causing the buggy to lurch forward.

'What is it, why have you speeded up?'

'Look over there, smoke, its coming from the direction of the house, something's wrong.'

They were returning from a day in Pretoria, a day of looking round and asking questions. Ellen had made up her mind to find a farm, somewhere to settle, a place where they could all be together and after a disappointing trip her mind was on other things until Patrick snapped her out of her gloominess.

'My clothes, what is happening to my clothes?'

'Ellen, your clothes are the last thing you should be worrying about, the valise is still in there remember,' snapped Patrick steering the buggy off the track and into some long grass.

'What are you doing?'

'Can you drive this thing if you have to?'

'I think so, why?'

'Because I might not come back and if I don't, then you drive as fast as you can to Pretoria.'

'Wha... do you think we are being robbed?'

'I don't know but that fire didn't start itself, someone started it and I aim to find out who. Here take the reins,' he said passing them into Ellen's hands before he jumped to the ground.

'Where are you going?'

'To have a closer look,' said Patrick pulling his revolver from his waistband.

The fire was an unexpected development and it was beginning to worry Georgie. He could hear the dry twigs and thatch crackling as the fire took hold and smoke was beginning to drift into the house. He looked for an escape but could see nothing obvious, even the water bucket was half-empty and would make little impression. It seemed that his only chance was to run for it but his fighting instinct told him it was a trap and he would be a sitting duck. He remembered those boys on the mountain, young lads fresh from England and the Boer sharp shooters picking them off. No, a mad dash would leave him dead, of that he was sure, there was only one thing he could do – surrender.

The first thing Hendrik saw was the door swing open and then the white sheet of surrender, limp and forlorn and he raised his gun.

'Come out with your hands up.'

'What guarantee have I that you won't shoot me?'

'None.'

'Then I'm staying put.'

'You won't last long,' said Hendrik squeezing the trigger.

The bullet whizzed close to Georgie, smacking with a thud into the doorframe and he withdrew further inside for some protection. Above him, the fire had taken hold and he knew it would not be long before the roof collapsed and frantically he looked for some relief. The house was beginning to fill with smoke and it would not be long before it forced him out into the open. Becoming worried he looked round for something, anything that might help his predicament and then his eyes alighted on a small trap door in the floor. Crossing to the flat wooden trap door, he reached down to grip the steel handle set into the wood and heaved. Gradually the rusty hinges succumbed and once he had it open, he could see that the void barely large enough for him, but it was all he had and so in he jumped.

Outside the building Hendrik was becoming agitated and called to his men to come to him and issued his orders.

'We will put a few shots into the place and wait for the roof to come down before we go looking for him.'

'He will not survive,' said Christiaan levelling his gun at the open door.

'He might and if he does he'll thank us for putting him out of his misery.'

'You will not be putting anyone out of their misery. Drop your guns – all of you,' shouted a stern and commanding voice.

Hendrik half turned, swinging his gun to take a shot at the intruder but did not make it. Patrick saw his movement and was in no mood to compromise shooting him full in the chest.

'Who's next?'

The men stood stock-still, apprehension spread across their faces and one by one let their guns drop to the ground.

'Right, get over there where I can cover you. One of you, see to him,' he said pointing his revolver at the squirming Hendrik lying on the floor.

'Sergeant McNamara, you can come out now.' he shouted.

Inside the burning building Georgie was only just pulling the trap door over his head when he heard the call. It must be Patrick he thought, no one else would call him that, not now, not after all this time. He was in a desperate situation and though he considered that it might be a clever trap he really had no option.

Jumping up from the hole, coughing from the smoke, he ran for the door and burst out into the sunlight, his intention to run for cover before his pursuers could react. However, the sight that met his eyes convinced him to stop.

'Am I glad to see you Sergeant Donovan; you seemed to have developed a knack of turning up at the right time.'

'Aye bonnie lad, now pick up one of those guns and let's decide what to do with this lot.'

Annika stopped her sewing, surprised to see riders approaching. She put down the dress she was making, looked into the cradle beside her on the verandah and, content Hans was asleep, called out to her mother.

'Mutti, someone's coming.'

'I see them,' said her mother appearing in the doorway and for several minutes, the two women watched the strangers approach. As he came closer, recognition dawned and Annika's heart missed a beat. The rider was Georgie, yet he was supposed to be in Pretoria, not to come back here until the Reverend Lemmer gave him permission. It was too soon for that surely, so why was he here?

'It's Georgie Mutti, and he has someone with him.'

Focusing her eyes, Annika's mother finally recognised Georgie and behind him two strangers in a buggy.

'Your father will not be pleased.'

Her father might not be but Annika was. She was pleased to see Georgie back so soon but at the back of her mind, she felt that something was wrong and as their visitors drew near, she stood up and gripped the verandah rail.

'Annika, Mutti,' said Georgie dismounting.

'Why have you returned so soon?' asked Mutti in a stern voice.

'All in good time. How is Hans Annika?'

Annika turned to the cot and lifted Hans for his father to see him and then the baby began to cry.

'You have upset him,' said Mutti accusingly.

'No Mutti, it is time for his feed.'

Annika frowned at her mother's hostility and holding Hans to her breast she covered him with her shawl while he fed.

'Papa is coming,' announced Mutti, 'he must have seen you coming.'

Georgie turned his head to see Jos and Petrus striding towards him, Jos with a face like thunder.

'I cannot believe Fraans Lemmer would send you back here so soon. Why have you come back without his permission, you have disobeyed me.'

'No sir, if you will listen I will explain.'

'Explain! I should run you off my farm and forbid you to marry my daughter and who are these people,' he said turning to the buggy.'

'They are my friends.'

'Christiaan!' exclaimed Petrus, seeing his brother for the first time, lying trussed up in the back of the buggy. 'What is going on, Papa they have Christiaan a prisoner.'

Jos strode to the buggy and leaned over to see his son lying with his hands tied.

'Papa get me out of here,' he called as Jos pulled out his hunting knife to slice through the bonds.

'Why have you brought my son home like a wild animal? What right have you to make him a prisoner?'

The old Boer was angry and Georgie became a little anxious, especially when Petrus seemed to turn against him as well.

'I fetch the gun Papa?'

'Yes.'

'Hold on, there's no need for guns, we've had enough of guns.'

'Then explain yourself,' Jos said helping a subdued Christiaan to his feet.

'Mister De Witt I love your daughter and want to marry her but a problem has arisen and I feel that I cannot solve it alone.'

'What problem?' asked Jos slowly, his eyes narrowing.

'This,' said Georgie turning to face away from the De Witt family and undoing the buttons of his shirt he exposed the scars on his back.

Horrified, Annika let out a muted scream and Petrus took a sharp intake of breath.

'What happened,' squealed Annika.

'This is a punishment for something,' said Jos. Who did it and why?'

'Christiaan and his friends,' said Georgie turning round to look at a sheepish Christiaan. 'I was making my way to the Kirk when I came across them in the square and Christiaan here asked what I was doing, and when I told him he accused me of rape. Then they attacked me, dragged me to a house and held a kangaroo court.'

'Hendrik De Klerq I think maybe Hendrik De Klerq had something to do with this,' said Jos slowly looking at his son.

'I heard the name Hendrik, yes, a self-styled judge who decided to have me whipped.'

'Those hot heads, they will drag us back into a war if they are left to their own devices. Christiaan has mixed with them ever since the rebellion, ultra-nationalists who want all Uitlanders out of the Transvaal and it seems they will stop at nothing. You have some explaining to do Christiaan.'

'My brother did this to you,' said Annika, regaining her composure, her face shaped by a look of contempt.

'Yes, but I don't want it to spoil things for us, this is why I have come back, to make it right with you all,' said Georgie fastening his shirt buttons.

'What should we do Papa,' asked a troubled looking Petrus. 'They have hurt Georgie and they have hurt my sister.'

'Christiaan, do you know what you have done, this hatred for the Uitlanders has gone too far. Did we not fight them, beat them and secure our freedom to live as we please? Why are you carrying on the fight that was finished years ago?'

Christiaan seemed lost for words under Jos's cross-examination and his sister's fixed gaze.

'I...it seemed the right thing to do, Hendrik told us that the Uitlanders would flood the country, take control of the government and force us to live under the British yoke.'

'That may be one day, but not now, not for a long time, the incomers are not farmers like us, they come for easy pickings and when they see how hard life is here most go away. Georgie, what have you to say on the matter, you are the victim.'

Georgie cleared his throat and looking first at Annika, then Mutti and finally Petrus he tried to judge their mood and then he glanced at Patrick and Ellen sat together on the buggy.

'Jos you insisted that I go to the Kerk for instruction in the ways of the Dopper. I did and I learned many things from the Reverend Lemmer. He taught me humility, taught me forgiveness, to live by the scriptures and because of that and because I love your daughter and our son I forgive Christiaan for all that he has done to me and hope we can live as a family without conflict.'

Georgie's eye briefly alighted on Mutti as he spoke and saw tears in her eyes. She loved all her children, Annika, Petrus and her eldest, Christiaan. She had seen trouble brewing for a long time but had kept her council, preferring instead to let events unfold in their own way and now she could not conceal the relief she felt. He looked at Jos and saw that he was smiling, a rare occurrence and finally at Christiaan who could not resist the temptation to rise to offer his hand in friendship.

'I have been foolish, foolish to destroy my family for an idea that is not true. I am sorry for the pain I caused you Georgie and I will welcome you into the family when you marry my sister.'

For a few minutes, there was silence as each of them considered Georgie's words and Christiaan's apology, finally nodding approval and then with a wide grin Jos lit his pipe.

The wedding was a low-key affair attended by the family and a few close relatives, Ellen, and Patrick as best man. The Reverend Lemmer made the trip from Pretoria to conduct the open-air service and after the blessing, the bride and groom he addressed the congregation.

'Friends, fellow worshippers we have witnessed many things in our lives, happiness, sorrow...conflict, and so it pleases me to see these two young people start out on their life together. As God's people, we have struggled to tame this wild land and he will look after us as he has done ever since Jan van Riebeeck first stepped foot in the Cape. God bless you all.'

A murmur of gratitude percolated through the congregation, their voices growing louder congratulating the newly wedded couple. There were still some who disapproved of a child born out of wedlock but it did not stop the womenfolk fussing over little Hans.

'Well I nivver taught I would see the day when my old army chum got himself married. Congratulations Georgie, she's a foine looking girl and the lad looks as if he will grow up big and strong like his daddy.'

'Thank you Patrick, thanks for everything, I don't think that I would be here now if it wasn't for you. How many times have you saved my life?'

Patrick said nothing, a wide grin spread across his face his answer and he slapped Georgie on the back.

'Congratulations cousin. You have come a long way since we roamed the East End and I wish you the best of luck. Tell me; what are your plans, what will you do now?'

'Er...I don't really know. Jos said I could live here, help on the farm. So much has happened that I have not really thought too much about it. I'm just happy to be married and have a family.'

Ellen looked straight at Georgie, her striking blue eyes cutting into him. 'Well you can't feed a family on thin air Georgie boy can you.'

'There's plenty of food here.'

'Maybe but you will be just one of the hired hands. Not a lot of fun in that is there.'

Georgie scowled at his cousin not sure what she was driving at.

'Patrick and I have been doing a lot of digging around since we came here. Originally we came to find you, I knew in my heart of hearts you were not dead and now we have found you I am looking to the future, our future,' she said, intimating that he was part of it.

Georgie had become aware that she had matured into a very astute woman and braced himself for what she had to say.

'What future?' he said.

'Farming, I am in the process of buying a farm, a big farm, six thousand acres. But not here near Pretoria.'

'Where?' asked Georgie, slowly, intrigued.

'South of Heidelberg, near the Vaal River. I employed the services of a local man to find someone willing to sell.

'You know nothing about farming Ellen, how will you cope?

'I won't have to, you and Patrick will run the farm, supervise any natives we employ.'

'You want me to help run it?'

'Yes, I have money to finance the whole thing. I cannot believe how cheap land is out here and native labour is just as cheap.'

For a few moments, Georgie stood looking at his cousin, amazed at her proposition but the logic was obvious. As a Transvaaler, he could probably escape the possibility of arrest as a deserter and earn a living unimpeded.

'I will tell Annika. When will you start?'

'Not for a month or so yet, tomorrow we are going to travel south to look the place over and then complete the purchase.'

'Where is it?'

'Half way between here and Middleburg, it's got a small house and an outbuilding, not much but I have plans.'

'Plans?'

'While I was in Kimberley I spent a lot of time watching what was going on, what made the place tick and I spoke to a few of the miners, men from distant parts, Americans, Australians and they told me a lot about mining.'

'Diamonds?'

'Some, but a lot of them were gold miners from California and South Australia. They have come here to work because lodes are running out back home and they believe there is gold here.'

'I have heard of prospectors searching the Transvaal for years but nobody has ever found very much.'

'No but they *have* found gold in many places, not large quantities but those experienced miners from abroad think that it is only a matter of time before there is a big discovery here. They said that they can feel it and I believe them.'

Georgie said nothing for a while, his eyes looking past her and out across the flat scrub to the distant horizon, his mind abuzz with all the things that had happening. The fighting at Laing's Nek, his time on the farm, Kimberly and now his marriage to Annika. He puffed up his cheeks as the thoughts intermingled and then he saw female guests fussing over little Hans. He had a wife and child to support and the prospect of farming with Ellen and Patrick was tempting but what most excited him was Ellen's belief that there was gold hidden in the Transvaal and that they would find it

Chapter 30

A storm began to break as Nkosinathi set out on his quest. Black, thunderous clouds filled the sky and every few minutes a rumble of thunder spread across the veldt. He looked up into the heavens, gaining strength from the turmoil above him, believing that it was Mondli stirring the cauldron of the weather, watching over him. Then he felt the first drops of rain begin to fall, large and cold and he shivered, more in apprehension than due to the drop in temperature.

It was twenty miles or more to the kraal of John Dunn and Nkosinathi knew that anywhere in his path; danger could be lurking. The last thing he wanted was to fall foul of the border patrol and looking towards the hills and the the bridleway that would lead him to the estate of John Dunn he decided that he would be foolish to follow it. Halting his horse amongst some tall bushes and scanned the landscape. The rain was grow heavier and slowly making its way towards him.

The bridal path was the quickest and easiest route to take but on occasion, the patrols also took the same route and any sharp-eyed scout would see him from miles away.

Field craft was required and a tree line some two miles away would provide cover. It was a good starting point and then he must take the more difficult route through the hills. He was safe for the present, invisible amongst the thorn bushes and visibility would be restricted in the rain. That would give him time to reach the trees line unseen, and when the storm finally reached him, he wheeled his horse round and coaxed her into a steady trot towards the distant trees where he took time to chew on some Dagga leaves until the worst of the storm passed by.

Rabanina felt pleased having just returned from a patrol along the northern border catching a group smugglers red handed. The men were leading a string of ten mules laden with goods to sell up in the Transvaal and because they had avoided payment, he had confiscated half of their wares and the mules with a warning that next time he would take everything.

'You have done well Rabanina; these are valuable goods. Take what you want and reward your men,' said John Dunn.

It was not often Rabanina received such praise from his father, after all he had almost forty brothers and half-brothers and had never received much in the way of personal attention.

'Thank you father, there are rich cloths from the east, I will take some and woo a Lady.'

'Ha ha, you are taking after me. A word of warning though, it does not do to get too close to one woman for there are always more to be had and you should try out as many as you can.'

Rabanina sneered more than grinned, he had been taking his father's advice for a long time and his reputation for sexual gymnastics was one of fear and loathing amongst the women. He was a cruel, unfeeling man and they avoided him as much as possible, leaving him to rape and kill the women of the outlying kraals rather than to suffer themselves.

'The chief Mondli, It was not a good idea to kill him. To kill a chief is to offend his people greatly and they could rise up against us.'

'Have no fear, there is only one amongst them who poses a threat and he is no more. We will have no trouble from this kraal be assured.'

Night fell; Nkosinathi was amongst low lying, wooded hills and looking for a suitable place to rest. He had been here before on his hunts and knew the place well enough, knew of several small caves and clearings where he would be safe. He climbed from the saddle, led his horse into a thicket pulling the branches apart as he went and after a few yards found himself inside a natural defensive circle. It was perfect, protected and invisible to anyone passing more than a few paces away. Tying his horse to a tree, he unsaddled her and left her grazing whilst he rolled out his sleeping mat and ate some mealie cakes.

Before settling down for the night, he quietly backtracked and stood listening to the forest. The animals of the night were waiting to come out as the last bird song echoed across the hills and he felt reassured that no predator was about. Even so, he slept lightly in these circumstances, his army training and hunting alone for days on end honing a sixth sense.

Suddenly he opened his eyes, his horse had snorted pawed the ground and awoken him. Instantly he was on his feet clutching his rifle and standing perfectly still, he reached out and touched his horse's snout to reassure her and he listened to the night as did a leopard hearing the same snort. It lifted its head, turned its nose towards the sound, sampling the air and silently moved across towards the thicket in search of a kill.

Nkosinathi was still unaware of the predator as he listened yet he heard something, a rustling no more than a few yards away and he felt the hairs on his neck rise up. He wondered if it might be a leopard or a lion. If it attacked it could only do so through the narrow entrance to the clearing and he would kill. The skin from such an animal was worth a lot and swallowing hard he gingerly stepped away from the horse to cover the most likely place a predator would attack from and readied himself.

There it was again, a gentle rustling of leaves and Nkosinathi turned towards the sound remaining as quiet as he could and then he heard the death roar as the predator charged. Aiming his gun at the sound, he waited for the inevitable, strained his eyes for his first sight of the charging animal and closed his finger round the trigger. There was roar, the sound of screaming, a thrashing sound in the undergrowth and after a final roar, silence.

The screaming had sounded almost human but Nkosinathi knew it was not that of a human but a hog. The predator had killed a hog and he could hear a self-satisfied purring as it tore into its meal.

He wondered then if he could kill it and peering through the thorns the moonlight shone down on the leopard as it tore into its meal. it was aware of him and turned its head and with a deep throated growl, warned him off. He had his rifle raised and was tempted to kill it but a gunshot in the middle of the night was not a good idea and so, for twenty minutes, he watched the Leopard devour the carcass and then it began dragging the remains away. Following at a safe distance he tracked the animal to a small cave and watched it drag the remains of the carcass in after it but in doing so left a trail of hair and skin and it gave Nkosinathi an idea,

After such a disquieting time he could not sleep and as the first grey shafts of light cut through the hills. He led his horse out of the small clearing, looking around for the leopard before mounting and heading towards the crest of a hill for a clear view across the valley. He knew that he was nearing John Dunn's camp and as he scanned the terrain he saw smoke from the cooking fires rising in the distance.

He dismounted and led his horse through the undergrowth and trees, keeping out of sight until he was no more than a quarter of a mile from several European style houses surrounded by numerous beehive huts and white tents. He was close enough and leaving his horse tethered he crept towards the settlement to see a corral holding more cattle than he had seen since the great days of the Kingdom.

The main living accommodation was still a long way off and Nkosinathi decided to stay where he was for the time being to observe the comings and goings and lay on his stomach to watch.

All day he lay there, noting wagons come and go, riders from a patrol arriving in late afternoon and he wondered if it might be Rabanina's. Straining his eyes, he looked at each man's face but they were too far away for him to be sure and it made him wonder how he would find Rabanina. He would have to enter the camp if he was to get close to him but then what. If he killed him, they might see him, catch and recognise him and then the kraal would be in mortal danger. He had to find Rabanina, lure him out somehow, and pick an isolated place to kill him.

Nkosinathi looked up at the sky, it would be dark soon and so he returned to his horse to make sure she was safe. He would need her to make his escape and, confident she was content and well hidden, he stealthy made his way back to the outskirts of the camp. Darkness was beginning to fall and he began to circle closer to the perimeter, noting everything and staying out of sight. He saw people, black, white and all shades in between and as it became late, most disappeared into their huts and tents save for a few. Then his heart missed a beat. Rabanina appeared from one of the huts followed by a young woman.

'I don't want to,' he heard her say and then Rabanina turned and slapped her hard across her face.

'When I say I want you, you will obey me,' he growled, grabbing her wrist. She struggled again but he was too strong for her and dragged her into the darkness.

Rabanina's sexual appetite was insatiable and he could wait no longer. He wanted the woman there and then and the only place he could see to perform the act was in amongst the cattle. Pushing the gate ajar with one hand, he dragged her in amongst a few complaining animals and pushing her against the side of one began to strip her of her flimsy dress.

The girl began to complain but Rabanina's hand stifled her protests, and then he was tearing her dress from her body. Nkosinathi caught sight of her nakedness as Rabanina lifted her squealing and with her legs entwined about him he thrust her against the side of the nearest animal.

Desire was the last thing on Nkosinathi's mind and as the lovemaking became intense, he crept closer, knobkerrie at the ready. The girl was facing him, her sweat-laden skin shining in the moonlight her eyes closed but then they opened and she screamed.

A fully occupied Rabanina realised the danger only by the tone of her voice and turned his head, but he was too late. Nkosinathi attacked, gripping Rabanina's tight black curls and pulling his head back, the girl shrieked in terror and the two of them disengaged. Rabanina tried to defend himself, swinging his arm to ward Nkosinathi off him, enough to stop the initial onslaught and to the sound of the girl's shrieks Rabanina turned and recognised Nkosinathi.

'You!' he hissed, reaching for his knife but the nimble Nkosinathi was already swinging the knobkerrie and there came a low, sickening thud as he smashed into Rabanina's skull.

The girl was the only witness to the crime and she knew what was coming. Her shrieks turned to whimpers as the knobkerrie found its mark for a second time leaving Nkosinathi standing over the bodies gasping for breath.

Suddenly there was a voice, a man calling into the darkness and Nkosinathi knew that he had little time left. Reaching into the leather pouch at his waist, he gripped the sticky, hairy body part and rubbed it into the nostrils of those cows nearest to him and as the animals picked up the scent of the leopard, pandemonium broke loose.

The scent of the leopard was enough to spook the herd and within seconds, the cattle were stampeding. Wild eyed animals thrashed around, bellowing in fear and in their panic broke through the fence. Nkosinathi dodged back and forth, lucky the beasts did not trample on him, unlike the two unfortunate lovers whose naked bodies the cattle trampled underfoot.

Exhaustion was taking its toll as Nkosinathi finally caught sight of his home kraal, smoke was rising from the fires and he could see the youths herding the few cattle they had left out to pasture. It had been a long night, a long and dangerous night, he had not stopped, not found a secure place to rest. The initial euphoria of avenging his father's death had driven him on and leaving the chaos of the stampede in his wake, he felt sure that no one would ever know that it was he Nkosinathi, the last Zulu warrior, who had killed Rabanina.

The Last Zulu Warrior